About the Authors

Cathy Williams can remember reading Mills & Boon books as a teenager, and now that she is writing them she remains an avid fan. For her, there is nothing like creating romantic stories and engaging plots, and each and every book is a new adventure. Cathy lives in London and her three daughters, Charlotte, Olivia and Emma, have always been, and continue to be, the greatest inspiration in her life.

Joss Wood wrote her first book at the age of eight and has never really stopped. Her passion for putting letters on a blank screen is matched only by her love of books and travelling – especially to the wild places of Southern Africa. Happily and chaotically surrounded by books, family and friends, she lives in Kwa-Zulu Natal, South Africa, with her husband, children and their many pets.

USA TODAY bestselling author **Janice Maynard** knew she loved books and writing by the time she was eight years old. But it took multiple rejections and many years of trying before she sold her first three novels. After teaching for a number of years, Janice turned in her lesson plan book and began writing full-time. Since then she has sold over thirty-five books and novellas. Janice lives in east Tennessee with her husband, Charles. They love hiking, travelling and spending time with family.

Boardroom

COLLECTION

February 2018

March 2018

April 2018

May 2018

June 2018

July 2018

Innocent in the Boardroom

CATHY WILLIAMS

JOSS WOOD

JANICE MAYNARD

MILLS & BOON

Published in Great Britain 2018
by Mills & Boon, an imprint of HarperCollins*Publishers*
1 London Bridge Street, London, SE1 9GF

Innocent in the Boardroom © 2018 Harlequin Books S.A.

At Her Boss's Pleasure © 2015 Cathy Williams
Her Boss by Day... © 2015 Harlequin Books S.A.
Special thanks and acknowledgement are given to Joss Wood
for her contribution to the Sydney's Most Eligible... series.
How to Sleep with the Boss © 2016 Janice Maynard

ISBN: 978-0-263-26632-0

09-0518

MIX
Paper from
responsible sources
FSC™ C007454

This book is produced from independently certified FSC™ paper to ensure responsible forest management.

For more information visit: www.harpercollins.co.uk/green

Printed and bound in Spain
by CPI, Barcelona

AT HER BOSS'S PLEASURE

CATHY WILLIAMS

CHAPTER ONE

FRIDAY. END OF JULY. Six-thirty in the evening…

And where, Kate thought, *am I?* Still in the office. She was the last man standing. Or sitting, in actual fact. At her desk, with the computer flickering in front of her and profit and loss columns demanding attention. Not *immediate* attention—nothing that couldn't wait until the following Monday morning—but…

She sighed and sat back, stretching out the knots in her shoulders, and for a few minutes allowed herself to get lost in thought.

She was twenty-seven years old and she knew where she should be right now—and it wasn't in the office. Even if it was a very nice office, in a more-than-very-nice building, in the prestigious heart of London.

In fact she should be anywhere but here.

She should be out enjoying herself, lazing around in Hyde Park with friends, drinking wine and luxuriating in the long, hot summer. Or having a barbecue in a back garden somewhere. Or maybe just sitting inside, with some music on in the background and a significant other discussing his day and asking about hers.

She blinked and the vision of possibilities vanished. Since moving to London four years ago she could count on the fingers of one hand the number of close friends she had managed to make, and since qualifying as an accountant and joining AP Logistics a year and a half ago she had made none.

Acquaintances, yes…but friends? No. She just wasn't the sort of outgoing, chirpy, confidence-sharing, giggling sort of girl who made friends easily and was always part of a group. She knew that and she rarely thought about it all—except…well…it was Friday, and outside the baking sun was fading into pleasant balmy warmth, and in the rest of the world people her age were all out there enjoying themselves. In Hyde Park. Or in those back gardens where barbecues were happening…

She glanced through her office door and an array of empty desks stared back at her accusingly, mockingly, pointing out her shortcomings.

She hurriedly made a mental list of all the wonderful upsides to her life.

Great job at one of the most prestigious companies in the country. Her own office, which was a remarkable achievement considering her age. Her own small one-bedroom flat in a nice enough area in West London. How many girls her age actually *owned* their own place? In London? Yes, there was a mortgage, but still…

She had done well.

So she might not be able to escape her past. But she could bury it so deeply that it could no longer affect her.

Except…

She *was* here, at work, on her own, on a Friday evening, on the twenty-sixth of July…

So what did *that* say?

She hunched back over the screen and decided to give herself another half an hour before she would leave the office and head back to her empty flat.

Thankfully she became so engrossed in the numbers

staring back at her that she was barely aware of the distant ping of the lift and the sound of footsteps approaching the huge open-plan room where the secretaries and trainee accountants sat, and then moving on, heading towards her office.

She was squinting at the screen and totally unaware of the tall, dark figure looming by the door until he spoke, and then she jumped and for a few unguarded seconds was not the cool, collected woman she usually was.

Alessandro Preda always seemed to have that effect on her.

There was something about the man…and it was more—much more—than the fact that he owned the company…this great big company that had dozens of satellite companies under its umbrella.

There was something about *him*… He was just so much larger than life, and *not* in a comforting, cuddly-bear kind of way.

'Sir… Mr Preda… How can I help you?' Kate leapt to her feet, smoothing down her neat grey skirt with one hand, tidying the bun at the nape of her neck with the other—not that it needed tidying.

Alessandro, who had been leaning indolently against the doorframe, sauntered into her office, which was the only area lit on this floor of his company.

'You can start by sitting back down, Kate. When I achieve royal status you can spring to your feet as I enter the room. Until then there's really no need.'

Kate plastered a polite smile on her lips and sat down. Alessandro Preda might be drop-dead gorgeous—all lean and bronzed and oozing sexy danger—but there was nothing about him *she* found in the least bit appealing.

Too many people were in awe of his brilliance. Too many women swooned at his feet like pathetic, helpless damsels in distress. And he was just too arrogant for his own good. He was the man who had it all, and he was very much aware of that fact.

But, since he literally owned the ground she walked on, she had no choice but to smile, smile, smile and hope he didn't see beneath the smile.

'And there's no need to call me *sir* every time you address me. Haven't I told you that before?'

Dark-as-night eyes swung in her direction and lazily inspected the cool, pale face that had not cracked a genuine smile in all the time she had been working at his company. At least not in *his* presence.

'Yes, you have…er…'

'Alessandro…the name is *Alessandro*. It's a family firm—I like to keep it casual with my employees…'

He swung round to perch on the edge of her desk and Kate automatically inched back in her chair.

Hardly a family firm, she thought sarcastically. *Unless your family runs into thousands and happens to be scattered to the four corners of the globe. Big family.*

'What can I do for you, Alessandro?'

'Actually, I came to leave some papers for Cape. Where is he? And why are *you* the only one alive and kicking here? Where are the rest of the accounts team?'

'It's after six-thirty…er…Alessandro… They all left a while ago…'

Alessandro consulted his watch and frowned. 'You're right. Not that it's stretching the outer limits of the imagination to think that at least a few members of my highly paid staff might be here. Working.' He looked at her, eyes narrowed. 'So what are *you* still doing here?'

'I had a few reports I wanted to get through before I left. It's a productive time of day…when everyone else has left for the evening…'

Alessandro looked at her consideringly, head tilted to one side.

What *was* it about this woman? He had had some dealings with her over the past few months. She was a hard worker, diligent, had been fast-tracked by George Cape. He certainly had not been able to fault the quickness of her mind. Indeed, she seemed to have a knack for cutting through the crap and finding the source of problems—which wasn't that easy in the fiddly arena of finance.

Everything about her was professional, but there was something *missing*.

The cool green eyes were guarded, the full mouth always tight and polite, the hair never out of place.

His eyes roved lower, taking in a body that was well sheathed behind a prim white long-sleeved shirt, neatly cuffed at the wrists and buttoned to the neck.

Outside, the temperatures had been soaring for the past three weeks—and yet you would never guess, looking at her, that it was summer beyond the office walls. He would bet his fortune that she would be wearing tights.

He, personally, thrived on a rich diet of sexy women who flaunted their assets, so Ms Kate Watson's severe veneer never failed to arouse his curiosity.

The last time he had worked with her—for several days, on a tricky tax issue with which she had seemed more adept at dealing than her boss, George Cape, whose head had recently been in the clouds—he had tried to find out a bit more about her. Had asked her a few questions about what she did outside work…her hobbies, her interests. Polite chit-chat as they had taken time out over the food that had been delivered to his office suite.

Most women responded to any interest he showed in them by opening up. They couldn't wait to tell him all about themselves. They preened and blossomed when he looked at them, when he listened to what they had to say, even though, in fairness, his attention wasn't always exclusively on what they were talking about.

Kate Watson? Not a bit of it. She had stared at him with those cool green eyes and had managed to divert the conversation without giving anything of herself away.

'You're here every evening at this hour?'

Still perched on her desk, invading her space, Alessandro picked up a glass paperweight in the shape of a goldfish and twirled it thoughtfully between his fingers.

'No, of course not.' *But far too often, all things considered.*

'No? Just today? Even though it's the hottest day of the year?'

'I'm not a big fan of hot weather.' She lowered her eyes, suddenly a little angry at some kind of unspoken, amused criticism behind his words. 'I find it makes me sluggish.'

'It would,' Alessandro pointed out, dumping the goldfish back on the desk where he had found it, 'if you wear long-sleeved shirts and starched skirts.'

'If you'd like to leave the papers with me, I'll make sure I give them to George when he's back.'

'Back from where?'

'He's on holiday at the moment. Canada. He's not due back for another two weeks.'

'*Two weeks!*'

'It's not that long. Most people book two-week holidays during summer...'

'Have you?'

'Well, no...but...'

'Not sure this can wait until Cape decides to grace us with his presence.'

He stood up and slapped a sheaf of papers on her desk,

then placed his hands, palms down, squarely on either side of the papers and leaned into her.

'I asked Watson Russell if he knew anything about the anomalies in the supply chain to the leisure centres I'm setting up along the coastline and he told me that it's been Cape's baby from the start. True or false?'

'I believe he is in charge of those accounts.'

'You *believe*?'

Kate took a deep breath and did her utmost not to be intimidated by the man crowding her—but it was next to impossible. Tall, raven-haired, muscular and leaning into her, he didn't cause anything but a rapidly beating heart, a dry mouth and perspiring palms which she surreptitiously wiped on her skirt.

'He's in charge of those accounts. Exclusively. Perhaps you could explain what it is you'd like to find out?'

Alessandro pushed himself away from the desk and prowled through the office, noting in passing how little there was of her personality in it. No cutesy photographs in frames on the desk, no pot plants, no gimmicky penholder...not even a desk calendar with uplifting seascapes ...or works of art...or adorable puppies...or semi-clad firemen...

He said nothing for a few seconds, then spun to face her, hands thrust deep into his trouser pockets.

'Quite by chance a batch of files was delivered to me— probably because "Private and Confidential" was stamped so boldly on the envelope that the post boy must have automatically headed up to the directors' floor. I scanned them and there appeared to be...how shall I say this?...certain discrepancies that need checking out.'

He couldn't keep his eye on every single small detail within his vast empire. He paid people very generously indeed to do that, and with the fat pay packet came a great deal of trust.

He trusted his people not to try and screw him over.

'There are a couple of small companies whose names I can't say I recognize. I may have a lot of companies, but generally speaking I do know what they're called...'

Kate paled as the significance of what he was saying began to sink in.

'You catch on quickly,' Alessandro said approvingly. 'I had actually come down here to confront Cape with these files, but in his absence it might be a better idea for *you* to have a look at them and collate whatever evidence is necessary.'

'Evidence? Necessary for what?' she asked faintly, and flushed when he raised his eyebrows in question, as if incredulous that the point of what he had said might have passed her by. 'George Cape is nearly at retirement age... he's a family man...he has a wife, kids, grandchildren...'

'Call me crazy,' Alessandro said, with such silky assurance that she wanted to throw the goldfish paperweight at his handsome head, 'but when someone I employ decides to take advantage of my generosity I tend to feel a little aggrieved. Of course I could be completely off target here. There might very well be a simple explanation for what I've seen...'

'But if there isn't...?' She was unwillingly mesmerized by the graceful way he moved around her small office, his jacket bunching where his hand was shoved in his trouser pocket.

'Well, the wheels of justice have to do *something* to keep busy...' He shrugged. 'So, here's how this is going to play out: I am officially going to hand the files over to you and you are to examine them minutely, from cover to cover. I am assuming you know Cape's password for his computer?'

'I'm afraid I don't.'

'In which case get one of the computer whizz-kids to sort that out. You're going to go through every single document that has been exchanged on this particular project and get back to me out of work hours.'

'Out of work hours? What are you talking about?'

'I think Cape's been embezzling,' Alessandro informed her bluntly. 'We could keep going round the houses, but that's the long and short of it. I had no idea that he was in sole charge of this project. Had he not been I might have been inclined to widen the net of suspicion, but it fundamentally comes down to just one man.'

He paused to stand in front of her desk and she reluctantly looked up—and up, and up—into his dark, lean face.

'From what I've seen there's not a great deal of money involved, which might be why no alarm bells went off, but not a great deal over a long period of time could potentially amount to a *very* great deal, and if there are dummy companies involved…'

'I hate the thought of checking into what George has been doing,' Kate said truthfully. 'He's such a lovely guy, and he's been good to me since I began working here. If it weren't for him I probably wouldn't have been promoted as quickly as I have been…'

'Blow his trumpet too vigorously and I might start thinking that you are in on whatever the hell's been going on.'

'I'm not,' she said coldly, her voice freezing over. Her green eyes held his. 'I would never cheat anyone of anything. That's not the sort of person I am.'

Alessandro's ears pricked up. He had dropped down to the third floor to deposit these papers with George Cape before heading out. He had no date—and no regret there either. His last blonde bombshell had gone the way of all good things, and he was back to the drawing board and more than happy to have a break from the fairer sex.

Kate Watson—*Ms* Kate Watson—was everything he avoided when it came to women. She was cold, distant, intense, unsmiling and prickly. She never let him forget that she was there to do a damn good job and nothing else.

But that single sentence…*That's not the sort of person I am*…had made him wonder.

What sort of person *was* she?

'You were asking me about my out-of-hours suggestion…' Alessandro moved the topic swiftly along, at the same time relegating her stray remark to a box from which it would be removed at a later date.

He had nothing to do on a Friday night. A rare situation for him. He dragged the single spare chair in the room across to her desk and sat down, angling it so that he could extend his long legs to the side, crossing them at the ankles.

Kate watched with something approaching horror. 'I was about to leave… Perhaps we could continue this conversation on Monday morning? I'm usually in first thing. By seven-thirty most days.'

'Laudable. It's heart-warming to know that there's at least one person in my finance department who doesn't clock-watch.'

'I'm sure you must have plans for the evening, sir… Alessandro. If I take the paperwork home I can have a look at it over the weekend and get back to you with my findings on Monday morning. How does that sound?'

'The reason I suggested that we discuss this situation out of hours is because I would rather not have it turned into a matter for speculation. Naturally you would be paid generously for your overtime.'

'It's not about being paid for overtime,' Kate said stiffly. She kept her eyes firmly pinned to his face, but she was all too aware of the lazy length of his body, the flex of muscles under the white shirt, the tanned column of his throat and the strength of his forearms where he had shoved the sleeves of his shirt to the elbows.

He had always made her jumpy, in a way other men never had. There was a raw, primal, barely contained aggression about him that threatened her composure, and it had done so from the very first time she had set eyes on him as a new recruit to the company.

It was dangerous. It was the sort of *dangerous* she could do without. She didn't like the way her body seemed to respond to him of its own accord. It frightened her.

Her upbringing had taught her many things, and the biggest thing it had taught her was the need for control. Control over her emotions, control over her finances, control over the destination of her life. She had grown up with a role model of a mother who had lacked all control.

Shirley Watson had adopted the frivolous name *Lilac* at the age of eighteen, and had spent her life living up to it—moving from pole dancer to cocktail-bar waitress to barmaid back to cocktail-bar waitress, flirting with men's magazine pin-ups along the way.

A stunningly beautiful, pocket-sized blonde, she had only ever learned how to exploit the natural assets with which she had been born. Kate only knew sketchy details of her mother's past, but she did know that Lilac had grown up as a foster-home kid. She had never known stability, and instead of trying to create some of her own had relied on being a dumb blonde, always believing that love lay just round the corner, that the men who slept with her really loved her.

Kate's father had vanished from the scene shortly after

she was born, leaving Lilac heartbroken at the age of just twenty-one. From him, she had moved on to a string of men—two of whom she had married and subsequently divorced in record time. In between the marriages she had devoted her life to pointlessly trying to attract men, always confusing their enthusiasm for her body for love, always distraught when they tired of her and pushed on.

She was a smart woman, but she had learned to conceal her brains because a brainy woman, she had once confided in her daughter, never got the guy.

Kate loved her mother, but she had always been painfully aware of her shortcomings and had determined from an early age that she would not live a life blighted by the same mistakes her mother had made.

It helped that she was dark-haired. And tall. She lacked her mother's obvious sex appeal and for that she was thankful. Her assets she kept firmly under wraps, and when it came to men…well…

Any man who liked her for her body was off the cards. No way was she ever going to fall into the same helpless trap her mother had. She relied on her brains, and goodness knew it had been tough going, ploughing through her school years, moving from place to place, never quite knowing what would confront her on her return home from school.

Her mother, by a stroke of good fortune, had been given sufficient money by her second husband in their subsequent divorce to enable her to buy somewhere small in Cornwall. She—Kate—would not be relying on any such stroke of fortune. She would provide for herself by hook or by crook and be independent.

And when and if she ever fell in love it would be with a guy who appreciated her intelligence, who was not the kind of man with commitment issues, who didn't abandon women after he had had his fill of them, who didn't go out with women because of the way they looked.

So far this paragon of virtue hadn't appeared on the scene, but that didn't mean that she would ever be distracted in the meantime by the sort of guy she privately despised.

So why, she wondered, did her stupid body begin a slow burn whenever Alessandro Preda was within her radius?

And now here he was, making noises about them working alongside one another *outside normal working hours*.

'Then what is it about?' Alessandro demanded, bringing her back to the reality of him sitting across from her with a bump. 'Hectic social life? Can't spare a week to sort this matter out?' He glanced around him before settling his dark eyes on her cool, pale face. 'Despite the extremely pleasant office you have here at the tender age of what…? Twenty-something…?'

'I've been promoted on merit.'

'And part of that promotion involves going beyond the call of duty now and again. Consider this one of those instances.'

Kate lowered her eyes, keeping her cool.

'You said you were heading off now…?'

'Yes.'

'In that case…' Alessandro stood up and sauntered towards the door, where he proceeded to lean against it, staring at her '…I'll walk you down. In fact, I'll go one better. I'll give you a lift to your house. Where do you live?'

Kate licked her lips nervously and ventured a polite smile as she stood up as well, and began tidying a desk that wasn't in need of tidying.

'How long have you been here?'

His voice had her head snapping up and she looked at him in bewilderment.

'How long have I been where? In your company? Working in London?'

'Let's start with in this office.'

Kate looked around her at her neat space, in which she felt so safely cocooned. These four walls were tangible proof of how far she'd come and how quickly—tangible proof of the solid income that marked her steps along that road called *financial security*.

Her mother had asked if she could visit her place of work when next she was in London but Kate had tactfully, and a little shamefully, killed the suggestion before it could take shape.

Lilac Watson, not yet fifty, and these days thankfully a little less obvious in displaying what she had to offer physically, would still never have blended into these muted, expensive surroundings.

This was Kate's life, built with her own blood, sweat and tears, and her mother had her own life. In Cornwall. Far away. Separate.

'What about it?' She shoved her work laptop into a leather briefcase and reached for the grey jacket she had slung over the back of her chair.

Grey jacket, grey calf-length skirt, flat, sensible patent pumps and, yes, definitely tights. Not stockings. *Tights.* Possibly of the support variety. Who knew? It was impossible to tell what sort of figure she had under the prim ensemble. Not fat, not thin, tall... The shirt managed to hide everything up top and the skirt did a similar job with everything down below.

And why the hell was he looking anyway?

'How long have you been here? *In* it?'

Kate paused and frowned. 'A little over six months. To start with I was moved in here because I was working late on a couple of very big clients and George thought that the quiet would help concentration. Not that it's a mad house outside. It isn't. And then, when I was promoted, I was offered it. I snapped it up.'

She reached for her briefcase, slung her black bag over her shoulder and straightened her skirt.

'Thanks very much for your offer of a ride home, but there are one or two things I need to collect on the way so I shall take the Tube.'

'What things?'

'Things… Food items. I need to stop off at the corner shop.'

Alessandro heard irritation behind her calmly spoken words. This was something he wasn't used to, and he was as bemused by his own reaction to it as he had been by his earlier curiosity as to what lay underneath the prissy work clothes.

'Not a problem.' He waved aside her objection. 'I've sent my driver home and I have my own car. Far more convenient if you load whatever you need to buy into my car rather than having to walk with it back to your house.'

'I'm accustomed to walking home with my groceries.'

Alessandro looked at her narrowly. He wouldn't have taken her for being skittish, but there was something skittish about her now. And why turn down a ride home? With him?

'It would be useful for us to decide how to approach this delicate problem with George Cape and whatever money he's been siphoning off.'

'*If* he's been siphoning off any. And I was under the impression that you had already decided what you would do if you found out that he had taken money from you… throw him in prison and chuck away the keys.'

'Let's hope I've got it wrong, in that case, and he'll be spared the prison sentence.' He stepped aside, leaving her just sufficient room to brush past him through the door, switching off the lights in her wake. 'You've been in this office for six months and this is the first time it's struck me that there's nothing personal in here at all. *Nothing*.'

Kate flushed. 'It's an office,' she said briskly, stepping in front of him, briefcase in one hand, bag over her shoulder, head held high and deliberately averted from him. 'Not a boudoir.'

'Boudoir…nice word. Is that where you stash all your personal mementoes? In your boudoir?'

Kate heard the amusement in his voice and turned to him angrily. *Get a grip*, she told herself sternly. *Don't let the man rattle you.* Green flashing eyes clashed with his oh-so-dark ones and she felt herself sinking into his gaze, had to yank herself firmly back to reality.

Alessandro Preda had a reputation with women. Even if the gossip hadn't reached her ears, one glance at any news rag would have informed her of that reputation.

He used women. He was always being snapped with models draped on his arm, gazing up at him adoringly. Lots of models. A different model for every month of the year. He could have started his own agency with the number of them he ran through. She wondered whether some of those models had been like her mother—sad creatures, blessed with spectacular looks but not enough common sense to know how to use what they had been given. Hanging on. Hoping for more than would ever be on the agenda.

'Shall I email you my findings?' Underneath the scrupulous politeness her voice could have frozen fire. She pressed the button to summon the lift and stared at him, as rigid as a plank of wood.

Alessandro had never seen anyone so uptight in his entire life.

This went way beyond self-control—way beyond a certain amount of composure.

What was her story? And didn't she know that all those 'No Trespassing' signs she'd erected around herself were enticing beacons to a man like him?

He was thirty-four years old, and he wasn't sure whether to be proud or simply accepting of the fact that he had never had to try very hard for a woman. They offered themselves to him.

But *Ms* Kate Watson had issues with him. He didn't know what they were, but he did know that they constituted a challenge—and since when had he ever been a man to turn down a challenge?

If he had, he certainly wouldn't have ended up in the exalted position of power that he had.

He suppressed the onslaught of thoughts that always managed to put him in a foul mood.

'I don't think so.' He stepped back as the lift doors slid open, allowing her to edge past him, making sure she kept her distance as much as she could, doing her utmost to be casual about it. 'Emails can be intercepted.'

'Aren't you being a bit cloak and dagger about all of this?'

Kate addressed the long metal case in the lift containing the various buttons, but she was acutely aware of him right next to her, of the warmth of his body wafting through the air and settling around her like a dangerous cloak that she wanted to shake off. She couldn't remember him having this sort of effect on her before, but then they had usually been in a room with other people around—not heading down in a lift, just the two of them.

She was alive to his presence in a way that made her whole body feel uncomfortable.

Alessandro stared at that pale averted profile. She was a beautiful woman, he realized with sudden surprise. It was something that wasn't immediately apparent, because she was at such pains to play down her looks, but studying her now he saw her features were perfect. Her nose was small and straight, her lips oddly full and sexy, her cheekbones high and sharp. Maybe the severity of her hairstyle accentuated all of that.

He wondered how long her hair was. Impossible to tell.

She swung round sharply and he straightened, flushing guiltily at being caught red-handed staring at her. *Not very cool.*

'I doubt George is going to do a runner if he gets wind that you're on to him. And that's *if* he's guilty of anything at all!'

'Why are you so keen to protect him?'

'I'm not keen to protect him. Just being fair. Innocent until proved guilty, and all that.'

The lift doors opened with a purr and she stepped out into the vast marbled foyer that still impressed her after nearly two years.

She wasn't protecting George Cape. Or was she? When she thought of George, a little guy staring down the barrel of a gun and not even realizing it, she thought of her own vulnerable mother, who had lived most of *her* life staring down the barrel of a gun and not realizing it, and when she thought about her mother she felt her heart constrict.

Which, of course, was *not* going to do. Least of all with a man like Alessandro Preda. And naturally she could see his point of view.

'Commendable,' Alessandro murmured. 'So we begin on Monday. The hunt to find out whether Cape is guilty of fraud or stupidity. Either way, he will doubtless end up being sacked. Now, where do you live…? My car's in the underground car park.'

CHAPTER TWO

IT HAD TAKEN a lot for Kate not to get in touch with George Cape over the weekend. *Was* he guilty of fraud? It was hard to believe. He was a true gentleman, courteous and kind, and he had taken her under his wing when she had started working for him. That said, he had not been his usual self over the past three months. Was there an explanation there somewhere?

She had looked through the files. Thankfully, no dummy companies had been set up—which she hoped ruled out fraud on a systematic large-scale basis. But the odd entries were definitely there, and...

She sighed and looked at her watch. She had managed to put off Alessandro the previous Friday evening, but he would be expecting her in his office now. At nearly seven p.m., the offices were again practically empty—aside from a few hard-core, nose-to-the-grindstone employees who barely glanced in her direction as she briskly walked out of the office with her files towards the bank of lifts.

It had been a while since she had been in Alessandro's office. Not since that tax problem that had needed sorting out. George and the head of finance had been there too, but there had been a brief period when it had just been her, doing the grunt work with the numbers, and Alessandro, who had been covering other aspects of the problem, and he had ordered in food for both of them.

It had been one of the few occasions when they had been alone together and she could still vividly recall the way she had burned when she had glanced up at one point and their eyes had met.

He had very dark eyes, fringed with thick, dark lashes, and that day he had had the sort of brooding, thoughtful expression that sent shivers racing up and down her spine. Having him look at her had felt like a very physical experience and she hadn't liked it.

And now that she was stepping into the lion's den again she was determined to bring her wayward reactions to heel.

Unfortunately her rapidly beating heart was already letting the side down, and by the time she heard that deep, masculine drawl telling her to enter her palms were sweaty and her nerves were all over the place.

He was sprawled in his leather chair, hands folded loosely on his stomach.

'Slight change of plan.'

They were his opening words and Kate stopped abruptly in her tracks. 'I could always leave the files and we can discuss them another time.' Disappointment warred with relief. 'If you're busy.' Her eyes flickered away from their compulsive visual tour of his body.

'We will discuss this over something to eat.'

That had her snapping to attention, and she looked at him with alarm. 'There's no need.' She had already recalled the last time they had shared a meal in this setting, and a repeat performance was something she could do without. 'I haven't managed to speak to the computer department about getting hold of George's password, but I don't think we will need to do that.' She took a few steps forward and thrust the files onto his desk. 'There are no dummy companies. I've checked that out thoroughly. And—'

'Over dinner.'

He slung his long body out of the chair and grabbed the jacket that had been tossed on the leather sofa by the wall. He didn't bother to put it on, preferring to hook it over his shoulder with his finger, and then he continued.

'I've asked you to work after hours. It's only fair that I take you out to dinner. I mean, we do both have to eat...'

'I hadn't thought... This really won't take very long...'

Alessandro had paused to stand in front of her, his lean, muscular body radiating a power that sapped her energy and threw her into a state of confusion. She resented both things. She was the consummate professional—a woman whose composed, efficient veneer was never dented. She had devoted her whole life to controlling the sort of feminine weakness that had reduced her mother to a victim over the years.

To combat the treacherous ache in her body she tightened her jacket around her, buttoning it and standing straighter—ramrod straight.

'This is a man's future we're talking about,' Alessandro's keen eyes had noted all her little defence mechanisms: the way her lips had pursed, the tension in her shoulders, the buttoning of the jacket. 'You wouldn't want to write it off in a five-minute summary just because you happen to have a hot date for the evening, would you?'

'I don't have a hot date.'

The words left her mouth before she could drag them back, and it was no big deal but she still felt suddenly vulnerable and exposed. Her cheeks were burning as curious eyes lingered on her face.

'I...I prefer to stay in on week nights,' she gamely went on, even though she knew she should just shut up, because now he was staring at her with even more curiosity. 'I often take work home with me. There's a lot to get through and I know how easy it is for…for…things to pile up…'

'You work late every evening, Kate. I don't imagine anyone would expect you to take work home with you as well.' He moved towards the door and opened it, standing back to allow her through. 'Which is all the more reason for me to take you out for dinner, so that we can discuss this in less formal surroundings. I wouldn't want you to see me as an unscrupulous boss who denies his employees a private life.'

Rattled, Kate walked briskly towards the lift. She turned to look at him. 'But aren't you?'

It was a daring question. One she shouldn't have asked. He represented everything she didn't like. In the normal course of events their paths would scarcely overlap. He rarely ventured down into the bowels of his offices, where the little people kept the wheels of his machinery well oiled and turning. But she didn't like what he did to her, what he did to her prized self-control, and some wicked little devil inside her had pushed her to be more daring than she normally would have been.

'Aren't I what?' He wondered how he had not noticed before the way her green eyes were the colour of polished glass.

Those polished-glass eyes slid sideways now.

'Unscrupulous.' Kate said eventually, although she still wasn't looking at him as the lift carried them downstairs in what felt like a step out of routine that she didn't want to take. Her heart was beating frantically inside her and she was thankful for the reliable armour of her neat starched suit. It gave her a confidence that was suddenly missing.

As they exited the building it was at least easier to talk to him when she was walking next to him and not staring directly at his face.

'What I'm saying is I thought that in order to make it to the top you would *have* to be unscrupulous. No one ever gets to play in the Champions League unless they're willing to…well…'

'Crush everyone and everything in their path?' He clasped her arm and turned her to face him.

'I didn't say that.'

'That's not my style. There's no need. And if this has to do with any decision I make about Cape, then you're way off target. If Cape's been defrauding my company then he'll take the consequences. It's an unfortunate truth that people must live and die by the decisions they make.'

'That seems a little harsh.'

'Does it?' His eyes darkened but he released her arm, even though he didn't immediately carry on walking. The crowds parted around them, shooting them curious looks.

Here, outside, it was very warm, and her suit of armour was beginning to feel more than a bit uncomfortable. Her skin prickled and she licked her lips nervously.

'Not that it's any of my business,' she was quick to add. 'Where are we going to eat?'

'Is that your way of telling me that you'd like to bring this conversation to an end?'

'I shouldn't have said…what I said.'

'You're free to speak your mind.'

They began walking to a gastropub that was tucked down one of the tiny side streets close to his offices in the heart of the city.

'Because it's really just a family firm…?' There was a smile in her voice as she tried to lighten the atmosphere.

'You've got it. One big, happy family—just so long as all my family members behave themselves. When one of them steps out of line, then I'm afraid I have to rule with a firm hand.'

'It's a very *big* family.'

'Which started small. And I suppose that's why it's important for me to take control when a situation such as the one we have now develops. I didn't create this baby for anyone to get it into their heads that they could climb on my bandwagon and begin looting. Here we are.'

He pushed open the door into a space that was so dark it took Kate a couple of seconds for her eyes to adjust. Dark and refreshingly cool, and quaintly higgledy-piggledy.

'This is not the sort of place I thought you would have liked,' she blurted out impulsively, and Alessandro smiled.

'I'm old friends with the man who owns it, and as a matter of fact coming here is something of an antidote to my frenetic pace of life. Why don't you take your jacket off?'

'I'm fine.'

Alessandro raised his eyebrows with mild disbelief. 'I expect you'd like to get down to work immediately…bypass all the pleasantries…?'

'I have all the files in my briefcase.'

'I hate to curb your enthusiasm, but I could do with relaxing for five minutes before I begin to hear about what George Cape's been up to. You might think I'm hard-line, but Cape's been with my company for a quite a number of years. It's regrettable that he could not have just approached me had he wanted a loan.'

She was spared the temptation of telling him that perhaps he needed to work on the whole *family atmosphere* approach by the arrival of the owner of the restaurant, who made a great fuss of Alessandro. They lapsed into rapid Italian and she covertly watched Alessandro, relaxed, gesticulating, grinning, showing her a natural warmth that was usually concealed under the forbidding exterior.

This would be the man who charmed women, she

thought. The guy who could have any woman he wanted at the snap of a finger and made full use of the talent.

And, of course, none of those women were Plain Janes or, God forbid, downright *unappealing*.

Drawn into their conversation towards the end, she smiled politely and offered the owner her hand in a businesslike handshake which, as they moved towards a table nestled in its own alcove towards the back of the restaurant, Alessandro told her had successfully nipped his friend's salacious ideas in the bud.

'I have no idea what you're talking about.' Once seated, she pointedly extracted the file they would need to discuss and placed it on the table next to her.

Wine was brought to them. On the house.

'You must know the proprietor very well,' she murmured, 'if free wine is part of the deal when you come here.'

'He would throw in free food as well.' Alessandro sat back and looked at her with lazy consideration. 'But I always insist on paying for what I eat.'

'That's very thoughtful of you.'

He laughed aloud and shot her an appreciative look. 'You have a sense of humour! I never realized.'

Kate thought that that was borderline rude, but how could she object when she had been pretty outspoken in some of the things she had said to *him*?

'Relax,' he urged, gently removing the hand that she held over her wine glass and pouring her some wine. 'We might be here to work, but you're not in the office now.'

And that, she thought, was the problem—because when she was in the office, surrounded by computers and filing cabinets and desks, and the constant buzz of ringing phones, she could be a cool, controlled professional. Whereas here…

The place was popular. Nearly every table was occupied, and the bar area was crowded with men in suits and women in sharp summer outfits and high heels.

'Why do you work so much overtime?'

Kate frowned and played with her wine glass before taking a sip. *What sort of a question is that?* she wanted to ask. He owned the company. Surely he should be congratulating her on her dedication to her job instead of asking her why she worked so hard?

'I thought that was the way to get ahead,' she said neutrally. 'But I might be mistaken.'

Alessandro grinned, enjoying her understated dry sense of humour.

'I mean,' Kate continued, warming to her theme because somehow, somewhere in his remark, there had been just the faintest hint of criticism. 'You *did* express some disappointment that the entire floor was empty when you came to drop those files off for George...'

'Quite true.'

'So why are you criticizing me because I happen to do a bit of overtime now and again?'

'I got the impression that it was more the rule than the exception. And I'm not criticizing you.'

'It sounds as though you are.' She could feel those dark eyes boring into her and had to restrain herself from squirming.

He was her *boss*. Actually, he was the lord of all he surveyed, and it was in her interests to remain as polite and detached as possible. Never mind all that tosh about his hundred-thousand-strong *family* of employees...he could ruin her career with the snap of his fingers. As he would doubtless ruin George Cape's career.

She bristled with anger, stole a resentful glance at his lean, beautiful face, and wondered what it would feel like to have those sensuous lips on hers.

She didn't even know where that errant thought had come from, but it was so vivid that her whole body responded. Her breasts ached, and between her legs…she was horrified to realize that she was dampening.

'I'm ambitious,' she told him heatedly, 'and there's nothing wrong with that. I work hard because I hope that my hard work will pay off, that I'll be promoted… I wasn't born with a silver spoon in my mouth and I've had to fight for every single thing I've got.'

It was more than she should have said, although not a word of it was untrue. It just felt weird—*wrong*—to be confiding in him. And why was she anyway? She wasn't here for an interview and he hadn't demanded that she explain herself.

Usually so reticent, she had been propelled into speaking her mind. She licked her lips nervously, realized that she was sitting forward, fists clenched on the table, and deliberately made herself relax and smile.

'You're implying that your colleagues come from a more privileged background than you?'

'I'm not implying anything. I was just…stating a fact.'

Alessandro noted the pink in her cheeks. Up close and personal with her—which he had never been before—he sensed that her reactions were honest. She blushed when he wouldn't have expected her to, because the impression she gave was one of complete self-control. He could remember asking her questions about certain technicalities in the jobs she had worked on and she had been cool, calm and knowledgeable, barely displaying any kind of personality at all.

But then…

He glanced briefly around him. This wasn't a cold, clinical office, was it? The neat little folder she had pointedly stuck on the table next to her was the only evidence that this was a work meeting. And without the backup of an office he had a tantalizing glimpse of the person behind the beautiful but bland exterior.

Did he want to bring the conversation back to work? Not yet.

'Maybe you think that *I* do...?' he murmured in a lazy drawl.

'I haven't given that any thought at all,' Kate lied. 'I'm here to do a job, not to pry into other people's lives.'

'Your days must be very dull, in that case.'

'Why? Why do you say that?'

'Because it's commendable to work hard, and to do a good job, but doesn't everyone get a little titillation from office politics? The salacious gossip? The speculating...?'

'Not me.'

Her voice was firm but her nerves were all over the place. She picked up the menu and stared at it but she could still feel his eyes on her.

'I think I might have the fish.'

Alessandro didn't bother to glance at the menu. He responded by keeping his eyes firmly fixed on her face while he beckoned with a slight raising of his hand and was rewarded when someone sprang to attention and hustled over.

How did he *do* that? Was there some poor sap hovering in the corner somewhere, waiting until the Mighty One beckoned him across?

Of course there would be. Money talked, and Alessandro Preda had a lot of it. Vast amounts.

People changed when they were around money. Common sense flew through the window. Subservience, slavishness and an awestruck inability to just *act normally* set in.

So she might feel *something*—a little insignificant twinge of awareness about the man—but that was natural. He was drop-dead gorgeous, especially when she was receiving the full, undiluted blast of his forceful personality. But she wasn't and never would be one of those simpering airheads who turned to mush around him. And actually not just airheads. Lots of clever women—definitely two in the legal department—giggled at the mention of his name and projected crazy fantasies about him over lunch in the office restaurant. Several times Kate had had to stop her eyes from rolling skywards.

Her body might be a little rebellious, but thankfully she had her head firmly screwed on.

She politely waited as he ordered, said no to a top-up of wine, and then relented because at least it made her relax.

'So, about George…' She flicked open the file and felt the weight of his hand over hers.

'In good time.'

'Sorry. I thought you might have finished relaxing.' Her heart was thumping so hard that she wondered if she might be having a mild panic attack. Or, worse, turning into one of those simpering airheads. Or even worse than that, one of those clever women whose brains went missing in action the second he came too close.

'Only just beginning.'

He dealt her a slashing smile that did nothing to steady her disobedient body and she pursed her lips in response.

'Perhaps I should have taken more of an interest in your career before…considering you're one of my rising stars…'

'I didn't think you got involved in doing appraisals on anybody in your company,' Kate responded politely. *Boss/employee*, she reminded herself. The boss got to ask all the questions and the employee got to ask none whatsoever.

'True,' Alessandro conceded.

He didn't look at the waiter as he placed their food in front of them and then did some annoying perfect positioning of their plates. All he wanted the man to do was disappear. Because he was pleasantly invigorated and didn't want to lose the moment. They were few and far between as it was.

'I like to think that's what my human resources people are all about. Although, in fairness, they probably work to rule like the rest of the occupants of your floor.'

'Everyone works overtime in the winter months. It's just that it's summer and it's baking hot outside—I guess they want to leave on time and enjoy the sunshine.'

'But not you?' Alessandro pointed out. 'Nothing urgent out of hours waiting for you?'

'I don't think what I do outside work is actually any of your business—and I apologize right now if you think I'm being rude when I say that.'

'No need for apologies. I just want to make sure. Do you feel the need to live in the office in order to get on?'

'I…'

She tried to imagine living a life in which that mythical other half was right now whipping up something in the kitchen for her, anxiously consulting his watch if she was running late. She would have to do something about that—turn the passing thought into reality. She didn't miss having a guy in her life now, but she would eventually. She wasn't meant to be an island, and if she wasn't careful she would wake up one day and find herself alone because she had sacrificed everything to her quest for security.

'Tell me what you're thinking.'

'Huh?'

'You're a million miles away,' Alessandro drawled drily. 'Simple question, really. I didn't think it would have required that much deep thought.'

'I…'

For a few seconds she nearly told him just how much deep thought that 'simple question' required. More than he could ever imagine because—like it or not—this man who saw his vast empire as a family affair was a man who came from money. How could he ever understand the drive inside her to fill all the gaps her upbringing had left?

'Sorry… No. Of course I know that there's no need for me to work long hours to get on—although, in fairness, I probably work fewer hours in winter than my colleagues.'

'Ah, yes. Because you're a creature of the night?'

And just like that Kate thought of her mother, of those jobs in dark bars earning money from tips, dancing and showing herself off in whatever nonsense she was told to put on. A creature of the night doing night-time jobs. *Nothing like her.*

'Don't you *ever* say that to me!' she blurted out before she could stop herself. She was shaking with anger and stuck her hands under the table on her lap so that he couldn't see that they were shaking.

'Say what?' Alessandro asked slowly, his sharp eyes narrowed on her flushed face. 'Did I say something wrong?' He frowned and saw her make a visible effort to gather herself. 'Tell me what the problem is.'

'There isn't a problem. I'm sorry. I overreacted.'

'Firstly, stop apologizing for everything you say that you think might offend me. I don't take offence easily. And secondly…there *is* a problem. You went as white as a sheet and now you're shaking like a leaf. What provoked that sudden bout of outrage?'

Curiosity dug deep. Underneath the calm surface, she was a hotbed of emotion and that intrigued him. He leaned forward, elbows on the table, crowding her.

'You're trying to think of a polite way of telling me that it's none of my business, aren't you?'

Kate shied away from his searching narrowed stare. She could feel the full force of his powerful personality like something raw and physical and it appalled and mesmerized her at the same time. This was evidence of the driving tenacity that had propelled him into the stratosphere of wealth and power and it went far, far beyond his formidable intelligence and his ambition.

She averted her face, her heart beating wildly. 'My mother worked in a cocktail bar,' she said flatly.

Why had she just come out with that? She never, ever went there with other people. Her past was a closed book to prying eyes.

'Amongst other things. I have no idea why I'm telling you this.' She looked at him accusingly from under lowered lashes. 'I don't usually confide in other people. I'm not usually a confiding kind of person. I know you think I'm strange, working long hours, but…'

'But you crave financial security?'

'*Crave* is a strong word.' She smiled tentatively. 'But maybe it's the right one.'

She felt a weird sense of release at unburdening herself. When she was growing up, those sensitive teenage years had been an agony of embarrassment. She had made sure never to get too close to anyone. She hadn't wanted them to find out that her mother worked as a cocktail waitress, brought men home who used her because of the way she looked, was a sad, desperate woman who knew only how to barter with her body to keep them going.

She'd loved her mother but she had been ashamed of her—and ashamed of being ashamed. And now here was her boss, Alessandro Preda, whose lifestyle repulsed her, who represented everything she found distasteful in a man, and the sympathy on his face was like a key unlocking her secrets. Stupid. Really stupid. *And somehow dangerous…*

'My upbringing was…unsteady. Mum never seemed interested in holding down a normal office job. I can only remember her going out at night, leaving me with some friend or other when I was young, and then the minute I hit twelve I was on my own. I loved my mother…I *love* my mother…but I hated the way she earned a living. I hated thinking of her in stupid skimpy clothes, with men staring and trying to paw her. And she was always falling in love—always thinking that Mr Right was the next handsome guy who paid her some attention and told her she was beautiful.'

'So when I called you a creature of the night…'

'I'm sorry.' Mortified, Kate stared at her empty wine glass and watched as he poured her some more wine. She hadn't planned on drinking anything at all. Now she wondered how much she had inadvertently downed. Maybe the alcohol had loosened her tongue? She didn't *feel* in the least bit tipsy, but why else would she have suddenly turned into a blabbering mess?

'What did I tell you about apologizing?'

'I work for you…'

'Which doesn't turn you into one of my subjects. Like I said, I have yet to attain royal status,' Alessandro drawled. 'Where does your mother live now?'

'Cornwall.' Kate shot him a quick glance and looked away just as fast.

He was just so sinfully *good-looking*! It shouldn't do anything for her, because she was the last person on the planet to judge a guy by the way he looked, but her tummy was in knots and she had to force herself not to stare at that dark, brooding, *interested* face. She almost had the feeling that, given half a chance, he would be able to reach into her head and pull out her deepest, darkest thoughts.

'She…she married twice. Her second husband, Greg, gave her sufficient money in their divorce for her to buy somewhere small, and she wanted to be by the sea.'

'And your father?'

'I had no idea I would be subjected to a question-and-answer session…' But she had initiated this whole conversation, and there was a weary acceptance of that in her voice.

Alessandro had never had the slightest curiosity about the back stories of his women. He was curious now.

'My father left soon after I was born. He was my mother's first love and her only love—so she tells me.' She cleared her throat and searched for the brisk, businesslike voice that was so much part and parcel of her persona. Sadly it was nowhere to be found. Just when she really felt she needed it. 'I think she's been trying ever since to replace him.'

'And now?'

'And now what?'

'There's someone in her life?'

Kate smiled and Alessandro felt the breath catch in his throat—a sudden, sharp, shocking reaction that came from nowhere. The woman was *beautiful*. Did she deliberately downplay that? This was a Pandora's box. She worked for him, and they were here to discuss the future of an employee. Serious stuff. But for the life of him he didn't want to let the conversation go.

'I'm proud to announce that my mother has been a man-free zone for three years. I feel she might be cured of her addiction to looking for love in all the wrong places.'

'And what about you?' Alessandro murmured huskily. 'Are *you* a man-free zone at the moment?'

His thoughts veered wildly into uncharted territory. He pictured her with a man. He pictured her with *him*. The face she chose to show the world was not the sum total of the person she was. In fact, scratch the surface and the cool, marble exterior gave way to swirling, unpredictable currents.

He had a driving, crazy urge to *test those waters*.

He had his own reasons, he knew, for the choices he had made and continued to make. His own parents and their all-consuming love had left little room for a kid and no room at all for common sense. Theirs had been a world with room only for each other, and their ridiculous choices had seen their joint family fortunes whittled away into nothing thanks to rash decisions, stupid blunders, irrational money-making ventures.

Control? They had had none of that. *He* did. He controlled every aspect of his life, including his love life, but suddenly all those beautiful, vapid, utterly controllable women who had cluttered his life seemed like *safe, dreary options*.

Insane. He had never mixed business with pleasure. *Never.* This woman was off limits.

But she had kick-started his libido and he felt the thrust of a powerful erection pressing against the zipper of his trousers, bulging and uncomfortable.

Kate detected something in his voice that sent the thrill of a shiver racing through her and desperately tried to squelch it.

How the heck had this happened? How had the conversation swerved from George and his misdeeds to questions about her private life? What on earth had possessed her to start sharing her life story like an idiot?

'I've been very busy getting my career up and going,' she said briskly. 'I haven't had time to cultivate relationships.'

'All work and no play…' Alessandro murmured. 'Personally, I've always found that a little bit of play makes the work go a helluva lot faster.'

'That approach doesn't work for me. It never has.' She

winced at the tenor of her voice—cold, prim, defensive. 'And now I think we ought to get the bill. I…it's later than I expected… I don't think it would be fair on George if we shoved our discussion of his plight into a few minutes tacked on to the end of a meal. I realize you've written him off as a master criminal, but I feel he deserves better than that.'

She automatically felt for the bun at the back of her head. Still firmly in place. Unlike the rest of her.

Alessandro mentally waved aside the topic of hapless George and his unfortunate wrongdoings. Tomorrow was another day. He would deal with that later. *They* would deal with that later. Right now…

'What approach doesn't work for you?'

Kate pretended to misunderstand his question.

'Ah. You've decided to retreat behind your professional mask. Why?'

'Because we didn't come here to talk about *me*. We came to talk about George.'

'But we didn't,' Alessandro pointed out with remorseless logic. 'We didn't end up talking about George, as it happens.'

'And that was a mistake.' She breathed a silent sigh of relief as the bill was brought to them, and then breathed an even bigger sigh of relief when the proprietor approached and began enthusiastically quizzing them on what they thought of their meal, his sharp black eyes dancing between the two of them.

So she hadn't answered his question. And he wasn't sure why he wanted to find out anyway. But he did. What was it they said about wanting what you couldn't get?

He watched as she rose, terminating all personal conversation.

'I shall get a taxi home,' she told him firmly.

He ignored her. 'I wouldn't dream of it.'

He ushered her out into a much cooler evening—suitable weather finally for her starchy suit and jacket. He made a call on his cell phone and his car, complete with driver, appeared from nowhere. It pulled over and he opened the passenger door for her. When she was inside, he leant down so that he was looking at her on eye level.

'You'll be happy to know that you'll be spared my company.'

He grinned, and she had one of those intuitive moments of knowing that he knew exactly what had been going through her head.

'I'll get Jackson to drop you home and we can pick up where we left off at a later date.'

'What later date?' She worried at her lower lip. If she could stick a few definite meetings in her work diary then she would be able to get a handle on seeing him again. And over her dead body if it was going to be in another cosy little restaurant.

'I'll get back to you on that one.'

'But don't you want to get this mess sorted out as quickly as possible?'

'You can keep an eye on all the business accounts for suspicious activity, but if there's none then why not let George enjoy his last supper, so to speak?' He stood up, slapped the hood of the sleek, black Maserati, and remained watching as it disappeared from view.

He hadn't felt so invigorated for a long time.

And what, he wondered, was a guy to do about *that*?

CHAPTER THREE

FOR THE PAST few years Kate had seen her place of work as a refuge. There, she had felt in charge of her life, had worked hard at putting together all the building blocks that gave it definition and purpose.

Now she felt jumpy. On tenterhooks. Always on the lookout for Alessandro who, for the past couple of days, had often appeared to talk to her. About a client with a thorny tax problem, two overseas companies whose vast returns had generated questions about splitting them into smaller fragments, an acquisition that would mark a significant branching out from electronics, shipping and the leisure industry into publications…

'Cape would normally handle this, but seeing that he's on an extended holiday abroad, and seeing that that extended holiday is likely to become permanent, you'd better start getting acquainted with some of his responsibilities…'

This at five-thirty earlier today, when most of her colleagues had mentally switched off in preparation for leaving and had been all agog at the appearance of the big man.

She had kept as cool and collected as she could but her nerves had been all over the place. Surely the head of finance should be handling this situation? she had ventured, watching askance as he had perched on the side of her desk and then dragging her eyes away from his muscular thighs and the way the fine fabric of his trousers was stretched taut over them. But, no. Watson Russell was swamped by several huge ongoing deals—and besides, these matters would qualify as fairly small peanuts for him.

Afterwards, some of the girls had hovered, waiting for her to emerge from her office, and had proceeded to ply her with questions. None of the questions had had anything to do with work. They had wanted her opinion of him. As a hunk. Kate had made it a point never to engage in conversations like that, but she had been pinned to the wall and had found herself admitting that he was all right but not her type.

So how come he's been around so much...is something going on...?

Argh! She had become just the sort of giggly, girly type she had never been, and it had left her all hot and bothered.

And he *still* hadn't committed to a meeting so that he could look through what she had found out—which, as it turned out, was not very much at all. George *had* been dipping his hands in the till, but it hadn't been going on for very long and the amounts, in the big scheme of things, weren't that significant.

She would talk to Alessandro about that—try and find some compassion in him for the older man—but she didn't hold out much hope.

Now, at home far earlier than she normally would have been, on yet another hot summer evening, Kate looked at her work computer with jaundiced eyes.

It wasn't yet six and she couldn't face sitting in front of her computer and picking up where she had left off during the day.

Wandering through her very nice little ground-floor flat, she had plenty of time to think about the social life she lacked.

The back door was flung open and she could smell the neighbours barbecuing. Aside from the pleasant couple with two kids living next to her, she had no idea who her neighbours were.

At work, having almost given up on asking her, two of her colleagues had invited her to go to the pub with them and she had felt a little surge of panic because…

Because her whole life was devoted to work.

How had that happened? Okay, she knew *how*, and she knew *why*, she just didn't understand how it had all run away with her so that she had lost all her perspective.

Not only was her social life practically non-existent, but where was the guy she should be dating? Where was the exciting sex life she should be having?

She had had one boyfriend, three years previously, and he had fallen off the face of the earth because he had wanted more attention than she had been prepared to give. He hadn't understood that she had been taking professional exams and had had to study when she wasn't holding down the demanding job at the accountancy firm she had left as soon as she had qualified.

At the time she had been miffed—because how hard would it have been for him to just give her some breathing space? Surely it had been enough that they'd had fun on the weekends? But he had wanted more than just fun on the weekends.

So now here she was—alone. She wouldn't have wanted to be with Sam still. No, in retrospect, he hadn't been the man for her, even though he had ticked a lot of the right boxes. But shouldn't she have *moved on*? Be having a good time finding his replacement? Somewhere?

She lived in *London*, for heaven's sake!

Frustrated with the direction of her thoughts, she slammed shut the French doors at the back so that she couldn't be reminded of what she was missing by the smell of barbecue wafting into her house.

Then she had a shower.

Then, in a pair of tiny shorts and a cropped top, she prepared to wait out the annoying train of thoughts that were suddenly bothering her.

For which she blamed her wretched boss, who had somehow managed to get under her skin, to make her feel somehow *inadequate*...

And as soon as she started thinking about Alessandro she found that she couldn't stop.

He was just so *alive* and *vital* and brimming over with restless energy. Next to him, she felt like a pale, listless shadow, going through the motions of having a fulfilling life when she wasn't.

Absorbed in pointless speculation, she was only aware of the doorbell when it was depressed with such insistency that she was forced to dash and pull open the door or else risk her neighbours complaining about noise pollution.

Alessandro Preda was the last person she'd expected to see standing on her doorstep. In fact she blinked rapidly, trying to clear her vision and turn him into someone else. But, no, he was still there. Tall, dynamic, broad-shouldered, and way too exotically good-looking for London suburbia.

He didn't say a word. Just looked at her. He had obviously come straight from work because he was still in his work trousers—charcoal grey, super conventional, and yet on him somehow *not quite*. But there was no jacket, and he had shoved the sleeves of his shirt up to his elbows, revealing muscled forearms liberally sprinkled with dark hair.

She seemed to have forgotten how to speak.

'Are you going to ask me in?'

Alessandro eventually broke the silence. It took some effort. He had wanted to catch her by surprise, had been driven by sheer curiosity to see her somewhere—anywhere—that wasn't to do with the office.

But he hadn't expected *this*.

This wasn't the starchy woman who occupied her own office three floors down in his building. Removed from the files, the computers, the telephones and the uninspiring range of suits in various shades of grey, this was a different woman altogether.

This was the woman he had glimpsed at the restaurant.

She was in a pair of shorts and a small top, and her hair was long and tied back in a ponytail that swung down her back.

Where had that body come from? She was long and slender, her stomach flat, her breasts…

He broke out in a fine film of perspiration. It was the sort of reaction he never experienced, and his awareness of her, his *physical* awareness of her, was intense, immediate—a rush of blood invading his body in a tidal surge.

She wasn't wearing a bra.

'What are you doing here?'

It was a breathless, angry question. She could barely deal with him at the office—was at war with herself and her puzzling reaction to him. How dared he now take himself out of that environment, which didn't even feel *safe* any more, and superimpose himself here? On her doorstep? In her apartment?

Suddenly excruciatingly aware of just how much of her body was exposed, she hugged her arms around herself and remained rooted to the spot. She hadn't shut the door in his face, but she wasn't inviting him in either.

'I've been busy this week,' Alessandro imparted roughly, raking fingers through his dark hair and staring away to one side while he tried to do the unimaginable and compose himself. 'I had every intention of going through this business with you, but I haven't had time. Like you said, Cape deserves more than five minutes of my attention when I can grab a moment.'

'You managed to grab lots of moments when you were in my office—piling work on me before George has even been given a decent burial…'

'Hell, why do you have to be so dramatic? And are you going to ask me in? Or am I going to have to stand outside and have this conversation with you? The neighbours might begin to wonder what's going on.'

Kate spun round on her heels, agonisingly conscious of her small shorts. She realized in a flash how important her formal work attire was. All those bland, off-the-peg suits in drab colours had been her way of keeping the rest of the world at bay. Even at the restaurant with him, when she had dropped her mask and actually spoken her mind, that suit of hers had still been a reminder of their respective roles.

But shorts and a cropped top? Since when could anyone call *that* armour?

Alessandro watched her extremely pert bottom as she stalked away from him. His erection was so ramrod hard that it was painful—and more than likely visible.

He wanted to ask her whether she made it a habit to open the door to anybody who might ring the bell dressed in next to nothing, because this wasn't Cornwall. He shoved both hands into his trouser pockets in an attempt to do some damage limitation with the serious bulge of his arousal.

'I'm going to change,' she told him ungraciously as she stood aside and indicated that he could wait for her in the kitchen. 'I'm sorry, Alessandro. I realize that you're the boss, and you probably think that you can do whatever you please, but I really don't think it's on for you to just call by unannounced.'

Her arms were still folded as she swung to look at him. Her heart picked up pace as their eyes tangled and held. Her skin felt too tight for her body. His eyes on her made her nipples tingle, made her want to rub her legs together to ease the ache between them.

'Why?'

He was now sitting at the kitchen table. *Thank God.* What the hell was going on here? He'd had his fill of stunning women, and none had had such an instantaneous effect on his libido. Was it because of the dichotomy between the consummate professional and the rangy, leggy, sexy woman she was under the uniform she chose to wear? Maybe it had been too long since he had had sex… He was a man with a high sex drive, and using his hand to do the job was far from satisfactory, given the choice of a woman's mouth doing the job for him.

He thought of Kate's mouth there, her pink tongue delicately flicking over his arousal, and he sucked in a sharp breath.

'Yes…' He cleared his throat. 'Go and change if it would make you feel better to slip into your suit because I'm here and you find it impossible to be anything in my company aside from an employee.'

'What's *that* supposed to mean?' Kate enquired tightly.

Alessandro sighed and sat back. 'It doesn't mean anything, Kate.'

It means you should leave now and return decently clothed. Sackcloth might do the trick.

'And you're right. I had no business showing up here on your doorstep without calling you in advance.'

'How did you know where I lived anyway?'

'Jackson was kind enough to provide me with the information.'

'And *that's* another thing,' she retorted, bristling as she thought back to her colleagues at work and their reactions to Alessandro descending from Mount Olympus to grace them with his presence. 'People have been talking…'

She reddened, but now that it was out what choice did she have but to stand her ground and say what was on her mind? Besides, he was in *her* territory now. If she couldn't speak freely in her own house, then where could she? He might be the ruler of all he surveyed in his towering glass house in the City, but he wasn't out here.

She quailed. Did he have to look so…so *ruler-like* even when he wasn't in his domain? She wished he would just look a little more *normal*, a little less…*intimidating.* Or sexy. Take your pick.

She suddenly felt her youth, her lack of experience.

'Talking?' Alessandro tilted his head to one side and looked at her intently. 'Talking about what? And who are these "people" who have been talking?'

'I maybe shouldn't have brought this up…' she began, chickening out.

'But you did, and now that you have you might as well finish. And for God's sake don't launch into any full-blown apologies when you've said what you want to say.'

'You seldom come down to our floor. In fact, I can only think of one time when you actually came to see me in my office, and George was there as well. Suddenly you've been appearing out of the blue and people…well, people have been wondering what's going on. They think… I don't know what they think… But I don't want them to think it. Whatever it is.'

'So these people think something…you're not sure what…and you don't want them to think it…?'

'I'm a very private person. Always have been.'

Except for one night in a restaurant, when I spilled my guts about my background to you…

'I'm at a loss as to what I can do to resolve this issue...'

He spread his arms wide in a typical gesture that was at once rueful and ridiculously phoney, because there was just a hint of a smile tugging at the corners of his mouth that made her feel like an idiot. His brows knitted in a frown which was also phoney.

'I guess you must think that Jackson thinks something too...although who knows for sure...?'

'It's all well and good for you to sit there sniggering, but I'm the one who has to live with other people's stupid speculations!'

'That's office life for you. Maybe you should climb out of your ivory tower and experience it. And don't worry about Jackson, by the way. Whatever he might think, or not think, he'll keep it to himself.'

Kate gritted her teeth together and remembered diplomacy. He was rich, and immune to the opinions of other people. Not that there would be many people willing to shoot their mouths off at him. The man was unbearably arrogant in his self-confidence. And he talked about *her* living in an ivory tower!

'Maybe I should,' she said, with a tight, forced smile.

'You look as though you've swallowed a lime.' Alessandro grinned. He hadn't noticed her freckles before, or the fact that her dark hair was more chestnut than brown, and golden at the ends.

'I'm going to change. If you want something to drink there's an opened bottle of wine in the fridge, or you can make yourself tea or coffee. It's not a big kitchen. I'm sure you'll be able to find what you need.'

With that she swung round and headed to her bedroom, fuming at the way he had invaded her privacy, fuming at the way he saw fit to say exactly what happened to be on his mind, fuming at her evening, which she had had neatly planned and which would now be spent in a state of edge-of-the-seat nervous tension.

She got to her bedroom and gazed at her mutinous reflection in the mirror. Her colour was up. Her hair was not in the neat little bun he was accustomed to seeing. The ponytail was coming undone and wisps of long brown hair trailed around her face. Which was completely bare of make-up…

She peered at the freckles which had always made her look so young.

Freckles, dishevelled hair, a pair of shorts that she would never in a million years have worn had she known that he—or anyone else, for that matter—would be turning up on her doorstep, and a small stretch top with no bra. The top might be navy blue, but she had generous breasts and it was perfectly obvious that they were not constrained.

If she half squinted and stood back just a tiny bit…well, she might pass muster as one of those cocktail waitresses she scorned. Small clothes, busty, legs everywhere, hair everywhere…

In the rational part of her mind Kate knew that it was just her imagination playing tricks on her. She wasn't dressed any differently from any young woman hanging around in her own home on a balmy summer evening.

But this was her tender spot—the place where her imagination took flight. She was ultrasensitive to any suggestion that she and her mother had *anything* in common when it came to the way they saw themselves and their bodies. Her mother had always been a benchmark as to how she, Kate, would *never* conduct herself.

She closed her eyes, breathed deeply, and hurriedly removed the offending attire, replacing the shorts and cropped top with a pair of jeans and a very sensible baggy tee shirt which revealed nothing but a faded logo on the front. She neatened up the ponytail, but drew the line at turning it into a bun.

When she made it back to the kitchen it was to find Alessandro well ensconced at her kitchen table, a glass of wine next to him, long legs extended to one side, relaxing back with his hands folded behind his head.

'I like your place.' He watched as she hovered for a few seconds by the kitchen door, the very picture of the disgruntled and reluctant host. 'Cool, airy, light colours… And nice that it's not in a big, impersonal block of flats as well. I take it there's just the one other flat above you…?'

'You've been poking around…' she said, eyes narrowed.

'You disappeared to change your clothes. What else was I supposed to do?'

'You were supposed to make yourself a cup of tea and stay put.'

'Wine seemed a better alternative. I try and avoid caffeine after six. You look nothing like her, you know.'

Kate stiffened. She took a couple of steps into the kitchen with about the same enthusiasm as someone entering a lion's den. This was *her* house and *her* kitchen, and yet he seemed to dominate it with his presence, making her feel as if she needed to ask permission to open the fridge.

'I have no idea what you're talking about.' She helped herself to a glass of wine and took up position at the opposite end of the table. 'And I would rather not get into any of that.'

'Any of what? If you don't know what I'm talking about?'

He slung his long body out of the chair and headed to the fridge, opened the door and peered inside.

'I see you're a very healthy eater,' he said conversationally, helping himself to the bottle of wine and bringing it back to the table, where he proceeded to pour himself another glass. 'Although the box of chocolates is a giveaway of a more...*decadent* nature...'

'If you give me five minutes, I'll go and fetch the file on George.'

'But returning to what I said...' This time his dark eyes were thoughtful, serious. 'And that remark you so adroitly tried to avoid. You're nothing like your mother. I looked at some of the pictures you have framed in your sitting room...'

'You shouldn't have come here and you shouldn't have nosed around...' For a few appalling seconds, Kate felt as though her little world was in the process of being tilted on its axis. 'I should never have told you any of that stuff.'

'Why? Is there something wrong with confiding in other people?'

'Do *you*?' She turned the question right back at him. 'Do *you* run around spilling your guts to all and sundry? What about all those models you go out with? Do you get deep and personal with *them*? Do you hold hands and sob over a bottle of wine while you pour your soul out?'

This was what it felt like to lose control. She had always had control, and now here she was, sitting at her own kitchen table, losing it with a guy who had the power to terminate the career she had so carefully built.

And the worst of it was that she didn't want to retract the accusation.

She was aware of him with every pore of her being. He swamped her. When she breathed she felt that she was breathing in his clean, masculine scent. When she leaned forward she could feel his personality wrap around her like tendrils of ivy.

She felt...*alive*.

But not, she told herself uneasily, *in a good way*. There was nothing about Alessandro Preda that could make her feel *anything* in a good way. She felt alive in a *very, very annoying* way.

'At least you're not apologizing for asking that daring question,' Alessandro drawled.

So she had ditched the shorts and the cropped top, but the jeans and the baggy shirt did nothing to reduce her sex appeal. Now he had seen that body shorn of its camouflage outfits the image was imprinted in his brain with the force of a branding iron.

'And you're right. I *don't* tend to do the personal touchy-feely business with the women I go out with. I can't recall pouring my soul out and sobbing in recent times.' His mouth twitched with amusement. 'In that we're strangely alike. But you wear your defence system on the outside. You cover up from neck to ankle but there's no need. You're not your mother. You may want to make sure you don't follow in her footsteps, but you don't have to dress like a spinster schoolteacher to do that.'

'How dare you come here and try and analyze me?' Tears stung the back of her throat but thankfully she was far too reticent a person to allow them access.

'I'm not trying to analyze you,' Alessandro told her in just the sort of gentle voice that she knew might prove her undoing if she let it. 'Don't you feel a little trapped by all the hoops you make yourself jump through?

'I don't feel trapped by anything. This is the life I've chosen to lead. You have no idea what it's like to be… insecure when you're growing up…'

'How do you know that?' Alessandro asked softly.

Her eyes widened. She paused for thought. How *did* she know that? Because of who he was? Rich. Powerful. Confident. *Arrogant.* Those were not the hallmarks of someone whose upbringing had been anything but exemplary.

Besides, he was the sole issue of the union of two wealthy families. If you looked him up on the internet—*which she never had*—you would discover that. She had overhead one of the giggly girls from the legal department imparting that titbit one day in the office restaurant. He occupied a stratosphere that was quite unlike hers. Actually, quite unlike most peoples.

'But you were right when you said that we're here to talk about Cape.'

For a minute there Alessandro had felt the pull to trade one set of confidences for another. He didn't know where that had come from, but it wasn't something he was going to give in to. Probably hearing her talk about her mother had naturally led him to think about his own parents. They too lived on the coast—probably not a million miles away from her mother. Small world…

'Of course. I'll just go and fetch the file I've compiled. I've summarized all my findings. I thought it might be easier for you to go through rather than follow the trail piecemeal.'

'Highly efficient, and just what I would expect of you!'

Kate frowned, but before she could rise to the bait he interceded with a grin.

'And, before you jump down my throat, I *wasn't* being sarcastic…'

'I wasn't about to imply that you were.' But she had been. And that made her feel a little uneasy. Either she was as transparent as a pane of glass, which was a bad thing, or else he could read her mind—which was a bad thing.

And what had he meant when he had hinted that it wasn't true that he wouldn't know what it might feel like to have an insecure background?

She felt her pulse race at the thought of him confiding in her and had to yank herself back to the reality that, when all was said and done, he was her boss and they had nothing in common.

Maybe he was right about that ivory tower, she thought feverishly as she fetched the file and headed back to the kitchen. Not as it applied to her in an office scenario but as it applied to her in a *life* scenario. Maybe she *had* lived life in the safe middle lane for too long. Maybe she *had* detached herself too much from the highs and lows of getting involved with people…with *men*. Maybe that was why she was behaving like this with him: disobeying common sense and flirting with something dangerous…

Flirting with an impossible attraction.

Shoot me in the head first, she thought.

But she had to take a deep, steadying breath before she pushed open the door and stepped inside where, thankfully, he was still in the same place and not snooping through the kitchen drawers and making himself even more at home.

'Would you like some coffee?' she asked politely, and Alessandro raised his eyebrows.

'I don't need sobering up,' he told her drily. 'So no, thank you. Besides, what did I tell you about caffeine after six?'

'Yes, you did say that—but I do remember you helping yourself to several cups of strong black coffee a few months ago, when we were working with George and a couple of others on that deal late into the night…'

'I didn't realize that you had been keeping a watch on what I was eating and drinking…'

God, but she was sexy when she blushed like that and looked away, as though she was in danger of giving away state secrets if she met his eyes. He felt himself stir again, aroused by images that had no place in his head.

He waved his hand for her to hand over her findings and

started reading. There wasn't a great deal to get through—less than he had been expecting.

'So all in all,' he said slowly, raising his eyes to hers, 'he hasn't been at it for very long...'

'Which I think is in his favour...'

'We'll have to agree to disagree on that one. The fact is that the man has stolen from me...'

'He must have had a reason.'

'Of course he must have had a reason. Greed. Possibly linked to a debt which had to be paid off. My money is on a gambling debt. Unless you've noticed anything out of the ordinary? Vodka bottles in his desk drawer, perhaps?'

'I can't imagine that George is a gambler,' Kate persisted, thinking furiously, trying to remember if she had noticed anything unusual about his behaviour over the past six months and coming up with nothing. 'And he certainly isn't an alcoholic, if that's what you're implying!'

'How would you know, unless you socialize with him out of work? On a regular basis?'

'He's a good guy.'

'Who has just happened to steal over a hundred grand from me over a five-month period. His halo's slipping slightly, wouldn't you agree? Still, he will have the opportunity to explain his borderline saintly status to a court of impartial jurors, and you are more than welcome to sign on as a character witness.'

'Sometimes—' She swallowed back something she would instantly regret saying and took a deep breath. 'Surely you could at least hear what he has to say before you condemn him and throw away the key...?'

Could he? Well, under any other circumstances there would be no question as to what course of action he would take. There could never be any excuse for fraud. Life was full of people forgiving the idiocy of other people, but in the end idiots deserved the punishment they got. The feckless deserved their fate.

He looked at that earnest face. That beautiful, earnest face. She should be as tough as nails—immune to feelings of empathy given her background. But she wasn't.

She was complex, intriguing, quirky… And all of this despite the fact that she was so desperate to be just the opposite.

He liked that.

Was there anything wrong with that?

When it came to women he had always been able to have what he wanted. This woman introduced a challenge to his jaded appetite and what was wrong with that? What was wrong if he wanted to explore that just a little bit further?

'I could…' he admitted, watching her carefully. 'Everyone has a story to tell…'

'I know!'

She hazarded a smile, leaned forward.

'You think I'm mad, but I just *know* that George isn't a bad guy. He…he's actually one of the kindest men I've met in my entire life! Although…' She laughed, and the sound was light and infectious, 'Compared to some of the guys I've had the misfortune to meet, thanks to my mother, that's not hard! Not that any of them threatened me in any way,' she added hurriedly, 'but I certainly grew up having first-hand knowledge of how scummy guys can be…'

She smiled shyly at him, marvelling that underneath that forbidding exterior and arrogant self-assurance he might not be quite as unrelenting as she'd thought.

'I'm really glad you're prepared to at least listen to what he has to say.'

Alessandro made a non-committal sound under his breath and smiled at her lazily. 'And wouldn't it be so much fairer if I had this discussion with him face to face? Outside the office? After all, the last thing I want is for the world to see him being marched out in handcuffs...'

'Absolutely,' Kate agreed, delighted at his turnaround. 'That sort of thing would just...*destroy* him...'

'Which is why we are going to fly to Canada and confront him there. Find out just what the hell has been going on. Surprise him, so to speak. But it will be a far less unpleasant surprise than if I do it in the office, with all those curious eyes peering through the glass, people jumping to conclusions and gossiping...'

'Sorry...*we*...?'

'Of course!'

He smiled broadly at her while she stared back, her brain moving sluggishly to compute the message it was receiving.

'You're the one who has influenced me into a decision I would never have otherwise taken. It's only right that you be there when the questions get asked...don't you agree?'

'Well...'

'Congratulations on changing my mind! It's a rare occurrence. I'll get my secretary to book flights out first thing on Monday morning. I take it you have a current passport? Yes? Well, then...' He looked at her with satisfaction. 'That's settled...'

CHAPTER FOUR

ALESSANDRO WAS WAITING for her five days later at the first-class check-in desk at the airport.

Kate spotted him from a mile away. Not hard. He stood out even in a packed terminal, where people were either rushing around frantically or else standing in long queues with blank *How much slower can this line move?* stares.

He was frowning at his smartphone, scrolling through messages, leaning against the counter with a solitary, very expensive holdall on the ground next to him. The picture of understated elegance in cream trousers, a white shirt and a lightweight jacket which he had tossed on top of the holdall.

Having planned on arriving bang on time, if not early, Kate was unavoidably running late and she was hassled.

She thought her neatly pinned-back hair might be unravelling. and her suit and pumps felt stiff and uncomfortable— unsuitable for the heat here in London, never mind abroad. Lord only knew how they would fare on a long-haul flight, but she had been determined to dress appropriately because, crucially, *this wasn't a holiday.*

She had allowed her rules to slip. She had found herself losing her self-control. It was going to be very important that she re-establish that self-control while she was in Toronto on this business trip.

Comfy trousers and a casual cotton jumper with loafers had thus been ruled out as suitable travel gear.

'You're late,' were the first words Alessandro greeted her with as he snapped shut his phone and straightened.

'Traffic. I'm sorry. It would have been quicker for me to have come by tube. But I'm here now, and I hope I haven't kept you waiting too long.' She managed to say all that in a cool, polite voice whilst not actually looking at him at all. 'Have you checked in?'

'I was waiting for you.'

'Is that all the luggage you've brought?' Kate asked incredulously.

Next to his holdall, her suitcase was the size of a small mountain—but they were going for a week, and she hadn't quite known which clothes to take for which occasion. So she had packed to cover every eventuality.

They had found out where George was staying with his wife without actually contacting him for the information—because, as Alessandro had persisted in telling her, the element of surprise would afford him no time to start thinking up fancy stories to cover up what he had done.

Kate hadn't said anything. Poor George. Little did he know what he was in for. Alessandro had assured her that he was prepared to listen, but was he prepared to absolve from blame and forgive?

In the world of Alessandro Preda there was no room for excuses or apologies. If you crossed him in any way retribution would be swift and unforgiving. She could only try and be the restraining hand on his arm, so to speak. It was a minor miracle that he was prepared to listen at all.

'I'm a believer in travelling light,' he said, checking in her suitcase and then taking his time to examine the picture in her passport, while Kate patiently waited for him to return it to her, teeth gritted. 'I take it you're not…?'

'I wasn't sure what to bring with me.'

'So you decided to bring it all? Including the kitchen sink?'

She reddened and mumbled something about it being so much easier for guys, who could fling two things in an overnight bag and disappear abroad for a month.

She might have added that she could count on the fingers of one hand the number of times she had been abroad in her entire life. She wasn't an expert when it came to working out what to pack. Aside from confronting George and ruining his holiday, they would be visiting a potential business opportunity on the outskirts of the city—killing two birds with one stone, so to speak, which was probably partly why Alessandro had chosen to make this trip in the first place.

So, yes, work clothes... But it wasn't really feasible to wear suits in the evenings as well, was it?

Not that she planned on spending a single one of those evenings in *his* company. Not one. She intended to draw some very clear and definite lines. Between nine and five she would be his employee, and after five she would disappear and do her own thing.

So she had stuffed some casual wear in her case as well. Jeans and loose, baggy tops. The woman in the tiny shorts and cropped top with the ponytail was *not* going to make an appearance.

'If I need more clothes,' Alessandro was saying, leading her through customs, handling everything so efficiently that she barely noticed them heading towards the first-class lounge, 'then I can always buy out there. I travel so much that I can be in and out of an airport a lot faster if I don't have to check in any luggage.'

'Hence the holdall?'

'Hence the holdall. Usually I bring something a lot smaller when I'm going to Europe.'

'I can't imagine what could be smaller,' Kate panted, walking fast to keep pace with him. 'A wallet?'

Alessandro chuckled and shot her an appreciative look—which she missed because she was trying to remain composed whilst half running beside him, one hand holding her neat little bun in place, the other dragging a pull-along case which she had stuffed with all sorts of useful reading matter.

'Occasionally,' he drawled, slowing down and veering off to the left, 'a wallet is all a man needs. It can hold a lot more than just banknotes and credit cards...'

'Really? Like what?' Kate retorted sarcastically, getting her breathing back and looking sideways at him. 'A change of outfit? Spare jacket? Pair of shoes?'

He burst out laughing, stopping and looking down at her with an unreadable expression that left her feeling a little dizzy.

'Where have *you* been hiding?'

'Sorry?' She stared back at him, confused.

'This witty, funny woman with the sharp tongue... Where have you been stashing her away? If I'd known she existed I would have taken some time out to try and find her...under the desk, maybe...or behind the coatrack...or in the stationery cupboard...'

Kate couldn't help herself. She blushed and smiled and looked away, and then caught his eyes again. And all the while she was doing that she could feel her heart pick up speed.

There was still laughter in his eyes as he continued to hold her gaze. 'A wallet,' he murmured, his dark eyes suddenly glinting with lazy devilry, 'can hold something that's even more vital than cash or credit cards...'

'What?'

'I'll let you think about it...' He grinned and began

walking again, pushing open the glass doors that led to the first-class lounge.

Kate paused and took stock. This was *amazing*. Here, the hustle and bustle of the airport terminal gave way to…well, peace, quiet…glassy counters groaning under the weight of food…men and women on their computers, comfy chairs and sofas…

'Wow.'

Accustomed to all of this, Alessandro took a few seconds to register her expression, and he felt a weirdly heady kick at having been the one to introduce her to the experience.

'So *this* is how the other half live,' she breathed, impressed to death. 'Am I standing out like a sore thumb?'

She looked at him anxiously and he smiled.

'I don't think there's a dress code in operation here,' he told her gently, guiding her forward and flicking their first-class passes to the well-groomed woman behind the polished curved counter.

Actually, there was. The dress code was *expensive*. He felt a sudden surge of protectiveness, which he dismissed as the normal reaction of a boss looking out for his employee. Having her insulted, stared at or criticized in any way was something he would not tolerate.

He ushered her to a long, low sofa, settled her down. When he asked her what she would like to drink he was amused to see her spring to her feet, eyes bright.

'I should do the honours,' she told him seriously. 'You *are* my boss, after all…'

'Of course,' Alessandro murmured. 'What was I thinking?'

So she didn't blend in? He was suddenly contemptuous of all those unspoken rules the seriously wealthy played by. A rich diet of supermodels had blinded him to the realities that everyone else lived with. And, of all people, shouldn't he know that the wealthy had their failings? Didn't always conform?

He frowned, distracted by the rare intrusion of introspection. He came from wealth—had known first-hand its ups and downs, had experienced the frailty of what could be so easily taken for granted. He was secure in his own personal fortune—had made sure of that—but it struck him that he no longer looked outside the box at lifestyles that weren't rich and privileged.

He was accustomed to his rare stratosphere because it was the one everyone he knew inhabited—including the women he dated. Although it had to be said that their passports came via their incredible looks.

She returned five minutes later with two plates heaped with various titbits, from little dainty sandwiches to cream cakes and packets of biscuits.

'I've gone a little mad,' she confessed. 'I know it's not cool to take a bit of everything that's there, but I couldn't resist.'

'You don't have to justify yourself to me, Kate. Take whatever you want. That's what it's there for. I'd bet that half the people here would love to do the same, but some warped sense of wanting to *blend in* and *look cool* stops them.'

Kate breathed a sigh of relief. 'I'm ravenous, anyway.'

'We could have a full breakfast if you'd rather?'

'You're kidding?'

'Perfectly serious. Airlines command fat fares for first-class travellers. Frankly, hot food in their lounges is the very least one can expect.'

'I'm fine.' She reminded herself that she wasn't there to have fun. Work was what was on the agenda—and not of a very pleasant nature either. 'But thank you for the offer.'

She tucked in as delicately as possible whilst noticing that he ate next to nothing.

'You can work if you want to,' she contributed awkwardly. 'You don't have to feel that I need entertaining.'

'I don't.'

She reluctantly looked at the little pile of uneaten sandwiches on her plate. 'How do you intend to…to confront George? Have you given it much thought? I know you have all the evidence compiled, but are you just going to present him with it in front of his wife?'

'Haven't thought that far ahead.'

'I'd hate him to think that I might have been the one to instigate this whole sorry business,' she admitted. 'Although if I show up at your side I guess that's the first thing he'll think.'

'Why does it matter?' Alessandro dismissed her concern with a careless shrug. 'So he gets the boot and puts it down to you? What's the big deal?'

'The "big deal" is that some of us actually *care* what other people think of them.'

'Why? Will you ever see him again? His family?'

'That's not the point.' She looked at him curiously. 'How can you be so…so cold and detached?'

And he was. Despite the fact that he socialized heavily, dated women by the bucketload if office gossip and the daily tabloids were anything to go by, there was something about Alessandro Preda that remained remote and untouchable.

She shivered. Was that all part and parcel of his incredible appeal?

In the City he was feared as a ruthless competitor. Men and women alike were awed by him. Even here, as she surreptitiously slid her eyes to the side, she could see the way people checked him out. He commanded attention and took it as his right. They all knew he was rich, or else he wouldn't be in a first-class lounge. They only wondered if he was famous—and if so famous, for what?

But, for all the attention he garnered, on some level he didn't *engage*. Why was that? she wondered.

'Trust me…cold and detached are two words that have *never* been used by a woman to describe me…'

And all at once Kate knew what he had been referring to with that little smile curling his lips, when he had told her that wallets held more important stuff than money and credit cards.

Condoms.

A man who could have whatever woman he wanted always had to be prepared, she thought, with a burst of cynicism.

It was incredible that she had managed to forget just what sort of a person he was. He might be remote, he might be as shallow as a puddle when it came to anything emotional, but he was also witty, intelligent, and when he focused those dark, speculative, brooding eyes on her, all her misgivings floated away like dew on a hot summer morning.

Which didn't change the fact that he was a man who made sure he carried condoms in his wallet—because who knew when some poor good-looking girl might cross his path, hoping for more than just a one-night stand or a one-month fling with a bunch of goodbye roses when she was on her way out?

'Well, this is one woman who's using them now,' Kate said coolly. 'When we've confronted poor George in his hotel room and you've shaken him down and booted him out of your company without a backward glance, will you be able to wipe your hands and walk away without giving him a second thought? Because if you can then you're cold and detached—and it doesn't matter how many adoring fans tell you the opposite.'

From any other woman Alessandro would not have taken this. He had his rules and his boundaries and those were lines that were never crossed. In truth, he never really even had to lay them down. They were unwritten, unspoken and obeyed without fail.

Kate Watson—who, on the surface, promised to be as non-committal as a plank of wood—chose to disregard every single one of those boundary lines, and her rampant disobedience intrigued him and he didn't quite know why.

Maybe it was the dichotomy between what she strove to conceal and what she was lured into revealing against her better judgement.

He might not be involved with her on a personal level, but there was something in her that aroused his interest.

'I expect you're going to remind me that it's not my place to voice opinions about you or what you do…' she muttered in a half-hearted apology.

'We're going to be in each other's company for a week. If you have something to say then you might as well get it off your chest. I don't think I can face your constant disapproval. And I'm guessing from those pursed lips that you *do* disapprove of me?'

'I… No, of course I don't…' Her voice fell away.

'Of course you do. You have opinions on the type of person I am, and admiration isn't one of them. That's something you've decided you'll leave to those adoring fans of mine.'

Hot colour crawled up into her cheeks. *Pursed lips.* She was a woman with *pursed lips* and *disapproval* and *starchy suits.* He was *fun.* And she was *the schoolmarm who always rained on his parade.*

Except it wasn't *fun* when there was some poor, deluded hopeful woman at the receiving end, was it?

'I have a lot of admiration for your business acumen,' she said stiffly. 'They say that everything you touch turns to gold. That's quite an achievement. I think it takes a lot to be a guy who builds all the businesses and it's something quite different from the guy who services them. You're the guy who builds the businesses.'

'Not exactly *adoring*, though, is it…?' he mused. 'When it comes to accolades…?'

He enjoyed the way she blushed. It was something he had never noticed before. Like a wayward horse tugging at its reins, his mind broke its leash and zoomed back to the picture of her in those shorts, long legs going on for ever, full breasts bouncing braless in that small top.

Great body sternly kept under wraps because she had learned lessons from having a mother who was too ready to flaunt hers.

Had she ever flaunted her body for a man?

'I don't have to be a member of your fan club to appreciate that you're talented at what you do.'

She wanted to tell him that this was hardly appropriate conversation, but she suspected that he didn't give a damn what was appropriate and what wasn't. He did what he wanted to do because he could.

If she annoyed him too much she would probably find herself next to George on a trip to never-never land.

'But when it comes to anything that isn't work-related your admiration levels drop off sharply—am I right?' Her face was averted and he absently appreciated the fine delicacy of her profile. He had a sudden urge to release her long chestnut-brown hair from its ridiculous clips and pins.

'I suppose I have different standards to you when it comes to relationships,' she said eventually, when the silence was threatening to overwhelm her. She wasn't looking at him, but she could feel his dark eyes boring into the side of her face.

What was this all about? He didn't give a hoot what she thought about his personal life. Maybe he was irritated because she was being a little more forthcoming than he was used to, but her outspokenness probably amused him.

She was providing him with a different taste sensation—why not try it?

'And tell me what those standards are…'

Kate swung to look at him and discovered that he was leaning towards her, far too close for comfort.

Dark, dark eyes with ridiculously long eyelashes clashed with hers and the breath caught in her throat. She inched back, furious with herself for feeling uncomfortable in his presence, for letting him *get to her*, when she had given herself a stern talk about all that nonsense before she had left her house.

'I…'

'You're not going to dry up on me now, are you, Kate? When you've come this far?'

And just how had she managed to do that? she wondered. One minute they were striding through an airport and the next minute she had launched into a personal attack on his moral standards. Or as good as!

Trapped by her own idiocy, she frantically tried to think of a clever way to change the conversation, but he was waiting for her to say something. And not a sudden commentary on the weather or the state of the economy. No such luck. Why would he rescue her from her hideous discomfort when he could get a kick from pinning her to the wall and watching her wriggle like a worm on a hook?

'I don't approve of men who…*use* women. Maybe that's the wrong word,' she corrected hastily. 'I mean I don't approve of men who slide in and out of relationships, trying them on for size and then discarding the ones that don't quite fit.'

'And what about women who try men on for size?'

'That doesn't happen.'

'No?' He raised his eyebrows in a cool question. 'Ever had a boyfriend, Kate?'

'Of course I have!' she said hotly. 'And I don't see what that has to do with anything!'

'Where is he now?'

'I beg your pardon?'

'Where is this wonder guy now?' He peered around him, as if at any moment the man in question would stride out from where he had been hiding behind a computer terminal.

'We… It finished…'

'Ah.' Alessandro sat back and linked his fingers lightly on his lap. 'So it didn't work out?'

'No, it didn't,' Kate said uncomfortably.

'Was it a case of him using you ruthlessly before tossing you aside on the discarded heap?'

'No!' she cried, as flustered as a witness sitting in the box, being picked apart by the prosecution.

'Well, what happened, in that case?' And now his tone had changed. Very subtly. Because he'd discovered that he was curious about this mystery guy who hadn't chucked her on his discards pile. 'And don't think about launching into a little sermon about it being none of my business. You don't seem to have too many qualms about speaking your mind, so you can answer one or two questions of your own.'

'We broke up.' She shrugged and tore her eyes away from his lean, aggressive face. 'The timing was wrong,' she admitted grudgingly. 'I was very busy. I wasn't in the right place to fully cultivate the relationship the way it deserved to be cultivated...'

'Ah...so an amicable parting of ways...?'

Kate could have thought of other ways of describing their inevitable split. *Amicable* didn't feature on the list.

'So here's the thing,' he said, voice as smooth as silk and yet razor-sharp. 'You seem to be under the impression that every relationship that doesn't end in a walk up the aisle is a relationship that involves one person using the other. But life's not like that. Yes, it may have been so for your mother, but your mother was a certain type of personality. Your mother—and I'm no expert on this—may have been searching for something, and the only way she could conduct her search was by offering what she had and hoping it got picked by the right kind of guy...'

'You're right. You *don't* know my mother.'

'Maybe your mother was fundamentally insecure,' he carried on relentlessly. 'But that doesn't mean that everyone is like her. She's not the benchmark.'

'I never said she was.'

'No?'

'I should never have said anything,' she breathed resentfully. 'It's awful when you tell someone something and they then proceed to use it against you like in a court of law.'

But didn't he have a point? She refused to concede that he did, but her conscience nagged in a way it never had before. He had stripped her of her convenient black-and-white approach and she didn't want that. It was easier to set a course when you weren't distracted by grey areas and murky questions.

'It's not about the outcome,' she muttered in a driven voice. 'It's about the intent.'

'Explain.'

'I don't want to be having this conversation.' She gazed at the tepid coffee in her cup and wished she had something to fiddle with. 'Maybe we ought to find out whether we should be boarding. Or something.'

'They'll call us when it's time for us to board the plane. Relax.'

She was as tense as a bowstring, her body rigid. So much emotion contained behind that bland exterior. He reached out and brushed his finger against the soft skin on the underside of her wrist and she tensed.

And *he* tensed.

Electric. Unexpected. A high-voltage charge that suddenly ran between them.

He withdrew his hand quickly. 'You initiate conversations,' he said coolly, 'and when the going gets a little tricky you back away because you're too scared to carry on. Weren't you ever taught to finish what you start?'

The lazy teasing had gone, wiped out by that ferocious assault on his senses when he had casually touched her. Watching and speculating was one thing. But what he had felt just then, when he had briefly touched her…

It had felt like a loss of control. For a couple of seconds he had been knocked back by a reaction he had not expected. Curiosity had stoked his libido, but now…now he felt something as powerful as a depth charge. The shock of the unexpected jacked his responses into full alert. For once, toying with the idea of a woman in his bed seemed a dangerous adventure not to be undertaken.

'Okay…' Kate surreptitiously rubbed her wrist where his finger had been. 'If you really want to know, there's a difference between starting a relationship in the hope that it'll develop into something and starting a relationship knowing that it's going to crash and burn when you decide it's time to move on.'

'And I'm a crash-and-burn guy...?'

She shrugged and he stared her down, his dark eyes cool, his expression unreadable.

Was he storing away everything she said to be used at a later date? Did he even care one way or another *what* she said? She decided that, no, he probably didn't. He wasn't the kind of guy who would tolerate personal comments on his moral choices. She couldn't picture any woman sitting him down with a cup of tea and sharing her opinions on his ethics and his principles. They might have a rant when he chucked them over for a new model, but that was different.

Yet here he was now, waiting for her to say something. If he didn't care about her opinions he wouldn't be allowing her this leeway. Would he?

'Sort of... I guess... It's not for me to say...'

'Easy to make assumptions, isn't it?' he said softly. 'You criticized *me* for making assumptions about how your background influenced you...yet here you are... A bit hypocritical, wouldn't you say?'

The question hung in the air between them. Suddenly it felt as though they were the only two people sitting here. Background noise—not that there was much of that—faded, until she could almost hear the beating of her own heart.

It had been easy to tell herself that she could redefine the lines between them. Sitting here, she couldn't understand how those good intentions had been swept aside so fast and so completely.

'If you can't take the heat,' Alessandro drawled, 'then you should stay out of the kitchen. You think it's okay to offer your opinions on what you imagine my personal life is like...? Well, it's a two-way street...'

He beckoned across a young girl who was on the hunt for empty plates and glasses and asked her to fetch him a cup of black coffee, and all the while his eyes remained fastened on Kate's flushed face.

'But I'm glad you brought this up,' he continued, obviously not getting the vibes she was transmitting, 'because, like I said, a week of constant silent disapproval isn't what I need...'

'I didn't *have* to come,' Kate muttered.

'But here you are. And, incidentally, you actually *did* have to come. You had to come because I requested it. So, now we're having this cosy little chat, let me fill you in on your misconceptions. I *don't* pick women up and drop them, having led them up the garden path. I don't make promises I have no intention of fulfilling in exchange for sex.'

Kate stared mutinously at the ground, wishing it would do her a favour and open up and swallow her.

She was being chastised. Like a misbehaving kid in a classroom.

'Trust me—I don't have to do that.'

Coffee was brought to him and Kate noticed the way the young girl half curtseyed and stared at him, goggle-eyed. He might make noises about not wanting to be treated like royalty, and laugh because maybe he really did mean it, but he *was* treated like royalty.

'So you don't leave any broken hearts behind you?' she finally asked, prompted into filling the silence.

He looked at her thoughtfully.

'Maybe I do,' he mused. 'But through no fault of my own.'

Kate's mouth fell open. Talk about ditching responsibility! Her face must have revealed what was going through her head, but this time he relaxed, sipped the coffee that had been brought to him and smiled.

'I don't want commitment and I never pretend that I

do,' he said, and she bit down hard on the ready retort rising to her lips. 'I lay my cards on the table from the start.'

'And what would those cards happen to be?' Kate asked politely. She thought that they probably came from the same deck that all commitment-phobes used.

'No strings attached. I tell them from the outset that I'm in it for fun. I give them the opportunity to walk away.'

How considerate.

'No sleepovers…no cosy nights in in front of the telly… no knick-knacks in the bathroom…'

'That's a lot of rules,' Kate said truthfully. 'And then what happens?'

'What do you mean?' Alessandro frowned in puzzlement, because how much clearer could he get with his explanation?

'What if some of the rules get broken? I mean, what if one of your dates decides that she'd rather stay in than go out. But, no… I suppose those supermodel types love the camera, so why would they ever want to do something as boring as *staying in*…?'

Alessandro grinned but didn't say anything. He didn't have to. Why would any woman want to go out when they had the option of staying in a bed with *him*? Kate could read that clearly from his wicked grin.

'My rules don't get broken,' he murmured with soft assurance. 'And if they do then it spells the end of a relationship. And now that we've cleared that up…' He leaned forward to flip open his laptop, which had been resting on the table in front of them.

Now that he had cleared that up she was dismissed— along with her opinions.

CHAPTER FIVE

IT WASN'T THE MOST relaxed of trips, even though it should have been. The first-class service was faultless. There seemed to be no end to the smiling girls waiting at the ready to bring whatever they were told to bring. They were, literally, primed to jump to attention. People paid a fortune—and they didn't just get hot breakfasts in the first-class lounges. The bowing and scraping followed them onto the plane.

Kate had been on a one-week holiday with her mother three years previously. They had flown to Ibiza for a few days of sun and the flight over had been cramped and unpleasant. The airline staff had been abrupt and indifferent and it had been a relief to land and get off.

On this flight she had endless leg room. The seat could be transformed into a bed. There was champagne and wine and the food was of fine-dining standard.

But she shouldn't have worn a suit. The pumps she could dispense with, but the skirt was horribly uncomfortable. Grey jogging bottoms had been thoughtfully provided in a sanitised plastic bag, along with a matching jumper, but she couldn't bring herself to wear either.

The only saving grace was that Alessandro worked and dozed, leaving her to get on with the business of dreading the week ahead.

There was a lot to dread. High on the list was the fact that she could give herself a million stern lectures on keeping her distance but none of those words of wisdom counted for anything—because he seemed to have the power to seduce her into whatever conversation he happened to want at the time.

She could wave the folder she had on George in front of his handsome face, but if he wasn't in the mood to get down to business then he just...*didn't*.

And something about him *propelled* her into speech. The hatefully arrogant man could just tilt his head to one side, direct that devastating half smile on her and off she would go, blabbering on about stuff that didn't concern him and pouring out confidences that she never shared with anyone.

Then he would grow bored and she would be dismissed—just like that.

If in the space of a few days and some snatched conversations she had managed to tell him about her insecure upbringing and how that had made her feel, not to mention her thoughts on men like him, then what was the week ahead going to bring?

And then there was the uncomfortable question of the way she couldn't seem to stop herself from *looking* at him—and not in the harmless way an employee was supposed to look at her boss. Nothing about what he aroused in her felt *appropriate*.

What was *that* all about? Was it because she had been so careful to put things into boxes—to put *men* into boxes—that the first time one had slipped through the net, she had not had the necessary weaponry to deal with the intruder?

That calmed her. It was easy to picture him as an intruder, muscling his way past 'Do Not Trespass' signs, making inroads into places he had no right to be.

She could deal with intruders. Even metaphorical ones. So she might have been caught off guard? That didn't mean that she was doomed to being caught off guard whenever she happened to be in his company. She might be inexperienced but she wasn't a complete idiot!

She was in a better frame of mind by the time the plane began taxiing down to land.

'Good flight?' he asked as everyone began to stand in preparation for disembarking. 'You look a little…rumpled. Didn't I question your choice of outfit? Why didn't you wear the comfy clothes provided? Or didn't you locate them…?'

'I had a very good flight,' Kate answered serenely. 'It was relaxing. I read my book, watched a couple of movies, dozed…and as a matter of fact I'm very comfortable with my choice of clothing.'

The damn man looked as fresh as a daisy—all bright-eyed and bushy-tailed and ready for what was waiting for them in Toronto.

She didn't dare glance down at her skirt, which would be horribly creased—a suitable companion to her shirt, which was also horribly creased. She wondered whether it was physically possible for a face to look creased as well. If it was, then she would bet that hers did.

But her smile was wide and bright.

'It beats travelling cattle class,' she volunteered, making sure not to watch as he hoisted his bag down from the overhead locker, as well as her own pull-along. 'I guess I should make the most of it. I don't see it happening again any time soon.'

'You aim too low.'

Alessandro looked down at her as they began the process of disembarking. Her neat bun was disobeying orders from above and staging a rebellion. Tendrils had escaped and she had tried to push them back into position without much success. She looked as though she had travelled prepared to step out of the plane straight into a board meeting, but had been dragged through a hedge somewhere along the way. *Cute.*

'I like to aim for what I can reasonably achieve,' she replied primly, stepping past him and out into the sweltering summer heat.

She felt his warm breath on her neck as he leant towards her from behind.

'Repeat. You aim too low. Reasonable achievements are for the unadventurous.'

'That's me,' she said sharply, half turning towards him. She spun back round and heard him chuckle behind her.

She had no idea what to expect of Toronto, having never travelled further afield than Ibiza, but whatever lay in store, it would flash past in style—because they'd cleared customs and outside there was a stretch limo waiting for them.

'Is this another *wow* moment?' Alessandro cupped her elbow with his hand and ushered her into the long, luxurious, totally over-the-top car.

There was lazy amusement in his voice.

When she had been feverishly writing him off as an intruder, who could be locked out with just a little bit of will power, she had been dealing with a cardboard cut-out in her head. Which was what she wanted him to be. An arrogant, obnoxious, ruthless cardboard cut-out.

Unfortunately the second he opened his mouth, her brain rebelled against categorizing him because he had far too many layers.

'It's just a car,' she returned politely.

It wasn't. Just a car was something small that took you from A to B, and fingers crossed it didn't decide to break down en route. At least, that would be the kind of car she would probably buy in a year or two.

'I'm not impressed because I don't see the point of something this big. I mean, you can't nip down to the supermarket in it, can you?'

'Good point. However you *can* help yourself to a glass of whisky from the handy little bar… Care for a drink?'

Kate shook her head. The last thing she needed was to start relaxing into yet another dangerous conversation with him.

She looked through the window, her whole body aware of him next to her, lazily lounging against the door, his long legs spread slightly apart.

'Have you been here before?' she asked eventually, turning to him, her body pressed against the door.

'If you'd paid attention to those reports on the company we're going to try and fit in while we're here, you'd have seen that I was here less than six months ago. Don't tell me you haven't scoured the file? I'll be bitterly disappointed.'

Kate cleared her throat. 'You enjoy doing that, don't you?'

'Enjoy doing what?'

'Winding me up.'

'Is that what I was doing? I thought I was paying you a backhanded compliment, as a matter of fact. You're such a professional that I expected you to have scoured that file from front to back and memorized everything in it.'

'I glanced through it. I wasn't aware that I was going to be actively involved in the acquisition.'

'Why wouldn't you be?'

'Because it's quite a sizeable…er…I just thought that perhaps someone a bit higher up the pecking order would be put in charge…'

'I don't see how that's going to be possible,' Alessandro

mused speculatively, 'when George will be busy packing up his belongings for the big goodbye. You waxed lyrical about your ambitions…'

'Of *course* I'm ambitious.' She automatically fell into familiar terrain. As long as they were talking about work then she was comfortable, and repeating her hopes for her career was a damn sight safer than getting lost in a personal conversation with him.

'Yes—you need to build financial security to protect you because you lacked it when you were growing up…'

'I want to get on,' she amended through gritted teeth.

'The work you did for me last week on those files I dropped off for you…good job…'

Kate flushed with pleasure. 'You mean it?'

'I can see why Cape decided that you had what it took to fast-track you. Mind you, I'm thinking he was busy directing his attention elsewhere, so it helped that you were so quick. You could pick up any slack.' He grinned. 'And before you launch into a defence of the hapless George, I have a proposition for you…'

'What?'

'Instead of recruiting from outside for a replacement for Cape, I am considering promoting you. Of course you won't qualify for Cape's vacated post, but you'll effectively be hoisted a couple of steps up the career ladder. You will be responsible for bigger accounts, and to alleviate any bad feeling with the people you work with I will reorganize the team. There will be a greater distribution of more responsible tasks and I'll bring in a few lower down the scale to be trained up. Effectively, you and your team will all benefit…'

'I…I couldn't…' Guilt swept over her. 'Poor George finds himself without a job, thrown on the scrap heap, and to top it all off I step into his shoes. I would feel like I was dancing on someone's grave.'

Alessandro frowned. 'You're being melodramatic. No one's dancing on anyone's grave. A vacancy will arise with his departure…it makes complete sense…'

'It might make sense, but it doesn't make it *right*…'

'He leaves and I either recruit from outside, with all the attendant hassle of training someone up, or I promote from within the company—and you're the obvious choice. You want financial security? This will lever you a couple of rungs up the security ladder.'

'It's not black and white like that!'

'Fine. *You* can get lost in the grey blurry bits, but it's pretty black and white from where I'm standing. Furthermore, would you deny your colleagues a golden opportunity to advance their careers because you're so concerned about a guy who didn't seem to care very much when it came to defrauding the company that's treated him very well for countless years?'

'You could still do something for them…I don't have to be part of the equation…'

'No deal. You accept the whole package or you don't. Simple as that. Think about it…'

'I…' Could she deny the people who worked alongside her their chance of getting pay rises? Of going further with their careers?

'Of course this would not be with immediate effect,' Alessandro said, watching her carefully. 'There would be a slow transfer of duties and when I'm reassured that you're up to the increased workload, you will be given a new title…and a suitable pay rise to reflect that. See this as my having faith in your abilities and not as twisting the knife in someone else's back. If any knife-twisting has gone on, it's been done by Cape to himself. He dug his grave the minute he decided to start embezzling.'

'I—I'm pleased that you have faith in my abilities,' Kate stammered. 'But...' She sighed. 'We don't know what will happen about George. We haven't...you know...heard what he has to say yet...'

'Don't really have to,' Alessandro told her gently. 'I could humour you by pretending that I give a damn about his explanation, but in my book theft is theft. My only concern is how he will be rewarded for his misdoings...'

'So this trip is...pointless...?'

'This trip is about you being on an essential learning curve when it comes to handling awkward situations. There's no room for grey areas or indecision. And whether you accept the promotion I'm offering you or allow your guilt to get the better of your good sense, you should know one thing: the higher up the ladder you climb, the more important it is for you to know how to do that.'

'In other words I have to become as ruthless as...as...?'

'As me?'

'I guess I believe there are other ways of...of...'

'There aren't.'

'You're so cut-throat...'

'Life has a curious way of shaping our responses.'

Kate looked at him and wondered what he meant by that. Was it just a general remark, or were there factors in his life that had made him the way he was? He was beyond rich, beyond powerful and beyond good-looking—and yet he moved from woman to woman with no intention of settling down. Why *was* that?

What it was, she told herself sternly, was *none of her business*.

'Of course...' Alessandro moved on smoothly. 'Before you accept your brand-new shiny job promotion—and I know you will because it would be stupid not to, and you're not stupid—there's something I should ask you…'

'What's that?'

'How reliable do you think you will be in this new role? You don't seem to object to putting in overtime in the steady climb upwards, but will that become difficult for you when and if you're given extra responsibilities and overtime ceases to be a choice and becomes a necessity? No, don't answer that. But think about it and we will discuss it over dinner. The back of a cab—even a very long cab—is no place to have this conversation.'

'Dinner?'

What dinner? What was wrong with room service in their separate rooms and a career discussion over a cup of coffee in the morning?

'It's all we'll be able to do with what remains of the day.' Alessandro was irked at the look of horror that had flashed across her face. 'We both *do* have to eat,' he said coolly.

'Yes, but I thought that I might just grab something in my room and hit the sack early. It's been a long day.'

'Well, you'll have to rethink your plans.'

'Of course.'

'And I trust your *entire* wardrobe isn't comprised of a selection of starchy suits…?'

'What difference does it make?' Kate asked tightly.

'It's not a working meal.'

Control. Yes, he understood. You didn't have to be a genius to join the dots. Her background had made her the sort of woman who felt a driving need to impose control in every aspect of her life. She controlled her appearance, she controlled her hair, she controlled her reactions, controlled her emotions. She was so serious that it was sometimes hard to believe that she was actually in her twenties. All over the world there were grannies out and about having

more fun than her. And he wasn't used to women looking appalled at the thought of spending five minutes in
his company.

'You can relax in my company for five seconds, Kate.'

Frankly, she thought she already had—and it hadn't
been a good idea. 'Right…'

'You *could* sound more convinced.' Irritation had crept
into his voice. 'We're here.'

She hadn't even noticed the stretch limo slowing. She
had missed most of the trip because her attention had been
exclusively focused on the man sitting next to her. So much
for dispelling the intruder by getting a grip.

She looked around her and saw a city that was like any
other—although there was something more peaceful and
less frantic about it than London. The hotel they were approaching was, as she might have expected, the last word
in expensive, from its imposing facade to the doormen
waiting to relieve the wealthy visitors of their baggage,
eager to make sure that they did absolutely nothing for
themselves if it could be helped.

The foyer was bustling with visitors, coming and going.
Next to them Kate felt the inadequacy of her carefully
chosen but now creased outfit. She didn't blend in. Even
some of the younger people in jeans and tee shirts managed to look staggeringly designer-casual, as though they
had randomly plucked something out of the wardrobe and
yet succeeded in looking effortlessly *cool*.

For a few rebellious seconds she wished that she hadn't
tied her hair back—wished that she hadn't worn a knee-
length drab skirt and a sensible blouse. She wished, for the
first time in her life, that she had taken a page out of her
mother's book and made the most of her assets.

She frowned. Alessandro had accused her of being a
hypocrite and she had predictably reacted by hitting the

roof—because who was he to pass judgement on her? Yet, wasn't she?

If she'd seen life in exactly the same black-and-white way that he did wouldn't she have worn more comfortable clothes for the flight over? Brought more to wear than stuff that could only be labelled as *excruciatingly business-like*…? Had a wardrobe that actually contained clothes a girl her age would wear? She was so scared of emulating her mother that she had veered off in completely the opposite direction, ignoring the fact that there was always a middle ground.

No wonder he was so entertained by her! No wonder he got a kick out of winding her up! She played straight into his hands by trying to control everything she said and did—way more than the occasion demanded.

Yet he *had* seen her in relaxed mode, she thought with a twinge of discomfort. And whilst that would have been nothing for him, because he was used to seeing far more beautiful women wearing a lot less, it had been something for her. She had felt exposed and vulnerable. Stupid.

She surfaced to find that she was being led out of the foyer and towards a bank of lifts up to her hotel room— which would give her welcome relief from her thoughts.

She was a lot less relieved when they were shown to the same door, which was flung open to reveal an absolutely enormous suite. She stared at it in horror.

'What's this?' She remained firmly planted in the door-way, only shifting to allow the porter inside, watching with her arms folded until he was dispatched and the only occupants of the vast room were Alessandro and herself.

Alessandro looked around, as though noticing his surroundings for the first time.

She was so predictable in her reactions. Dismay at the prospect of being in his company, horror at imagining dinner with him, and now downright shrieking tension, barely kept in check, at the idea that this vast suite might be a shared situation.

Was it any wonder that he couldn't seem to stop himself from goading her?

Especially when, as it was now, the colour staining her cheeks looked just so unbelievably appealing?

As was her half-opened mouth, her flashing eyes, and the way her pink tongue had sneaked out to moisten her lips…

'It's a room, Kate,' he said, in the patient voice of someone explaining the obvious. 'Hotels tend to have them. It's a must when it comes to attracting potential guests.'

'Ha-ha.' She wasn't budging. She could feel her pulse racing as she craned her neck from her position by the door to try and ascertain just what the situation was regarding sleeping arrangements.

He couldn't possibly expect them to share *a bedroom*, could he? No. No way.

As if reading her thoughts, and reluctantly deciding to put her out of her misery, he said without looking at her, strolling towards the huge bay window to gaze idly outside, 'No need to panic. This is where I'll be staying.'

He turned to face her and saw her visibly relax.

'I asked my secretary to book two adjoining rooms. It wasn't a necessity, but I thought it might be more convenient if this deal kicks off and we find ourselves having to work late. I only realized when I read through the confirmation that my instructions were taken a little too literally…'

He took his time walking towards a door which she hadn't noticed and flung it open.

'You're in there… Actually, if you'd looked at the bedroom you would have noticed that your case is nowhere in evidence. You could have spared yourself your giddy meltdown.'

'I was *not* having a *giddy meltdown*… I was just curious as to… Well…'

'You may have your opinions on my relationships with women…' Alessandro's voice was cool and hard '…but I draw the line at sharing a bedroom with one of my employees when we're on business…'

And when we're not?

Kate shoved aside the immediate thought that sprang into her head on the back of his remark. She walked towards the door and peered into a suite that was almost as big as the one in which she was standing.

'And, before you ask, yes, there's a lock on the interconnecting door—so you'll be quite safe should I find myself accidentally trying to sleepwalk into your bedroom.'

His voice left her in no doubt that that was the last thing he would consider doing. There was laughter just below the surface and she flushed. *She* might be having a hard time disassociating the sex-on-legs guy from the guy who actually paid her salary, but that was because of her own overactive imagination.

'In that case,' she said stiffly, 'I think I'll freshen up… have a bath.' She looked at him. 'I wonder whether it might not be a better idea for us to continue our discussion about my job in the morning. When we're more alert.'

'It's not even seven-thirty in the evening,' Alessandro said drily. 'I think I'm alert enough to focus. And in the morning we can both look forward to a fun-packed full day tracking down our adventurous crook. So…' He looked at his Rolex and then back at her as she waited, ready to sprint to safety. 'I can either come and get you in an hour, or so you can meet me in the bar downstairs…which would you rather?'

'I'll meet you,' Kate muttered.

'Fine. In an hour sharp.' He grinned. 'You can scuttle off and have your bath now…'

Scuttle.

Horrible word. *Scuttle* was the sort of thing timid little creatures did to get away from danger. Admittedly Alessandro might easily be classed as a dangerous species—at least to her peace of mind—but she had never particularly considered herself a timid little creature.

She had had to develop a tough streak just to get though most of her childhood. In addition to her mother's guilelessly flamboyant jobs, her shocking naivety when it came to the opposite sex and her casual disregard for most aspects of parenting, Kate had also had to be on standby for her mother when her heart had inevitably got broken.

In the framework of things, being timid was a luxury she had never been able to afford.

But was that how Alessandro saw her? If so, wouldn't that come into play when it came to sealing the deal on any job promotion for her? Who wanted someone *timid* handling important accounts and clients?

The clothes she had packed all fell into the category of *timid*. When she had chosen what to take she had made sure to pack stuff that conveyed the right message—she was a working woman on business. A few less formal things had been brought for those evenings that she had intended spending on her own, discovering the city at her own pace and without her challenging boss for company.

Prospects on that particular front now looked anything but sunny. Overcast with the threat of downpours might be more like it.

She took her time enjoying her bath, absently marvelling at the size of the bathroom, and then, with a sigh, opted for a variation on the eternal suit. The navy skirt was, like all her work skirts, knee-length, but instead of a white blouse she chose a red one. And after a lot of hesitation decided against the bun—because she could already visualize those mocking dark eyes taking in the ensemble and having a laugh at her expense.

It took her a while to find the bar. The hotel was enormous, with extensive shopping within it and several dining areas. Eventually, however, she was directed to one of the less casual bars, which was where she expected he would be. Relaxing over a whisky and soda and amusing himself with various scenarios involving George and his dismissal.

Sure enough, he was there, nursing a drink, although it looked like wine instead of whisky.

He glanced at her as soon as she began heading in his direction.

He had changed out of his travelling gear into a pair of cream trousers, an open-necked pale shirt and some loafers. He looked completely at ease—which had the perverse effect of making her feel totally out of place.

She had brought her tablet, which she placed on the table before sitting down.

'What's that for?'

Alessandro poured her a glass of wine before she could tell him that she wasn't going to be drinking.

'Have you decided that you'd rather watch a movie than talk to me?'

Instantly flustered, Kate adjusted the tablet and then sat back, hands on her lap. 'I thought I'd take notes on it rather than on paper,' she told him.

'We're having an informal chat.' Alessandro finished his wine, and before he could top up his glass someone materialized and did it for him before subsiding back into the background. 'I'm not dictating terms and conditions.'

'Yes, I know that. But…'

'No matter. If it makes you happy to busy yourself on a tablet then who am I to tell you otherwise? I thought we'd eat here. It's less formal than one of the hotel restaurants and it saves us the trouble of venturing out… Unless you'd rather do a bit of city exploring…? See what's out there…?'

He waited for a heated negative to that idea—which, predictably, he got.

Did she ever let her hair down? he wondered. Aside from when she was closeted away in her house, safe in her territory, where no one could see her? Unless they unexpectedly dropped by and refused to go away without being invited inside… What did she do *for fun*? Did she have any? Or was that an alien concept to be avoided at all costs?

Curiosity niggled away at him, and he wasn't sure whether he was impatient with that, exasperated or invigorated—because curiosity and women was a combination that didn't occur in his life.

His dark eyes lazily fastened to her face, he summoned the same guy who had leapt to refill his glass and somehow managed to convey a request for menus without actually saying anything.

Kate watched this interplay between power and subservience, unsettled but fascinated.

'I sincerely hope you've brought something else to wear tomorrow, Kate. It's boiling here at this time of year…'

'I'll be fine,' Kate said airily.

'Sure? Because if you've brought those shorts of yours then feel free to wear them. They'd be far more appropriate, given the weather. The food here's excellent,' he carried on, as menus were placed in front of them. 'I stayed here the last time I was in Toronto and I couldn't fault the food. Or the service.'

'They're very obliging,' Kate said politely. 'I guess it's

the least you'd expect, considering what you're probably paying…'

Alessandro grinned. 'A bit like the service and the hot meals in the first-class lounge…? Touché…'

'I don't suppose you ever slum it…'

'I try and avoid that. Why? Have I been missing out?'

At the prospect of another detour into a personal conversation she didn't want—one she would have to manoeuvre through with the adroitness of someone walking in a minefield—Kate brought the talk firmly round to business and the reason why she was sitting opposite him in the first place. In a darkened bar. Knees practically touching under the table. Chilled wine in front of them. She inched her knees to one side and hoped he hadn't noticed.

'You mentioned in the car on the way here that there was something you wanted to talk to me about in connection with this job promotion…that's why I've brought my tablet, as a matter of fact. I thought it might be an idea to make some notes on the various responsibilities I'll be taking on board.'

'Ah, down to business straight away…'

Kate reddened, resenting the way that simple observation made her feel instantly like a bore. A bore in a semi-suit.

'Good idea. You're right. We'll probably both need our beauty sleep if tomorrow's going to be a long day.'

Kate searched his face for typical Alessandro irony but he returned her gaze seriously. Not that she believed *he* needed to go to sleep at this hour. She doubted he needed much sleep at all. Maybe even none. He struck her as the sort of guy who could just keep going…and going…and going…taking the occasional power nap while the rest of the world collapsed, exhausted, in his wake.

And he'd be able to do that whilst still managing to look, frankly, drop-dead gorgeous.

They both ordered something light from the menu and then she nervously gulped down a generous mouthful of wine and looked to him to carry on the conversation. He didn't.

'Yes…' she returned feebly at last. 'So…'

'So here's the thing, Kate.'

He leaned forward, suddenly all business, and she inched back in the chair, taking the wine glass with her.

'If you recall, I expressed some concern that you might find the hours attached to your new role a little tedious if you're forced to do them…and that's something we should clear up right here and right now before going any further…'

He really had the most amazing eyelashes. He hadn't shaved, and there was a shadowy stubble on his chin that also looked pretty amazing.

Kate tore her eyes away from both those *amazing* features and focused on him with a slight frown.

'There's nothing to clear up,' she told him crisply. 'I have no problem working long hours, if required. I one hundred per cent realize that that's all part and parcel of any job that entails responsibility.'

Alessandro made a non-committal sound under his breath and sat back, pushing his chair away from the table so that he could cross his legs. He looked at her long and thoughtfully.

'What about your personal life? Not to put too fine a point on it, I wouldn't like to find that I've promoted you and you're not up to the challenge because there's some guy in the background, waiting for you to return home to cook his dinner…'

'That won't be the case,' Kate responded hotly. 'Firstly,

there's no man in the background—and secondly, even if there was, I certainly wouldn't expect him to be a demanding kind of guy who wants his dinner cooked by me! In fact the reason I broke up with my last boyfriend—' She clamped shut her mouth and stared at him, aghast.

He returned her stare, unperturbed.

'Those sort of demanding men are to be avoided at all costs,' he murmured softly. 'I'm taking it that the boyfriend wanted more than you were prepared to give…? Hence he was given the heave-ho…?'

'I… It was a very busy time for me… I…' She cleared her throat and attempted to recover her lost composure. 'So you needn't fear that my mind won't be completely on the job.'

'I'm relieved. Although,' he mused, 'I sympathize. I guess he must have been an important person in your life, because you did tell me that you don't believe in transitory relationships…'

'It didn't work out,' Kate told him firmly, as she frantically sought an exit from the conversation. 'I don't dwell on the past.'

'Very wise. Although you *do* allow it to influence certain aspects of your life. For instance, your dress code.'

At which point she decided that the next thing she would do, just as soon as she got the chance, would be to wipe that smirk off his face by making a point of showing him just how much it did *not* affect her dress code.

One slip-up—*one* slip up and the wretched man thought that he knew everything there was to know about her.

'And now that we've settled that,' she said calmly, 'maybe you could let me know how you plan on handling tomorrow…?'

CHAPTER SIX

KATE SPENT A restless night, even though she'd checked and double-checked and, just for good measure, triple-checked that the interconnecting door was firmly locked.

She didn't expect him to waltz into her room—not at all—but she knew that she would have no peace of mind unless he was physically incapable of doing so.

As it was, she didn't have much peace of mind anyway.

Her brain was buzzing with thoughts of promotion, of George—poor George—and the surprise he was going to have delivered to him the following morning in the form of Alessandro and herself, of her helplessness when it came to taking a step back from Alessandro…

She had left him sauntering towards one of the hotel lounges, where he'd intended to relax and work. She had no idea what time he had eventually returned to his bedroom, but *she* had not settled into sleep until after midnight.

Now, with her alarm buzzing her awake at seven sharp, she felt tired and unrested.

She took a few minutes just to lie there, appreciating the splendour of her surroundings. The sleeping area of her suite was twice the size of her bedroom at home. A super-king-sized four-poster bed dominated the space—wickedly, decadently romantic, with gauze curtains—and through the shimmery cream veils she could make out the sleek fitted wardrobes, the clutch of chairs by the window for relaxing…

Beyond the bedroom was an exquisite sitting area, with sofas, a concealed plasma television, a drinks cabinet…

It was a home away from home—except Kate felt anything but relaxed as she contemplated the day ahead.

Alessandro had the name of the hotel where George and his wife were holidaying. Somewhere slightly outside the main hub of the city. They would get the whole thing over and done with and then, from there, devote the remainder of the day to arranging meetings with the company he wanted to buy and two others he might or might not want to have a look at.

He had made no appointments ahead of their arrival but she knew that that would not matter. He had such clout that doors would open before he even got round to knocking on them.

'You look tense,' were his opening words as she took a seat opposite him in the dining area where they were having breakfast. He indicated the buffet area, which was extensive, and told her that a cup of strong coffee and plenty of food would settle her nerves.

'I'm not nervous,' Kate lied. 'Yes, I'm tense, because what we have to do will be unpleasant, but I'm not nervous.' Because nervousness was closely related to timidity, and they were not up sides when it came to a job promotion.

At any rate, Alessandro thought wryly, she was doing her utmost to ward off the nerves she claimed not to have by wearing yet another suit and having her hair scraped back into its habitual bun. Just in case he didn't get the message, her choice of clothes would remind him that she was here to do a job and relaxing wasn't part of the programme.

He had almost had to drag her down to have dinner with

him, and even then she had kept up the professional facade that he was increasingly tempted to shatter.

The glimpses he had had of the real, living, breathing, passionate woman underneath the straitjackets she insisted on wearing 24/7 had whetted his appetite.

Of course it didn't make sense. He had enough choice in his life when it came to women not ever to make the mistake of hunting one down in his own office building. He also had enough choice to avoid any woman who gave off signals of looking for more than he was prepared to offer, and Kate Watson was definitely one of those women. He liked no-strings-attached, no-demands-made sex. She wanted strings and he was pretty sure she would be demanding. Not for her a few casual words of warning and then full steam ahead.

But he couldn't get that image of her wearing those shorts and that cropped top out of his head. He couldn't forget how she looked without make-up, with her hair swinging in a ponytail and those cute little freckles sprinkling her nose.

'I'm relieved to hear it,' he said.

Alessandro wondered whether she was aware of the challenge she was posing by wearing those unappealing suits at every opportunity. Maybe he should tell her that all items of clothing that were buttoned to the neck begged to be ripped off. Perhaps he could slip that into the conversation somewhere along the line. Her white, sensible blouse was buttoned to the neck…

'Are you insisting on taking me with you to dispatch George as some kind of test?'

Alessandro's eyebrows shot up. 'You mean to see if you pass out at the ordeal? We'll be dealing with a common criminal, Kate. I'm not asking you to visit a morgue and identify a body. But, like I said, it's important to know how to be tough when the occasion demands. I'm surprised that you're fixating on the stress of this fairly straightforward situation,' he added with silky assurance, 'when you brushed your last boyfriend aside because he wouldn't do as you wanted…'

Without giving her a chance to say anything, and with his eyes firmly pinned to her face, he summoned one of the many hovering waitresses and ordered them both a full breakfast.

'You'll need it. If we're heading up to see Wakeley's there's no guarantee that lunch is going to be on the agenda. We might have to grab something on the way. Now, you were about to explain how it is that this situation is bringing you out in a cold sweat when dispatching the potential love of your life didn't…'

'I was *not* about to explain any such thing!'

'Apologies. I had no idea that it was still such an issue for you…'

'It's not an issue for me!' Kate felt like a swimmer, desperately trying to fight against a current. Why had he ordered breakfast for her? She was fine with fruit and a croissant! Fine with removing herself from his suffocating presence on the pretext of taking her time to choose items from the buffet table.

'There's no need to explain why you'd rather not discuss this. I was only making conversation, Kate. No need to panic.'

'I am *not panicking*,' she gritted tightly, and he threw her a kindly smile which implied that he didn't believe a word she was saying.

'And why,' she pressed on, snatching at the coffee and taking a restorative mouthful, 'do you insist on asking me loads of personal questions? Which have nothing to do with my job?'

'Like I said, I was only making conversation. If I'd known that you were still sensitive on the topic of your ex-boyfriend then I would never have gone there. Trust me.'

Kate resisted the urge to burst into manic laughter. Trust him? She would rather trust a river seething with hungry piranha.

'And as to asking you "loads of personal questions"…I like knowing a bit about the people who work for me—especially those higher up the pecking order, in positions of responsibility. Which, I'm sure, is where you will be very soon, given your talents… It helps if I know whether they're married, involved in a serious relationship, have children… That way I can tailor the needs of the job to accommodate their needs as much as is possible…'

He had never given it any such thought before, but now that he had it sort of made sense. Not that he would be playing by those rules. *Ever.* Still, never let it be said that he wasn't a man who didn't see things from every angle.

Kate allowed her ruffled feathers to be soothed. She had overreacted. Breaking up with her ex was not exactly state-secret fodder. Who cared? Did Alessandro Preda *really* give a damn whether she had called off a relationship years ago with a man who no longer featured in her life? Wasn't he telling the truth when he said that he was just making conversation? *Polite* conversation? The sort of polite conversation that was made every second of every day between people who didn't know one another all that well?

'It didn't work out,' she told him. 'Simple as that. And before you tell me that I'm a hypocrite, because I make such a big deal about the importance of taking relationship building seriously…'

'*Relationship building? What's that*?'

Something my mother never did, was the reply that immediately sprang to mind, but she bit it back because that would be perfect proof of just how much she had been influenced by her mother's behaviour.

In truth, looking back on her relationship with her ex-boyfriend, she could see that it had been built on hope—hope that he might be the one because they got along and because he ticked all the boxes. Like her, he had been studying accountancy. He had been reliable, feet firmly planted on the ground, a solid, dependable sort. He had been just the type of guy who *made sense.*

'It's when two people take the time to really establish the building blocks of a future together.'

'It sounds riveting. How do they do that?'

Kate lowered her eyes and remained silent.

'Please don't tell me you're going to slip back into *I couldn't possibly say because I'm just your employee* mode...'

'I *am* just your employee.'

'I'm giving you permission to speak your mind. Believe it or not...' he sat back as enough breakfast to feed a small developing country was placed in front of them '...I *do* have conversations with some of my employees that don't revolve exclusively around work...'

'I doubt you'd understand the sort of building blocks I'm talking about,' Kate told him politely. She stared at the mound of food facing her and wondered where to begin. She speared some egg and then eyed the tempting waffles at the side. 'Considering you're not into building relationships.'

'Fill me in. I want to see what I've been missing.'

Kate looked at him with exasperation. The man was utterly impossible, even though the smile on his face was so charming that it would knock any woman for six. She hurriedly focused on her food as her heart picked up speed and started relaying all those taboo messages from her brain to her body.

'I know you don't mean a word of that,' she retorted, glaring. 'But if you're really interested then I'll tell you. Relationship building is taking time to get to know someone else—to find out all you can about them, to open up so that they can find out all about you, and to plan a future together based on love and friendship and respect.'

'You're not selling it.'

'I'm not interested in whether I'm *selling it* or not,' Kate snapped. 'And I wouldn't expect to *sell it* to *you*, anyway!'

'So, having spent time on this relationship building exercise, at what point did you discover that the fun element was missing…?'

'He was lots of fun.'

He hadn't been. He had been nice and he had been steady, and he had been all those things she had thought she wanted, but when it had come to the crunch he had also been ultra-traditional. So traditional that he had wanted her to be the little lady whose career was secondary to his, who did as he asked, who dropped everything because he came first…

She felt a wave of self-pity as she realized that she would probably never find anyone. She would end up with a terrific career but next to no friends—and certainly no significant other doing the barbecue thing in the back garden.

And she would never know what it was like to *have fun* because she had always been adamant that having fun wasn't important—so adamant that the only important thing in life was being in control and never letting herself get swept away by emotion as her mother had.

But right now, in the depths of Cornwall, and despite her chequered past with men and jobs, Shirley 'Lilac' Watson was pretty contented.

Kate abruptly closed her knife and fork and fought against the sudden confusion rolling over her like fog.

'It just didn't work,' she said flatly. 'The time wasn't right. But that doesn't mean I didn't put my heart and soul into it. And that's all I have to say on the subject—I don't want to discuss it again. It's not relevant. And it's not always just about *fun*.'

This to try and stifle some of the sudden misgivings that had swept over her—dark thoughts that some of the choices she had made in her life might not have been the right ones, even if they had been made with all the right intentions.

'You're probably right.'

But she barely heard him. His soothing agreement floated around her and dissipated.

'I know for…for some people…' she only just managed not to pin *him* as one of those people she was talking about '…*fun* is all about *sex*, but as far as I'm concerned there's a great deal more to relationships than sex…'

She glared at him defiantly, challenging him to argue with her, but Alessandro had no intention of doing any such thing.

He had never registered much interest in analyzing women, or trying to plumb their hidden depths, but in this instance he could see the pattern of her life as clearly as if it had been printed in bright neon letters across her forehead.

She had instilled such a strict code for herself that she was a prisoner of it. He doubted she had ever had any sort of fun with that ex-boyfriend of hers, and he wondered what fun she had now, with her stable job and her bright future. Her head told her what she needed, but what she needed was not necessarily what she *wanted*.

And he got the impression that she was thinking about that conundrum for the first time in her life.

Because *he* had rammed it down her throat.

On the one hand he had done her a favour. She was so uptight that she would snap in two given a slight breeze. Life was not kind to the seriously uptight. He was certain of that. They were always the ones who ended their lives thinking about all the things they'd strenuously resisted doing.

On the other hand she was visibly upset—and that was hardly a positive way for a boss to encourage his employee to start the day.

'You haven't finished your breakfast,' he told her, indicating her plate.

She smiled, thankful for the change in conversation and the reprieve from her thoughts.

'I don't think I've ever sat in front of a bigger breakfast.'

'Bigger is better—that's the motto, I think. We can stick to the buffet tomorrow.'

'I didn't have much appetite anyway,' Kate admitted. 'I guess I really *am* nervous about what today's going to bring. Normally I eat like a horse. Perhaps we should think about going.' She dug into her capacious handbag and extracted her tablet. 'I've brought along all the information I have on George, in case you want to sit down with him and go through it.'

Alessandro had no intention of doing any such thing, but he was relieved that she was back to normal—back to her usual efficient self, back to being the woman who matched the uniform of suits she always wore.

Even though those moments just then, when he had seen her vulnerability, had merged into the other moments when he had glimpsed the woman underneath the navy suits... strangely alluring, weirdly appealing...

Impatient with himself, he signalled a waiter in order to sign for the breakfast and flung his linen napkin next to his plate. 'Right.' He stood as he signed the bill. 'Let's get going.'

It was as though their very personal conversation had never happened. He was all business. Even without the business suit.

'Shall we get a taxi there? Do you know whether it's a long drive out of the city centre?'

'We won't need a taxi.' He flicked his cell phone out of his pocket and scrolled though the numbers. 'I've arranged to have my own driver for the duration of our stay here. More reliable and more convenient than trying to find a taxi when we need one.'

'The limo…?'

'No.'

They began strolling out to the street and she followed him as he expertly made his way through the grand hotel and the designer shopping centre that circled it.

He looked at her, his eyes creased with amusement. 'I didn't think that my conscience could stand the guilt caused by the carbon footprint.'

There he went again, she thought with a little flurry of desperation. Undoing all her plans to ignore him by being…*funny*. By saying something that made her want to smile, even though half an hour before she had been mentally snarling at him for invading her private life and asking personal questions.

He was also in business mode. She could sense that as they settled into the back of the car—a far more modest affair than the limo, though still sleek and impressive by most people's standards.

The hotel was forty minutes' drive away, which made it quite a distance out of the hub of downtown Toronto, and he turned to her and said, with a thoughtful frown, 'Seems a little odd to head for a hotel in the hills when you're spending vast sums of money on a city holiday—wouldn't you agree?'

Kate gave that some thought and nodded. 'Although some people hate cities.'

'Then why holiday in one?'

'His wife might like shopping.' She grinned. 'That's one of those building-block situations I was telling you about. He hates cities and shopping, she loves them—so they go somewhere in between.' She surprised herself by harking back to a conversation she wanted to forget, but at least it distracted her from the unpleasant task that lay ahead.

'I'm not sensing an element of compromise here…'

'Well, the next time it's her turn to give in and allow him more of what he wants.'

'For instance…?'

Kate shrugged. 'He might want to…I don't know…go fishing, rent a cottage in the Cotswolds and have long walks, head up to Scotland to appreciate the wild, stunning scenery…'

'My take is that *that* particular couple aren't suited. She wants to shop…he wants to half freeze to death in the middle of nowhere to appreciate the scenery… It'll end in tears. You wait and see…'

Kate laughed. Really laughed.

She felt all her concerns melt away and their eyes met. Her breath caught in her throat because she felt as if it was an intense moment, when something intangible had been shared. Though what, she couldn't say. A shared sense of humour? A certain way they both had of finding the same thing funny…?

'Here, it might make a little more sense. You don't have

to travel too far out of the city before you come slap-bang into some remarkable scenery…'

He began giving her a potted history of the place, telling her about its geographical splendours, the thousand and one sights that made it so special.

What the hell had happened just then? he wondered. He had got caught out by a curveball—had had the oddest sensation of stepping onto quicksand, a place where he was no longer in complete control but at the mercy of reactions and responses that went against the grain, against his rigidly imposed rules.

The hotel, when they finally arrived, was a modest building, with a car park in the front, sandwiched between a fast food restaurant and a shop advertising all manner of office supplies.

Kate could see that Alessandro was taken aback at the place George and his wife had chosen to stay for their vacation, but he said nothing as they walked through the glass revolving doors and straight to the reception desk, which was manned by a bored-looking girl, twirling her hair and chatting on her mobile.

Kate wondered whether they had chosen this spot because it offered access to the city but also access to the outlying countryside…pine forests, lakes…beautiful terrain to explore. She didn't know what George and his wife did for fun, aside from family stuff with their kids and grandkids. Maybe they loved mountaineering, hiking…who knew…?

The blonde twirling her hair instantly hung up and straightened as they approached the desk.

Mr and Mrs Cape… Would she buzz through to them…? Tell Mr Cape that Alessandro Preda was in Reception and wanted to have a word with him…? Tell him that Kate Watson was there as well…?

The blonde shot Kate a covert look that simmered with envy.

'Mr and Mrs Cape aren't in.' She didn't need to consult the register for this information. 'They leave at the same time every morning. Eight sharp. I can leave a message for them and get them to contact you—or you can leave a note and I'll make sure they get it as soon as they're back.'

'Which would be at what time...?'

'This evening. Six sharp.'

'Unusual sightseeing activities that can be planned with such precision,' Alessandro said with stinging sarcasm, and he received a shocked and surprised look from the blonde in response.

'Can I ask whether you're related to George and Karen?'

Alessandro raised his eyebrows expressively. *Cosy relationship with the girl at Reception?* he thought. Bit odd... Admittedly the hotel was only the size of a bed and breakfast. For all he knew that was exactly what it was, despite its grandiose name: the Ruskin Hotel. But still...

'I'm his boss, and I'm here to see him on a business-related matter.'

'If you're his boss then I'm surprised... Didn't he mention...?'

'Mention what?' Kate asked gently, reading sudden confusion in the receptionist's blue eyes.

'They go to the hospital every day. They're allowed some leeway with the visiting hours, but they tend to stay there pretty much for the whole day, so that they can be there for Gavin and Caroline.'

'Caroline's their daughter...' Kate turned to Alessandro, her mind a whirl. 'Gavin's their son-in-law. I know that because there's a family photo on his desk...'

'Right. Hospital. Perhaps you could tell us which hospital this is...?'

They arrived at the hospital in under an hour. It had been a largely silent journey. For the first time Alessandro had been caught on the back foot—handed information he had not been expecting…information that altered the straightforward situation he'd thought he would be dealing with.

Despite the fact that George and his wife had chosen to stay outside the city, the hospital was actually in downtown Toronto. Kate guessed that either the little hotel was very reasonably priced, or else they had some experience of being there before. Or maybe they just needed to be outside the main drag of a city to clear their heads at the end of the day.

A long day.

Because the days *would* be long. In the back of the car Alessandro had looked up the hospital on the internet, so they both knew that it was a centre for the treatment of sick children.

Now, as they approached the white-fronted building visible through a bank of trees, Alessandro turned to her and spoke for the first time.

'This is not what I expected,' he said roughly, raking fingers through his dark hair. 'And you won't be accompanying me into the hospital.'

'Perhaps we should wait until they're back at the hotel this evening. And I *will* be accompanying you, by the way.'

'It wasn't a suggestion, Kate. It was an order.'

'And my answer wasn't a suggestion either. It was a statement of fact.' She sighed. 'I'm very fond of George. He's been good to me, and I want him to know that I'm here for him and his wife. Whatever the outcome of your… *talk* with him.' She paused and looked at Alessandro's averted profile. His beautiful eyes were veiled.

He turned to her before opening his door. 'Stubborn.'

'Yes, I can be.' She stuck her chin out defiantly, prepared to go all the way into an argument, but there was no argument as he shrugged and stepped out of the car, waited for her to join him.

She wished she could reach into his head and see what he was thinking. She had the strangest urge to rest her hand on his forearm in a gesture of comfort, although she had no idea what she would be comforting him *for*—unless it was just for getting something wrong, for showing himself to be fallible like the rest of the human race.

She didn't imagine that he liked being wrong. She thought that he had probably never been wrong about anything in his entire life—at least not when it came to business. In business—and this *was* a business matter after all—his judgement would always have been faultless.

'Stubborn can sometimes be a good thing,' he mused, glancing down at her.

'What…what do you intend to do?' she ventured, half running to keep up with him and longing for a bit of cool, because she was beginning to overheat in her outfit.

'I intend to play it by ear…'

'Can *that* sometimes be a good thing?'

'I'll let you know later. Can't say it's something I've ever done before.'

They entered the cool foyer of the hospital, and after that everything seemed to happen very quickly.

Alessandro commanded attention. How did that work when he wasn't Canadian, wasn't a doctor and had no connections to the hospital? It just did.

Within half an hour they knew where they could locate George, and after an hour and a half—during which time they sat in a very modern, very nice restaurant in front of cups of coffee, with Alessandro working via his smartphone and Kate pretending to be hard at it in front of her tablet—George came to meet them.

A wearily resigned George, who had obviously sussed why they had landed up in Toronto and at the hospital.

Kate's heart went out to the older man. He was in one of his usual trademark brightly coloured outfits. She had always smiled at that. Even when he was in a suit his shirt was always jolly, his tie was always patterned, his hankies were always ridiculously gimmicky. He had told her once, laughing, that his wife chose his shirts, his daughter chose his handkerchiefs and his grandchildren chose his socks. So what chance did he ever have of looking debonair?

He seemed to have shrunk—or maybe she was only noticing that now because he looked so weary.

'I know why you've come,' were his opening words as he sat opposite them with a cup of coffee. He looked at Alessandro with resignation. 'Of course I was going to be found out. I'd hoped that somehow I would have managed to start repaying what I… I want to say what I *borrowed*, but I realize, Mr Preda, that you probably won't see it that way…'

'You have no idea how I'm going to see it, George. So why don't you start from the beginning and leave nothing out…?'

It was after six by the time their day was done. And every second of it had been spent at a high-voltage pace that had left Kate breathless, barely able to keep up.

Now, as she tripped along in Alessandro's wake, she ran her fingers through her hair, which had unravelled, been scooped back up again, and then unravelled again—so heaven only knew what she looked like now. Not the consummate professional, she was betting.

'Alessandro…' she breathed, only realizing afterwards

that it was the first time she had addressed him by his Christian name without feeling awkward.

Alessandro stopped en route to his very patient driver, who had been on call throughout the day and was probably as exhausted as she was.

He shot her an expressive and very wry look. 'Well? Get it over and done with…'

'What?'

'A tender-hearted comment about my soft side… Have I turned into one of those, caring, sharing touchy-feely types who do foot massages for their loved ones every evening before running them a hot bath and cooking them a slap-up meal?'

'I *have* seen a different side to you…'

'Same side as always,' Alessandro told her drily. 'You're just choosing to interpret it in a different way. There would have been no point prosecuting George.'

'You did more than just not prosecute him,' she pointed out.

But she wasn't going to run away with a long explanation of exactly what had transpired over the past few hours. He might tell her that he had been as tough in his dealings as he always was, but he hadn't.

George's granddaughter was ill. Tears had sprung to his eyes as he had described the speed of little Imogen's disease and their dismay when they had discovered that the prognosis in the UK was not favourable.

They had scoured the internet—searching for hope, really—and it had come in the form of a revolutionary breakthrough treatment in Toronto. But it was treatment that came at a price, and hence his dipping into money that didn't belong to him. Because he had already used all his savings—every scrap of money that had been put aside for his retirement—on the initial consultations and the first lot of treatment.

Alessandro could have listened and stuck to the programme: *You ripped me off and you're out—save your excuses for the judge.*

Even at her most optimistic she'd thought he might have acquitted George of blame, understood the extenuating circumstances and been sympathetic when it came to a repayment scheme.

Instead, he had not only heard the older man out and absolved him of having to repay the debt, but he had taken charge of everything. He had dealt with the bank, set up an account for George's daughter, then spoken to the hospital, assured them that the treatment would be covered whatever the cost. He had also—and this had made her heart constrict—informed George that he would not have to see out his old age in penury.

Alessandro Preda, a hard man in the world of finance, a guy who was ruthless in his business dealings, had gone beyond the bounds of duty.

'True,' he agreed, stepping aside so that she could precede him into the car. 'And of course he should have spoken to me before he did what he did…' He sprawled back against the door, facing her, his handsome, lean face amused and speculative.

'But all's well that ends well…' Kate inserted hurriedly. 'Although we didn't get to visit your client. Will that be on the agenda for tomorrow?'

'Tell me you're *not* about to stick on your business hat after the day we've had?'

Kate licked her lips, nervously aware of his eyes fastened to her face. She had completely forgotten throughout the course of the day that she had to be careful when she was around him. She had seen another side to him and had been swept away by the revelation.

Which didn't change the fact that she still heartily disapproved of him on a number of fronts…

'Because I'm too tired to start thinking about cutting deals…'

'Of course.'

'And I'm surprised you don't feel the same.'

'I suppose I could do with a little downtime…'

'Splendid. Because tonight we'll go out for dinner, do a little city exploring. We can both knock business on the head for a couple of hours—wouldn't you agree?'

'Dinner…? City exploring…?' she asked, dry-mouthed.

'Or you can call it "downtime". Whatever you prefer. And you're *not* going to be wearing a suit.'

'But that's pretty much all I—'

'Then use the company account to buy something more suitable to wear. You *have* got a company account, haven't you?'

'Yes, but—'

'Then it's settled. Today has been a day full of surprises,' he murmured, in a soft voice that was as devastating to her senses as a caress. 'I've surprised you. Now it's your turn to surprise me… Be someone more than just the prim and proper busy little bee. Do you think you can do that? Or is it too much of an ask…?'

CHAPTER SEVEN

"Is it too much of an ask?"

If he had just insisted on dinner, ignored her protests, basically commanded her to relax in his company, then reluctantly she would have agreed, because she would have had no choice. And she would have donned one of her various suits because it was vitally important to maintain the boundary lines between them.

Boundary lines that, yet again, were in danger of being breached.

But that amused, mocking, *"Is it too much of an ask?"* question had got her back up.

How buttoned up did he think she was? Did he imagine that she was incapable of ever letting her hair down? Did he think that she was such a dull Miss Prim and Proper, glued to her tablet, that she quailed at the prospect of shedding her work clothes and taking time out to be a normal young woman?

Or maybe he thought that she just quailed when the shedding of her work clothes threatened to take place *in his company*. The man might have shown her a side that was curiously empathetic in his dealings with George, but that didn't mean he wasn't still the arrogant guy who took what he wanted from women and chucked them out when he decided the time had come to move on.

But if he insisted that she go shopping—that she use the company account to buy stuff she probably would never wear again—then why not?

Toronto was full of wonderful shops. Shops that lined the streets or were packed into malls.

It was still so hot outside that she opted for the Eaton Centre. She had no idea what she intended buying. It wouldn't take long. She loathed shopping. It was just one of those things that needed doing now and again, under duress.

Her mother had been a shopper. Kate could remember being dragged from shop to shop, spending money they could ill afford on garish outfits. By the age of eleven she had grown accustomed to sitting outside changing rooms, her head firmly planted in a book, while her mother tried on clothes. It had been toe-curlingly embarrassing. She had so desperately wanted her mother just to…*to look like all the other mothers*. How hard would that have been? Plain trousers? Tops that didn't cling or have plunging necklines? Shoes that didn't have five-inch heels and were never, *ever* worn with tight white jeans? How hard would it have been for her just to *avoid wearing bright red*?

Her mother had never complained at the little digs she had thoughtlessly inflicted over the years. The not-so-gentle hints that maybe she should *tone it down*. She had laughed and told her to loosen up a little—had tried to get her out of her jeans and baggy jumpers into the occasional dress. Shirley Watson might not have been good when it came to all the stuff Kate had considered crucially important, she might have failed to take the appropriate level of interest in parents' evenings and homework projects, but she had never tired of trying to dress her up.

Kate had resisted all those efforts, and had continued doing so even when her mother had no longer been around, trying to steer her in a different direction from the one she wanted.

So now here she was.

And as she browsed through the shops she saw herself through her mother's eyes. Always a little drab. Never making anything of what she had been given.

Those were Alessandro's eyes also.

A streak of rebellion coursed through her, and as she shopped she was guiltily aware that she was enjoying shopping for maybe the first time in her life.

She wasn't buying clothes to project the image she wanted the world to see. She was buying clothes because she liked the way they looked on her. Two dresses, a skirt that reached to mid-thigh, tops that had no buttons…and shoes that had heels and weren't black.

Though she still avoided red.

She had no idea where they would be going after the 'city exploring' Alessandro had suggested, but she didn't care.

She took her time soaking in the bath, washed her hair and *left it loose*, so that it tumbled down her back in a cascade of waves, and wore one of the dresses she had bought—a sleek, pale coral affair that did a little clinging. And she wore the high sandals she had bought too.

As she stared at her reflection in the mirror she could feel her heart beating wildly. Because this was not the Kate Watson she had spent her life cultivating.

This was a young woman who *had a life*—and an exciting one.

'Okay…' She grinned sheepishly at the stranger in the mirror. 'So we both know that that's a bit of an exaggeration—but what's the harm in having a life for one evening? Dispelling the ideas Alessandro has about me? Mum, if you could see me now, you'd be proud.'

On the spur of the moment she took a selfie and sent

it to her mother, and minutes later, as she headed down to meet Alessandro in the bar, she smiled at the response she got—which was a series of exclamation marks and smiley faces.

They had arranged to meet in one of the trendier bars in the hotel and it took her a few minutes to locate Alessandro, who was sitting at the back, shielded from view by the crowds of young people milling around.

Some of those young people were turning to *look at her.* Kate was conscious of that out of the corner of her eye, and it gave her a heady little thrill as she took some time to look at Alessandro…

He glanced up and there she was. For a few seconds Alessandro's mind went completely blank. He had thrown down a challenge to her—*dress like a woman and not like a robot*—but he had doubted she would pick up the gauntlet. He had fully expected to see her in yet another tiresome version of 'The Suit', complete with discreet blouse buttoned all the way up, just in case a glimpse of her neck made her feel like a tart.

Not for a single passing second had he expected…

A vision.

He had seen her in a pair of shorts and a cropped top, but not even that had prepared him for just how beautiful she was when she stripped off the suit of armour.

She was tall anyway, but her heels escalated her to nearly six foot. Her long brown hair, streaked with shades of chestnut and deep gold, flowed down her back and over her narrow shoulders, and the dress, in some peachy colour that would have made most women look washed out, was glorious against her skin tone.

Glorious, and clinging in all the right places.

A surge of purely masculine appreciation kicked in with force. He watched as she glanced through the crowded bar, noticed as eyes were turned in her direction, realized that he wasn't the only one in the room feeling a surge of purely masculine appreciation.

He relaxed back, half smiling as she sashayed towards him.

Who would have guessed that she could *sashay*? But then prissy, starchy suits weren't conducive to sashaying, were they? Neither were sensible flat black pumps…

But a peach-coloured dress that lovingly cupped generous breasts, clung to a slender waist and fell to mid-thigh with a frilly little kick was definitely the stuff that sashays were made of…

He wondered whether it would be politically incorrect to insist in the contract for her promotion that she only wear clothes conducive to sashaying…

'I see you went shopping…' he said, rising to his feet as she approached him. In heels, she was almost at his eye level. Eye make-up. A charcoal colour on her lids that gave her a sultry, sexy look. And just a shimmer of lip gloss, emphasizing the fullness of her lips.

An inconvenient erection was making itself felt, pushing against his zipper.

'You were right.' Kate sat down hurriedly. Because, unusual and satisfying as it was to garner stares from other people, her prurient streak was just a little too insistent to ignore for very long. 'My suits are way too formal and hot for the weather over here, so I've invested in one or two things…'

She discreetly tugged at the hem of the dress, which had ridden up and was exposing too much thigh for her liking.

'Very wise,' Alessandro murmured gravely. 'Although you might have gone to the other extreme. If you plan on wearing sexy little numbers like this during the day…it might be a little too dressy…'

Kate's breathing hitched and her eyes widened at the slow, lazy smile that lightened his features.

'This is just a normal…er…dress,' she stammered, mesmerized by the gleam in his eyes. 'Nothing that any other woman in here isn't wearing.'

Alessandro made a show of looking around him before resting his dark eyes on her flushed face. 'But not many of them have the body to pull it off. You must know that.'

'I…'

'I admit I was a little surprised when I saw that you had taken me at my word. Aside from the time when I surprised you in your house, I honestly thought that your entire repertoire of clothes was comprised of suits in various shades of grey and navy…'

'I don't have much use for… I don't usually…'

'Paint the town red in snappy little numbers that attract attention?'

So what had she expected? That they would talk about work? When he had specifically told her that work was the last thing he wanted to think about after the day they had had with George and his sad, disturbing revelations?

'I've never been one for going to clubs.' She couldn't conceal a shudder. 'So, no, this is the one and only dress I have along these lines. Well, aside from the other one I bought today. Now I have two.'

'Two? I don't know why, but that strikes me as a little sad…' He grinned, and she blushed and looked away.

'You're winding me up again, aren't you?'

'More stating a fact,' Alessandro told her drily. 'Maybe we should play truant tomorrow and go shopping again…'

'Haven't you made arrangements for us to visit the company that you're interested in buying? I heard you on the phone when we were driving back from the hospital…'

'Arrangements are made to be broken. The company

isn't going anywhere, and besides…' he shrugged carelessly '…they're keen to sell and they won't find a better buyer than me.'

'Well, thanks for the offer, but I'm all shopped out. It's not something I do unless I have to, and—'

'You really need to start living your own life, Kate, instead of the one prescribed by your mother's lifestyle.'

He poured her a glass of wine from the bottle that was chilling in a cooler on the table. 'Your mother liked shopping for clothes you deemed inappropriate, so your instant reaction was to dislike shopping and to dress in clothes your mother probably wouldn't be seen dead in.'

Kate gulped down some wine and glared at him. 'I'm getting paid to work while we're over here,' she pointed out.

He smiled at her. 'And I'm telling you that you're off the hook tomorrow. If you don't tell, then I won't.'

'You *like* shopping? With a *woman*?'

'In answer to question number one—can't stand it. I have someone who knows the sort of clothes I wear. I leave it to her to stock my wardrobe.'

'Who? Who *does* that?'

'Let's just say that a long time ago I went out with a woman who got a little more involved than she should have…'

'You mean she wanted more than just a one-night stand?'

Kate couldn't believe she had actually said that to Alessandro, but this whole expedition was beginning to take on a slightly surreal air—and, frankly, if he wanted to command her to relax, then he would just have to take the consequences. The thrill of being *daring* and *reckless*, of releasing some of her tightly wound strings, soared through her veins, making her giddy.

'I don't do one-night stands,' Alessandro informed her.

Kate laughed aloud.

'Where's the joke in that? I'm missing it.'

'I thought…I thought you were a guy who didn't do long-term relationships?'

'The opposite of *long-term* isn't *one-night stand*. There's a very happy middle ground—trust me. Now, drink up and let's go out. I've asked the concierge for a couple of recommendations and he's booked a restaurant for us within walking distance.' He eyed her shoes. 'Are you going to be mobile in those?'

Kate stuck out her foot and inspected it, turning it round in a circle. The shoes were wonderful. The first pair of high, strappy sandals she had ever owned.

'Yes, you have a lovely foot,' Alessandro told her. 'Nice toes. Very good ankle. Would you like to twirl the other one for my inspection?'

'I wasn't fishing for compliments.'

'Of course you were. Woman's prerogative.'

'They're a little tricky to walk in…'

'We'll take it slowly—and if you feel yourself toppling over, don't worry. I'll catch you.'

Kate's head filled with that thought. It was as if someone had switched on a lightbulb, illuminating dark corners and lots of murky thoughts she had been shying away from.

Alessandro Preda might represent everything she disdained, but he was sexy and he was charming—was it any wonder that she was attracted to him? Against all odds? For so many reasons it was all wrong. She worked for him. He was a player. He was way too good-looking, too rich and too self-assured for his own good. And, yes, she was inexperienced.

All those things combined into a heady mix—which was why, as they left the bar, she could feel a powerful thread of excitement racing through her veins, so that she was hyper-aware of him next to her, practically brushing her arm with his.

The restaurant was much further from the hotel than she had thought, and she could feel the steady burn of developing blisters as they navigated the crowds, but there was no way she was going to mention that to him. Besides, what could he do?

She sighed with relief as they entered the blessed cool of a fish restaurant and discreetly kicked off the sandals underneath the table as they sat down.

The backs of her feet stung and her toes were throbbing. Thank God he had begun to talk to her about the electronics company he wanted to take over, because she could plaster an interested look on her face and focus on that instead of trying to subdue the pain.

'And so,' Alessandro concluded, 'the entire company was sucked into a black hole, to disappear into the ether...'

'Absolutely!' Kate chirped, tentatively feeling one blister with her toe and trying hard not to wince. 'It's *such* a good idea and I'm sure it'll all work out. I'll make sure to look up the company and do some research...er...later tonight...'

'I've never been able to resist a woman who hangs onto my every word,' he drawled. 'Have you heard a word I've been saying for the last ten minutes?'

'You were talking about the electronics company...'

'Care to recap? Ah. Thought not. Tell me I'm not such a bore that you lost interest in my conversation after five seconds...?'

'I'm sorry. I was miles away.'

'Anywhere in particular?'

Yes, in a world of pain and agony where my only mission was to get hold of some blister plasters and paracetamol.

'Nope. Just...just thinking about being here in North

America… You know, I've done next to no travelling? I guess I was just overwhelmed by all the sights and sounds. I got lost filtering them all in my…'

Wine had been brought to them. When had that happened? She gulped down most of her glass in the hope of discovering some restorative or anaesthetic qualities to help her get through the evening without making a complete fool of herself.

'You must have been abroad, though, at some point in your life…?'

'Ibiza.' She rolled her eyes and grimaced. 'I took my mum.'

'And?'

'And it was…fun—although Mum did spend quite a bit of time flirting with the waiters.' Kate laughed. 'But, thinking about it, it really *was* fun. She made me put away every single textbook I had taken with me—I had been studying for exams—and she forced me to repeat that I was there to *relax* whenever I mentioned tax laws, or corporate finance laws, or profit and loss columns or dividends. She also made me wear my swimsuit *without* a great big tee shirt over it—even though I told her all about the dangers of too much sun and overexposure.' She sighed and looked at him. 'You must think me the last word in dull…'

'Not dull, no. Just a little…cautious…'

'And I guess you've never been cautious?'

'None of us is exempt from being careful when it comes to certain situations,' Alessandro murmured. 'Now, choose whatever you want from the menu—and don't be afraid to eat to your heart's content. The concierge tells me that the chocolate brownie pudding on the menu is famous…'

Lots of very good food, far too much very good wine and Alessandro Preda as a dinner companion—it all went a long way to numbing the pain in her feet, and she only woke up to the reality that her blisters were still there, alive and kicking, as she wriggled her feet into the sandals at the end of the meal.

The walk was less than half an hour, the air was still warm and they weren't jogging at speed—but every step was agony and it was only when the hotel was in sight that she heard herself give a soft moan, partly out of relief that her ordeal would soon be over, partly because she just couldn't help herself.

'What?' she asked brightly when he stopped and looked at her narrowly.

'What's wrong?'

'Nothing. Just taking it easy...enjoying the buzz... It's very different from London, isn't it? Not as hectic.'

Alessandro cocked his head to one side, then took his time looking at her, those clever dark eyes travelling the length of her body until they rested on her feet.

'Hell!' He stooped to examine her feet and she uttered a little shriek of mortification.

'Get up!' she whispered. 'Please, Alessandro! People are looking at us! They're going to think...to think that you're *proposing* or something!'

'To your feet?' He glanced up at her and she kept her face firmly averted. 'How long have you been in pain?'

'I'm not *in pain*. My feet might be a bit sore because I'm not used to wearing heels. Or sandals...'

'Good God, woman.'

He vaulted upright and then scooped her up in one fluid, easy movement. She squealed and clutched him, shocked rigid as he began striding towards the hotel while people turned to stare and laugh.

'Put me down!' she wailed. 'Everyone's staring!'

'You worry too much about what other people think. And I'm not putting you down. I'm only just about hanging on to my temper. Why the *hell* didn't you say something earlier?'

'They were fine at the restaurant!'

It was hard to talk whilst trying to wriggle into some sort of position that wasn't utterly humiliating. Was her underwear on display for everyone to have a look at? She wriggled frantically, ignoring his commands to keep still, hating him at that moment in time even if he *had* rescued her from having to hobble for the rest of the way.

'*Please* put me down when we get into the hotel. I can manage from there.'

He ignored her and headed straight for the reception desk. In her head she could picture the curved marble counter, manned by banks of cruel, sniggering young girls, as she heard him ask for a comprehensive first-aid kit to be sent to his suite immediately. No, a doctor wouldn't be required—just get the kit up to his quarters double quick.

She gave up protesting and clung to him, arms around his neck, fingers clasped, eyes squeezed tightly shut—because that way she could kid herself that none of this was happening.

She only opened her eyes when she was gently lowered onto his bed, and then she watched as he even more gently removed the offending sandals and cursed softly under his breath.

'You've probably done your back in,' was all she could find to say.

'My back is fine—which is more than I can say for your feet. They're raw.'

'I'm not used to wearing heels. Or shoes like this.'

Embarrassment washed over her as he rested her aching, swollen feet on his lap and reached for the first-aid kit, which had already been placed on the bed.

'You're right. I should have mentioned earlier that I was

developing one or two blisters… But, please, I can take care of this myself.' It was a last desperate plea that she thought he might ignore—and he did.

His hands were so soothing… Kate closed her eyes and her breathing slowed as he dealt with her blisters, gently cleaning them, putting cool cream on them, and then the special plasters from the kit. Maybe blisters were a common occurrence here? she thought drowsily. Maybe every silly tourist took to the streets in inadequate footwear and returned to the hotel in need of a first-aid kit?

'I had no idea that you were a doctor along with everything else,' she murmured, joking because the silence was so intense and somehow so *intimate*.

'I had planned on doing medicine, as a matter of fact…'

Her eyes flickered open. She looked at his dark head, bent down, those long brown fingers working quickly and efficiently on sorting out her feet. 'Really?'

'Really,' Alessandro said drily, without glancing in her direction. 'It was a short-lived ambition.'

'Why?'

This time he did look at her. Briefly. Dark eyes serious. 'My feckless parents needed me to set them on the financial straight and narrow.'

Now why had he said that? When he never confided in anyone—least of all a woman? When he knew that confidences encouraged women to think that they could inch their way beyond his barriers…when he knew that a woman in possession of a confidence was a woman who felt she had the upper hand…

But it had been an unsettling day. He had had his preconceived notions smashed, had been forced to re-examine the black-and-white approach to life that had always stood him in good stead. Things were always so much clearer without grey areas. And now this… His body messing with his head in a way it had never done before, controlling him as he sat here with her feet on his thigh…

'What do you mean?' Kate asked curiously. 'I thought…'

'That I was born with a silver spoon in my mouth?'

'More golden,' she admitted haltingly.

'In a way you'd be right,' he said thoughtfully, drawing back to look at his handiwork with satisfaction. 'I *am* the product of two wealthy families. My parents had more money than they knew what to do with. Unfortunately neither of them possessed the common sense to manage their fortunes properly.'

He smiled wryly and stood up, flexing his muscles, packing away the first-aid kit and then strolling to the window, where he stood for a few seconds gazing down at the street below before turning to her.

'That's love for you,' he said, and walked slowly back towards the bed, then stood at the side, hands shoved into his pockets, his lean, handsome features hard. 'The soulmates, let's-put-together-the-relationship-building-blocks kind of love you find so seductive…'

'What do you mean?' She looked at him in confusion.

'I mean…' He smiled with cool introspection. 'I have first-hand experience of how a couple of soulmates can encourage each other into lifestyles that are self-obsessed and destructive. My parents married young, and by the time they hit forty they'd managed to squander most of their joint inheritances on…well, frankly, on crap investments and eco-nonsense schemes. They lived with their heads in the clouds. Yes, they were in love—but, personally, I think if there had been a little less love and a little more common sense they might have not spent their lives hurtling from one ridiculous investment to another. Until, of course, it was up to me to bail the pair of them out.'

'*You* had to bail them out?'

'They misguidedly thought that the well would never run dry.'

'So you gave up your dreams of being a doctor for a...a more profitable lifestyle...?'

'Don't get carried away, Kate. Being in my position is hardly a hardship.'

'No...but money doesn't really matter, does it?'

'Is that why you spend every second being a business-woman in an attempt to advance your career and get financially stable? What did I tell you about hypocrisy...? Tut-tut...'

Kate reddened. Standing over her, he was so damned tall, overwhelming her with his physicality. Her mouth dried. She couldn't tear her fascinated gaze away from him. She was suddenly conscious of her bare legs, the small dress, of the heat racing through her body inflaming her pulse, tightening the buds of her nipples into hard, pointed peaks.

'Now, here's the strategic difference between us,' Alessandro drawled softly.

She had propped herself up against the pillows and he took his time following the long, slender lines of her body before leaning down, palms flat on the bed, so that his face was only inches away from hers.

'*I* haven't abandoned having fun in favour of some never-never dream of perfection that won't be happening.'

'I haven't done that!'

'No? So when was the last time you had sex?'

Just like that the room shrank to the size of a cardboard box and breathing became difficult. Her heart was beating so hard that she could almost hear it. When she opened her mouth the professional woman with an agenda not to be affected by him had vanished. In her place was a woman in the grip of desire, a woman with needs—a woman who could feel those needs in the liquid moistening between her thighs, dampening her underwear.

'I… Well…'

'When was the last time you just *let go*, Kate…? Here's what I'm thinking… Tonight was probably the first time in years that you went out in something other than the sort of clothes someone's great-aunt would be proud to be seen in…'

'That's not fair,' she whispered, stung because it was true—horribly, mortifyingly *true*.

'It may not be *fair*, but it's true. When was the last time you felt anything but a need to work, so that you can avoid ending up in the same pickle your mother did? It's a dry life.'

'It's…'

'Dry, sterile… You're hiding away from emotion, waiting for the Big Thing to happen, and in the meantime life's passing you by.'

'It's not all about sex…'

He didn't answer. He didn't have to.

She could read the intent in his eyes and she knew that he was going to kiss her—*and she wanted him to*. She wanted him to with every fibre of her sex-starved being… even if it made no sense.

His mouth covered hers, and it wasn't with the possessive hunger of a man who wanted to take without giving. No, it was a slow, lazy, lingering kiss…a melding of tongues that had her whimpering. She linked her fingers behind his neck and drew him to her—only to pull back and look at him with huge, bewildered eyes.

'We shouldn't be doing this,' she whispered huskily.

What a joke! She still had her hands behind his head and her body was still leaning towards his.

Tell me about it, Alessandro thought. This was probably the *last* thing he should be doing. But for the first time in his life his control had slipped and he had no intention of trying to claw it back. He was so turned on that he could barely think clearly. He wanted to feel her hand on his erection, feel her rubbing him, licking him, taking him into her mouth…

Instead they were both still fully clothed, and it was driving him crazy.

'It's better to do the things we know we shouldn't do than live an empty life resisting all temptation,' he husked. 'But if you want me to stop…'

'I don't even approve of you…'

'I know.'

He silenced her with another kiss, and this time it was hungry, urgent, demanding and utterly, utterly devastating.

She was barely aware of him getting onto the bed with her, or of him rearing up to strip off his shirt. She was too fascinated by the sight of his bare torso…bronzed, broad-shouldered, every ripple of muscle defined.

She moaned and levered herself up, licked his stomach. It felt so decadent and so wanton that she could scarcely believe she'd done it. He flung back his head and she felt him suck in his breath. Lord, but that made her feel powerful.

Tentatively, she placed her hand on the bulge pushing against his trousers, and was thrilled when she heard him groan and felt him press her hand down hard.

'Just…wait…' Alessandro held his breath, gathering his scattered self-control, then released it in a long, slow hiss.

'Wait for what?'

'I…have never…been so close to doing the unthinkable…'

'What's that?'

Alessandro looked down at her flushed face and grinned with wicked enjoyment. 'Coming before I want to—shall I show you what it feels like?'

His dark eyes were bold as they raked over her. She had no idea how he could do this, but she knew that he had done it before—looked at her and made her feel as though she was being touched, caressed.

So it was a bad idea. It didn't make sense. It went against every principle she had ever held. Sex was not something to be given away lightly—it should be part of a developing relationship, a journey of discovery and exploration.

Alessandro Preda had about as much interest in journeys of discovery and exploration as a pirate sizing up his next conquest. *See, take and move on* was not the motto of the sensitive kind of guy she needed.

But, God, she wanted him. And wasn't he right? She had been so busy building her secure little nest that she had forgotten there was a world out there—a world of experience and fun and adventure and...*challenge.*

Why shouldn't she accept the challenge and go with the flow for the first time in her life?

'I work for you...'

'I think it's too late for us to throw that into the mix...'

He straddled her and reached for the button on his trousers. One hundred per cent dominant alpha male...*one hundred per cent heartbreaker*...

But she was safe. Her heart could never be broken by a man like Alessandro Preda. Men like him had broken her mother's heart time and again. Men like him led women on, led them astray, made them forget reason. Her lifetime's work had been to make sure that she was emotionally immune to men like him. So what if it turned out in this instance that she wasn't *physically* immune? She could deal with that...

This was living in the moment. It was something she had never done. And she was going to do it now because he was right. Regret would always make a bitter companion.

CHAPTER EIGHT

THE LITTLE SILKY nothing of a dress had ridden up her thighs as she lay sprawled on the bed, watching him with bated breath.

Still straddling her, not taking his eyes off her heated face, he reached behind him without looking and cupped her between her legs.

She was melting. When he moved his hand, pressing down, she moaned and her eyelids fluttered. She was wet… so wet. She let her legs go limp, inviting him, and he took advantage of the invitation to slip his hand under her damp panties so that he could rub two fingers gently, insistently, finding the throbbing nub of her clitoris and making her gasp with pleasure.

'You like what I'm doing to you?' he murmured.

She nodded, dazed, hardly able to believe that this was *her*—sensible, practical, ever-watchful Kate Watson, who had always planned her life right down to the very last detail, who had never allowed herself to get swept up in anything she couldn't control.

She moved against his questing fingers, groaning softly, feeling the waves of pleasure beginning to rise to a crest.

'Not like this…' she managed to croak, in a voice she didn't recognize, and he withdrew his fingers immediately, leaving her aching down there. 'Beast.' She smiled at the wicked glint in his eyes.

'I'll let you do the same to me,' Alessandro soothed. 'Sometimes it works…getting so close to the finishing line and not being able to cross it…it makes the eventual crossing so much more thrilling…'

He eased his big body off the bed and took his time removing his clothes. He found that his hands were unsteady, his pulse racing, and he was momentarily confused… Because this had never happened to him in his life before. He couldn't remember *ever* having to struggle against a desire to come before the time was right. When it came to making love he had always had the ultimate control over his body.

Not now.

Now he knew that if she touched him down there, in all the ways he wanted her to, he would ejaculate. He would have to take his time, move slowly, and whilst it wasn't his style to rush, this time rushing was exactly what he wanted to do.

This loss of control was…destabilizing. It made him feel like someone tipping over the edge as they bungee-jumped into the unknown.

Her eyes were on him, fascinated, apprehensive, weirdly shy, as he stood in front of her clad only in his boxers.

'Like what you see?'

Kate nodded, her mouth dry. *Like?* That word didn't begin to sum up what she was feeling. The man was the ultimate in physical perfection. How was that even possible for someone who spent the majority of his time on a plane, or behind a desk, or clutching a cell phone…?

'You must exercise a lot,' she ventured, and he grinned. 'I'm taking that as a compliment.'

He slipped off the boxers and she nearly fainted at the

sight of his impressive arousal. Her eyes were half-closed as he slipped back onto the bed next to her.

Nerves threatened to overwhelm her. For a wild moment she wondered how she had managed to end up lying in his bed, his naked body hot and demanding against hers, her own body tingling, perspiring, aching to have the flimsy dress off her—because even the slightest bit of material felt like an iron barrier between them that *had* to be removed.

This wasn't *her*. Yet, in a way, nothing had ever felt so natural. Her heart was beating like a sledgehammer as she curved onto her side so that they were facing one another, and she marvelled at the depth of his eyes, the shades of navy that flecked the black.

'You were telling me how impressed you are with my body...' he murmured, pushing her hair back and planting a trail of delicate kisses on her face. He *wanted* to hear her say it, which was a feeling he'd never experienced before.

'Was I?'

'I do work out, as a matter of fact.'

'When? I thought you lived at the office?'

'I work hard, but I play hard as well... I like to think that that's what makes for a balanced life.'

Kate knew what he meant by *playing hard*. It wasn't trips to the gym twice a week. It was sex. No-strings sex. With beautiful women who didn't make demands because the second a demand was made their time was up.

The operative word was *play*.

It occurred to her that his sudden attack of desire for her had only surfaced when he had seen her out of her work uniform—when he had seen her dressed to kill and showing off her assets. As her mother had. He had gone for the body, and how many times had she told herself that she would never be—could *never* be—attracted to any man who wasn't interested in her *for who she was*.

So much for being able to rely on her brain to tell her what to do…

She wanted this man. She couldn't think past the heat sizzling through her veins, making her feel treacherously *alive* for the first time in her life.

'Why me?' she whispered.

Alessandro drew back to look at her. Up close, she was even more stunning. Her face was dewy, satiny smooth, her lips full, her eyes the purest green he had ever seen.

But he wasn't lying in this bed, his body on fire, because of the way she looked. The world—especially *his* world—was full of stunning women. After a while they simply merged into one. No, he was here because she was…*different*.

And because she had witnessed him in a rare moment of confusion—when he had had all his preconceived notions about George Cape thrown over, when he had had to think on his feet and behave in a way that hadn't been predicted by his assumptions.

Vulnerable.

He hated the word, but there it was. She had seen him strangely vulnerable.

Had that created some sort of weird bond between them? It was a thought he didn't bother to follow through to a conclusion because it made no difference. The reality was that he was here, she was here and they were going to make love.

'These things happen,' he murmured. 'Who knows what generates physical attraction? You have skin like a peach… Stop talking. There are better ways for us to expend energy.'

He ran his hand along her thigh, under the dress, along her waist. He was almost *nervous*, and that shook him a little.

Against her, Kate could feel the hardness of his erection,

massive, stirring as he touched her. She reached down and held it and had another near-fainting moment.

'I'm not…experienced…like those women you go out with. I just thought I should warn you…'

'Okay. Warning duly noted. Now, I want you to get out of that dress. It's a nice dress, but I'd rather see it on the floor…'

She hitched her hands under the hem, ready to wriggle it over her head, but he stopped her.

'Not so fast…'

'What do you mean?'

Alessandro propped himself up on one elbow and looked at her with a little half smile that did all sorts of things to her already escalating levels of heat. Spontaneous combustion might very well be on the cards.

This was lust. *This* was what women went on about when they whined that they *just couldn't help themselves*. Kate had never had any sympathy at all for women like that. As far as she was concerned there was never any *not being able to help yourself* when it came to men and sex. You could *always* help yourself. She was a prime example of that and it was called self-restraint. Easy.

Except right now, if someone had told her to walk away from the man staring at her with eyes that could start a forest fire, she wouldn't have been able to move a limb.

'Time for you to do a striptease…' He lay back on the bed, hands folded behind his head, and looked at her. 'Fair's fair, after all.'

'I've never done a striptease before in my life.'

Nor had she ever wanted to! In fact, on a scale of one to ten of activities she would have avoided at all costs, performing a striptease was off the scale completely.

Just thinking about it now brought her out in a cold sweat, and yet underneath there was a dark stirring of excitement when she imagined those dark, dark eyes focused on her, enjoying her…

Did that make her weak…like her mother? Helpless in the company of an attractive man? Unable to obey what her head was telling her? Ruled by responses over which she had no control?

No. Kate knew that with gut instinct. It didn't. But she had the scariest feeling that she was letting go of the old Kate…although she had no idea where that notion came from. Or where the old Kate was going and whether she would be returning any time soon.

'You don't have to if it makes you feel uncomfortable,' Alessandro said, in a tone of voice that made her realize he could see from the expression on her face exactly what she had been thinking.

'Why would it make me feel uncomfortable?'

'Tell me something,' he said, watching as she hovered, half-sitting, poised between climbing out of her box and hanging on in there for dear life. 'When you made love in the past, was it always in the dark?'

Kate blushed—which was an answer in itself.

He reached out and lazily stroked the side of her arm. 'Have you never wanted to see what you were doing?'

'I've slept with a guy precisely four times,' she confessed in a harried rush. 'We never… I never… I suppose if things had worked out…'

No. Even if she and Sam had *not* ended up crashing and burning, she still wouldn't have become the wanton hussy she was now capable of being. Given the right guy. Or rather the wrong guy—the utterly, utterly *wrong and inappropriate* guy. She would have still insisted on having the lights out when she got undressed, because he had not induced these crazy feelings of uncontrollable yearning in her.

She slithered off the bed and stood just where Alessandro had previously stood. His discarded clothes were right there on the floor by her feet. Very slowly, and with a lack of self-consciousness that amazed her, considering she should be ravaged by it, she drew the slip of a dress over her head and tossed it on the ground, where it joined his clothes.

Then she reached behind her and unclasped her bra.

Alessandro touched himself. His breathing faltered. She was slender, but not skinny, and her breasts were generous, barely contained within the flimsy bra. Her nipples were large, pink, begging to be sucked. Just thinking about it made the breath hitch in his throat even more.

She stepped out of her underwear and then drew herself up proudly, all woman, curves in all the right places, the downy patch between her thighs proclaiming her as one of the few who *didn't* think it necessary to depilate every square inch of her body.

Alessandro had never been so turned on in his entire life.

As if suddenly remembering that she should be quivering with embarrassment she lowered her eyes and blushed madly, before making a dive for the safety of the bed. But he stopped her in her tracks by placing one big hand on her stomach.

'Your feet still look tender,' he murmured, gazing at her plastered heels and arches.

Blistered feet should do *something* to get his raging libido a little under control—but actually, as he stared down, all he could see were her extremely shapely ankles, and all he could smell was the heady, musky perfume from between her legs.

He groaned and curved both hands to cup her bottom, tugging her gently towards him.

Kate had forgotten about the sore feet that were the reason she was in this bedroom in the first place. They were consigned to oblivion now, as she took those tentative steps into…the unknown…

'I…I can't…' She managed to articulate those strangulated words while, of their own accord, her fingers curled into his hair.

She gasped when he parted those soft folds, and gasped again as his tongue flicked against the wet, sensitized flesh, and then she stopped gasping and drew in her breath, holding it as that exploring tongue began to explore some more.

It was exquisite. She was transported to another dimension. And she parted her legs, accommodating that questing tongue as it located the throbbing nub of her swollen clitoris. She arched back. Her whole body was covered in slick perspiration. If a bomb had dropped on the hotel right now she was pretty sure she wouldn't have noticed—because the only thing she was capable of noticing was the sweep of sensations racing through her body at breakneck speed.

When he withdrew she practically sobbed with the sense of loss.

'*Now* you can come to bed,' Alessandro commanded softly.

He patted the space next to him and she slid like a rag doll into the allotted spot, her body turning and curving against his, loving the feel of the heat he was emanating.

He pushed his thigh between her legs and moved it with just the right level of pressure to ensure that she picked up where she had left off when he had removed his tongue from her.

Kate grasped his shoulders, feeling solid muscle under

her fingers, and looked at him drowsily, drugged, completely in his power.

And he liked that.

He kissed her—a hungry, very thorough kiss, that made all her bones feel just a little more jelly-like—and then he carried on kissing her. The slender column of her neck, her shoulder blades, working his way down until he was circling her nipple with his tongue and then taking it into his mouth and suckling on it, lazily, in no rush to go anywhere.

She had died and gone to heaven. There wasn't a single part of her entire body that wasn't buzzing with all sorts of new, wonderful, pleasurable sensations, and they only increased when his hand wandered down to her thighs, slipped between them, his fingers idly playing with her in a way that was screamingly intimate and utterly erotic.

She squirmed and felt him smile against her breast. He was enjoying himself—but he couldn't be enjoying himself half as much as she was enjoying *herself.* He did this all the time. He had a reputation that preceded him wherever he went. He was a guy who had wined, dined and bedded some of the most beautiful women in the world. This was probably routine for him.

Not that she liked the thought of that. But she hadn't been born yesterday, and even while she was losing herself in the pleasure he was bringing her she was still realistic enough to know that he was an expert at this sort of thing. An expert when it came to giving sexual pleasure.

Whereas *she* was in a whole new territory—one she had never visited before—and she was loving it.

Loving what he was doing to her.

Loving the way her body felt—as though it was waking up for the very first time.

She closed her eyes and sighed as he moved from one tingling nipple to the other.

She had always thought her breasts to be overtly sexual —had always secretly longed for little ones that didn't require the heavy-duty support of a bra—but, watching his dark head exploring them, she was enormously proud of them, of their fullness, the prominence of her dusky nipples, which he couldn't seem to get enough of.

She moved against his fingers and he thrust them a little deeper into her, arousing her yet further.

'Please…' she pleaded, and he stopped sucking her nipple to look at her.

'Please what…?'

'You know…'

'Okay, so maybe I do, but I still want to hear you say it…'

'You want me to tell you that…that I want you? Right now? That I can't hold on for much longer? That—'

'That you'd like to come into my hand but you'd much rather feel me moving inside you…thrusting hard and deep… Repeat all that after me…'

'I can't!' she gasped breathlessly, and Alessandro grinned. Because the chasm between her wet, hot body and her prurience, to which she couldn't help but carry on clinging, even if it was just a little, fascinated him.

'You can…'

She did. And just saying those things out loud was a huge turn-on.

She was aware of him leaving her for a few seconds, felt the mattress depress when he returned, and knew that he was donning protection.

She was open and ready for him when he entered her. Although it had been a while and he was big—very big. Her tight muscles relaxed, closed round his hardened sheath, took every glorious inch of him in. And when he began moving inside her it was like nothing she had ever experienced in her life before.

Her short nails dug into his back. Both their bodies were slick, sliding against one another. He reared up just as the groundswell of sensation inside her cascaded and splintered, sending her into orbit and making her cry out.

Utterly spent. That was what Kate felt as she descended from the peak to which she had been catapulted at supersonic speed. Utterly spent and very much aware that, like it or not, she had been as vulnerable to this man's sexual charisma as all those supermodels he had dated and dispatched with monotonous regularity.

Alessandro rolled off her, took a few seconds to gather himself—because the experience had left him on a different planet. He felt amazing—as though he had discovered the ability to walk on water…

Where had *that* feeling come from?

He lay on his side and looked at her body. He cupped one breast with his hand and felt its weight.

Kate edged away and scrabbled for the duvet, which was solidly planted underneath them. Horses, stable doors and bolting sprang to mind. What was the point in succumbing to a sudden attack of shyness when she had been uttering things that made her blush only minutes previously?

That said, what on earth had she gone and done? Shouldn't she be in the grip of remorse? Regret? Mortification?

'My feet feel much better…' That was the prosaic statement that came out of her mouth—because she was too busy looking at the man she had just had sex with to think of anything wittier or more profound to say.

'Sex has a way of sorting out most of life's little problems.' He toyed with a few tendrils of her hair, tucked them behind her ear. 'Including sore feet.'

'Really? I never knew...'

'That's because you've spent all of your adult life avoiding it.'

And you've spent all of your *adult life avoiding commitment.*

It was something she wanted to say. She found that she wanted him to talk to her—talk to her the way she had inadvertently been persuaded into talking to him—but that was a line that could not be breached. She knew that with every gut instinct inside her. Step over that line and she would be dismissed as casually as a stranger he had happened to bump into.

She didn't want to be dismissed. Not yet. Not when she had discovered this crazy, sensual side to her that made her feel so great—as though she could walk on water. She wanted to hang on to it for just a little bit longer.

What was wrong with that? It was human nature, wasn't it? The desire to cling on to something that made you feel good?

Not that she had any intention of being clingy. She might have taken an unexpected detour with him, but in the process she hadn't steamrollered over all her principles. She was as strong as she always had been.

She swatted away the uneasy realisation she had had earlier that she had fallen for his charm, succumbed to his animal magnetism, trodden the same mesmerized, idiotic path that those women he dated had trodden before her.

Now that the haze of unbridled passion had dissipated she decided that she was the same person she always had been but with *added dimensions.* And how could *that* not be a good thing? How could *that* not stand her in good stead for the future that was out there waiting for her?

Mr Right was out there—and not only would he be waiting for her with a glass of chilled wine when she had

had a long day…after the chilled wine he would sweep her off her feet and carry her into the bedroom and make her feel just the way the very inappropriate Alessandro Preda was capable of making her feel.

Because now the sensual side of her had been unleashed. Her ex-boyfriend might not have been the full package, but now she knew the full package was practically round the corner.

And the relief of knowing that knocked her for six.

Only now did she realize how much she had begun to accept an inevitable future in which she found no one, remained a lonely career woman, heading up the ladder with no one at her side.

She snuggled against Alessandro and laughed when she realized that their recent bout of mind-blowing sex had done nothing to depress his very active libido.

'The reason I asked you how your feet were,' Alessandro murmured in between kisses to the side of her mouth, 'is that it's occurred to me that walking is going to be fairly difficult for you tomorrow. Possibly for the next couple of days.'

Kate stilled. In a horizontal position, with this gorgeous hunk next to her and her body already eagerly anticipating round two in the sexual stakes, her feet had been the last thing on her mind. They felt right as rain, in fact.

Now she pictured shoving them into her little black pumps, feeling the tight leather pressing against the plasters, and knew that he had a point. But she was here to work. And he was first and foremost a man who put work ahead of everything else—and that would include a romp in the hay with one of his employees.

Which was what she was. An *employee*.

'I'm sure I'll be able to walk if I get some flip-flops.' She drew back and pressed her arms in front of her, shielding her bare breasts. 'It may not be the most professional look, but as long as I don't wear closed shoes I think I'll be fine. There's no need to imagine that I won't be able to do my job.'

And there's no need to imagine that because we've slept together I'm suddenly going to become anything less than the efficient person who reports to you... No need to fear that I'll turn into one of those clingy types who don't know when the party's over.

She had a desperate urge to fill him in on how she felt— to let him know that she was still in the driving seat...to let *herself* know that she was still in the driving seat.

'That's not why I mentioned the feet,' Alessandro drawled. 'Although I'd be curious to see how flip-flops work with your navy suits...'

'I did bring a beige one. It's my summer suit.'

'Oh, the levels of daring to which you've aspired... You forget: you can get rid of the suits. I've seen you in all your non-suited glory. You can actually feel free to dress down a little now when it comes to your work attire. I mentioned the feet because if you can't walk then we might have to resign ourselves to being holed up in this suite for the next couple of days...'

'What do you mean?'

'You *know* what I mean. You can feel the chemistry between us. I can't keep my hands off you.'

All her old principles rose to the surface but she fought them down—because hadn't she *wanted* to embark on this challenge? She wasn't going to get cold feet now.

'But what about the client you wanted us to visit?'

'He won't be going anywhere. At least not for a couple of days.'

'Is that the time limit you've set on this...er...situation?'

The sexy warmth on his face evaporated just like that.

She could feel him pull back and knew that he was gauging the situation—weighing up the pros of having good sex against the cons of what might prove to be an awkward situation.

She hadn't heard his warning speech about not getting wrapped up in him. Was he trying to work out how he could give it now, having had mind-blowing sex with her?

'I know what you're thinking,' she said casually, lowering her eyes and trying to stanch the sudden pain twisting inside her.

'Really? You're a mind reader?'

'I'm not a mind-reader, but I'm not stupid either. I've told you how I feel about meaningless relationships. I've told you that I've never seen the point of one-night stands and sex just for the sake of sex. So you're probably scared stiff that we've slept together and now suddenly I'll be trying to drag you down to the local jeweller's to see what the rings there look like. But you couldn't be further from the truth.'

'No?'

'No,' Kate told him firmly. 'I don't know what happened here…things went down an unexpected road…but that doesn't change the fact that you're you and I'm me. For a start, I work for you. You're my boss. And that makes this all wrong.'

'Let's get past the boss/employee situation…'

'It's all right for *you* to say that.' Kate was suddenly angry at his complete self-assurance that he was entitled to do exactly what he wanted to do, without any repercussions whatsoever. 'You can turn round and sack me if you decide I'm some kind of liability.'

'And will you be? A liability?' He hadn't even thought of her as the sort to sell some tacky kiss-and-tell story to a newspaper—not that that would turn his world on its axis. He couldn't care less what people thought of him. But the idea that she might go down the tawdry route of gold-digger, out to siphon off money after sleeping with him...well, that was a horse of a different colour.

And why *hadn't* he thought of that possibility?

Because she'd struck him as a person of integrity. Was he about to be proved wrong?

But, no. He could tell instantly from the look of distaste that crossed her face that he had insulted her.

'I had to ask,' he said with cool detachment, rolling onto his back and staring up at the ceiling with his arms behind his head.

'Of course you did.' Kate's voice dripped sarcasm. 'It's only natural after you've slept with a woman to ask her whether she's about to phone a tabloid and spill the beans about sex with billionaire Alessandro Preda. If you think that I hopped into bed with you because I fancied my chances of fleecing you for money—'

He turned to her and stared her down unsmilingly. 'When you live my life you don't take anything for granted.'

'Then you must lead a sad life.' She sighed. 'I shouldn't have said that. I'm sorry. But I don't know how to behave around you now that this has happened. Every time I say something a little too frank I remember who you are. And then I start wondering how we got into this...this mess...'

'Situations like this are only a mess if they get out of hand—and they only get out of hand if one or the other becomes too involved.'

'And that would never be *you*.' She shot him a rueful glance, because whatever mess she had found herself in she was too greedy to want to get out of it just yet.

But get out she would. And before he gave her his lecture she thought that she might give him *hers*—set his mind at ease, pave the way for a dignified retreat when this little one-week working holiday was over. Because, as sure as the sun rose and set every day of every year, there would be nothing between them when they returned to London.

'Don't worry—it won't be me either,' she added quickly.

'I know.'

'You do?'

'You're looking for a soulmate, and it's not me. What we have is a purely physical thing.'

'It's not like me to do a purely physical thing…'

'Which makes me feel sorry for you.' He coolly returned her criticism of him back to her and she blushed. 'You look very fetching when you blush,' he murmured, distracted. 'And, just as an aside, don't feel that you have to tiptoe round me as though you're walking on eggshells. When you're lying in bed naked you cease to be my employee…'

And when I'm no longer lying in bed naked…? When I'm back sitting at my desk, wearing one of my many suits…? Working on the deals you're throwing at me…?

She had got caught up in a riptide, had lost all her prized control, and there was only one sure way she could think of regaining it—because if she didn't then she would be lost. It was a terrifying prospect. If she got lost where would she be? How would she ever be able to find all the landmarks that defined her life?

'You have to promise me something,' she told him seriously.

'I dislike making promises. Especially to women.'

'Well…' She drew in a deep breath and exhaled slowly. 'You're going to make *this* promise—if you don't then I'm going to…to get dressed and hobble back to my room…'

'Is that blackmail?' Alessandro asked coldly. 'Because that's something I dislike even more than I dislike making promises.'

'No, it's not *blackmail*. Are you always so suspicious of everyone's motives? No, don't answer that. You are. You can't help yourself. I want you to promise me that when we return to London this ends. And we never talk about it. Ever again. We pretend none of it happened and I go back to being your employee and nothing more.'

Alessandro raised his eyebrows, for this was the first time in his life he was being dismissed prematurely. Actually, it was the first time in his life he was being dismissed *at all*.

He shrugged and decided that it was a promise he was more than happy to make. He would have her for a week, and by the time the week was done he would be ready to move on. Kate Watson, stunning and sexy as she might be, wasn't his type. She wanted more from a man than a passing fling, and he suspected that if they were to continue their liaison all her good intentions not to get wrapped up in someone who wasn't her soulmate would be ground down—because that was just the way it was.

'So it's a deal?'

'It's a deal, and we can shake on it—but who's to say that you won't find it impossible to stick to your side of the bargain?'

'I may have…given in…but…but…I see this as a kind of adventure. I mean, I've never allowed myself to get carried away. I never thought I would either. But I'm glad that I have. I suppose, in a weird way, I should thank you…'

She looked at him with shining sincerity and Alessandro looked back at her, amused.

She was complex. An ambitious professional who was endearingly inexperienced, a sensible suit-wearing employee who still blushed like a teenager. She was scrupulously honest, and seemingly unaware that scrupulous honesty was *not* part of the game when it came to sex and seduction. She spoke her mind and ignored the potential fallout.

All told, she challenged him.

Women generally didn't.

He wondered idly whether he had just been looking in the wrong places. He wondered whether the time wasn't drawing near for him to move on from hit-and-run romances with obliging but empty-headed supermodels. He was no believer in romance, but maybe the time was drawing near for him to test the waters for something more solid.

Kate Watson had shown him that a good brain certainly broadened the appeal. Tie that up with a woman who wasn't searching for love and romance, who was as down to earth as he was when it came to relationships—a woman who could challenge him intellectually, could see marriage as something blessedly free from the vagaries of so-called *love*—and who was to say that it couldn't work?

He had become jaded. This interlude had demonstrated that. The novelty of having someone out of his comfort zone had been telling. Hell, he could hardly think straight with her lying here next to him! He needed to move on...

'Maybe...' he pulled her towards him '...I should be the one thanking *you*...'

CHAPTER NINE

ALESSANDRO SWIVELLED HIS leather chair away from his desk towards the floor-to-ceiling windows through which, at several floors up, he had nothing more inspiring than an uninterrupted view of grey skies. In the week and a half since they had returned from Toronto the blue-sky summer had morphed into a more traditional London summer of leaden skies, intermittent drizzle and the low-level complaints of a nation who had become accustomed to going out without the back-up of brollies and cardigans.

His temper should have improved by now. It hadn't. He scowled and allowed himself a few satisfying seconds of thinking that change might be on the way in the form of a very shapely, very sexy lawyer, who had been nestling in his little black book, waiting for him to get in touch after their brief meeting several months previously. At the time he had been involved with a frisky little redhead, but frisky was no longer on the agenda and the lawyer seemed a far more promising bet.

True to her word, Kate had shut the door on him the second they had taken off from the airport in Toronto.

'It's been fun,' she had informed him, with a cheerful smile.

Thoughts of the sexy, shapely lawyer vanished as he remembered his response to that.

'I'm not ready for the fun to end just yet,' he had told her in a lazy drawl, absently noting that the suit was back in place.

And he hadn't been. As far as he'd been concerned the fun had only just started—so why should it end the second they touched down at Heathrow Airport? His diet, when it came to women and sex, didn't include self-denial, and he had seen no reason why that should change.

They had had an outrageously sexy week in Toronto, only just managing to squeeze in a brief visit to his potential client. It had been enough to secure the deal, and the remainder of their time in the city had been spent exploring the tourist attractions, getting more adventurous as her feet had healed, and making love. Surprisingly, he hadn't tired of her. He had felt none of his usual irritation or mildly suffocating claustrophobia at being in a woman's company even when they hadn't been in a bed.

That being the case, why *should* they have called it a day? She hadn't been of the same opinion.

He scowled and glanced at his watch. Every time he thought about the outcome of that conversation he wanted to hit something. She hadn't only kindly, *gently*, told him that it was over, she had also carried on smiling, a little puzzled smile, as though she hadn't quite understood why he wasn't *getting it*.

His ground his teeth together in smouldering fury as he recalled that.

He'd had no idea that a little dented ego could prove so difficult to shift. Was he really *so* conceited that he couldn't handle someone wanting to quit an affair before he was ready? Especially when he knew it was something that wasn't destined for the long haul anyway?

Because it wasn't. Simple as that. Kate Watson might have stepped out of her box, to do something that had never been on her agenda, but that didn't change the fact that what she wanted in life was completely different from what *he* wanted.

She wanted a long-term, no-holds-barred relationship, and that came with all the trappings he had no time for. Getting wrapped up with someone wasn't for him. Long-term, for him, would be something far more controllable—something that didn't risk disrupting the primary focus in his life, which was his work, something that wasn't…*intrusive*.

His cell phone buzzed.

Rebecca—or Red-Hot Rebecca, as she was called in certain legal circles. Long legs. Short hair. Good-looking with a seriously high-powered brain. Once upon a time, the seriously high-powered brain would not have been in his search engine, but now—yes, it definitely worked. In fact he couldn't understand what he had seen in his previous girlfriends. He couldn't envisage dating anyone now who didn't have a brain. The long legs helped—as did the attractive short bob. And when he had bumped into her a few months ago she had left him in no doubt that she was up for some quality time together.

And she wouldn't be on the hunt for romance and fairy-tale endings. She wouldn't want to take him over. She was a career woman, on her way to becoming the youngest ever lawyer to take silk. She didn't give the impression of someone who would be ready to jack all that in for a guy—any guy.

Big plus.

He picked up the call. She was on her way over. Opera was to be followed by a slap-up meal at one of the most expensive restaurants in the city. And then…who knew? Actually, he did.

His brain skidded to an inconvenient halt and veered off in a completely different direction.

Kate. In his bed at the hotel. Her long hair spread across the pillows, her arms resting lightly on her flat stomach as he undressed. Her eyes heavy with desire, turning him on until he could barely control himself—and that had been before he had even touched her.

Kate laughing, her hair blowing around her face, in the car they had rented so that he could show her some of the wild scenery that lay just a hop and a skip out of the city. She had insisted on taking a picnic and he had concurred, even though there had been a string of more-than-decent restaurants along the way.

Kate asking him gently about his past, trying to work out why he was anti-love and all its trials and tribulations... And him talking to her, telling her things he had never shared with anyone else...

He focused on that, pushing aside every other memory that threatened to rise to the surface.

He had been so damned wrapped up in the whole mind-blowing sex thing that he had dismissed her curiosity as an inconvenience rather than what he now knew it to be.

A way in.

It enraged him that even with that evidence of boundary-crossing he still hadn't been able to get her out of his head—still found himself taking cold showers in the middle of the night.

He had made sure to stay clear of her ever since they had returned to London. She was back in the bowels of the office, several floors down, busy as a little bee, he presumed. Her promotion was now general knowledge, as was George Cape's early retirement, which had been put down to him wanting to spend more time with his family during difficult times. Not untrue. Happy campers all round.

Which was not what he had originally foreseen when this mess had erupted.

Kate: new job. Cape: retired with his dignity intact—a decision for which Alessandro had not catered but one with which he was pleased. Several members of the accounts team had been reshuffled, much to their individual satisfaction.

Unfortunately *he* didn't feel like a happy camper, and it was getting on his nerves.

He was pinning a lot on the curative powers of Red-Hot Rebecca.

On the spur of the moment he dialled through to Kate's cell phone, wanting to remind himself of what was history. He was branching out in a different direction with a different woman, and from nowhere came the urge to satisfy himself that he was over his brief liaison with Kate. Aside from which he had a couple of things to ask her. Rebecca would be more than happy to wait for five minutes for him downstairs if traffic was light and she arrived sooner than expected. She wasn't the clingy sort who would throw a fit if he was a little late.

Her cell phone was answered immediately.

'It's Alessandro.'

On the other end of the line, Kate felt her heart skip a beat.

There had been no need for him to announce himself. She would have recognized that deep, dark, lazy drawl anywhere. And after nearly two weeks of trying to get it out of her head she found that it still did the same crazy things to her nervous system it had done when they had almost lived in each other's company.

She had done the right thing in ending it. She knew that. He had wanted to carry on until he got bored, but she had noticed that he hadn't put up much of a fight when she had swept past that interruption. Just as she had noticed that he had made no effort to try and contact her since they had arrived back in London.

He had delegated all the work for her hand-over to his financial director. She had got the message loud and clear. If she'd been up for a little more fun and frolics then he would have happily obliged, but the second she had refused he had shrugged, backed away and headed off in the opposite direction. No big deal.

Except for her it was all a big deal. She missed him. She missed everything about him. On paper, it didn't make sense. On paper, the only thing that should have glued them together was the sex. But unfortunately life couldn't be worked out on paper—even though she had spent years trying to make sure that it did.

Unfortunately for her the guy who made no sense was also the guy who had made her ridiculously happy. He was the guy who had bandaged her feet and carried her to that spot where they had had a picnic because he had told her that he didn't want her feet to be aching when they headed back to the bedroom later. He was the guy who had made her laugh, and he had shown her a side of himself that was empathetic and considerate in the way he had dealt with George.

He was also the guy who had refused to discuss anything he considered too personal.

And what did that say? Several times she had tried to talk to him about his childhood, about his parents. After all, he knew all about hers! He might have confided a little, but beyond that *little* there had been no more on the table.

What that said to her was that he was not prepared to take things a step further, and she hated herself for knowing that that was what she had ended up wanting. Ended up *craving*.

Because she had fallen in love with him.

She'd gone and torn up the rule book and done the one thing she had promised herself she *wouldn't* do. In fact she had done the one thing she had been so convinced she wouldn't be in danger of doing because Alessandro Preda and her, as a couple, *made no sense*.

So much for relationships that made sense. Another myth to be chucked out of the window.

At least she hadn't gone running back to him with a change of heart, greedy to take the crumbs that might still be on offer. Not that she hadn't thought about that on more than one occasion. Knocking on his door…telling him that she had thought things over…that he was right… that she wanted to carry on sleeping with him until the fire burnt out…

He wasn't to know that there was no danger of *her* fire burning out, was he?

But she had resisted.

It was only now, when she heard his voice, that she realized just how much she'd ached for him to get in touch with her.

And he had.

She didn't dare contemplate what that meant, but she dared to hope…

She wasn't sure that she would even be able to play it cool. Of course she wouldn't *leap* into immediate acquiescence… She might allow a heartbeat's pause, so that he could understand that she was actually considering turning him away, but then she would crack. She knew she would because the past eleven days had been the worst in her entire life.

'I was just about to leave,' she said, in what she hoped

was a cool, calm and collected voice—as opposed to one that sounded breathless, excited, which was how she was feeling. 'I guess you're phoning to talk about the problems with the Wilson deal? Watson Russell told me that you were concerned they were going to pull out at the last minute and that I was to do whatever was in my power to stop that from happening. I'm pleased to say that I think I may have persuaded them to go ahead...'

'The Wilson deal... Yes...of course...'

'I really do think that it's a brilliant direction to go in...electronics and telecommunications might be right up there when it comes to making huge profits, but it's important that we keep publishing companies alive. And this small one, if it's developed and run properly, stands a good chance of making a profit. I told Ralph Wilson all of this, and he seemed very happy.'

'Drop the files up for me,' Alessandro told her abruptly.

'Sure. I'll make sure they're on your desk first thing in the morning.'

'Wrong response. When I said *drop the files up for me,* I meant bring them to my office—right now.'

Did he want to see her? Hell, why not?

He phoned through to Rebecca, told her to wait for him in Reception...that he had some last-minute business to tie up...and was told, in reply, that there was no rush. She was working on her laptop in the taxi because her working day never seemed to end...blah, blah, blah...

Alessandro barely heard the tail end of her sentence because there was a knock on his door and his whole body tensed in anticipation of seeing Kate...

Which enraged him.

His face revealed nothing, but in the space of a few seconds his cool dark eyes had clocked her from head to toe.

And he didn't like what he saw.

Where the hell had the suit gone? Aside from that little window in time when she had let her hair down she had always worn suits. Grey suits, black suits, navy suits, the daring cream one...

No suit. She was wearing a floaty dress in smoky blue colours over which a businesslike blazer did absolutely nothing to hide the sexy body underneath. And she wasn't wearing pumps. She was wearing sandals. Flat blue sandals with diamanté on the straps. And she had painted her toenails—a pale transluscent pink that matched the polish on her fingernails and also her lip gloss.

'So sorry,' he drawled, turning his back on her and walking towards his desk. 'It appears I've stopped you on your way to a cocktail party...'

Kate reddened and said nothing.

She had hoped for...*what*, exactly? Disappointment raced through her and she could have kicked herself. She had thought...*what?* That he had called her to his office as an excuse to see her?

'Here are the files.'

She held them out and was ignored, although he did signal to his desk, where she dropped them before spinning round, ready to head for the door, mortified at the optimism that had made her reapply her lip gloss and straighten her hair. Which was tied back but no longer in its severe bun. Instead it was loose, with only two blue clips on either side restraining the riot of tumbling waves.

'Wait a sec...' Alessandro drawled, ignoring the files. 'How are the team settling into their new roles?'

She turned slowly to face him and focused on a spot just beyond his shoulder. Safer. No perilous eye-to-eye contact. 'You should know how they're settling in. It's early days, but I did have a debrief with my new boss... I filled

him in on how everyone's adapting to their new roles…
Hasn't he reported back to you?'

'I take it from your remarkable shift in dress code that
you've vacated the ivory tower…?'

'I don't know what that's supposed to mean.'

'It means that after a lifetime of suits you seem to have
adopted a different dress code for work…'

'I've adopted the same dress code as everyone else…'
She glanced down at her very respectable outfit, feeling
the rake of his dark eyes on her and remembering everything she knew she should be forgetting.

Alessandro saw the buzz of his mobile and ignored it.
Red-Hot Rebecca could wait for a couple more minutes.

'And what else has changed…hmm?' he enquired softly.

'I have no idea what you're talking about,' Kate answered tonelessly. 'But if that's all I'll be on my way.'

'On your way where? You never said…'

'Actually, I *do* happen to be going out tonight…' Did the
supermarket qualify as 'going out'? she wondered. 'And
then I shall be spending the weekend away. So…'

Alessandro clenched his jaw. *Where?* Where was she
going later? And with whom? And would it just happen
to be the same person she would be spending the weekend with?

Demanding questions surged through his head with
angry force, and making him even angrier was the fact that
his libido was rising faster than a rocket from a launch pad.
That flimsy dress was made to be ripped off. That little
line of tiny pearly buttons would challenge any man with
the slightest sex drive—and *his* sex drive was unstoppable.

Another buzz on his mobile. He shoved it into his pocket
and ignored it.

'Are you going anywhere exciting?' he asked through
gritted teeth.

Kate laughed gaily. 'Oh, is there anywhere in London that *isn't* exciting? So many clubs and restaurants! Although I shall be heading out of London for the weekend. It's always nice to have a change of scenery...'

What the hell could he say to *that*?

Hadn't he told her often enough that it was all about fun? All about sex and letting her hair down?

She *had* let her hair down...and who the hell was she having sex with...?

He was spared having to say anything else because just at that moment his office door was pushed open and his date...Red-Hot Rebecca, with the medicinal powers to rescue him from his ongoing foul mood...was stepping into his office.

He forced himself to smile. Rebecca was in red. Red dress barely skimming long white legs...red clutch bag... scarlet lipstick... Red was the one colour Kate always avoided. He remembered her saying so. Some passing titbit of information that had stuck in his head.

The hotshot lawyer was dressed for play—and all of a sudden she was the last thing Alessandro wanted. Why hadn't she waited in Reception?

Kate, positively demure by comparison, still managed to have the sex appeal of a siren, luring him on, making him blind to his date and everything he had hoped she might do for him.

'Kate...this is...Rebecca...' He shot his date a sideways glance before his eyes returned compulsively to Kate, keenly noting the barely there flush that tinged her cheeks.

Something insane and ridiculously childish made him want to sling his arm around Rebecca just to see what reaction that would evoke in Kate, but he resisted the impulse. He was jealous of whoever she was about to see...whoever she was going to be spending the weekend with…and he wanted her to be jealous too…

It felt like an incontrollable weakness.

Kate was already looking at Rebecca, her eyes guarded and unrevealing.

'You must be the finance bod.' Rebecca broke the silence. 'You poor dear… I do hope the brute pays you well for working late…?'

She flashed Alessandro an intimate, raised eyebrows smile that made Kate's teeth snap together.

'Although my sympathies are with *you*, my dear…' she continued in her cut-glass voice. 'I'm about to take silk and working late is something of a habit now…positively dreadful…'

'Dreadful,' Kate agreed dully.

'Alessandro…' The striking brunette turned to Alessandro and coiled her arm into his. 'Shall we let this poor thing get on with the rest of her life…? It's too, *too* naughty of you to keep her here—especially when we should be getting on…'

'We have tickets to the opera,' Alessandro said roughly. 'Although…' he disengaged his arm and stepped to one side, shoving both hands in his pockets '…I'm afraid that might have to be put on the back burner…'

'Why?' Rebecca demanded. A querulous note had crept into her voice.

'Because the file Kate has brought up requires some urgent work…'

'I think I've covered all the tricky bits,' Kate said tightly. 'Please… Don't let me keep you both from…' Words failed her and she took a deep breath. 'From your plans for this evening.' She smiled at Rebecca and cool blue eyes met hers. 'I'm in a bit of a rush as well…' she explained faintly.

'That's as may be… But part and parcel of your new

position is a willingness to do overtime when it's necessary. It's necessary *now*.'

Alessandro looked at Rebecca. It had been a major mistake to renew contact with the lawyer. It had been an even bigger mistake to summon Kate to his office. And even worse than both those big mistakes had been the mistake of seeing them both alongside one another—because it had only fuelled his frustration at not having Kate to himself.

Not being able to touch her.

He raked his fingers through his hair, realized that he was shaking—but because of what, exactly, he wasn't sure.

'Apologies.' This to an increasingly annoyed Rebecca. 'My driver will return you to your house—unless you'd like to take someone to the opera with you…'

He was already flipping open his cell, giving instructions to his driver to come to the office.

'Are you telling me that I'm being *stood up*?' Rebecca hissed as she was ushered towards the door. She tugged free of his grasp and spun round to face him, hands on hips. 'Believe me, Alessandro, I have better things to do than to come here and find myself without a date for the evening!'

'Again… I apologize…'

'Not good enough!'

'Unfortunately…' he eased her out of the door '…it will have to do…'

'There was no need to…to do that…' Kate felt the tiny pulse in her neck beating as she stared at him. 'There's really nothing…nothing that can't wait until next week… to be sorted…'

'You've been in your new role for under two weeks,' said Alessandro, knowing very well that she was right. 'Do me the courtesy of not overstepping your brief.'

'Your date must have been disappointed.'

'That's very considerate of you… I can't say I'm half as considerate towards yours…'

'Sorry?'

'The clothes…the make-up…the sexy little sandals— which, I notice, you can now wear *without* a serious onset of blisters. I'm not an idiot, Kate. You might not be on the way to a cocktail party, but you sure as hell won't be having a meal in on your own tonight…'

He swung round and strolled towards the window, trying hard to get his act together.

He turned to face her, back to the window, arms folded. 'You move fast.'

'That's rich, coming from you!' Patches of angry colour stained her cheeks.

How dared he accuse her of moving fast when he was already involved with another woman?

'Who is he anyway?'

'We're no longer an item, Alessandro. My private life is none of your business now…'

'It is when it involves you playing hanky-panky with a colleague!'

'That's ridiculous. Who am I supposed to be…? To be…?'

'Say it, Kate! Spit it out! *Playing with… Having an affair with… Having sex with…*'

'I would *never* do anything with a work colleague,' she flung back at him.

But she wasn't denying that she was seeing someone…

Maybe not someone she worked with, but nevertheless she was still flaunting herself…parading her femininity where before she had concealed it…

And it was driving him crazy.

He wanted to point out that she was in a position of responsibility, that climbing the career ladder *didn't* involve wearing clothes that turned men on… But where the hell

would he be going with that anyway? He wasn't a dino-
saur, and there was no rigid dress code within his company
aside from the fact that his employees had to look 'smart'.

'You're *jealous*…'

And that angered her—because he had no right to be.
Not when he was seeing another woman. Not when he
had moved on at the speed of light. *He* had no right to be
jealous just because *she* had been the one to walk away.

She felt sick when she thought of him and the lawyer
in the short red dress.

She felt sick because he had broken with tradition
and was going out with someone smart, someone high-
powered, someone with a cut-glass accent—someone just
like him.

Alessandro had never been jealous in his life before,
but he couldn't contradict her.

'*You've* found someone else,' Kate threw at him, 'but
you still can't bear the thought that I was the one who
walked away from you, can you?'

He no longer wanted her, but he wasn't quite ready for
her to want anyone else.

Was that it? Alessandro thought.

He didn't say anything. Instead he strolled slowly towards her and Kate backed away, as terrified as a rabbit
caught in the glare of oncoming headlights.

Terrified because she knew that he could still have her.
It was mortifying.

Her breasts felt heavy, as if remembering his touch. Her
nipples tightened as she imagined his mouth on them, his
tongue licking and teasing them, and between her legs she
knew that she was wet for him.

She half closed her eyes, dazed at the graphic memory
of him down there, sucking her, taking his time, his big
hands on her inner thighs, making sure her legs were open

for his lazy exploration. She remembered what it had felt like to gaze down at that dark head between her legs, to have her fingers coiled in his hair as she urged him on.

She bumped into the edge of his desk and didn't even know how she had managed to stumble back there.

'You still want me,' Alessandro growled.

She shook her head in helpless denial but her eyes, pinned to his face, were telling a different story.

He was so hot for her that it hurt. Very slowly he dragged his finger gently along her cheek. She turned her head away sharply. But her breathing was ragged, all over the place, and he could *feel* her body burning up for him.

Kate licked her lips.

'I… I…' Her throat was so dry that she could barely get the words out.

You have a girlfriend…you have a hotshot lawyer… Okay, so you might have dispatched her tonight, but she'll still be hanging around, waiting for you to say the word, because that's just what women do for you… But not me.

'Tell me that you don't…' he murmured roughly. 'Tell me that whoever this guy is…whoever you've picked up… he can make you feel the way I make you feel. Tell me that if I were to slide my fingers into you right now you wouldn't open up for me…'

'No!' Kate pulled away and managed to galvanize her unsteady legs into action. 'You've moved on. I've moved on. Nothing…nothing else matters…'

She couldn't look at him. If she looked at him—looked into those deep, dark eyes—she would be lost.

She fled.

She was so scared he would follow her that she didn't dare look round. Her whole body prickled with tension. Her fingers were trembling as she repeatedly jabbed the button to call the lift. When it finally whirred up she leapt through the doors and pressed herself against the mirrored back, only breathing out when she was disgorged onto the ground floor.

He'd played with her the way a cat played with a mouse—toying with her to prove a point.

He'd proved it.

For the first time ever she had a driving need to talk to her mother—to actually *talk* to her about her feelings.

Nothing had gone according to plan, and that was something Shirley Watson would understand. None of *her* life had gone according to plan. She had lurched from one guy to another in search of love. And she, Kate, had tried so hard to make sure she went in the opposite direction to her mother.

She had formulated her Plan A and had been determined to stick to it. *Now* look at her! Whatever plan she had ended up on, it certainly wasn't Plan A. She wasn't even sure it was Plan B.

She dialled her mother's number and burst into tears at the sound of her mother's voice.

'Mum,' she finally hiccuped, 'I've made such a mess of things... I've just gone and done the stupidest thing... I've fallen in love with the wrong man...'

'Oh, Katie. It's not the end of the world... You're crying, my darling. Please don't cry. You're such a strong young woman. What can I say? I've always known that you disapproved of my lifestyle, but it's better to have fallen in love with the wrong man than to never know what it is to fall in love. Come down to Cornwall...spend a few days. Sea air is very good for clearing the head...'

There was no Red-Hot Rebecca spending the night for fun, games and a future of intellectual stimulation. She had been permanently dispatched.

Alessandro had spent the past hour wandering from room to room in his enormous house, unable to settle down. Work was no distraction from his thoughts, and right up there when it came to those thoughts was: Who the hell was her date and where the hell was she going to be spending the weekend?

And hard on the heels of that thought was another disturbing one... Why did he care? Why did it make him feel slightly sick whenever he thought of her with another man?

She still wanted him, but having proved that left him empty. She might burn for him but she had run away... hadn't looked back.

And it wasn't in him to chase a woman. He had never done that and never would. Chasing implied a lack of control, and he only had to look at his parents to see where that led. Their crazy love had resulted in an utter lack of control. They were so similar that they couldn't help but egg each other on in their harebrained antics. For them, the rest of the world didn't really exist—and that was a dangerous place for them to occupy.

That said, he spent the evening on his own, drinking too much and then suffering the after-effects with a sleepless night and a headache that kept him in bed until eight the following morning.

Where could she possibly be going for a weekend with a guy she'd only just met? Was the woman completely off her head? Had she flung herself into some kind of random affair with a man who could turn out to be anybody? Wasn't she aware that that was a dangerous game to play?

And how could she get involved with someone else when she was still wrapped up in him?

He couldn't. He'd tried, but he hadn't been able to.

Kate might think that she was a tough, sassy career woman but she wasn't. Dig a little and what you found was someone who was vulnerable—someone who was waiting to be taken advantage of, someone who wouldn't be able to spot danger if it approached ringing bells and announcing itself through a megaphone.

She had been as safe as houses with him, but who knew what she would find with some man she had probably picked up in a bar somewhere? Because sure as hell she didn't keep a little black book full of useful rainy-day numbers. Whoever this mystery guy was, she would have found him in just the sort of place where predators waited for gullible single girls to appear. A sexy-as-hell single girl would be like manna from heaven.

She might think that she was forging ahead on some new, independent path, but she was too naive to realize that any path that involved sex would be littered with potholes and pitfalls for someone who still believed in fairy tales.

He didn't think twice. He knew where she lived.

What harm was there in just going over? Making sure that she hadn't found herself in some sort of perilous situation she couldn't cope with? Or even some sort of fairly harmless situation she couldn't cope with?

What was the big deal in being a guy who could see the bigger picture? He was magnanimous enough not to be churlish just because she had decided to move on with her life. Even though she still fancied him.

Besides, he was pretty sure he needed to go out to buy something anyway. Coffee… Newspapers…

This would be a multipurpose trip.

CHAPTER TEN

KATE HAD NEVER in a million years thought that her mother could be a source of comfort when it came to the whole big love thing. But Shirley Watson had risen to the occasion and surprised her. She was, as she had said with an uninhibited laugh, the queen of broken hearts.

'But, really, my heart was only broken once,' she had said. 'And that was when your father left. I just needed to find my way via a lot of frogs to realize that I could never replace him. I had to look in different places for a different sort of man. But guess what? Even if I could have turned back time and saved myself the heartache of falling for a guy who would leave me, I would have said no. Because falling for your dad was the best bit of falling I ever did.'

Kate double-checked that everything in the house was as it should be and glanced down at the holdall in which New Kate had been packed. New Kate being the Kate who wore clothes that suited a girl her age instead of the clothes of someone three times her age.

Unfortunately Old Kate was not managing to keep pace, and Old Kate was the one who had fallen in love with the wrong man, who didn't fit the pretty, carefree outfits, who still wanted to hide behind her armour of suits and flat shoes and high-necked blouses and baggy jackets.

She sighed and thought that there was no point in killing

time. It was going to be a long trip—although her mother had told her that she intended shopping in Exeter, that she would get the train and meet her there, and then they could continue the remainder of the journey together. At least she wouldn't be on the road alone for longer than three and a half hours, all being kind with the traffic.

It was just as well, because she felt exhausted.

How *could* he have just replaced her with someone else in such a short space of time? And how could he have done what he had—turned her on, made her remember what she didn't want to remember?

Speculation took root and had a field day in her head.

Had Alessandro been seeing the lawyer before he had decided to indulge in a fling with her? Maybe they had had an argument. Two high-powered people…that would be fertile ground for all sorts of arguments. Perhaps their timetables had clashed. Perhaps he had *wanted more*.

Or maybe he had come to his senses and done the comparisons… An employee who believed in love was a waste of energy next to a lawyer who was heading in the same direction he was. They could make appointments to meet up and book dates in bed to accommodate their frantic timetables. For a man who had no heart that would be the ideal arrangement, and perhaps he had worked that out for himself.

Or maybe…

Maybe it was even simpler than that.

Maybe he had realized that he was way too good for the daughter of a cocktail waitress. The sex had been good… *great*…but it paid to pay attention to the detail, and one big detail was the ease with which he had accepted her decision to end things. If he had wanted her enough he would surely have put up a bit more of a fight… He had just been soothing his ego by proving that she still wanted him. If only he knew…

So, all in all, good riddance!

She pressed on the accelerator of her hire car and a glance at the dashboard showed her that she had been driving for over an hour. She had been operating on autopilot, barely noticing the motorway whizzing past.

The grey summer skies had finally cleared and it was a beautiful morning. She turned the radio on, adjusted the channels until she found one that had suitably peppy driving music, and then resigned herself to the remainder of the journey being spent in a state of pointless introspection.

There were only so many distressing scenarios she could play over and over in her head, but she thought that she might quite like to wallow in them.

In fact she was sure that she could add to the tally, and thereby get even more depressed than she already was.

It was a little after one by the time she made it to Exeter, which was thick with traffic on this Saturday afternoon.

She had suggested that her mother live in Exeter when she had planned on making her big move to the coast. She had thought that her mother would find it impossible to live in the middle of nowhere, but she had been wrong.

Not only had her mother loved Cornwall from the very second she'd gone there, but she had thrived.

And for the first time she was realizing that there were other things about her mother she had maybe not quite appreciated.

True, Shirley Watson had flung herself headlong into love after love after love, with the desperation of a starving man trying to grab at food that was always just out of reach, but she had not become embittered.

When it came to parenting Kate had summed her up

as fragile, but she had been strong enough to do a pretty good job as it turned out.

She, on the other hand, with all her preparations and her precautions, her wariness and her insistence on being able to control her choices, had been the one to end up making the biggest mistake of all in falling in love with Alessandro.

Kate turned the volume up, crawled through the outskirts of the city and after a lot of hunting, managed to locate a car park.

She'd managed to complete the entire journey without really being aware of her surroundings except to marvel at how light the traffic had been.

Forging her way through the crowded streets, she decided that that was probably because everyone had already descended on the city. It was a tourist hotspot and packed.

When she finally made it to the Cathedral square, she couldn't help but notice all the loved-up young couples lazing in the sunshine.

Some people made smart choices.

She was hot and flustered when she spotted her mother, sitting in front of a glass of wine with a pot of tea next to it, as though the healthy beverage atoned for the slightly less healthy one.

Kate smiled.

Thank goodness she was out of London. The long drive had helped her put a lot into perspective—such as how you could think you knew someone only to find that you didn't…not really. She was looking forward to getting to know her mother a whole lot better.

Over tea or wine or whatever…

Now that he knew where she had gone Alessandro slowed his pace, for the first time really questioning why he had made this trip, why he had followed her like a police of-ficer hot on the trail of a wanted felon. He had arrived to see her driving off, had spotted the pull-along case—the same one she had brought with her to Toronto—and he had seen red.

Part of him had thought that all her talk about having a date and being booked up for the weekend had been noth-ing but hot air. She just wasn't the type who stepped out of one relationship only to immediately fling herself into another, especially when she still fancied him as much as he still fancied her.

He had been wrong.

God only knew where this sex-fest weekend was going to take place, but he'd intended to find out—and rather than overtake her, force her to pull to the kerb and then demand an answer which she was unlikely to give him, he had decided just to…follow her.

It hadn't been hard.

She had no idea what car he'd be in. He had several cars, and the black Range Rover was a whole lot less con-spicuous than the Ferrari. He had made sure to keep a safe distance behind her, but he probably could have been at-tached to her bumper and she wouldn't have noticed. Who really ever paid attention to other cars on the road unless they were misbehaving?

He'd known from the route she was taking that she was heading for the West Country and he hadn't been able to believe it.

She was going to spend the weekend with a perfect stranger, miles away from her home ground? Who the hell did that?

And now here he was, in a picturesque city square, with quaint Tudor-beamed buildings lining it, standing in front of a coffee shop, for the first time in his life hesitating.

A coffee shop was hardly the raunchy, seedy motel he had been expecting. A coffee shop smacked of a nerd—or some clever smart-ass *pretending* to be a nerd. Someone who didn't make her lose control…someone who wasn't… *him*.

But, having come this far, he had no intention of leaving without first confronting his *rival*.

Because that was what it felt like. Sitting somewhere in that coffee shop was his rival—some man he didn't know from Adam, who was laying claim to his woman. It was a possessive feeling, it was unwelcome and it was…the way it was.

He strode forward.

'Good heavens.'

'What?'

'There's a gentleman by the door…quite arresting…'

Kate had had her fill of 'arresting' men. She had come to the conclusion that they all spelt bad news. She wasn't interested—and besides, she was too busy getting rid of her misery via the plate of cakes that had been put between them. Her mother had nibbled one. She was on her fourth. Not only was she destined to be a spinster, she would end up being a fat spinster.

'He's coming over here…'

If she had never agreed to go to Toronto with him she wouldn't be sitting here now, stacking on the pounds and fighting off a crying jag. If she hadn't be so arrogant as to think that she could control the situation—could sleep with him and still hang on to her heart—she wouldn't be here. There were so many steps along the way that could have saved her from being where she was now that she felt giddy when she thought about them.

She was lost in her thoughts, and when she heard that

deep, sexy drawl she immediately put it down to the fact that she was probably hallucinating.

Except her mother was still staring, the voice had said something else and the young waitress who had been walking towards them had stopped and her jaw had dropped.

Heart beating fast, Kate slowly twisted round and there he was—larger than life and just as devastating.

Staring down at her, his dark eyes unfathomable.

'You played fast and loose with the speed limit on the motorway,' Alessandro murmured, instantly clocking the situation and feeling light-headed with relief because *this* was her weekend date.

There was little doubt that the older and still stunningly attractive woman staring at him, open-mouthed, was her mother.

'I'm Alessandro, by the way...' He turned to the blonde, hand outstretched. 'I'm guessing you must be Kate's mother...'

'What are you doing here?'

Kate found her voice at last and anger surged up through her—anger that he had the barefaced cheek to have landed himself here when she was on the verge of congratulating herself on having put some temporary distance between them...anger that her whole body had lit up like tinder in receipt of a life-giving flame...anger that none of the bracing little homilies she had given herself on the drive down counted for anything when he was standing right here in front of her...anger at the power he had over her...

Had he come here for a repeat performance of proving just how much he could affect her?

'Why are you *here*?'

'Darling, I shall leave you two to get on with things. I have a bit more shopping to do, as a matter of fact.'

Shirley Watson was already standing and reaching for

her handbag, ignoring the desperate yelp coming from her daughter.

'Shoes...' She addressed Alessandro. 'A girl's best friend... I've tried my entire life to instil that into my beautiful daughter, but I see that it actually took you to succeed...'

Kate watched in horror as her mother—*her treacherous and disloyal mother*—disappeared with a cheery wave, leaving her seat vacant for Alessandro to sit on.

Which he did. Not once taking his eyes from her face.

'How *dare* you follow me? What were you *thinking*? I can't *believe* you followed me here!'

'I was worried.'

'You were *worried*? What's *that* supposed to mean?'

She couldn't peel her eyes from his face. God, he was handsome. A little drawn, perhaps, a bit haggard, but even drawn and haggard he was still drop-dead gorgeous.

'You just took off.' Alessandro loathed the defensive note that had crept into his voice. 'On a so-called *weekend away*. I assumed—'

'Oh, I get it,' Kate said with blistering resentment. 'You decided that I was going to meet some man, and also decided that I was too incompetent to look after myself. Or maybe you thought that I didn't dare meet up with anyone because there's a bit of you still in my system...?'

'What was I supposed to think when you refused to tell me where you were going?' So she had admitted it—and it thrilled him.

'I didn't *refuse* to tell you anything! I assumed that it was none of your business! And what would your lawyer girlfriend say if she knew you were here?'

It took him a couple of seconds to comprehend what she was talking about, and a few more seconds to bypass the instinctive clamp-down on explaining himself—which was something he never did. 'There's no connection there...'

'Oh, right. You mean you slept with her and then decided that she didn't fit the bill after all?'

She hated the weakness that was driving her to find out whether he and the lawyer had ended up in bed. It didn't matter! What mattered was that he had rushed down here in her wake because he had some stupid, over-developed he-man instinct to make sure she wasn't going to do anything crazy. Like actually get a life.

'We never made it to the bedroom,' Alessandro admitted in a driven voice.

That stopped Kate in her tracks. It wasn't just what he had said, it was *how* he had said it—it was the way he was pointedly not looking at her, the way he had flung himself back in the chair and was staring around him as though fascinated by his surroundings.

'Well, it doesn't matter anyway.'

'This is not the place for this conversation.'

'It's *exactly* the place for this conversation!' She breathed deeply and then sighed. 'Look, I don't need this. What we had is over. Finished. I just need you to get out of my life—and if you can't do that then I'm going to have to hand in my resignation.'

'It's not finished,' Alessandro muttered in a low, unsteady voice.

He leaned towards her. He was a man with one foot dangling over the side of a cliff and he knew he was going to jump and damn the consequences.

'Not for me. Please, Kate. Let's go somewhere—anywhere. It's too small here...too packed...too mundane and busy for what I have to say...'

'Which is *what*? No, let me guess! You want me back so that you can have a little more *fun* before I end up next to the lawyer who never made it past first base before boring you…'

'Something…happened…'

'Yes, I know what happened,' Kate intoned bitterly. 'You couldn't stand the thought of me walking away from you, so you decided to prove to me that I still wanted you. That's why you summoned me to your office, isn't it? So that you could play with me?'

'I summoned you because I…I needed to see you…'

Needed to see me to prove a point.

'You're just so arrogant that you didn't see why you should let me get on with my life. It didn't matter that you were busy getting on with yours. As far as you were concerned, I didn't *have* a life to get on with because I still felt something for you. You just couldn't accept that I wasn't interested in carrying on with a fling that wasn't going anywhere, because in your world the only thing that matters is sex.'

'I wasn't getting on with my life,' Alessandro muttered under his breath.

There was no guidebook when it came to this kind of conversation, but he was still condemned to have it… Because she just mattered so damn much…

'I tried,' he continued. 'But I couldn't. And I couldn't because something happened when we were in Toronto…'

'Something *happened*…?'

'I never meant to…to get involved…'

He raked his fingers through his hair and his hand was not as steady as it should have been.

'Let's get out of here…please—' He broke off gruffly and, without giving her the chance to lodge another protest, signalled across to the waitress and asked for the bill. 'And you can stop fishing around for money, Kate,' he grated. '*I'm* getting this.'

'Well?'

This when they were outside, heading towards the grass, joining the milling crowds of couples who had made smart choices. She turned to him, shading her eyes from the glare of the sun, and he just looked at her.

'Come on.'

He reached out, clasped her hand, and her whole body quivered. The feel of his fingers linked with hers was like an electric charge, and under its impact her brain shut down. All those protesting voices were silenced as they found a shady spot close to the Cathedral and sat on the ground.

'Just say what you've come to say, Alessandro, and don't bother dressing it up with words you don't mean. You didn't get *involved* with me…not in the way that most people think of involvement. You *sexually connected* with me and you weren't ready for it to end. You couldn't produce proper involvement out of a hat, but you still had to show me that it wasn't over…'

She hugged her knees up to her chest, suddenly drained.

'How was I to know the difference between involvement and a sexual connection?' he said, half to himself. 'How was I supposed to recognize the difference when I had never been presented with the situation before in my life? When we returned to London I figured that I could put you behind me by dipping into someone else…'

'That's just *horrible*.'

'I'm being as honest as I can. It's what I've always done. I've gone from woman to woman, never realizing that the time might come when I would find myself incapable of doing it…'

'You're doing it again, Alessandro,' Kate whispered. 'You're confusing me with words.'

'I'm using words to tell you how I feel… You asked

me why I followed you. Well, I followed you because… because I couldn't stand the thought of you touching another man, seeing another man, laughing with another man…'

'You were only jealous because you weren't ready for me to let you go—you would have seen any man as competition—but that's not real jealousy. Real jealousy has its basis in something bigger…stronger… It's different.'

But hope flared…

'In my world there was never a place for jealousy of any kind. It's not an emotion I've ever experienced. But I…I recognized it…' He smiled crookedly. 'And you're right. Real jealousy *does* have its basis in something bigger— much, much bigger than lust. It wasn't just imagining you getting into bed with another man…'

He clenched his jaw and shook away the violence of emotion that assailed him when he thought about that.

'What I felt… I couldn't even bear the thought of you looking at anyone else…talking to anyone else…'

He risked grazing her cheek with his finger. It was enough to send his libido soaring into overdrive and he wanted nothing so much as to take her hand and place it firmly on his erection, so that she could feel what she did to him. He wondered whether she was feeling it too… the current zipping between them, electric and impossibly alive.

'I'd never planned to… God, Kate, you have no idea how much I want you right now…'

'Wanting just isn't enough for me,' she whispered, and a wave of misery threatened to engulf the fragile shoots of hope that had been growing.

'And it's not enough for me either…'

He tilted her face so that she was gazing at him, locking her in their own private world even though they were surrounded by people.

'I never planned on losing control of my emotions,' he told her seriously. 'I've seen what that can do. I watched my parents get lost in each other and I lived through the ramifications. I thought that it was just about money...' He hesitated.

'But it wasn't, was it?' Kate said softly. 'It was more than just having feckless parents who encouraged each other to blow their respective fortunes, who had no self-control... It was about being shoved aside, wasn't it?'

'They were very good at employing nannies. My parents were so wrapped up in one another that they had no time for a kid. No time for anything. I resolved never to let myself succumb to that kind of emotional excess—and, for me, falling in love with a woman constituted that kind of emotional excess...'

Kate found breathing difficult. She feared that if she exhaled she would somehow blow apart the atmosphere.

'But I fell in love, my darling... I didn't plan to, and I don't know when it happened... I just know that when you walked out on me my world stopped turning...'

'You hurt me. I know I walked away, but I still waited for you to come—waited for you to just...*miss me* so much that you couldn't help yourself. I waited for you to catch up with me, and how I felt about you, but then there was that woman in your office and suddenly it was like my whole stupid world really and truly fell apart.'

'I thought I could find myself some clever woman who would give me an uncomplicated life...with none of the inconvenient loss of self-control that came with you. It was a knee-jerk reaction. You had me wrapped around your little finger and I knew that the second I saw you in that dress. God, you have no idea what that did to me...'

'I love you,' Kate said simply. 'I fell in love with you and I knew I had to walk away because I would just end up getting more and more hurt. You couldn't commit and I couldn't settle for anything else.'

'You love me?' Alessandro said shakily, enjoying this loss of self-control with the woman he had given his heart to. 'I guess your mother is going to be in for the surprise of her life, then, isn't she?'

Kate chuckled, delirious with happiness, sliding close to him and knowing that he was as aroused as she at their physical contact. 'I think that she's already had the surprise of her life—when I confided in her, when I stopped pretending to be an emotional robot and showed her that I was human and fallible and an idiot…'

'And how do you think she'll react when we tell her that we're going to be married? Because I can't imagine my life without you, Kate. So…will you marry me? Be my wife? Never leave my side? Have lots of babies for me?'

Would she marry him? Try stopping her!

'Wild horses couldn't stop me!' She laughed and flung her arms around him.

Who said that fairy tales couldn't come true?

* * * * *

HER BOSS BY DAY...

JOSS WOOD

For my sister, Jen Seymour-Blight,
who lives far too far away in Australia.
Miss you.

CHAPTER ONE

'YOU WILL NOT get me into bed tonight. Tomorrow night isn't looking good for you, either.'

In the huge bathroom mirror of the upmarket Saints restaurant in Surry Hills, Willa Moore-Fisher practised the phrase and shook her head in disgust. She was being too nice and her sleazy blind date didn't deserve that much consideration. Obtuse to a fault, he might think that there was a chance of sleeping with her in the future. Which there wasn't—ever. She'd rather gouge her eye out with a blunt twig.

'I'd explain why I think you're an arrogant jerk, but then your brain would explode from you trying to understand.' Willa tested the words out loud.

And wasn't that an image to make her smile? *Ka-boom!* She could just imagine that smirking, arrogant expression blown apart by the suitable application of high-impact explosives. There were, she decided, very few personal problems that couldn't be solved by a little C4.

Willa imagined that the explosive would work really well on soon-to-be-ex-husbands too...

Maybe you should just go back in there and give him another chance, suggested nice Willa, doormat Willa. *It might be that this disastrous date is your fault; if you were a little better at drawing him out, at asking the right questions, at being more interesting...*

Wild Willa dropped doormat Willa with a snappy kick to her temple. *That's what you did for eight years, moron; you tried to bring the best out in Wayne, tried to change yourself so that he would change. And how did that work out for you?*

'Catch a freakin' clue, dumbass.' Willa pointed a finger at her reflection. 'Find your balls, metaphorically speaking, tell him he's wasting your time and get the hell out of here.'

Yeah, like you'd ever actually say that aloud, taunted wild Willa. *You're the world's biggest wuss and you'd rather put up with someone's crap than take the chance of making anyone mad at you.*

Maybe some day she'd learn to stand up for herself.

Wild Willa just snorted her disbelief.

God, these voices in her head exhausted her.

'So, is this talking to yourself something new or did you always do it and I didn't notice?'

In the mirror Willa saw the slick blonde and admired her exquisitely cut and coloured short, smooth bob. Then she clocked the mischievous tawny-brown eyes and spun around in shock.

'Amy? My God, *Amy*!'

'Hey Willa.'

Amy walked towards her on spiked heels. Her shift dress showed off her curves and her make-up and salon-perfect hair were flawless. Willa scanned her face and there, in the tilt of her mouth and in the humour dancing in her eyes, she saw her best friend at eighteen—the mischievous flirt who, just by being Amy, had opened up a world of fun to her that summer so long ago.

'Amy. My God…what are you doing here?'

Willa leaned in for a hug and was surprised by the fact that she didn't want to let Amy go. Why had she *ever* let her go? Let her fade from her life? That summer in the Whitsundays, their core group of friends—Amy, Brodie, Scott, Chantal, her older brother Luke—had been her world and, like so much else, she'd given them up when she married Wayne.

Stupid girl.

'Having dinner with my flatmate before we go clubbing,' Amy replied, keeping hold of Willa's hand. 'But you—why are you talking to yourself?'

'Short answer…an excruciatingly bad blind date that I am trying to get out of.' Willa tipped her head to the bathroom window. 'Do you think I'm skinny enough to slip through there?'

Amy looked her up and down. 'Actually, you are far too skinny—and back up. What about Wayne? You married him, didn't you?'

Willa lifted her ringless left hand. 'About to be divorced. That was a…mistake.'

Hmm…a mistake. That was a major understatement, but she'd go with it.

Amy pursed her lips. 'I'm sorry… God, Willa, so much time has passed. We need to catch up. *Now.*'

'What about my date and your friend?' Willa asked. She had already been in the bathroom for an inexcusably long time—she was being so rude.

So what? Wild Willa rolled her eyes.

'*Pfft*…your date sounds like a moron and Jessica was exchanging hot looks with a guy across the room. She won't miss me.'

Amy stalked to the door, yanked it open and let out one of her high-pitched, loud and distinctive whistles. Willa wasn't surprised when she soon saw a Saints waiter outside the door.

'Is the small function room empty?' Amy asked.

'Yes, ma'am.'

'Good. Tell Guido that I'm using it for a while, and ask him to please bring me a bottle of that Burnt Tree Chardonnay I like and put it on my tab,' ordered Amy, and with a luscious smile sent him on his way.

The kid, drooling, whirled away to do the goddess's bid-ding. It seemed that Amy, always a good flirt, now had a PhD in getting men to jump through her hoops.

Amy turned back to Willa and shrugged at her astounded expression. 'I hold a lot of work functions here. Guido owes me.'

Amy led Willa out of the bathroom, down a decorated passage and into a small function room that held a boardroom table at one end and a cluster of chairs at the other. She pulled Willa to the set of wingback chairs and gestured to her to sit.

'It's so good to see you, Willa,' Amy said, taking the seat opposite her. 'You look so…different. Classy…rich.'

Willa knew what she saw: it was the same face and body she looked at every day. She was still the same height, taller than most woman but skinnier than she'd been at eighteen. Thick, mocha and auburn shoulder-length hair, with a heavy fringe surrounding a pixie face dominated by silver-green eyes.

'That's because I *am* classy…and my husband—ex—whatever—is rich,' Willa said, making a conscious effort to keep the bitterness from her voice but doubting that she'd succeeded. 'Gym, designer clothes, best hairdresser in Sydney.'

Amy lightly touched her knee. 'Was it awful…being married to him?'

Willa considered lying, thought about glossing over the truth, but then she saw the understanding and sympathy in Amy's eyes and realised that while she wouldn't tell Amy—tell *anyone*—the whole truth, she didn't have to blatantly lie. She and Amy had been through too much for her to lie.

'Not awful, no. Boring—absolutely. Wayne wanted a young, gorgeous trophy wife, and that's what I've been for the past eight years.'

An eight-year marriage condensed into two sentences…

'God, a trophy wife.' Amy winced. 'But you're so damn

bright…you always wanted to study accountancy, economics, business.'

'Yeah, well, Wayne wanted beauty and acquiescence, not brains. I kept up with the markets, trends, but he'd didn't like his wife talking business. I was supposed to be seen and not heard.'

'I always thought that he was waste of space.'

At the knock on the door Amy got up to accept a bottle and glasses, thanked the waiter profusely and adeptly poured them both a glass.

Amy took a sip of her wine and took her seat again. 'Why do I get the feeling that I'm getting the sanitised version here?'

Because she wasn't a fool. 'My dead marriage is a very boring topic, Amy.'

'You were never boring, Willa. Quiet, maybe—intense, shy. Not boring. And I know that you probably gave Wayne-the-Pain a hundred and fifty per cent because the Willa I knew bent over backwards to make everyone happy. When you make a promise or a decision it takes a nuclear bomb to dislodge you.'

'I'm not that bad,' Willa protested, though she knew she was. She didn't give up—or in—easily.

'You hate going against your word.' Amy sent her a strange, sad smile. 'You were distraught that you had to ask Luke for help that night in the Whitsundays because I'd begged you not to.'

Willa bit her lip, still seeing Amy, battered and bloody, tears and crimson sand on her face. Her black and blue eye and her split cheek from fighting off Justin's unwelcome advances on the beach. Sometimes she still saw her face in her dreams and woke up in a cold sweat.

'I'm sorry, but I needed Luke to help me to help you.'

Amy looked into her wine glass. 'I know…it's okay. It was all a long time ago. How *is* Luke?'

There was an odd tremor in her voice which Willa instantly picked up. Amy and Luke had always had some sort of love-hate, weird reaction to each other that Willa could never quite put her finger on.

'He's fine...still single, still driven. He's working on a massive hotel development in Singapore—the biggest of his career.'

Amy eventually raised her eyes to meet Willa's. 'Are you still in contact with the others from the resort? Brodie, Chantal, Scott?'

Willa shrugged. 'Loosely, via social media and the very occasional e-mail. Chantal is still dancing, Scott is one of the city's most brilliant young architects, and Brodie is the heart and soul of a company that runs luxury yacht tours down the Gold Coast. I haven't seen them or socialised with them....nothing has been the same since the week you and Brodie left.'

Happy to be off the subject of her dysfunctional marriage, Willa cast her mind back to that summer they'd spent in the Whitsundays, when a group of strangers had arrived at the very fancy Weeping Reef resort, ready and rocking to start a holiday season of working all day and having fun all night.

It still amazed her that the five of them—six if she included Luke—had clicked so well. They were such a mixed bag of personalities.

They'd laughed and loved and drunk and partied, and then laughed and loved and partied some more. They'd been really good at it, and the first two months of their summer holiday had flown past. Then their idyll had been shattered when two dreadful incidents had dumped a bucket of angst and recrimination and guilt over their magical interlude and ripped their clique apart.

And set Willa on a path that she now deeply regretted.

'To go back a whole bunch of steps—we were talking

about you and Wayne and what caused the split,' Amy said, pulling her back to their conversation. She refilled their glasses and lifted an eyebrow.

'Oh…that.'

'Yes, that.'

How strange it was that after so long she and Amy could just fall into conversation as if it was yesterday… how strange and how right.

In the natural order of things they shouldn't have been friends… Amy was bright and flirty and outgoing, and Willa was quiet and naïve and a lot less boisterous than her friend. She couldn't just spill all the beans about her less than happy marriage—not even with Amy, so successful, confident, sophisticated. With Amy those qualities went deeper than her looks and clothes right into her psyche. Unlike Willa, whose confidence and sophistication was just a fabric layer deep.

'I wanted to be something other than his pretty arm decoration. He didn't see why being that wasn't enough for me.'

'It got ugly. I called him a balding, ageing git and he called me a shallow bimbo. The words "separation" and "divorce" emerged and we were both very happy with the idea.'

Amy closed her eyes in sympathy. 'Sorry, Wills.'

Willa shrugged. 'Eight months ago he booted me out of our apartment and into a waterfront mansion in Vaucluse—'

Amy whistled at the mention of the very upmarket Sydney suburb. 'Why didn't *he* move into the waterfront property?'

Willa smiled. 'He hates water and open spaces. Anyway, he moved Young and Dumb into the apartment the afternoon I moved out. Now the divorce just needs its court date and I'll be free!'

'What are you going to do then?'

Willa shrugged. 'Still working that out… I have a degree, but no experience, and—worse—no contacts. Money is not a problem, but time is. I battle to fill my day, and rattling around on my own in that mausoleum doesn't help.'

She glanced at the Rolex on her wrist, a twenty-first birthday present from Wayne. It was boring enough living her life, she didn't need to dissect it as well, so she attempted to change the subject.

'We've been in here for about twenty minutes. Do you think my date from hell has got the hint?'

'I told Guido to tell him that you weren't interested.' Amy shrugged at Willa's quick, questioning look.

'Hey, you wanted to make his brain explode. I thought I'd save you a prison sentence.'

'True,' Willa admitted as she stood up. 'Okay, well… it was great seeing you but I suppose I should get home.'

'To do more rattling?' Amy shook her head. 'Oh, hell, no. If I ever saw someone in need of a party it's you. I've just signed a huge PR deal—'

'You're in PR? You're far too self-effacing, modest and shy for PR, Ames,' Willa said, her voice deceptively gentle.

Amy just laughed, and instantly catapulted Willa back the best part of a decade. It was a killer laugh—dirty as mud.

'There's that sarcastic mouth I used to love. Anyway, I've just signed a huge deal to launch a new franchise of sports shops selling clothes and equipment—my client is also setting up some hardcore men-only gyms—and a couple of my workmates and I are going out to celebrate. We're taking my new client clubbing. And *you* are going to join us!'

'Uh, I don't think so…'

'I do! My client's name is Rob, he's gorgeous and gruff—but not my type, unfortunately.' Amy led her out of the pretty function room and back towards the main dining area. 'He might be yours.'

Willa scoffed. 'If he's like any of the men I've recently come into contact with he'll need a hug…around the neck… with a rope.'

'Am really *loving* this whole bloodthirsty serial killer vibe you've got going.' Amy shot her a grin. 'I sense sexual frustration.'

Willa grinned at her. 'I sense that I am going to kick you soon.'

Amy tucked her arm into Willa's as they walked towards the exit. 'Oh, yeah…the girls are back in town. And it seems like I am going to have to teach you how to party… to cut loose.'

'Again.'

Rob Hanson looked at the sharply dressed partygoers dutifully lining up outside Fox, waiting in anxious anticipation to get into the popular club, and shook his head. Pulling on a pair of Levi's and a button-down white shirt with its sleeves rolled up was about as dressed up as he got…besides, it wasn't what you looked like that got you into a club—unless you were female and had a great cleavage, blonde hair down to your waist and legs up to your neck— it was attitude…

And he had lots of it.

Rob caught the eye of a bouncer, jerked his head and received a quick nod to go in, bypassing the queue. He slipped a bill into the guy's hand in a slick movement as the rope was lifted and cursed when his mobile vibrated in his pocket. Stepping back from the door, he shoved his finger in his ear and answered the call.

'Rob, it's Gail.'

'Hey, Snail.' At twenty-two, his sister was ten years younger than him and the best thing in his life. 'What's up?'

'Not much—just checking in,' Gail replied. 'Whatcha doing?'

'About to go into a club.'

'Have you met anyone yet?' Gail demanded.

'I haven't even been here two days!' he protested.

'My man-about-town bachelor brother is slacking,' Gail teased and he rolled his eyes.

'I won't have the time in Sydney and I don't have the inclination,' Rob retorted.

Gail's laugh tickled his ear. 'Did the screaming match with Saskia put you off? Judging by the way she flounced out of here, she obviously didn't take it well when you told her that she'd hit her expiry date?'

'Jeez, Gail! Her *expiry date*?'

'I call it like I see it. You never go over the three-month-fling mark and she was due.'

Not as obsessed with the time-frames of his dates as his sister, Rob counted back. Yeah, it *was* nearly dead on three months. He'd started getting twitchy as Saskia started making noises about 'formalising' their relationship, dropping comments about needing cupboard space in his bedroom. She had left a box of tampons in his bathroom cabinet and he'd realised that it was time to bail. She wasn't someone he wanted around long-term...

He'd never met anyone he wanted around long-term.

'One day you're going to meet someone who blows your socks off,' Gail warned him.

He doubted it. Remembering that the best way to get Gail off the subject of his love-life was to comment on hers, he said: 'Are you still dating the tattoo artist? Does he make enough money to take you to the movies occasionally?'

Gail sighed. 'Well-played. Deflect and distract.'

'I try. Don't do anything stupid with this one, okay, honey?'

After witnessing the best and worst of love, he and

Gail approached relationships from opposite directions. She thought that true love and happily-ever-after was just around the corner, and he knew that there was only one person he could ever fully depend on and that was himself.

He and Gail adored each other, but they didn't understand the other's choices when it came to the opposite sex.

'How long are you going to be in Sydney?' Gail asked. 'This house is like a morgue without you.'

'A month…six weeks,' Rob replied. 'Do not let Mr Body Art move in while I'm gone.'

Gail laughed again. 'I'll just move into his place… Bye—love you!'

Rob looked at his dead phone and shook his head. He was convinced that Gail only called him to wind him up and raise his blood pressure. That, he supposed, was a younger sister's job.

Rob looked at his watch…ten p.m. here, and that meant it would be around two in the afternoon back home. Snail was home from her morning classes at uni and she was bored—and a great way to relieve that boredom was to take pot-shots at his love-life.

Revenge, Rob decided as he stepped into the heaving club, would be sweet and designed to embarrass her to the max. Because that was what his job as her older brother was.

Slapped in the face with the noise and smell of the club—alcohol and perfume and sweat mixed together in an almost palpable fug—he immediately asked himself what he was doing. Apart from the fact that he was still exhausted from the long flight from Johannesburg the day before yesterday—he really had to learn to sleep on planes—and the fact that he'd been working sixteen-hour days for months, he also hated clubs and clubbing.

Too loud, too packed, girls too obvious and generally far too young and too eager. Call him old-fashioned but he liked to do a little work before a piece of tail fell into his lap. And, really, at thirty-two, dating kids his sister's age or younger made him feel like a dirty old man.

Rob brushed off a hand on his behind and ignored a proposition from his left as he scanned the bar. He'd find his new firecracker of a PR person, make his excuses and then head back to the flat he'd rented and fall face-down onto the bed.

Rob ran a hand over his short dark brown curls and squinted into the low light of the club. Finding Amy in this madhouse was going to be a nightmare, he thought as his mobile vibrated in his pocket. Or not, he thought, looking at the text message.

At the entrance, hook a left and head towards the back of the club. Table in the back corner.

God bless technology. Rob smiled, shoved his mobile back into the pocket of his jeans and took her directions.

Ah, a table full of women…not too young, thank God, but obviously, judging by the bottles and glasses on the table, well on their way to being cabbaged. *Shoot me now,* he thought. Half an hour, one beer, and he was out of there.

At least they were gorgeous women, admittedly. Amy, confident and glossy, led the pack. There was her colleague—he couldn't remember her name—and her assistant. Couldn't remember her name either. The other two women he didn't recognise at all. He dismissed the tomboy blonde who, he saw when he looked over his shoulder, was swapping some major eye contact with some dude at the bar, and focussed on the woman with mahogany hair tucked into the corner of the table, a cocktail glass in her hand. She had a wide-eyed, Audrey Hepburn waif look to her that instantly made a man regress to being a caveman.

You woman, I protect you. Lie down and I make you happy. Grunt. Grunt.

He'd known a lot of women—sue him…he was in his thirties and had been consistently single all his life—so he was old enough and wise enough to realise that waifs and strays, romantics and women who seemed helpless and hopeless, normally ended up tearing strips off him.

Women, as he'd learnt, were seldom what they portrayed themselves to be. Scrap that. *People* mostly weren't who they said they were.

Amy sprang to her feet. 'Rob—yay, you're here!'

Yeah. Yay.

'You know Bella and Kara, my colleagues—' their names went in one ear and out of the other '—the creature ignoring you for the rock star wannabe at the bar is my flatmate Jessica—oi! Jessica! This is Rob.'

The blonde whipped her head around, flashed him a smile. 'Hey, Rob.'

Quick eye contact and a super-fast scan to determine whether she found him attractive. She hesitated, suggesting that she did, but then her eyes slid back to the bar. Rob smiled inwardly. Someone, if he played his cards right, was getting lucky tonight.

Amy touched his wrist to get his attention. 'And this is my old, old friend Willa. Willa, this is Rob Hanson.'

'You make me sound like a crone with all the olds, Ames,' Willa complained good-naturedly, before lifting amazing silver-shot-with-green eyes to his. 'Hi.'

'Hi back.'

Rob took the open seat next to her and eyed the full beer bottle on the table, icy cold. It was his favourite brand.

He cocked an eyebrow at Amy. 'That for me?'

'Sure.' Amy pushed the bottle and glass across the table. Ignoring the glass and picking up the bottle, he lifted it to his lips and allowed the liquid to slide down his throat. One beer, half an hour and he'd leave...

'Rob owns a chain of sports equipment and clothing stores in South Africa, Willa. And some gyms. He's looking for franchisees to open branches of the stores everywhere, and the gyms will be here in Sydney, Perth and Melbourne initially.'

'Brave...' Willa murmured. 'Especially the gym part, since the marketplace is dominated by Just Fit. And Just Fit has gone on an acquisition drive to buy up the rats and mice gyms that aren't allowing them marketplace domination.'

Rob lowered his bottle and sent her a long look. Then he lifted his eyebrows at Amy, who just laughed.

'She's not just a pretty face,' she said.

Intriguing...

And she wasn't done. 'It takes a set of brass balls to take on two competitors, firmly established and synonymous with Australian health and fitness, one of which is about to list on the ASX. I intend to buy some of their shares when they go public in...' Smarty-Pants squinted at her watch '...six weeks' time.'

Rob just stared at her as she rested her chin in the palm of her hand and gave Amy a puppy-dog look. '*I* want a set of brass balls, Ames. How do I acquire my own?'

Amy threw back her head and laughed. 'Wills, how many of those Screaming Orgasms have you had?'

Willa slid her eyes to the row of cocktail glasses in front of her and counted them off. 'Not enough real ones and four fake ones.'

Willa and Amy exchanged a long look before they both bellowed with laughter.

Oh, jeez—drunk girl humour. About orgasms. Shoot him now. But he had to admit it wasn't fake girl laughter but a real, joyous exchange of humour between two friends who understood each other's subtext. Their laughter made him smile.

'So how long have you been friends?' he asked, picking at the corner of his beer label with a short, blunt fingernail.

He hoped that his question would distract them from further Screaming Orgasm humour—especially since, A. He hadn't had one recently, and B. He'd just decided to stay for another beer, another half-hour.

'Eight, nearly nine years—with far too many lost years in between,' Willa replied.

Seeing the confusion on his face, she placed her hand on his bare forearm and—*whoa*! What the hell…? Lust and attraction shot up his arm and exploded in his brain. He went stock-still and tried to work through his reaction. He'd never, since the time he'd found out that girls had fun things he liked to play with, had such a rocketing blood from his head reaction to the simple touch of fingers on his skin.

He looked at her again and realised that she wasn't just pretty—she was damn sexy. High cheekbones, a pouty mouth and those amazing siren eyes. He allowed his own eyes the pleasure of skimming over smooth shoulders, smallish breasts and that too thin but utterly feminine body.

He tipped his head slightly to the side and saw that her sage-green sleeveless dress disappeared under the table. He needed to see more. On the pretext of bending sideways to scratch his foot, he looked under the table. The dress ended mid-thigh and, holy Moses, those legs were long and toned. Since one nude heel had dropped off a slim foot, he saw that her toes were tipped in tropical orange polish.

Hot, *hot*.

'…and then Amy left the Whitsundays—'

Rob blinked as he lifted his head and came back to the conversation. He was both amused and irritated with himself. He never went on mental walkabouts—and especially not over women.

'You're going to have to back up, Wills. Rob didn't hear a damn thing,' Amy drawled, lifting her beer bottle to her lips and raising a knowing eyebrow in his direction.

Rob felt an urge to pull out his tongue at her, which he manfully suppressed. He quickly rewound and took a stab in the dark. 'So, have you kept in contact with your other mates from those days?'

'Well, I talk to Luke my brother all the time. He was the resort manager.'

Amy sat up straighter and leaned forward. Hmm, Rob thought, interesting reaction to the mention of his name. Something churning there.

'We barely talk nowadays, but I have all their e-mail addresses, and I'm friends with them on social media,' Willa answered, her lips around a purple straw.

Rob, forcing the mental picture of what he'd really like to see those lips wrapped around from his mind, thought that there was no way he could go so long without connecting with his own tight circle of friends.

'You all should get together some time—catch up.'

Amy clapped her hands together with delight. 'That's such a fantastic idea. We should do that, Wills. We can invite them for a barbie…it'll be a Whitsundays reunion,' Amy gushed.

'Let's do it! When?' Willa asked, eyes sparkling.

'The sooner the better… Tomorrow is Sunday! A perfect day for a barbie by the pool…beers, bikinis… We can have a seafood Barbie,' Amy babbled. 'Invite them, Willa! *Now!* I betcha they will all come.'

Willa reached for her bag, her enthusiasm elevated by those Screaming Orgasms. She pulled out the latest smartphone and Rob raised his eyes as her fingers flew over the touchscreen. 'Okay, I've tagged Scott and Brodie and Chantal. Luke is in Singapore, the jerk. Who else?'

'The bartenders—Matt and Phil. Invite them! They were

fun… Tell them to bring booze for cocktails.' Amy leaned forward. 'And Jane and Gwen who were part of the entertainment crew.' Amy looked at Rob. 'We were quite sure that they provided extra "entertainment" to the guests, but they were such a riot.'

'And the lifeguards—I hope they're still hot! Tagged them… Come on, Ames, there were at least twenty of us who ran wild… I've tagged the girls who helped me entertain the rug rats.'

'The rug rats?' Rob asked.

'I looked after the kids at the resort… I kept them entertained so that their parents could have a break. And afternoon sex,' Willa explained without looking up from her smartphone. 'Come on, Amy—think!'

Amy rattled off a few more names and Willa bobbed her head in excitement. 'Okay, anyone else?'

'Nah. I think that's it.'

Amy leaned back in her chair and looked over to her flatmate. She let out a loud whistle that felt like an ice pick in Rob's brain, but it had the desired effect and Jessica turned around.

'Hey, Jess, want to go to a barbie with me and Willa?'

'Sure,' Jessica replied, turning to Willa. 'When?'

'Tomorrow. What time?' Willa asked Amy.

'Eleven. Bring your own bottle,' Amy replied, and Rob watched, amused, as their impromptu party started to take shape.

Whether their guests would appreciate—or accept—an invitation at half-ten at night for a party the next day was another story, but it was fun watching their cocktail-induced excitement. That being said, he knew that they were *so* going to regret their impulsiveness in the morning, when their heads woke them up, screaming that they had had brain surgery without anaesthetic.

'Okay, eleven…bring my own bottle…where?' Jessica asked.

'Yeah, where? Maybe I should add that.' Willa squinted at her phone.

'That would be helpful,' Rob murmured, but no one heard him.

Amy pretended to think, her eyes dancing. 'Oh, I don't know…who do we know who has an empty Sydney water-front property with a pool?'

Willa shrugged. 'Who?'

Then the penny dropped with a clang and Willa bounced up and down in her chair like a first-grader.

'Oooh, *I* do! Me! Me, me, me, me…*me*!'

'Attagirl.' Amy lifted her bottle in her direction.

Even Rob, stranger that he was to the city, knew that waterfront property in Sydney meant big bucks. Who *was* this waif? An heiress? A celebrity?

'Hey, if I'm finally going to host a party of my own then I'm going to invite who I want to invite,' Willa stated emphatically. 'Like Kate!'

'Who's Kate?' Amy asked.

Yeah, who is Kate, gorgeous?

'My lawyer.'

Why would a woman in her mid to late twenties have her own lawyer? Interesting… Then again, the whole package was fascinating… Brains and beauty and those brilliant legs that were made to wrap around a man's hips…

Okay, slow down there, Hanson.

Willa's phone beeped and her face fell. 'Poop. Kate can't come. Oh, well.' She looked around for a waiter. 'I need another drink.'

Some liver pills, a litre of water and a few painkillers wouldn't hurt either, Rob told her silently.

CHAPTER TWO

SHE WASN'T DRUNK, Willa told herself. Happy, relaxed…
slightly buzzed, maybe, but not drunk. And she was having fun, she realised on a happy sigh. *Fun*… She rolled
the word around her tongue. Well…hello, there, stranger.

She was twenty-six years old—jeez, nearly twenty-
seven—and she'd played the part of young, gorgeous, thick
trophy wife all her adult life because Wayne and what he'd
wanted had been important…her, not so much.

She was a great example of why you shouldn't be in
charge of your own destiny when you were too young and
too dumb to be making decisions more complicated than
how to operate a teaspoon.

Willa pushed her heavy hair back from her face. She'd
stopped loving Wayne years and years ago, and now she
just wished she could finally be free of him—legally, mentally, comprehensively. And when she was she could fully
enjoy men like…Rob.

Willa sneaked a look at that face and swallowed her lusty
sigh. He was scruffy in all the right places, she thought.
Sable-coloured curls that she longed to touch to see if they
felt as soft as they looked, a four-day-old beard, a shirt that
skimmed long muscles and tanned skin, giving hints of
well-defined pecs, and an impressive six-pack.

Those grey piercing eyes seemed to be shockingly ob-
servant and yet basically unreadable.

Rough, rugged, and completely at ease in his skin.
She couldn't help but to compare him to the only other
man she'd ever slept with—she was biggest of big girl's

blouses!—and it was like comparing instant coffee to Mountain Blue. Simply an exercise in stupidity.

Wayne was smart Italian suits and hair gel to cover the bald patch on the crown of his head. Cologne, cufflinks and designer labels. Rob was…*not*. He didn't need to accessorise—he was excellent just as he was.

Sexy. Masculine. Nuclear-hot.

'Honey, you keep looking at me like that and I'm going to have to do something about it.'

Willa blinked as his drawling voice pulled her back into the moment and she noticed Amy leaving the table with a tall blond guy. They were heading towards the dance floor in the centre of the club. When had that happened? Maybe while she'd been spending the last five minutes drooling over Nuclear-Hot across the table.

She turned back to Rob and blinked like an owl. 'Hi…' she whispered.

'Hi back. You okay?'

'Mmm. I'm having fun. I haven't had fun for a long, long time.' Willa tapped her fingers on the table in time to the music. 'Do you dance?'

Rob's mobile mouth kicked up. 'If I have to.'

Willa looked from the dance floor to him and nibbled on the bottom of her lip. The last time she'd danced—really danced, with feeling and heart and soul—had been in the Whitsundays at that dive bar where all the staff employed at the hotels in the area had congregated to hook up, break up, kiss and make up.

She wanted to feel young again—eighteen again—when the nights had been long and had held a myriad of possibilities.

She wanted to dance with Rob…

Maybe it was the cocktails making her feel brave. If it was she'd have another three or four Screaming Os, thank you very much. *Then you'd be face-down on the floor*, commented doormat Willa.

Willa took a breath and blurted out her question. 'Will you dance…with me?'

Rob immediately rose to his feet and held out his hand.

Willa took a moment to find her shoe before standing up and placing her hand in his much bigger one. She followed in his wake as he pushed through the packed crowds to the edge of the dance floor. Instead of finding a spot on the edge, Rob pulled her into the centre of the floor, flashed her a grin and started to move.

Willa stared at him in shock as he immediately picked up the beat and moved his hips in a sinuous rhythm that dried up all the moisture in her mouth. Dear Lord, those hips… If he took the same skill to the bedroom he would be declared a lethal sexual weapon in several countries.

'I thought you said you don't dance!' Willa shouted.

Rob flashed her a smile as his shoulders lifted and rolled. 'I said that I dance if I have to.'

Willa stepped closer to him so that she could speak directly in his ear. 'You're pretty good.'

'Just one of my talents.'

Rob placed his hands on her hips and before she knew it her thigh was between his and they were rocking together. Willa swallowed the lump in her throat as Rob's hand lifted to encircle her neck, using his thumb to push her jaw up so that their eyes met. Willa wasn't that out of practice that she couldn't recognise the attraction in his eyes, the accelerated pulse under the wrists she loosely held.

'Man…you are seriously gorgeous. And to think that I nearly blew this off,' Rob muttered, mostly to himself, as his other hand slid around her back and yanked her towards him so that their bodies were pressed flush against each other.

His chest was wider and bigger and harder than hers,

Willa thought as she dropped her nose to the V of skin his shirt revealed and inhaled his man smell, his heat. Lust boiled and roiled and her happy place throbbed, echoing the beat of the music. His surprisingly soft chest hair tickled her nose and she felt rather than heard the rumble of a moan in his chest, his throat. One hand splayed across her back, between her shoulder blades, and the other dropped lower onto her ass, holding her firmly in place against him. And that, she could feel, made him *very* happy indeed.

Somehow he kept them swaying to the beat, pretending to dance.

'So, twenty questions time?'

Rob's deep voice in her ear did nothing to assuage the heat between her legs—in fact it sped up her sluggish blood.

Questions? Was he mad? Between him and the cocktails she'd didn't have an operational brain cell left.

'Yes…no…I don't know,' Willa murmured back.

'Wrong, wrong and wrong,' Rob responded with an appreciative grin. 'Let's try that again. Why do you have a lawyer?'

She didn't feel like explaining about Wayne and her imminent divorce. She wasn't going to see Rob again after tonight, but she still thought it would be tacky to explain about her ex while she was pressed up very close and very personal against him. Besides, she didn't want memories of Wayne to taint this experience of her first fun night out in for ever. Her ex and her old life were in the past.

Rob was here—now.

Carpe diem, Willa.

'Pass.'

'Okay…next one. What do you do that you're such an expert on the health and fitness market? Stockbroker? Financial analyst?'

She wished—she really, *really* wished.

'I read. A lot.' Even she, novice that she was at this flirting and seduction stuff, knew that he didn't need to know that reading finance and business magazines was one of her favourite ways to pass some time. Willa squinted at him and pulled a face. 'These are very boring questions...'

Rob laughed. 'Okay, then—you hit me with one.'

Willa sucked in her cheeks. There were a million things she wanted to know about him, but the least important flew out of her mouth.

'Boxers or briefs?'

Bad girl, Willa.

Rob's laugh brushed over her skin.

'Why don't you drop your hands and find out?' Rob suggested, and her face immediately pinked up. Taking one of her hands from his neck, he guided it around his hips and slapped it on his butt. 'Feel free to explore.'

Oh, that was a mighty fine ass, she thought as she took him up on his offer. Hard, muscular...male.

'What do you sleep in?' he asked, his breath teasing her ear.

A pair of sleep shorts and a ratty T-shirt. That wasn't sexy, Willa thought. She tossed back her hair and widened her eyes as she prepared to lie. 'I sleep naked. All... the...time.'

His eyes dilated and Willa remembered how much fun it was to flirt, to tease, how thrilling it was to get a hard-eyed and hard man—in every way that counted—all flustered. Sometimes being a girl was such a kick.

'Bet you look damn good naked.'

'I do. As, I suspect...' Willa gave his butt a squeeze '...do you.'

In her head wild Willa tried to high-five doormat Willa, but she was banging her head against an imaginary wall.

Rob let out a muffled groan and rested his forehead on hers. 'How hot is it, exactly, in here?'

'It's cookin',' Willa agreed, surprised at their effortless banter, her ability to flirt so easily.

Maybe it was the Screaming Os, the obvious appreciation and attraction in Rob's eyes, his hot hands sliding over her arms, back, hips, that made her feel bolder and brighter—the best version of herself. Confident, slightly crazy, prepared to take a risk.

One night, she told herself. Didn't she deserve one night of uncomplicated pleasure with a hot man who looked as if he wanted to gobble her up in one big bite? *Hell, yes!* shouted wild Willa, thoroughly over-excited. Didn't she deserve a night of stupendous sex after more than eight months of sexual drought? Her house was empty, her bed was empty...she was all but free.

You betcha, sister!

Doormat Willa groaned and slapped her hand over her eyes.

Before she could lose her courage and change her mind, Willa tipped her head back and nailed him with her silver-green eyes. 'Got condoms?'

'Yes. Why?' Rob replied carefully as his hands tightened on her hips. 'You offering to let me use a couple?'

'Yeah...you interested?'

Rob sucked in a breath. 'Yeah—to the max. I've been thinking about it...'

'Since when?'

'I've been having X-rated fantasies about your fabulous legs encircling my hips since I first clocked them.' He stepped back and looked at her legs. When he lifted his eyes again they'd turned sombre and serious. 'You sure about this, Willa? Why do I have the feeling that this isn't the way you normally operate?'

It isn't—we don't know what we're doing here! Doormat Willa wrung her hands, whimpering.

Well, she wasn't in charge tonight. Wild Willa was going to have some fun. 'I'm very sure.'

Relief flashed across Rob's face. 'Where would you feel more comfortable? My place or yours?'

Oh, her place—absolutely. And if she was silently raising her middle finger to her ex by sleeping with someone else in a bed that he'd paid for, then nobody had to know but her.

Oh, dear God, she was *sleeping with someone else…* someone other than her forty-something husband who didn't exactly encourage creativity in bed. Mr Missionary Position, she'd privately called him. Wham, bam…skip the thank-you, ma'am.

Rob's thumb brushing her cheekbone pulled her back to reality. 'Hey, where did you go?'

Willa grabbed his wrist. It was only fair to give him a heads-up so that he didn't feel cheated when he realised that she was more below par than porn star. 'Look, you should know that I don't do this…often.' *Try never.* 'And I'm not…'

'Not what?'

'Experienced.'

Rob looked at her for a long time without saying anything. Before he spoke, he brushed her lips with a kiss and Willa quivered. 'Feel that?' he murmured against her mouth. 'Feel the electricity between us?'

'Mmm-hmm.'

'I'm old enough and experienced enough to know that doesn't happen often, and when it does you don't need anything else but to give yourself over to it. But, since you were honest enough to tell me that you aren't a pro at this, let me remind you of the rules.'

There are rules? God! Seriously? Her lower lip pushed out. Wild Willa didn't like rules.

'Okay,' Willa agreed, although she'd really much prefer Rob just to kiss her again.

'This is a one-night thing, so no thinking about hearts and flowers.'

Willa felt the power of his honest statement.

'I'm attracted to you, and the little I've seen of you, I like. I don't sleep with women I don't like, but tonight is it…there will be nothing more than a couple of laughs and some good sex.'

'*Good* sex is the minimum I require,' Willa said, making herself sound innocent.

Rob's lips twitched. 'Why do I suspect that when you widen those eyes and sound naïve you are at your most sarcastic?'

Because he wasn't a fool, Willa realised, but she didn't confirm or deny his statement.

'And if you change your mind at any point—any point at all!—you say so and I back off. I can't guarantee that I'll be happy about it, but I'll back off. You don't like anything I do, you say so and I don't do it again.'

Willa blinked. 'My God, you are direct.'

'No point in being anything else,' Rob retorted. 'I'm uncomfortably honest, or so I've frequently been told. It's the only way I know how to be. Can you handle that?'

After the last eight years, honesty was a brilliant change of pace. 'Since you're only going to be around for the rest of the night, I think I can cope.'

Rob grinned at her jibe. 'There's that gentle sarcasm again…I love it. So, let's go—so that I can get you naked sooner rather than later.'

Willa felt his hand wrap around hers—solid, masculine and sure—and she allowed him to tug her off the dance floor and towards the exit of the club.

We're gonna get laid, Wild Willa shouted, *thoroughly thrilled. Whooo-hooo!*

Willa didn't bother to switch on any lights as she entered the double-volume hallway of her Vaucluse waterfront property—she just kicked the door closed behind Rob and immediately reached for him.

They'd found a taxi as they'd left the club and a heated silence had filled the interior of the vehicle. Yet she hadn't needed words to know that he couldn't wait to get his hands on her. His warm hand had started off on her bare knee and slowly worked its way up her thigh, so that when the taxi had pulled up in front of the massive mansion her dress had been skimming her crotch line and his fingers had been not too far from her happy place.

Now she was damp and hot and horny, and if she didn't get him touching her soon she was going to cry like a little girl.

Rob, finding her plastered against his chest, didn't need any encouragement and immediately yanked her dress up and palmed her butt with his masterful hand. He shoved his other hand into her heavy mass of hair, clasped her head and angled her face to receive his no-holds-barred kiss. Tongues danced as he devoured her mouth, learning her, tasting her, pushing her for more.

Emboldened by his passion and his groans of appreciation, Willa pulled his shirt up so that she could touch his hot body. So hard, she thought. Muscular, but not over the top…just pure masculine strength. Her fingers traced the rows of his six-pack and the long muscles that covered his hips, brushed over the hard erection that tented his jeans.

Ooh, she liked that, so she traced his long length with the tip of her finger. Yeah, she liked that. *A lot.*

'Yeah, that's it,' Rob muttered against her mouth, pulling her dress up and over her hips, revealing her tiny black thong to his hungry gaze.

His hands gripped and released her hips as he looked down at her, past her flat stomach to her long legs. She was still in her heels.

'Perfect,' he breathed. 'Is the rest of you as pretty, Willa?'

'Maybe,' Willa replied, undoing his belt buckle.

Rob slid his hand between her legs and cupped her, his thumb immediately finding and brushing her clitoris through her thong, causing her to yelp into her mouth.

'So good...so good,' Willa moaned against his lips. 'More...more.'

Rob's hand stilled and his breath was hot and laboured. 'If we don't stop now I'm going to yank these off and take you right here, right now. Against the front door or on this Persian carpet under our feet.'

Willa tipped her head back to look up into his fabulous passion-soaked steel-coloured eyes. 'Yeah...either. Both. Just do it *now.*'

Rob smiled and reached for the foil strip of condoms he'd shoved into the back pocket of his jeans. He ripped a packet off with his teeth and allowed the rest to drop to the floor. He placed it in her hand with a wicked grin.

'Put it on me while I get rid of your panties.'

Willa popped open the first button of his jeans, then the second, and when they were loose around his hips she shoved her hands inside his briefs and pushed both his underwear and jeans down. His erection stood tall and proud, and Willa sighed at how big he was... It seemed that Wayne wasn't nearly as well-endowed as he'd claimed. Well, he'd lied about everything else so she wasn't particularly surprised.

But Rob was long and thick, and she knew that taking him inside her meant she would have to stretch and... She licked her lips... She couldn't wait. She wanted to be pushed, filled, taken to the limit. She wanted to feel like a woman being possessed by a man...in the best way possible.

Willa ripped the packet open with her teeth, pulled out the condom and swiftly rolled it over his penis, sucking in her breath as he hardened even further.

Above her head, Rob swore. 'Honey, this is going to be hectic…we'll keep slow and sexy for later.'

With those words, he hooked his big hands under her thighs and lifted her up, spreading her legs so that the head of his penis probed her wet and moist feminine core. It was only then that Willa realised he'd magicked her panties away without her even realising…

Rob pressed her against the massive wooden front door and pinned her there with his body, sliding into her with one long, sure stroke. Willa felt herself dissolving from the inside out as her world narrowed to what was happening between them. Her surroundings faded away and there were only Rob's hands on her thighs, his tongue in her mouth mimicking his thrust of his hips, the sure strokes as he lifted her higher and higher.

'You need to come, honey, 'cos I'm not going to be able to hang on,' Rob muttered, his forehead against hers.

'Don't you dare stop!' Willa shot back, grinding down on him as lightning bugs danced along her skin.

Rob dropped his head to talk in her ear. 'That's it, Willa, take all of me. Yeah, move…use me…higher, dammit!'

'Harder…' Willa demanded, reaching for her release.

Rob slammed her against the door and she shouted as stars exploded behind her eyeballs and her body splintered into a million billion pieces. She vaguely heard Rob's roar in her ear, felt his orgasm deep inside her, but didn't particularly care. She'd come and it had been magnificent…

Rob moved his hips again and, still mostly hard, touched something inside her. She rocketed up again, harder and faster than before. She slammed her eyes shut and screamed his name before she fractured again in a big bang of cosmic proportions.

Minutes, hours or years might have passed before she came back down to earth, her head on his shoulder, pinned to the door by Rob's strength.

'I really don't think you hit the mark, Willa. We might have to do that again.'

She heard Rob's smile in his words, felt the curve of his lips against her temple.

'Slow and sexy this time?' Willa agreed on a happy smile, sliding to the floor.

Early the next morning, after another round of blow-her-head-off morning sex, Willa, her head on Rob's shoulder, felt well satisfied with herself. She thought that she'd feel dirty and guilty, going to bed with a complete stranger, but all she felt was...satisfied—and strangely safe.

Sure, he was good-looking—what was the point of having a one-night stand with an ugly man?—and he had a body that spoke of a lifetime of physical fitness. He smelt good, and he had treated her with care and made sure that that she was fully satisfied—every single time—before climaxing himself.

He was as close to a perfect lover as she'd ever encountered—okay, *that* didn't mean anything at all!—and she idly wondered whether it was his skill in the sack or her previous lack of satisfactory sex that had had her coming over and over again.

She suspected that it was mostly Rob. He was an amazing lover. She'd felt safe enough to allow herself to lose control—to touch, to explore, to taste—and she had lost all her inhibitions in her quest to explore those long, lean muscles. That had never happened to her before.

With Wayne... *No.* No comparisons—no thinking about him.

Suffice to say that with Rob she felt energised. Sleep had been forgotten in the delight of his body. She remembered thinking that she hadn't wanted the feast of touch and textures and taste and masculinity to end.

She still didn't.

'I need sustenance,' Willa said on a long yawn. 'What's the time?'

'Half-eight.'

Rob patted her butt to get her to move. He slid out of bed and walked across the ridiculously enormous bedroom to the balcony doors. He gripped the top of the doorframe and Willa rolled over on her stomach to look at his beautiful back, tight ass and long, muscular legs.

Hot damn, the man was sexy. Willa licked her lips and was suddenly conscious of her pounding head and the fact that her mouth felt as if a herd of llamas had bedded down in it during the night.

'This is a hell of place you have here, Willa. Yours?'

'Yeah.' Well, it would be in a few weeks' time.

This massive house she'd moved into eight months ago still didn't feel like her home. But the exclusive property would form part of her divorce settlement—along with her Mercedes and a hefty donation to her bank account. She'd wanted to walk away with nothing, just to get rid of Wayne, but Kate, her lawyer and now a good friend, had refused to allow her even to go there.

'He cheats, he pays,' Kate had told her, over and over again.

'Where exactly are we?' Rob asked. 'Is that Sydney harbour bridge?'

'Yep.'

Willa stood up, wrapped a sheet around her torso and ducked under his arm to move onto the veranda off the bedroom.

She leaned against the railing and pointed down to the jetty that kissed the crystal-clear water below. 'At the end of the garden is a gate that leads onto that path, and via that jetty I have direct access to Parsley Bay. I can swim, snorkel, kayak, or picnic in the beautiful neighbouring parkland.'

Willa turned her back to the bay and looked at him.

'It's a big house on a big plot of land—six bedrooms, four bathrooms, lots of living space and decks. Double garage. Private.'

'And you live here all alone?' Rob asked, sceptical.

'Ridiculous, isn't it?' Willa replied lightly, not wanting to go into details about her failed marriage. 'The house is cold and empty and it should have kids running around in it, pets, people visiting and loud parties...'

'Well, it will today.'

Willa looked at him blankly.

Rob grinned and she caught a flash of white teeth and the glint of the sun in his stubble. 'Honey, you have a bunch of people arriving for a barbecue...' he looked at his watch '...later this morning.'

It took a moment for her to remember that she'd invited the entire Whitsundays gang—not just her old friends—for a barbecue this morning.

Grabbing Rob's wrist, she looked at the dial of his watch and let out a low wail of panic. She had nothing in her house to eat, no booze, and the fact that she had to entertain people she hadn't seen in years—not to mention dealing with this very sexy souvenir from the night below—had panic crawling up her throat.

She couldn't do this,—she really couldn't. Maybe she could hustle Rob out through the front door and she could escape out the back—hightail it to her canoe and belt her way up the bay.

Opening her mouth like a fish desperate for oxygen, she stared at Rob in horror.

'Take a breath, Willa,' Rob suggested on a slow grin.

Willa slapped her hands against her cheeks and gasped as the sheet dropped and fell over the lounger. Rob's eyes darkened with passion and his penis started to swell. Willa saw what was happening, lifted her hand and tried to step away from him—she really did. But her legs weren't doing much listening. In fact they were taking her to him!

'No! No! No, no, no, no, no, *no*! I don't have time, Rob!'

Rob's thumb drifted over her nipple and Willa felt her resolve weaken. How could she just look at him and feel prickly and horny and…wet? *Get a grip, Willa.* But one more time her body whispered its demand. One more thrilling, amazing orgasm or…four.

'I want to take you here, on this lounger, in the morning sun.'

'God, Rob… It's out in the open. The neighbours….'

Why was she even thinking about doing this? Was she mad?

'Nobody can see us, Willa. This balcony was built for privacy,' Rob said, sliding his hand between her thighs.

Willa instantly melted.

'Here…in the sun, Wills. Say yes.'

'Yes.' Willa sighed, looping her hands around his neck and slapping her naked body against his. As if she'd ever had any chance of saying no.

Ding-dong! Ding-dong!

Willa's eyes shot open and she bolted upright in bed. Fudge, was that the doorbell? That couldn't be the doorbell, there was no way that it was eleven already…

Ding-dong. Ding-dong.

Dammit, it *was* the doorbell, and the doorbell meant guests. *Arrrggghhhhh.* She was in such trouble…

Rob groaned and opened one eye. Willa glared down at him. 'This is your fault!' she hissed.

'Huh? Why?'

Willa shot out of bed and ran to her walk-in closet, reaching for clean underwear and a pair of shorts. Grabbing a denim pair that were more holes than fabric, she yanked them on.

'"I want to take you here, on this lounger, in the morning sun…"' Willa growled, imitating his deep voice. '"Just come back to bed for a little while," you said. "we have time," you said!'

'We must have dozed off.' Rob rolled over, taking the sheets with him, and squinted at his watch. 'Huh—ten-forty. Someone is early. Either way, it seems we're out of time.'

'You *think*, Einstein?' Willa barked, yanking on a tank top and pulling her hair up into a haphazard tail. 'I need a shower, to brush my teeth…'

'Slow down, gorgeous…' Rob suggested, standing up and stretching.

Willa glared at him as the doorbell chimed again. 'Keep your pants on,' she muttered, and then pointed to Rob. 'You too, hotshot.'

Rob grinned at her. 'I'm going to have a shower first…'

'I hate you!' Willa barked, before rushing out of the bedroom and down the stairs.

Through the stained glass windows of the door she could see two people on the other side. Yanking it open, she was relieved to see Amy and Jessica on her front steps.

'Thank God it's you!' she stated, holding her hand to her head, hoping to keep it from exploding. God, she had the headache from hell. What had been in those cocktails? Liquid mercury?

'Are you okay, Wills? You look…frazzled,' Amy said.

'I *am* frazzled,' Willa admitted. 'God, can I cancel this?'

Amy stepped into the double volume hall and whistled her appreciation as she turned in a circle. 'Hell, no, you're not cancelling a damn thing—and…wow, Wills, this house is a hell of a divorce settlement.'

'Kate's a hell of a divorce lawyer.'

And she wasn't letting Willa settle for just a house. She was, as she frequently told Willa, better and meaner than that.

Willa took a seat on the bottom step of the floating staircase. 'She's the sharpest tool in the shed; you'd like her, Amy.'

'If she's helping you bury Wayne-the-Pain then I like her already,' Amy agreed.

The Pain. *Such* an apt moniker.

'Anyway…can we concentrate, here? I have a cracking headache from those cocktails, I have God knows how many people arriving at any minute, and I have nothing—repeat, *nothing*!—in this house to feed or lubricate them.'

Amy frowned. 'Did you forget you invited us?'

'Sorta…kinda….yeah.' She couldn't tell her friend that she'd been having too much fun playing with Rob to think about her guests. 'What am I going to *doooooo*?'

'You are going to go and have a shower. Jessica will greet anyone who arrives and Amy will shoot to the shops and grab food and drink.'

The deep, masculine, made-for-sin voice floated down the stairs.

Willa watched as Jessica and Amy's heads shot up and quickly turned to see Rob, his hair wet from his ultra-quick shower, dressed in his clothes from the night before, walking down the stairs, bare feet sticking out from the ragged hem of his jeans. Their surprise turned to feminine approval and she groaned as two sets of perfectly arched eyebrows lifted in a silent question.

'Way to go, Wills.'

Willa threw her hands up in defeat at Amy's mischievous murmur. 'Ah…Rob. Rob stayed over…'

'I can see that,' Amy stated with a grin.

Willa caught Amy's eye and saw the glint of sisterly pride in her eye. *So, didja have fun?* she could imagine her asking, if Jessica and Rob hadn't been there.

So much fun.

Thought you would. He looks the type who knows what he's doing.

You have no idea, old friend.

'You two done with your telepathic conversation?' Jessica demanded as she put out her hand and hauled Willa to her feet. 'Go shower, Willa. Amy, let's take a look and see what Willa has so that you know what to buy.'

'Nothing,' Willa said mournfully. 'I have nothing.'

'Why do *I* have to get the food?' Amy wailed.

'Because it was your idea to do this,' Willa retorted, hand still on her head. 'There's a deli down the road. They have everything… Just buy them out and I'll pay you back.'

Willa looked at Jessica and pointed to her left.

'Kitchen that way. Through the French doors of the kitchen—and off all the rooms on that side of the house—is a covered patio and the pool. Chairs, tables—all outside. Outside kitchen…grill. Go wild.'

Amy whistled her appreciation. 'As I said, Wills, it's a helluva settlement.'

Yeah, Willa thought as she climbed the stairs to the second floor and her bedroom. *All I had to do was put up with crap and be an aimless, thick trophy wife for eight years.*

CHAPTER THREE

ROB TOOK A call on his mobile and thought that if he didn't get coffee into his system in the next few minutes he'd find himself face-down on Willa's expensive floor, whimpering like a little girl.

He'd thought he had stamina—he regularly took part in triathlons, ran eight miles five days out of seven, and hit the gym several times a week. Yet rolling around in the sheets with Willa had sucked every last atom of energy from him...

Rob grinned. Best fun he'd had—in or out of bed—for ages.

But now coffee...*stat*. He'd grab a cup, kiss Willa goodbye and move on out. It was what he did and he did it well... He should—he'd had a hell of lot of practice at it.

Shoving his mobile into the back pocket of his jeans, he walked across the hall towards the feminine voices drifting down the passage from what he presumed was the kitchen.

'So, did you ever meet Willa's husband?'

Rob slammed to a stop and cursed... She was *married*? Crap, crap, crap. He didn't do married women—it was one of his *hell, no!* rules. She didn't wear a ring but...*crap!*

'About to be ex-husband,' Amy corrected, and he resumed breathing again. 'They've been separated for about eight months.'

Good—that was good. Not perfect, but a helluva lot better than married.

'What's he like?'

Rob leaned his shoulder into the wall a couple of metres away from the kitchen door, knowing that if he went in Willa's friends would stop talking. Girls tended not to dish the dirt on about-to-be-exes when the guy one of them had had a one-night stand with was in the room.

But he was curious.

He wanted more information on Willa, who interested him far more than she should for a one-night stand. That was something he needed to think about...but only when he'd had coffee and a solid eight hours' sleep.

'Wayne... Yeah, I was with Willa when they met for the first time.' Amy's voice had a faraway quality that suggested she was recalling memories from long ago.

'And?' Jessica's voice sounded impatient.

Amy took a while to answer and Rob mentally urged her to get a move on.

'Slick,' Amy said eventually. 'Slick as snot. A lot older than Willa—I think he was in his mid-thirties when they first met...'

'You didn't like him,' Jessica stated.

'Yeah, instinctively didn't like him,' Amy agreed. 'I was just frustrated, I guess. Willa was a kid so desperately in need of fun, a good time, letting her hair down, and I was showing her how to do that... God, we were having a blast! Partying up a storm, flirting up a bigger storm...we ruled the resort.'

'You mean *you* ruled and Willa was your sidekick,' Jessica said, dryly.

Rob grinned at that.

'Then she met Wayne and she... How do I explain this? She shrank in on herself and became the perfect girlfriend—cool, calm, collected. With him she was eighteen going on eighty. Crazy Willa left the building.'

'Since she was slamming down those cocktails last night, I think crazy Willa is back,' Jessica said, and Rob could hear the grin in her voice.

'Not by a long shot. And she wasn't anywhere near being drunk, trust me, that girl can hold her booze. When she's really drunk she ends up singing eighties ballads and taking her clothes off.'

Rob's eyebrows lifted with surprise. He'd like to see *that*.

'She can be a wild woman,' Amy added.

Rob had the nail-marks on his butt to prove *that* point.

'But with Wayne she stopped having fun. I suspect that last night was the first time she's had some real fun—proper fun—since she got married. She's a little sad, scared, and a lot lonely. I feel sort of protective of her...'

So did he.

Huh?

Rob looked down at his bare feet and instead of heading for the kitchen—caffeine, shockingly, could now wait—he walked through the sun room and headed for the sunlight-dappled deck: expensive outdoor furniture, a pizza oven built into the wall and an island holding a gas stove and a fridge. A ten-seater wooden dining table with benches on either side dominated the kitchen end of the deck, and cane couches and chairs with blue and white striped cushions filled the rest of the space. The large, rectangular pool looked cool and inviting and he wished he could dive into its clear depths.

He loved to swim—did some of his best thinking in the water.

So Willa had been married...was still, technically, married...to a guy who was a lot older than her and obviously rich. Her eyes held shadows within them that suggested long-term unhappiness; he recognised those shadows—he'd seen them in his mum's eyes every day she'd been married to Stefan.

Which was all on him. Because when she'd told him that Stefan had proposed, wondering what he thought, he'd said that she should take the plunge. Stefan had been his dad's best friend—*her* friend. Their second dad. She'd liked him, they'd liked him…what could go wrong? He'd just wanted her to be happy again, and—he had to be honest here—he'd known he would feel a lot more comfortable going off to uni across the country if he knew that Stefan was looking after Mum and Gail.

That hadn't worked out the way he'd thought it would.

When he'd finally got to the root of the problem—when his family had disintegrated around him for the second time—he'd felt his heart rip apart. It had been like losing his father all over again, and along with that he'd waved goodbye to his innocence and his faith in people.

And he'd kicked trust over a cliff.

Rob ran his hand along his scruffy jaw. Where was this coming from? He'd been thinking about Willa's sad eyes and then he'd started thinking of his past and his failure in the interpersonal relationships department.

Huh…

But the fact remained that he didn't like the idea of Willa feeling sad…

He'd slept with her once and he was already giving her more thought than he'd given all his past flings put together. Something was *very* wrong with this picture…

Because he didn't play games with other people—and especially with himself. He had to admit that he kind of liked the fact that Willa was still married, if only legally. It was a minor barrier, but a barrier nonetheless—something to help him keep his emotional distance, to remind him not to become any more involved than he should be. Than he liked to be, wanted to be, could afford to be…

One friggin' night and she's turning your head upside down. Get a grip, Hanson! You just want to sleep with her again, his sensible side argued. *There's no need to go all dark and broody and—what was the word Gail had used the other day?—'emo' about this. It's just sex. You know that after a couple of days you'll get bored and want to move on. So ask for another night, or two, or three, but just stop bloody brooding already. And get it into your thick block that she's no different from the others...*

Except that she is, he thought.

Very different... She *had* to be if he was thinking about her like this.

Rob dropped his long frame into the nearest chair and groaned loudly.

Get the hell out of her house and her life, moron, he told himself. *Now. You're looking for trouble—inviting complications in through the door. The night is over, the sun is high in the sky and if you're thinking that she is remotely special then your ass should be on fire, trying to get the hell away. Be smart about her, dude. Get your cup of coffee, say your goodbyes, and get the hell out of Dodge. You never stay this long—you rarely spend the night.*

Yet despite running through his long list of why he shouldn't be contemplating another night, a fling, a short-term affair with her, he was unable to walk away.

Rob placed his head on the back on the chair and groaned again. *You are utterly and completely screwed, man.*

Even that thought wasn't enough to pull himself out of the chair and out of her house.

Screwed to the max. And still caffeine-deprived.

Rob tapped on the frame of the open bathroom door and grinned when Willa, standing in front of the huge bathroom mirror above the double basins in a pale yellow bra and thong, reached for a dressing gown to cover up.

'Bit late for that, seeing as I've seen and kissed most of you.'

Fighting her blush, Willa dropped the gown. He had seen—stroked, tasted—everything, so it was a silly, pointless gesture. Willa picked up a square black box and, flipping it open, brushed a pale pink blush over her cheekbones. Rob placed a cup of coffee on the counter and went back to lean his shoulder into the doorframe and cross his legs at the ankles, holding his cup in his hand.

'Thanks,' Willa said.

'That was the last of the milk, and there's nothing but a half-tub of cottage cheese and some yoghurt in your fridge...what do you eat?'

'Not much,' she admitted in a jerky voice. 'I hate cooking for myself.'

Rob saw the confusion in her eyes, knew that she wasn't quite sure what to do with him, how to behave. While he knew her body inside out, he was still, to all intents and purposes, a stranger.

'So, some of your friends have arrived. Do you want me to go?'

Willa bit the inside of her lip. 'You don't have to... Stick around if you don't have anything better to do.'

Thank her for a good time, kiss her goodbye and walk on out...

'Thanks, I'll do that.'

His sensible side cursed him a blue streak for staying exactly where he was and stalked off. Since Patrick—his cousin, partner and accountant, who'd accompanied him from South Africa to work on establishing their companies here—was spending the weekend with an old university friend, Rob rationalised, why should he spend the day alone? He liked people, and they, despite the fact that he could be blunt and frequently tactless, liked him. So Rob thought he might as well hang around... He could always change his mind and leave. That was one of the cool benefits of free will.

He folded his arms against his chest and his biceps stretched the fabric of his creased shirt. He kept his eyes and tone inscrutable. 'So, apparently this house is part of your divorce settlement? You are still technically married.'

Willa sent him an uncertain look and for a moment she looked a lot younger and a great deal more vulnerable than he'd expected. His heart shuddered and he told it to get a grip... He wasn't a sap about women and their wobbly lips and soft eyes.

'We've been separated, officially, for a little more than half a year; in reality we haven't had a marriage for more years than I can count. Should I have told you?' she asked, unscrewing and then replacing the cap of her mascara in a movement that suggested OCD or nervousness.

If she had mentioned the M-word in the bar he would have run as fast and as far as he could, not even sticking around long enough to hear that she was separated. Was he crazy about the fact that she was still married? No. Was it going to stop him from sleeping with her again? Hell, no.

'I don't sleep with married women,' he stated, and wasn't sure if he was informing her or reminding himself.

Willa met his gaze in the mirror and her aqua eyes were direct and honest. She tossed the tube of mascara onto the counter and slapped her hands on her hips. 'I don't cheat. I haven't slept with anyone else and I would not have slept with you if I'd still felt morally married.'

Rob lifted his hands, slightly amused at her spirited reply. 'Easy there, tiger.'

Willa glared at him. 'So, would *you* cheat if you were married?'

Of course not. But it was a moot point because he had no plans to get married—he couldn't, because marriage meant that he had to trust himself and his judgement when it came to women. And people.

Not gonna happen.

'Well? Would you? *Do* you?' Willa demanded, pulling

him back to this house, on another continent, a lifetime later.

'Sorry—missed that. What did you say?'

'Would you cheat on your wife? On your girlfriend? Is that something you already do?' There was no judgement in her voice, just curiosity.

'What? Cheat?' Rob twisted his lips. 'I'm single, and I don't get involved with anybody long enough for the question to arise.'

Willa released a long, surprised sigh. 'God, you're honest. I haven't met an honest man in a long, long time.'

'You've been hanging around with the wrong crowd, gorgeous; it's the only way to be,' Rob stated. 'So, in the spirit of honesty...do you want to do this again?'

He really didn't want her to say no, Rob realised. He wanted to make love to her again... If she didn't have a house full of people downstairs he'd lift her up onto that counter, spread her legs and pull her panties out of the way. He'd be inside her in a matter of seconds...

And there he went, rising in anticipation.

'You're talking about having sex again?'

At least she hadn't called it *making love*; if she had, he'd have had to correct her.

'Yeah. You keen? Pure sex, pure fun, no obligations or strings.'

'For how long?'

He wasn't idiot enough to make promises he couldn't keep. 'I have no freakin' idea. Once more? Twice? Sixteen times? I don't know...let's just play it by ear.'

Willa was so still and so quiet for such a long time that Rob thought she was about to say no and his heart plummeted. As earlier suggested: *Get a freakin' grip, dammit!*

'Yeah,' Willa said eventually. 'We can do that. Play it by ear.'

'Excellent.'

Rob slowly slowly, put his cup on the shelf next to the door and walked into the bathroom. Then he gripped her hips and easily lifted her up onto the bathroom counter, placing her between the two basins.

'Let's start right now.'

Since she'd just placed her hands on his chest and sucked his lower lip between her teeth, Rob assumed that she had no objections to his suggestion.

When Willa finally made it downstairs and stepped onto the outside entertainment area, still cross-eyed and lost in a lustful funk—she had a lover...*whoo!*—it felt as if she had been transported back eight years to the magical Whitsundays and the Weeping Reef resort. It was in the laughter she heard, the excitement in the voices of her guests, the rhythm of their speech.

She pulled in her breath and allowed the years to roll back to when she'd felt free and happy and sexy and... *happy.* Back then she'd thought that nothing bad could ever happen...and then it had. Amy was attacked and Scott and Brodie's friendship had blown up and everything changed.

She didn't respond well to change or to pain, and her distress that her friends had been hurting, that their magical time on the Whitsundays had ended so brutally, had just pushed her further into the arms of the older, romantic, tell-her-exactly-what-she-needed-to-hear Wayne. She'd felt safe there—cosseted, protected. After all, she'd been shielded from the vagaries of life since she was thirteen by her father, who didn't see why her being an adult should change that.

Note to Dad: life doesn't work that way.

Willa shook off her memories, put a smile on her face and ignored the flutter of nerves in her stomach. Nobody was judging her, waiting for her to fail, she told herself as she was recognised, as conversations were muted and a cluster of her old friends walked over to greet her.

'Oh, it's so good to see you.'

'You look fantastic.'

'Thank you for coming… Have a drink…help yourself to food.'

Willa kissed and hugged her guests, making her way across the veranda, and then Scott was standing in front of her, his arms open wide. Willa gave a cry of delight, stepped into his arms and Scott picked her up and swung her around. She could feel the strength in his arms, the power of his chest. His fabulous green eyes sparkled down at her and he smelled terrific. He was sexy and solid… But, nope, he didn't make her heart or her hormones hop.

'Scott, it's been so long!' she cried, and kissed his cheek.

'Looking good, Wills,' Scott said in his drawling voice, before stepping back to jam his hands into the pockets of his cargo shorts.

Willa, seeing Jessica standing next to Scott, and remembering that, without her help she'd be buzzing around like a demented fly, reached over and squeezed her arm. 'Thanks for setting everything out, Jess.'

'No worries.'

Amy's flatmate, wearing very dark glasses, was nursing what looked like a Bloody Mary. Jeez, she could do with one of those… Her booze hangover was gone, but she suspected that she now had a hangover thanks to too much sex. Don't get her wrong, she wasn't complaining…

Talking of spectacular sex… She turned around and saw Rob helping himself to a beer. 'And this is Rob…'

'Rob Hanson.'

Rob held his hand out for Scott to shake and within minutes was enveloped in his and Jessica's conversation. Seeing that her brand-new lover didn't need babysitting—

thank goodness—Willa sent him a slow smile and turned away to catch up with her friends.

While she played host, gently flirted with her old male friends and caught up with her old girlfriends, she exchanged hot looks with Rob. Even though he was still dressed in last night's jeans and shirt, he looked as if he'd stepped off the cover of a men's magazine. Broad shoulders, long legs, white teeth, and those silver eyes slightly shadowed by blue.

Willa couldn't believe that out of all those sexy girls in the club last night he'd come home with her—that he still wanted more from her. Again, she wasn't complaining… *at all*. She was just surprised and grateful.

Grateful that he was nice and fun and, yeah, *hard*. Skilled…hot.

Willa's conversation with Jane—if she could call Jane's wittering on about pottery classes and her not hearing a word a conversation—was interrupted when Amy grabbed her arm and whirled her away.

Willa sent Jane an apologetic smile but allowed Amy to pull her into a quiet corner. Remembering how curious Amy could be, she waited with lifted brows.

'How long does it take you to shower—or did you get distracted by the good-looking bloke with the funny accent?'

'He doesn't have a funny accent,' Willa protested, hoping to deflect Amy's nosiness.

'*Pfft*. We both know that I'm asking if you got shagged again,' Amy demanded.

'Ames, that's none of your…' Willa looked around and dropped her voice. 'Okay, I did. Again. On the counter of the bathroom and it was *fabulous*.'

'We can all tell,' Amy said dryly. Her expression changed and became a lot more sober. 'Look, I know I sort of pushed you towards him last night, but I thought you'd just flirt with him and it would cheer you up. All this… Well, do you know what you're doing, Wills? He's a nice guy, but he has short-term written all over him.'

Eight years on and she was being shooed away under Amy's wing again. Willa rubbed her shoulder with her hand, thinking that she was a big girl and didn't need to be shooed anywhere any more.

'So he told me. Relax, Ames, I'd be an idiot if I fell for the first man I had sex with after The Pain, and I really am trying not to be an idiot about men any more.'

'Promise?'

'That I'm not going to be an idiot? Well, I promise to try…' Willa smiled. 'So, what are we eating? Drinking?'

Amy gestured to the dining table, piled high with salads, a couple of loaves of fresh bread and various dips. 'I bought enough to feed an army. There are prawns and crayfish in the fridge that the boys can throw on the barbie… wine, beer, coolers to drink.'

Willa looked from the food to her friend. 'You need to tell me what I owe you.'

'Later.'

'Can you believe how many people came? It's amazing…'

'You were always a lot more popular than you realised, Willa,' Amy replied. 'I just wish…'

'That Luke and Brodie and Chantal were here?' Willa finished her sentence. 'Me too.' She took Amy's hand. 'Thank you for doing the food—thank you for making me do this. I feel like the others are just around the corner… like we're waiting for them to arrive.'

'Me too.' Amy looked down at their clasped hands and licked her lips. 'Talking of friends… Did I ever say thanks, Willa? For helping me that night? For picking me up and patching me up?'

Willa looked at the faint scar just below Amy's eye and

acid rolled through her stomach. 'God, I am just so glad that he didn't…you know…'

'Rape me? Yeah, me too. Though he packed a pretty mean punch,' Amy said in a low, bitter tone. 'If it wasn't for you—for Luke—I don't know if I could've got through that night.'

'I wish you hadn't left, Amy. It wasn't the same without you.'

Amy shook her head. 'Honey, how could I stay? I was front of house and I looked like a raccoon, with two black and blue eyes, a split cheek and a fat lip. I couldn't work like that, I didn't want to answer questions from our friends and I couldn't tolerate the idea of seeing Justin again.'

'Luke kicked him off the property and told him never to return. I suspected he also might have punched him… I saw that his knuckles were a bit sore and raw for a couple of days after you left.'

Amy's eyes softened. 'That Luke. I was crazy about him. I only went to the beach with Justin in an attempt to make Luke feel jealous.' Amy looked out onto the harbour. 'Is he okay, Willa? Really?'

Oh, hell, how did she answer that? 'Oh, Ames, I don't know. We're not that close, and he'd never talk to his younger sister if something was worrying him.'

Amy tilted her head. 'Why not?'

'I was thirteen when my mum died and it messed me up. Messed *us* up. Dad wrapped me in cotton wool, and then in bubble wrap, but he left Luke to flounder.'

'I don't understand.'

Hell, she didn't either.

'Luke dealt with Mum's death on his own. Maybe it was because he was older and a young adult already, away at uni, but Dad cosseted me and pretty much ignored Luke. It created a distance between us.'

Her father hadn't done them any favours… She'd grown

up to be spoilt and naïve and Luke had remained on the outside of a family circle reduced to two. She still felt guilty about that, and wished that her father had handled the situation—them—differently. Wished that he'd allowed her to grow up and make some mistakes, allowed Luke to grieve with them instead of encouraging him to work and study his way through his pain.

As a result she'd come to believe that all she needed was a strong man to sort her problems out and protect her from the nasties life could throw her way. Luke had become a highly self-sufficient and extremely independent businessman, with an inability to become emotionally engaged.

'What are you trying to tell me, Willa?'

Don't pin your hopes on him; find a nice man who will love you with everything he has. Luke is too complicated, too self-sufficient, too distant.

Willa started to say the words and then shook her head. The heart wanted what the heart wanted, and nothing she could say would have any effect. And for all she knew she could be barking up the wrong tree.

Willa snagged a cold beer from the fridge and lifted her shoulders in a what-the-hell-do-I know? shrug. 'I don't have a clue, Ames. Ignore me.'

Later that afternoon Willa, with Scott, Rob and Amy, sat at the round wooden table at the far end of the pool, under the shade of a large umbrella. Her other guests—including Jessica, who'd caught a ride with one of the old Whitsundays lifeguards…cute, but not a rocket scientist!—had all left, and the four of them were lazily picking at a selection of snacks as a late-afternoon treat.

Amy leaned across the table and lightly touched Scott's arm. 'I haven't had a chance to speak to you, Scott, and I want to catch up with what's going on in your life. Willa says that you're an architect.'

'Yep.'

'And how's Chantal?'

Willa sucked in a deep breath and winced. With all the craziness she hadn't had time to fill Amy in on exactly what had happened after she'd left the Weeping Reef. 'Uh, Ames…'

Amy ignored her interruption. 'She's not here with you… why not? Are you two still together?'

Scott stared hard at his beer bottle. 'No, we broke up,' he answered eventually.

'When?' Amy demanded.

'How are your folks, Amy?' Willa asked, desperately hoping to change the subject.

Amy waved her question away. 'Fine. I really wish she and Brodie were here. Okay, you obviously don't want to talk about Chantal. Then tell me about Brodie, Scott. How is he? *Where* is he?'

Willa groaned. *Shoot me now.*

Scott smiled thinly, drained his beer, stood up and held out his hand for Rob to shake. He bent down and kissed Willa's cheek. 'Thanks for a great day, Willa. Let's get together again and catch up.'

'No, don't go,' Willa said.

Scott's smile didn't reach his eyes. 'I need to get moving. You stay and tell Miss Curiosity, here—' he ruffled Amy's hair '—about the last episode of the soap opera that was the Weeping Reef.' He lifted his hand and shook his head. 'No, don't get up—I'll let myself out.'

Willa felt sad as she watched Scott walk away. He was such a good guy, but the situation with Brodie and Chantal, old as it was, obviously still bugged him.

She turned to Amy and sighed. 'Well, didn't *you* put your foot in it?'

'In what?' Amy asked, looking around, her expression pure confusion. 'What did I say?'

'I keep forgetting that you weren't there when it all happened…' Willa mused.

'*What* happened?' Amy demanded.

Willa took a breath, leaned back in her seat and rewound. Scott and Chantal: the golden couple of the resort. Scott the head sailing instructor, and perky, talented Chantal—Head of Entertainment—had been an item, and everyone had assumed that they were perfect for each other. No one except her had seemed to notice the sexual tension between Chantal and Brodie, Scott's fellow sailing instructor and his best friend.

It had been a recipe for disaster and it had exploded in their faces the night after Amy had left town.

It had taken one song, one slow dance between Scott's girlfriend and his best friend, for Scott—and everyone else in the room—to see that they both wanted to get naked very, very soon. With each other. The sexual tension and electricity had crackled around them as they'd danced, seemingly oblivious to the fact that everyone—and Scott—was watching them. The song had ended and so had their friendship…

Scott's fist had connected with Brodie's face—resulting in the second black eye in consecutive days—and wild accusations had bounced off the walls. Willa knew that nothing had happened between Scott and Chantal except for excessive heat, but Scott had felt betrayed and Brodie guilty, because he'd firmly subscribed to the notion of 'mates before pretty much everything else'.

Brodie had left and Chantal had walked around as a shadow of her former perky self. Her remaining weeks at the resort, *sans* Amy and Brodie, had been miserable—as Willa now told Amy

When she was finished Amy shook her head. 'But that's stupid,' she stated. 'They only danced! That wasn't a good enough reason to break up—for Brodie and Scott to fight.'

'Yeah, it was,' Rob said quietly. When both pairs of feminine eyes landed on his face he shrugged. 'Guy dances with his best mate's girl and looks like he wants to do her—best mate has grounds to be pissed off. Big-time.'

Amy looked scornful. 'But he didn't *do* anything!'

'It doesn't matter. It was a metaphorical kick to Scott's balls…' Rob rolled his beer bottle between the palms of his hands. 'Did Brodie hit Scott back?'

Willa shook her head. 'No, he just stood there, taking it. Then he walked away and just…left.'

Rob nodded. 'Sounds about right.'

This all seemed very natural and normal to him… Willa pulled her eyebrows together. Were she and Amy missing something critical here? Some subtle male nuance that had completely escaped them because they lacked testosterone and masculine bits and bobs?

'But they haven't spoken for eight years!' Willa protested.

'They'll talk when they're ready to…or not.' Rob stated. 'My advice? Stay out of it.'

Like Amy, Willa just stared at him.

Willa eventually sighed and shook her head. 'Boys are just weird.'

CHAPTER FOUR

AMY, FED, WATERED and out of reminiscences, didn't leave until after six that evening and Willa was exhausted. Her house looked as if a bomb had hit it, and she groaned at the thought of clearing up; she just wanted to climb into a shower and then into her bed.

She stepped into her hall, looked at those steep, floating stairs, walked over to them and sat down on the bottom step. Rob hadn't left yet, and she wasn't sure how she felt about that. Part of her desperately wanted to be alone, to process the fact that in the space of twenty-four hours she'd had her first one-night stand *and* reconnected with most of her friends from Weeping Reef. She was very used to being alone—not so much to having so many people in her space.

'Willa…?'

Willa looked up and smiled at Rob, who'd come into the hall, holding his mobile in his hand. 'Sorry, I just sat down for a moment.'

'You must be exhausted. I know I am.' Rob sat down on the stair next to her. 'I've called for a taxi. It'll be here soon.'

'You don't need to leave…' Willa protested, innately polite but secretly relieved.

Rob briefly touched her hand with his. 'Yeah, I think I do. Neither of us got much sleep last night and it's been a long day.'

Willa picked at the frayed cotton on the hem of her denim shorts. 'I had fun.'

'I imagine that reconnecting with your friends has brought back a truckload of memories,' Rob commented.

Willa smiled. 'Some good, some that make me cringe, or laugh, and others that make me want to cry.'

'Where *are* the...?' Rob snapped his fingers. 'I can't remember the name of the place you met them.'

'The Whitsundays? It's a group of islands in the heart of the Great Barrier Reef.'

'Tell me about them,' Rob commanded gently.

Willa placed her chin in the palm of her hand and her eyes went soft and dreamy. 'Jeez, where do I start? Brilliant sunsets, white sands, fantastic shades of clear water. I dived and snorkelled whenever I could—I was absolutely fascinated by the fish and corals. There's a coral called the weeping coral—that's where the resort we all worked at got its name.'

'And you looked after kids?'

'Yeah, I loved running the kids' activity programme. It filled the days—and at night we partied. Amy taught me to flirt—well, she tried to—and to party. I fell well short of her legendary standards. But I learnt to hold my drink and—as much as I could—to cut loose. I...blossomed.'

'You met your husband there?'

Willa nodded a little forlornly. 'He was older, wiser, and to me—being from a small town where everyone knew, loved and protected me—he seemed so refined. Charisma, confidence and charm. Being noticed by Wayne was a huge ego boost, and after I realised that he was actually interested in me I felt sophisticated and special.'

'As you would.'

She'd tumbled into love with him. In hindsight, she'd probably been more in love with the way he'd made her feel—strong, sexy and stylish. Amy had thought Wayne was too flash, too demanding, and Luke had questioned what a thirty-three-year-old man saw in his country bumpkin teenage sister, but she'd brushed their concerns away... She'd been in love and she'd felt marvellous.

'I was eighteen years old and I thought I knew what I was doing and nobody was going to spoil it for me.' *Yeah, right.*

'I have a theory that there should be a law against anyone making life-changing decisions before they're twenty five.'

Willa picked up the sour note in his voice and tipped her head. 'Did you make some bad choices too?'

'You have no idea.' Rob gestured for her to continue her story. 'Carry on.'

'Something bad happened to Amy that made her leave the resort, and then there was the blow-up between Chantal, Scott and Brodie. I shoved my head into the sand and started spending more and more time with Wayne.'

The dissent at the resort had shoved her further into Wayne's arms… She'd felt safe there, and protected. When she'd been with him she'd had a break from worrying about Amy, and she'd been able to escape the tension between Chantal and Scott.

'At the end of the season he proposed and I accepted. I was marrying a gorgeous, romantic older guy, who would love and take care of me for the rest of my life. What could possibly go wrong?'

'Things obviously did?'

'Yeah—big-time.'

Rob didn't push for more and she appreciated his tact. She'd said more than she'd meant to and she couldn't explain that while there had been love, it had been a distorted version of the emotion. Love on his terms. He'd taken care of her financially, not emotionally, and cheated on her constantly.

His had been a love that was rude, conditional, disparaging. Controlling. That was why she was embarking on this short-term fling with Rob—it was healthy, a positive step in the rehabilitation of Willa. It was honest, it was temporary, it was…straightforward. Direct, undemanding, clear-cut. It was everything she'd never had with Wayne…

And the sex—well, that was nothing like she'd had with her ex. Just the thought of Rob's hot, muscled body made her mouth dry up; she felt tingly and dizzy, feminine and free.

This was the way she'd felt that summer at Weeping Reef—before all the drama. Strong, healthy, sexy…free. Her freedom had been taken away for eight years, but she was not going to waste a second of it now.

Rob spun his mobile around on the palm of his hand with his finger. 'So, you're still okay with the no-strings sex decision we made earlier?'

There was that in-your-face honesty again. God, she loved it. 'Yes.'

Rob placed his hand on her slim thigh and squeezed. 'Good. I'll call you.'

'You don't have my number,' Willa pointed out, leaning her elbows on the step behind her.

'I found your phone and dialled my number—saved my number to your contacts,' Rob explained on an easy grin. 'You don't have that many contacts on your phone, so I should be easy enough to find.'

'I figured that if I didn't have to talk to my ex then I sure didn't have to talk to his snooty friends either. Another of the many benefits of getting divorced. Can I ask you a favour?' she asked, looking at his strong profile.

'Mmm? What?'

'On the day the divorce becomes final, if you are still around, will you help me celebrate by doing something completely wild with me?'

Rob tipped his head. 'Like…?'

'Like a motorbike ride, or bungee-jumping, or sky-diving… Flying to the Whitsundays for a couple of days and doing a wreck dive—I'll pay. I want do something that makes me feel crazily alive and free, and I think you might be the type of guy who would be up for doing that with me.'

'What do I get out of it?' Rob asked, his mouth twitching in amusement.

'Um…crazy sex?' Willa suggested.

'Oh, I intend having crazy sex with you anyway.'

Rob picked up her hand and kissed her open palm, his fabulous eyes hot and heated as they connected with hers.

'Sure, I'll help you celebrate your freedom, Willa. Let me know the day and we'll do something to mark the occasion.'

Rob leaned forward and brushed her lips with his and Willa's heart sighed. His kiss was gentle and sexy—a nibble here, a lick there. It was as if he knew he couldn't take it deeper or further, that they were out of time…for now.

And they were. They had barely started when they heard the toot of a taxi horn.

Rob pulled away and stood up, jamming his hands into the pockets of his jeans. 'I'm going to go…get some sleep. And, Willa?'

'Mmm?'

'The phone works both ways.' Rob waggled his eyebrows. 'You need me for a booty call—don't be shy.'

Willa grinned. 'I might take you up on that.'

'Feel free.'

After kissing Willa's cheek, Amy slid into a chair on the other side of the small table in the outside shaded seating area of Saints, which morphed into a trendy bistro during the day. Amy pushed her designer sunglasses up into her hair and scanned the specials board, quickly ordering a frappe and a goat's cheese salad from the hovering waiter—whose knees, Willa was sure, buckled under the force of her smile.

'Sorry, I'm late. I was in a meeting with Rob.'

Willa, who hadn't heard from Rob since he'd left her house on Sunday, tried not to sound too eager. 'Oh…?'

'Poor guy is looking a bit frazzled. I told him we were meeting for lunch.'

And did he have anything to say to that? Willa growled her frustration as Amy picked up her phone, checked her messages and smiled at a cute guy who was walking past. Ah, this was vintage Amy, who could be annoying as all hell.

Willa picked up her fork and not so gently poked the back of Amy's hand with the tines.

Amy attempted to look innocent, but since the last time she'd been innocent had been when she was in utero, she didn't quite pull it off. 'Oh, you want to know if he gave any reaction…?'

Willa growled again, and lifted the fork in a threatening movement.

'How old did you say you are again?' Amy asked. 'Fifteen?'

Willa sighed and drew patterns on the colourful tablecloth with the fork. 'I know. I'm such a dork.'

Amy laughed and held up her hands in surrender. 'He said that if you asked I was to remind him of your last conversation… Which means what?'

The phone works both ways…booty call.

Willa explained.

'He's right,' Amy said. 'But he doesn't know that you would rather chop off your own head than risk being rejected…'

Willa glared at her. 'I am not eighteen any more!'

'Then call him—tell him you're horny and you want him bad,' Amy challenged her, one eyebrow raised.

Willa felt her neck and cheeks heat up. Hell, she couldn't do that—could she?

'As you said…you are such a dork,' Amy said, with absolutely no malice in her voice. 'Newsflash, honey: girls are allowed to ask boys out.'

'Asking someone out on a date is a bit different from asking someone to come over and take you to bed,' Willa protested.

'Why? It's the twenty-first century.' Amy took the fork from her hand and set it on the table, waited for Willa to meet her eyes. 'That being said, you *are* playing it cool with him, aren't you, Willa?'

'Of course I'm playing it cool, Amy—not that I have much choice. Rob is unfailingly honest—haven't you noticed? I know exactly where I stand and I'm very comfortable being his sex-with-no-strings girl.'

'Okay, as long as you know what you're doing.' Amy grinned. 'He *is* honest, isn't he? Today he told the director of marketing—my boss—that his ideas were crap and that he was paying them for my expertise not his. Since the director has the marketing smarts of a moose, and is only there because he married the owner's daughter, I was cheering. But the sensible part of me remembered that he's my boss, so it was only on the inside! Anyway, are you going to call him?'

'No.'

'Cluck-cluck.'

Willa rolled her eyes. 'You're not going to dare me into making a booty call, Amy.'

Amy said nothing and lounged in her chair, her eyes laughing.

'I'm okay with being a dork, a wuss, a chicken,' Willa protested.

Amy used the same look she'd used to get her to do all those things they shouldn't have as staff members at the Weeping Reef Resort. Skinny-dipping and raiding the kitchen for late-night snacks had been minor transgressions. Doing golf cart doughnuts on the greens of the golf course had been a major misdemeanour—amongst others.

Amy would just wait her out until Willa did what she wanted her to do... Hell, when Willa did what she herself wanted to do. She wanted Rob back in her bed, back inside her, making her eyes cross with pleasure.

Huffing a frustrated sigh, she dug in her bag for her mobile and found the number she now knew by heart.

'Gorgeous,' Rob said, after answering on the second ring.

And that one word and his amused voice gave her courage.

'Booty call,' she whispered softly, ignoring Amy's triumphant grin.

'Tied up until late tonight,' Rob answered, just as briefly. 'I can be there around eleven.'

'I'll be up.'

Willa disconnected and held up a finger. 'Not one word!'

'Not one word except that I am mega impressed. Short, succinct, direct,' Amy said cheerfully. 'Okay, that was a whole bunch of words. Changing the subject.... I love your shoes.'

Willa looked down at her strappy high-heeled sandals. 'I'd like them more if I'd paid for them... I need a job, Amy. I need to *do* something.'

'You've got your degree, Wills, and you've got a Masters! Surely there must openings somewhere?' Amy sat back as the waiter placed her iced coffee in front of her.

Willa sighed. 'I was offered a job about two months ago—a really nice position with a new clothing brand—but Kate didn't want me to take it in case it jeopardised my divorce claim. I kept telling her that I'd rather have the job than the money, but she advised me to sit tight.'

'I'd like to meet her,' Amy said. 'She sounds nice.'

'She really is—and she's a damn good lawyer. I want

to be her when I grow up. She's a high-achieving, competent and highly confident woman—she definitely doesn't need a man. That being said, she does get very protective over her clients… You should have seen her wipe the floor with Wayne's smug attitude. She had him tied up in knots—his lawyer too.'

Amy smiled in appreciation. 'Just for that she has my unending appreciation. Anyway, getting back to you and a job…have you applied anywhere else?'

'I haven't seen any openings and I've been looking. I think the type of accounting job I'm aiming for needs experience, or contacts, or a network—or something else that I don't have. I'm *good*, Ames—or at least I could be good if someone gave me a damn chance,' Willa replied bitterly. 'I just feel so…useless. I sneaked around for years, getting that cursed degree, and nobody seems to want to see me put it to use!'

'I take it The Pain wasn't exactly supportive of your studying?'

Willa snorted.

She'd begged Wayne to allow her to study but he'd laughed away her ambitions. Even if he had said yes she'd known that keeping up with her course work while following her husband around the world like a lapdog would be impossible.

It had only been when Wayne had started leaving her at home in their luxury penthouse apartment—probably around the time he'd engaged in his first affair—that she'd signed up for an online degree and studied in secret, knowing how dismissive and cruel Wayne could be. There had simply been no point in giving him more ammunition to take pot-shots at her…

When he'd found her graduation papers, hidden under the lavender-scented drawer lining of her lingerie drawer—why he'd been looking in her panty drawer still boggled the brain—he'd been, as she'd suspected, completely dismissive, belittling her dreams of having any type of professional career, and also furious because she'd pulled the wool over his eyes.

That argument—and the fact that he'd had smudged lipstick on his jawline—had been the final straw, the last nail in the coffin, the excuse she'd been looking for to walk away from him...and to keep on walking, straight into a lawyer's office.

'No, he wasn't supportive. Anyway, let's not talk about him. But if you hear of anything will you let me know?'

'Sure. So, I had a drink with Scott and he told me that you guys met for coffee yesterday?'

'We did. And Brodie sent me a message apologising for not making the party. He's invited us both out to lunch next week as he's in Sydney.'

'But he didn't invite Scott?'

Willa's chest lifted in frustration. 'Nope. Anyway, I looked at Brodie's photos online and, while he was always a good-looking guy, it looks like he's lifted *sexy* to a whole new level. So has Scott, actually.'

'I know. I thought that too,' Amy replied, wrinkling her nose. 'But the thought of doing either of them is like...'

'Creepy? Incesty?'

'Yeah—that! I feel like I'm perving over my brother!' Amy looked relieved. 'I thought it was only me...I'm glad you feel the same.'

'Maybe it's got something to do with the fact that we've seen them snot-drunk and puking?' Willa mused, but knew that, for her, it was more the fact that neither of them—good-looking devils that they were—could hold a candle to the man who'd shared her bed on Saturday night. Who'd share her bed tonight...

And she suspected that, for Amy, neither of them

matched up to a certain man in Singapore who was also her brother.

Dammit.

The doorbell rang at about eleven-thirty and Willa put her hand on her stomach as she left the library and walked down the passage to the hall. She was dressed in a brief T-shirt and briefer denim shorts and her feet were bare... This was a booty call and she hadn't bothered to dress up—mostly because she wanted to get naked as soon as possible.

Willa opened the front door and there he was, standing beneath the porch light. Her heart bounced off a rib and she licked her lips, looking for any moisture she could find. In a pair of smart grey suit pants, a pale blue shirt and grey tie, he looked tall, rangy, fit...businesslike.

Willa connected with his eyes and sighed... Along with lust—and there was a lot of that in his eyes—she saw frustration and stress and a whole bunch of exhausted.

'Hey...' she murmured, grabbing his tie and pulling him inside.

'Hey back.' Rob put his hands on her hips, his thumbs skimming the strip of bare skin between her shorts and T-shirt. But instead of kissing her, he laid his forehead on hers and sighed.

Willa hooked her hand abound the back of his neck and felt the tension in his rock-hard muscles. 'Bad day?'

'Frustrating rather than bad. Sorry I'm late.'

'No worries. Want a drink?'

Willa took his hand and led him to the kitchen, directing him to a bar stool before opening the fridge door and pulling out a bottle of wine.

Rob wrinkled his nose. 'Light, calorie-free wine? Got any whisky?'

'Sure.'

Willa replaced the wine and turned to a cupboard next to

the fridge. She pulled out a bottle of Macallan and swore she heard Rob groan in appreciation. Pouring two fingers into a tumbler, she added ice and handed it over. Rob sipped, closed his eyes, and rested the glass against his forehead.

The man was exhausted, Willa realised. The shadows she'd seen under his eyes at the weekend were now solid purple stripes. He'd scraped the scruff off his face, but she could see stress in his hard jaw, in the deepening of the fine lines around his face.

'You okay, Rob?'

Rob ran a hand across his face. 'Yeah, sorry…little distracted. It's been a couple of long, tense, tough days.'

'Any particular reason?'

'Just the normal stress when you're trying to set up a business in a foreign country. The rand also weakened substantially today, which shrinks our capital.'

His days had been more than difficult—they'd been brutal. She could tell by the stress in his shoulders, the banked anger, the waves of frustration.

'We don't have to do this tonight. If you'd rather go… do.' Willa licked her lips. 'Don't feel like you have to stay.'

Rob put his glass down on the granite counter-top, leaned forward and hooked his finger in the V of her shirt, pulling her gently towards him. 'There's nowhere else I'd rather be. I've been thinking of you, remembering you… under me, wet and warm…every night and a whole lot during the day. Sexy daydreams of you have been hell on my productivity.'

Well, then… Okay…

Rob's hands skimmed up her sides and his thumbs whispered over her breasts—a teasing hint of pleasure to come. Willa felt warm, moist lust between her legs as she stepped between Rob's open thighs, almost swallowing her tongue at the sight of the long, thick ridge in his pants.

'I need to be inside you,' Rob muttered, his mouth against her neck, making her shiver.

Willa pulled his tie, then left it loose as she worked to undo the buttons on his shirt. Then she pulled his shirt apart and placed her hands on his warm, masculine skin. She could smell his deodorant, soap, and warm, excited, turned-on male.

'I need you to be inside me.' Willa told him, scraping her nails across his flat nipples, down his ribcage and over his ridged abdominal muscles.

And she did. She'd never felt quite as alive, as fulfilled, as she had when Rob had been inside her, rocking her into oblivion. Willa dropped her hand over his crotch and lightly cupped him. She tipped her head back to smile into his eyes before stepping away from him and holding out her hand.

When he stood and enveloped her hand in his much broader, stronger one she sent him a slow smile. 'Come to bed and let's get naked.'

Rob's eyes lightened and he flashed her one of his devastating grins. 'You really are getting the hang of this booty call stuff.'

Setting up a business in a foreign country was a pain, Rob thought, pressing the doorbell of Willa's idiotically big house, and it was full of stupidities and intricacies that he didn't find back home. So why, instead of working his way through the pile of documents that sat on the desk—as Patrick was doing at the moment, in the two-bedroomed apartment he'd rented in the city—was he standing here hoping she'd open the door?

And why *wasn't* she opening the door? he wondered, looking around. Her little Mercedes sat in the driveway and he could hear music—hard rock and loud—coming from somewhere inside the house.

Turning the knob on the door, he frowned when it

opened soundlessly. Burglars? Rapists? Murderers? *Willa... haven't you heard of those?* He walked into the massive hall, deliberately ignoring the green monstrosity that called itself art on the wall.

Rob left the keys to the SUV he'd rented and his wallet and mobile on the hall table, made sure that the front door was locked, and then walked through the house in the direction of the music, looking into rooms as he walked down the passage.

Massive reception room with heavy furniture and an air of emptiness, a library/TV lounge that looked messy and lived-in, and a formal dining room with a huge dining table and more weird art.

The music was increasing in volume and he looked to his right, where he saw a short flight of stairs. Walking down them, he lifted his brows when he saw the fully equipped gym downstairs. He whistled in appreciation at the up-to-date equipment: she had most of what he intended to put in *his* gyms.

A massive plasma screen TV covered half of one wall and on the mat in front of it was a sweaty and puffy Willa—dressed in the tiniest pair of gym shorts and a T-back crop-top—trying to follow the instructions of a Tae Bo instructor. Kick, punch, side kick...

Rob smiled, Willa was about as co-ordinated as a newly born giraffe—all arms and legs heading in different directions.

Rob looked around, found the music system and hit the 'off' button. Willa whirled around at the silence. She caught a glimpse of him and screamed, instinctively lifted a barbell above her head.

Rob grinned and lifted up his hands. 'Relax, Wills, it's me.'

Willa lowered the weight and glared at him. 'Thanks

bunches—you just took ten years off my life. Do you normally stroll into people's houses and scare them to death?'

'I wouldn't have strolled in at all if you hadn't left your front door unlocked! That's stupid!'

Willa tapped her foot on the exercise mat and he could see the irritation on her face.

'And do you normally stroll into people's houses with no notice and call them *stupid*?'

Rob nodded, acknowledging the criticism. She might have got married when she was a baby but she wasn't anyone's push-over—or at least not any more.

'Sorry...let's start again. Hi, how are you?'

He could see her debating whether she should give him more grief, but then her shoulders dropped and the moment passed.

'Hi back.' She ran her hand over her forehead and grimaced at her sweaty fingers. 'Yuck. Sorry—not at my freshest...'

'There's nothing wrong with a bit of sweat.' He looked around again. 'This is impressive, Willa. Did you buy the equipment?'

Willa picked up a gym towel and rubbed the back of her neck and her face. 'No, it all came with the house. Wayne-the-Pain bought the house shortly before we separated; the entire house and all its contents were up for auction. That's one of the things he does—snaps up properties for a song and resells them. He bought the place—all furniture, art, gym equipment included—and moved me into it until we finalised the divorce. Then I hired Kate as my lawyer and she decided that I should keep it as a sorry-I-cheated present.'

'Hell of a present,' Rob said, inspecting a brand-new, never-been-used rowing machine. 'So you don't use the equipment?'

'It intimidates the hell out of me,' Willa replied, heading for a small bar fridge and pulling out a bottle of water.

He nodded when she offered him one and caught the bottle she tossed in his direction with one hand. After cracking the lid and swallowing half the bottle, she nodded at the instructor on the big screen, who was still kicking and punching.

'I stick to Tae-Bo and Pilates. And I run.'

'I could show you how to use it properly if you'd like,' Rob suggested, moving to a treadmill and pressing the computer to see its functions. He whistled, impressed. It was top of the line and, again, unused. What a waste.

Willa walked back to the mat and sat down under the air-conditioning vent. 'Have you always been sporty?' she asked. 'Is that why you do what you do?'

Rob shot her a quick look, about to give her his stock answer—that he'd always been sporty and going into the fitness industry had been a natural progression for him. He *was* sporty, and it *had* been a natural progression for him. But his Uncle Sid's gym—that smelly, masculine environment—had been the place he'd run to after his dad died.

'My dad died when I was sixteen, I used to go to my uncle's gym with him. It was the place where I still felt connected to my dad.'

After his mum had split from Stefan, leaving him with an inability to trust and a zero tolerance for bullies, exercise had been the way he'd held the demons of guilt and recrimination at bay.

'My Uncle Sid wanted to retire, and when I had the opportunity to buy a half-share of his gym along with Patrick, his son, I jumped at the chance.'

And three years later he and Patrick had had a string of sports equipment and clothing stores and a handful of men-only gyms. Now, ten years later, they were expanding into Australia.

'And that was your first business?'

'Mmm. We kept the gym a men-only operation—kept it low-key and unpretentious but brilliantly equipped—and it started gaining a reputation as a place for serious athletes who paid less attention to how they looked and more attention to how they felt. We encourage our clients to be strong, healthy, balanced, fit—we don't support bodybuilding for the sake of bodybuilding.'

Rob lifted his eyes from the monitor to see Willa looking quizzically at him.

'I don't believe in it. I use the machines because they have a place in a workout, but I—and my staff—encourage our clients to use a range of exercise techniques. Martial arts, Pilates, running, swimming, boxing...'

Willa leaned back on her hands and stretched out her legs. 'I still don't think that opening another gym in today's market is a good idea.'

Rob swung the punchbag as he moved over to the mat and sat down next to her. 'You need to stretch or else you're going to stiffen up.'

He waited until Willa had grabbed her toes and groaned as her muscles pulled.

'I have actually done some research, Willa,' he said mildly. 'I've visited a number of the competition's gyms in various areas and, while they are suitable for daily use, the staff and the atmosphere don't work for a serious athlete. The people I am targeting for my three gyms are hardcore athletes—sportsmen who need more intensive training. My gyms come with personal trainers who are a class above; they can design programs tailored to individuals. I'll have physiotherapists and dieticians on the premises, biokinetics.'

Willa just looked at him and he could see the wheels in her head turning.

'Sounds expensive.'

'It *is* expensive, but market research tells me that there are many people—and sports organisations—willing and prepared to pay the price to get the results. There's a big gap in the market and I intend to fill it.'

'You sound confident,' Willa said, stretching her arms over her head.

Her breasts lifted and her nipples, easily discernible through her crop-top, pebbled. His mouth dried up and his shorts tightened.

'I am confident…if we get through the damn paperwork required to set up a business by a foreigner in your country.'

Willa's face brightened. 'I could help you with that.'

Yeah… Sorry, gorgeous, but I'm not trusting my brand-new business to someone with a degree but no experience. Even if *I* think you're smart…

'Patrick, my cousin, is an accountant, and he's here with me. He's sorting it out.'

'Okay.' Willa's lips twisted as she stood up, hurt flashing in her eyes.

Feeling as if he'd kicked her cat, and not sure why, Rob gently hooked his leg around her calves and tumbled her back down to the mat. She fell on her back, as he'd intended her to, and within seconds he was leaning over her, his hands on either side of her face.

Brushing her mouth with his—once, twice—he smiled. 'Want to fool around?'

He saw her intake of breath and watched as her neck and cheeks flushed at the memory of shared pleasure. Her eyes deepened with lust as her hands sneaked up under his shirt and skittered over his abs, around and down…

'I'm all sweaty,' Willa protested, but not very convincingly.

'I own gyms. Sweat doesn't scare me.' Rob grinned his pirate grin. 'And, honey, you're about to get a whole lot sweatier.'

CHAPTER FIVE

WILLA AND ROB were on the pier below her house. His feet were dangling in the warm waters of Parsley Bay, the sun was setting, and she was lying flat-out, her head resting on Rob's muscular thigh.

She looked up at him. His eyes were hidden behind wraparound sunglasses but he practically oozed testosterone. She was quite certain that if she looked closely she would be able to see it bubbling out from every pore. And it wasn't only his hard, muscular body that screamed it—he had a don't-mess-with-me attitude that melted women's panties and made men wary.

Yet he was, to all intents and purposes, still a stranger. It seemed strange that he could know her body so well, and she his, but she didn't even know the bare bones of his life.

'Where do you live in South Africa?'

Rob, his palms behind him on the deck, looked down at her. 'Jo'burg...Johannesburg,' he corrected. 'I live in a suburb called Sandton in our family home.'

Okay, he'd said that there was no significant other in his life, but she thought she'd check. 'Alone?'

'No, I live there with my six wives and ten kids,' Rob said wryly. 'Actually, I share the house with my younger sister Gail.'

'Parents?'

'My mum lives about ten minutes away. I told you that my dad died when I was a teenager.'

Willa knew that his hard-as-nails, don't-go-there voice was enough warning for anyone to back off and change the subject—but, strangely, Rob didn't intimidate her at all. He could be gruff and tactless and brutally honest but he was a straight-shooter. If he didn't want to talk, he wouldn't.

In case he felt like volunteering any more personal information she kept her eyebrows raised, pushing for more.

'Stop batting your eyelashes at me, Willa. Won't work.'

Rob brushed her hair from her face before putting his hand back on the deck. See, he could be all grumpy and grouchy and then he did something tender that blew her away.

She loved his tender…

Well, he didn't have to talk—but she could. And maybe her opening up would encourage him to do the same. So she sat up and sat cross-legged on the deck, facing his shoulder.

'My mum died when I was thirteen,' Willa said, after topping up their wine glasses. 'Brain aneurysm. One moment I had this perfect life and the next it was shattered. Luke, my brother, was at uni, so it was my dad and I. We lived in a small town, and everyone was *so* determined to make sure that nothing dreadful happened to me again.'

'Did that work for you?' Rob asked, bending one knee and resting his forearm on it.

'Nope—life doesn't work like that.' Willa flashed him a quick smile. 'I sort of believe that life is a series of lessons you are sent here to learn and no one can stop you learning them—no matter how hard they try.'

Intriguing, Rob thought. 'And what lessons have you been sent to learn?'

'Well, I haven't figured them all out yet, but I think that one of them is that I'm stronger than people thought I was. Stronger than *I* thought I was.'

'Explain.'

He sounded bossy, but Willa didn't mind. Rob wouldn't use ten words when one would do.

Willa was about to speak when she pulled back and

shook her head. No, she didn't think she would, thank you very much. Talking was a give and take affair, and if he wasn't prepared to reveal his secrets then neither would she.

'Another time,' Willa said, her voice resolute but not bitchy. She knew that he wouldn't push for more…she wasn't giving any man anything that she didn't get in return.

Besides, she reminded herself, this relationship was about fun and sex—not about probing each other's psyches.

'This is a beautiful spot, Wills,' Rob said, looking across the bay and the harbour towards the bridge.

'It is, isn't it?' Willa agreed as the setting sun hurled streaks of red and yellow across the sky. 'I'm not overly fond of the furnishings, but I love the house.'

'You didn't bring any stuff from your previous place?'

'Nothing to bring,' Willa explained. 'I have some furniture of my mum's that's in storage. Wayne wouldn't let me put it in our house because it didn't fit in with the vision of the interior designer.'

Rob muttered an expletive under his breath and Willa grinned.

'He is exactly that. Anyway, I'll use my mum's stuff when I know what I'm doing with this place.'

'Are you going to sell it?'

'Dunno. As I said—love the house, hate the furnishings. I don't *need* to sell it. Kate's negotiated me quite a settlement and I could live off that for a long, long time if I'm careful. Selling the house would mean that I could live very comfortably without ever lifting a finger, but I want a job—want to kick-start my career. I'm ten years behind everyone else—which is stupid because I *am* smart, dammit!'

'Never said you weren't,' Rob said, keeping his voice even. 'But what you are is inexperienced.'

'And how am I supposed to get some experience if no

one will give me a chance?' Willa cried. 'I'm so frustrated I could spit spiders.'

'You've just got to keep knocking on doors.'

'Easier said than done,' Willa muttered into her glass.

'It could be worse. You could be sitting in a crappy apartment, drinking cheap wine and eating a hunk of stale bread,' Rob pointed out.

'True. Did I start whining there?' Willa asked, cocking her head.

'It was close. And I don't do whining...it makes me impatient.'

'I think you're impatient anyway.'

'True enough,' Rob agreed, looking as if he was mulling an idea over in his head. 'You should sell the contents of the house if you hate them—the art has to be worth something—and keep the house if you like it. I'd be willing to make you an offer on the gym equipment you're not using.'

Willa frowned. 'Seriously? Why?'

'Because it's never been used and because it's top of the range—the latest models. You interested in that? I'd leave you with a couple of machines, after showing you how to use them correctly—the basics of what you'd need to train.'

Willa mulled his suggestion over. 'Let me think about it...talk to Kate. There's nothing I can do until I sign the papers anyway.'

'Do that,' Rob said. 'I'll put the offer down on paper in the meantime.'

'Yeah, okay... Kate would insist on that. She loves paper,' Willa said. 'I suppose I should get an art appraiser in.'

'Wouldn't hurt,' Rob replied. 'Sorry—won't make you an offer on the art; it's bloody ugly.'

'I think so too,' Willa agreed. 'And it gives me the creeps.' She drained her glass and, putting it down, whipped her shirt off, revealing the top of a lime-coloured bikini. 'I'm going to swim. You coming?'

'Only if I can feel you up underwater.'

'I'm sure that that is one offer I *can* take you up on.' Willa dropped her shorts and dived off the pier, surfacing a long way away. 'Come on in—the water is divine!'

Rob pulled off his shirt, dropped his glasses and dived into the bay, and Willa sighed in pleasure as he swam to her, his long length cutting through the water with ease. When he popped up next to her she looped her arms around his neck and her legs around his waist.

Deciding that he was fit enough to tread water for both of them, she brushed her lips against his, then again with more heat as his hand slid beneath her bikini bottom and covered one butt cheek.

Willa nipped his bottom lip and then soothed the bite of pain away with her warm tongue. He immediately shot up—zero to let's-get-naked in three seconds—and from the glint in his eyes she knew that he wanted to haul her back to shore and get her to a place where he could bury himself, long and deep, inside her.

This was crazy, she thought, and wild. And because it was so crazy, and so wild, it couldn't last.

Willa felt a pang somewhere in the region where her heart resided and scoffed at herself.

You don't need it to last, Moore-Fisher, you just need to enjoy it.

Enjoy him.

And that, she admitted as his mouth settled over hers and he whirled her into another soul-scorching kiss, she had no difficulty doing.

Rob and Patrick left the building housing Amy's marketing company and stepped into the late-afternoon, still furnace-hot sunshine. Yanking their sunglasses from their jacket pockets, they slipped them over their eyes and immediately shrugged out of their suit jackets. Walking down the pavement to their rented SUV, which they'd miraculously found parking for two blocks down, they rolled up their shirt sleeves and yanked down their ties.

Rob was checking his mobile messages when his cousin's fist ploughed into his bicep.

'What the hell…?' Rob snapped his head up and glared at Patrick, who was pretending that he hadn't just sucker-punched him. 'What was that for?'

'That was for you wandering off into Never-Never Land and letting me answer all those marketing questions!' Patrick lifted his hand and pointed his thumb at his own chest. 'Me accounting—you marketing and sales and blowing smoke up people's butts.'

'I was there,' Rob protested, but without conviction.

He hadn't been, really. He'd spent most of the meeting staring at a picture on Amy's office wall. It had been of Willa and Amy, younger, plumper and a great deal happier, mugging it up for the camera. Willa's face radiated happiness and joy and a love of life. *That's how she should look all the time*, he'd thought.

Patrick's fist made him take a step sideways again, and he felt pins and needles rocket up his arm. He cursed Patrick roundly. 'What did I do *now*?' he demanded.

'Who are you? Freaking Peter Pan? You keep wafting away—dreaming of Tinkerbell, probably!' Patrick stopped as they approached the SUV and put his hands on his hips. 'Is this about the girl? The one you and Amy talked about before we started the meeting?'

'What girl?'

'Now he's going to be coy. The girl you've been sneaking out to see. The one whose bed you frequently sleep in. *That* girl, moron.'

Rob opened the car doors and they climbed inside. Rob immediately started the engine to get the air-con going.

'Willa—her name is Willa,' he finally admitted. He took a deep breath and jumped. 'Want to meet her?'

If he hadn't been so surprised at the words that had come out of his mouth he would have laughed at Patrick's bugged-out expression. Then his smart-ass cousin recovered and put a hand behind his ear.

'Sorry, run that by me again. Did you invite me to *meet her*?'

'More fool me,' Rob muttered.

'You *never* introduce me to your women. What's different about this one?'

There was a question he couldn't answer.

'I'm going to dinner and you're going back to the flat. I thought you might like to get out instead,' Rob stated as he adjusted the vents to get cold air blowing at his face.

Patrick called BS, as he'd known he would. Then he reached for his mobile and grinned gleefully. 'I've *got* to tell Heather about this.'

'You are such a girl,' Rob grumbled as he pulled out into the traffic. 'Willa is a woman I met. There's no need to get excited. It's food, some beers—that's it.'

'Followed by hot sex for you and for me Mrs Hand—'

Rob rocketed a fist into Patrick's shoulder. '*Blergh*. Thanks for the visual. Now I need to bleach my brain. Look, about Willa—we're just having a...a thing while I'm here.'

'A thing, huh? Well, that's got to be an improvement on one-night stands.'

'Don't get excited. She's not a keeper.'

'Is she hot?' Patrick demanded, before banging the side of his head with the flat of his hand. 'Sorry—stupid question. They are *always* hot.'

'Do you want to meet her or not?' Rob demanded, irritated.

'Hell, yeah.'

'Then shut the hell up and do *not* embarrass me at dinner. No stories about high school or university or anything else,' Rob threatened.

Although this conversation was *very* high school, he admitted.

Patrick grinned. 'You, the king of I-don't-care-what-anyone-thinks, wanting to make a good impression?' He lifted his mobile again, waving it around. 'Heather, baby, get your ice skates on—because hell just froze over!'

'I really don't know why Heather married you and not me. One of these days she's going to realise that you're a pain in the ass and she'll dump you for me,' Rob grumbled.

'You wish,' Patrick snapped back, but his face softened at the thought of his wife and four-year-old daughter.

Rob softened too; little Kiley was his goddaughter and the unofficial love of his life.

'Can I at least tell Willa about the time you streaked across that polo field at James Golding's wedding?'

Rob's look threatened to cut him off at the knees.

'Or the time you drank that red wine and spewed all over your girlfriend's mother's priceless Persian rug?'

God, what he wouldn't do to be able to kick Patrick out of the vehicle. Had he always been this much of a pain and he just hadn't noticed?

Patrick's mobile rang in his pocket.

'Saved by the bell… Hey—hi, Dad. I'm having a freaky moment because your favourite nephew is taking me to meet a *girl*!'

Patrick listened for a moment, and then Rob sucked in his breath when all the colour drained from his cousin's face.

'What?' Rob demanded. 'What is it?'

'You need to get me to the airport. Now.'

* * *

After she'd received a text from Rob saying that he couldn't make dinner at Saints, Willa spent the evening trawling the net, looking for job opportunities in accounting and business and wishing plagues of blood-sucking locusts on every advertiser who used the words 'experienced' or 'proven track record'. And there were a lot.

Willa banged her head against the sleek desk in the study-cum-library, empty of books but full of light, and cursed the prickling in her eyes that suggested tears were a hair's breadth away.

She was starting to get desperate, and was actually thinking that she should call the one person who could land her a job with just a call or two. Wayne-the-Pain had connections on Mars, and any of the many accountancy firms he'd had dealings with over the years would find a position for anyone he suggested.

There was just a tiny problem with that scenario—actually, two problems. The first was that she'd rather boil her head in tar than ask him for anything, and the second was that he thought she had the intelligence of a tree stump.

Oh, and there was also a number three problem. The Pain thought that she had bought her degree with *his* money.

So, to summarise, calling her ex was not an option.

Willa banged her forehead on the desk again and just stayed there, her cheek lying on the cool surface.

'You look like I feel,' Rob said.

Willa lifted her head and looked at him, tall and strong, standing in the doorway to her study, hands gripping the doorframe above his head, biceps bulging. He often stood like that, and Willa knew that he had no idea how sexy he looked.

'Your front door was unlocked again.'

She had to start being more conscientious about that.

She was no longer living in an apartment with a private lift and a twenty-four-seven doorman.

Rob walked over to her, briefly covered her lips in a kiss hello, and perched his butt on the edge of the desk. He ran his hand through his hair and looked out of the window. He looked tired again, she thought, and worried. The fine lines around his eyes were deeper and his lips were compressed in a tight line.

Willa placed her feet on the desk and nudged his thigh with her big toe. 'Are you okay? You look played out.'

Rob picked up a glass paperweight and tossed it from hand to hand. 'I just had to take my cousin to the airport. His wife and little girl—my goddaughter—have had a car accident and both are in hospital.'

Willa dropped her feet with a bang. 'Oh, no! Are they okay?'

'Kiley, their baby girl, is in for observation, and Heather has a broken collarbone and a couple of broken ribs. Lacerations. Obviously Patrick needs to be with them, so we raced to the airport and got him on the first flight out. I thought about going with him but he said that it's not necessary; we have lots of family in Jo'burg to help out and there's so much to do here.'

'I'm sorry, Rob. I'm sure they'll both be fine.'

A muscle ticked in Rob's jaw as he stared out of the huge windows that overlooked the pool.

'I know…and I really feel crap and selfish for thinking this…but…' he dropped an F-bomb '…this couldn't have happened at a worse time. I need Patrick *here*. He was wading through and more importantly understanding the minefield we're negotiating to get these companies set up. I thought that the officials back home liked red tape, but your government is giving them a damn good run for their money. It should be simple. I want to open a business, pay your exorbitant taxes, employ some of your people and make some money. Why does it have to be so frigging difficult?'

'It's not—'

Rob spoke over her. 'Patrick won't be back for weeks, and now I have to find someone I can work with in a city where I know no one. I suppose asking for someone I can trust would be like asking for moon dust.'

'You know *me*. And you can trust me.'

'I don't trust anyone—and, sorry, but I don't think you can help me out with this particular problem,' Rob muttered, jumping off the desk to pace the area in front of the windows.

Willa glared at his back. 'And what does that mean?'

Rob ignored her question, his mind millions of miles away. 'Didn't you say that your ex is a hotshot businessman? Who does *he* use?'

'Excuse me?' Willa managed to get the words out as a fine red mist descended in front of her eyes.

'Who are his accountants? Come on—surely you know that much?' Rob retorted, impatient.

Willa climbed to her feet, pulling in deep breaths as she struggled to hold on to her bubbling temper. 'Are you *kidding* me?' she gasped, feeling side-winded by his lack of sensitivity. And, worse, hurt. Dammit, she'd promised herself that she wasn't going to allow men to hurt her any more! 'You son of a bitch!'

'What?' Rob frowned. 'What's your problem?'

'You! *You're* my friggin' problem! Asking me about Wayne's connections! In between shagging me, did you even hear anything I said about what I studied? What I'd like to do?' Willa shouted. Oh, wow, another part of her wondered, when had she last shouted? Lost her temper?

That would be, like, *never*.

'You studied accounting… What's that got to do with me?' Rob asked.

Willa felt like launching the glass paperweight at his head. She waited until he'd connected the dots and then he looked puzzled.

'Oh, come on, Willa—you don't *really* think that you can take Patrick's place?'

Willa slapped her hands on her hips. 'Why the hell not?'

'Because he's got fifteen years of business experience, has been a CA for ten, and I trust him with my life and—more importantly—with our business!' Rob snarled. 'Are you seriously suggesting that you can do his job? You don't even have any experience in bookkeeping!'

'I'd like someone to give me some damn credit!'

Willa bent down and yanked open the deep drawer of the desk. She pulled a folder out of the concealed filing cabinet. Slapping it onto the desk, she flipped it open and removed some pages. Stomping over to him, she smacked the papers against his chest.

'I have a Master's degree in commerce. I graduated summa cum laude. In case you've forgotten what that means, that's the highest honours. I majored in accountancy and business law. I am *not* a freaking bookkeeper!'

Willa's chest heaved and bright splotches appeared on her throat and neck. 'You insensitive, insulting…*clod*! Now, take a walk back through my unlocked door and keep walking! Not even your excellent skills in the sack are worth putting up with this amount of BS and such lack of respect from you!'

Rob looked at the certificates in his hand and closed his eyes. 'Dammit, Willa, I'm—'

If she couldn't have his respect then she definitely didn't need his apologies.

Holding up her hand to stop him talking, she shook her head. 'Stop. Just get out.'

Rob looked stubborn. 'I'm not leaving.'

Willa narrowed her eyes; he was either six one or six

two of solid muscle, and she'd need a crane or the police to shift him if he didn't want to move. She had no intention of using either. 'Fine. Then I'll leave.'

Striding towards the door, she blinked back tears as she looked at the ceiling. *One teeny, tiny break here, universe? Any chance of that, huh?*

Hours and too many tears later, Willa walked into her kitchen and closed her eyes when she saw Rob at the stove, a pink apron tied around his hips. It took a man very secure in his masculinity to pull that look off—then again, she knew that Rob had no issues with his masculinity. Neither did she. But as cute as he looked—and he did look cute in his black basketball shorts, red T-shirt and the frothy pink apron—she was still not happy that he was in her space, in her house, in her life…

Okay, that was a lie; maybe she was a little happy. He might be a stupid, insensitive male, but he was still pretty. And it looked as if he was making…was that pot roast? Striding over to the oven, she yanked open the door, nearly smacking Rob in the shoulder as she did so. Damn— missed. She wished she'd had a better aim or he'd had slower reactions.

Pot roast, roasted vegetables, peas…all her favourites. She was instantly catapulted back to helping her mum make Sunday lunch.

Willa bit her lip as Rob gently shut the door, and she didn't resist when he linked his arms around her stomach and pulled her back into his chest.

'How did you know?' she whispered.

'Know what?'

'To make me that…it's my favourite meal ever.'

Rob turned her around and pushed her fringe out of her eyes. 'I didn't. I was just hungry and I was looking for something to do while you got over your—'

Willa glared at him and he was smart enough to snap off his words.

'While I waited for you.' Rob rubbed her cheekbone with his thumb as his hand clasped the side of her face. 'I'm sorry that I hurt you. That what I said came across as me insulting your intelligence.'

Willa sighed. 'You *did* insult my intelligence,' she pointed out.

'I questioned your experience, Willa, not your degree— which is impressive, by the way.'

Willa stepped away from him and held her hand against her forehead. 'It doesn't make the sting go away, Rob! Tell me, please, how am I supposed to prove to anyone—you— that I can do the job if no one—you—will allow me to prove that I can?'

Rob walked away from her and went to the fridge, pulling out a bottle of beer. 'Want a glass of wine?' he asked.

Willa glanced at the wall clock, surprised to see that it was past nine—way past wine o'clock. And, dammit, she needed a little pick-me-up. 'Hell, yes.'

Rob pulled a bottle of wine from the fridge and took the glass that Willa handed him. So working for him was out of the question. She understood, intellectually, that she was too inexperienced for him to trust her with his precious company. Her business brain understood his reluctance, but the rest of her wanted to pound her fists against his chest and wail like a child, screaming that the world was a horrible, unfair place.

Nobody had ever said that life was fair, she reminded herself.

Rob took a long pull of his beer and Willa couldn't help noticing the masculine up and down movement of his throat, the width of his shoulders. His eyes were more blue than grey today. He met her gaze and passion, hot and wild, arced between them. Instead of moving towards her, as she'd expected him to, he lowered the bottle and slid onto a bucket-shaped stool at the granite counter.

'I went to every single bank I could to raise the money to buy into my uncle's gym. Every single bank manager I met—all of them fat and unfit, I might add—told me that I had no collateral. I didn't. And, worse, I had no experience.'

Willa leaned her arms on the counter, interested despite her irritation. 'So how did you raise the money?'

Rob peeled the sticker off his beer bottle. 'My mum cashed in her pension fund. I nearly had a heart attack when she gave me the cheque. I was so angry with her; my father had left her some money—but her pension fund? Craziness.'

'Did you refuse to take it?'

'I did. Until she told me that I either took it or she was going to go on a world cruise and pick up as many disreputable men as she could who would help her spend it.'

Willa smiled.

'She would've too; she's the most stubborn woman I've ever met. Anyway, I bought the gym. Then Patrick and I opened another one, and the old saying that it's easy to get money out of the banks when you already have money turned out to be true. I repaid my mum,' he added.

'Of course you did.' Of that she had no doubt. The man was a clot, not a scummy conman.

'I'm trying to make a point here...'

He was? Willa had just thought they were having idle conversation. 'Which is...?'

'No one would give *me* a chance either and I proved them wrong. Maybe I should give you the same chance.'

It took a moment for the words to sink in, to make sense in her jumbled brain, but when they did Willa felt the sweet sensation of joy roll through her.

Telling herself not to get her hopes up, she lifted her eyes to Rob. 'Please don't toy with me,' she pleaded with him.

'I'm not. But I'm also not risking my business on your inexperience. So I'll make you a deal.'

'What deal?'

'You start at the beginning—pretend that I'm a new investor. Make a list of the steps I need to take, detailing what you think I should I do, look out for. Back your opinions up with the relevant legislation... If you come up with a plan of action that is the same as Patrick's we're in business and I'll hire you as my Australian accountant.'

Willa looked at him in astonishment. 'Are you being serious?'

Rob's mouth twitched at the corners. 'Not up for the challenge?'

'Of course I am!' Willa swallowed her squeal. 'How long do I have?'

Rob cocked his head. 'Two days?'

'You're on.'

Willa slid off her chair and walked past Rob, who grabbed her by the seat of her pants and pulled her back.

'Where do you think you're going?'

Willa looked at him, surprised. 'To work. I've got a stack of research to do.'

Rob spun her around and pulled her between his open thighs. 'Your pot roast will be ready in fifteen minutes.'

Willa looked longingly towards the oven. 'Okay, I'll work after supper.'

'After supper you *will* work—and it will have nothing to do with corporations and trusts and Inland Revenue,' Rob said against her mouth.

Willa placed her hands on his thighs and felt the long muscles under her hands contract.

'Tomorrow will be soon enough for you to get all nerdy and geeky and accountanty,' Rob told her.

'I *am* geeky and nerdy,' Willa told him. 'I even have those big black nerd glasses.'

'I *love* those. You'll have to wear them for me—naked.'

Willa pulled her head back and laughed up into his eyes. 'Give me the job and I will.'

CHAPTER SIX

TWO DAYS LATER, after a long, long day interviewing personal trainers and admin staff, Rob was grateful to be off the clock—or as much off the clock as you could be when you owned your own business. It was a stunningly beautiful summer's evening, still hot, and it was way past time for a beer and some downtime.

He was at Willa's house—palace, mansion, whatever—and inside was a woman, cold beer and fantastic sex.

He'd certainly landed with his bread butter side up woman-wise, he thought as he dropped his keys and mobile into the ceramic bowl on the hall table. Willa was fun and uncomplicated, easy to be around, and—perhaps surprisingly—she enjoyed sex as much as he did. In his arms, naked, she became a sensual, demanding woman who wasn't afraid to tell him what she wanted and how she wanted it.

Yes, the gods of a good time were sure smiling on him. If they could bring the gods of getting his business up and running to the party he'd be eternally grateful.

'Oh, good, you're here. *Finally.*'

Rob turned, looked at the creature who'd spoken to him, and blinked. Tailored black pants, stark white shirt, thick mahogany hair pulled back into a severe twist. Willa nearly always greeted him in shorts and a tank over a bikini—why was she dressed up like corporate mannequin?

'Hi. You look…businesslike.'

'That's the point. But before we get to that, how is your cousin's wife, his daughter? I've been thinking about them.'

Rob felt touched that she'd thought to ask. 'They are both at home, recovering. Patrick has started to breathe again.'

'I'm so glad,' Willa replied. 'So…can I see you in my study?'

Rob frowned at her crisp voice and briefly wondered—okay, hoped—that this was the start of a role-playing game in which he ended up taking her from behind as she leaned over her desk, that delicious butt in the air.

'Can I get a beer first?' he asked, veering off towards the kitchen.

'Afterwards,' Willa insisted, taking his hand and pulling him down the passage.

Rob allowed her to push him into the chair on the other side of her desk and waited from her to straddle him—because if he couldn't get a beer then he wanted sex. Then a beer, then a swim, then more sex and possibly dinner. Then more sex—if he hadn't passed out or dropped dead by then…

Rob jumped as Willa tossed a thick bound document into his lap. Frowning, he flipped it over. 'What's this?'

'You gave me two days to gather information for you on setting up your company in Australia.' Willa sat down in the chair behind her desk and looked at him. 'That is what I came up with.'

Rob looked down at the professional-looking document in his hand and back to Willa, who was looking nervous and hopeful and…petrified.

Rob ran his hand over his jaw. *You're treading on some-one's dreams here, Hanson, do not open your big mouth and shatter her illusions. For once in your life be gentle. Or at least tactful.*

When Willa hadn't mentioned his little test again he'd almost presumed that she'd thought it too much of a has-sle. He'd sort of thought that she liked the *idea* of working more than she was actually prepared to work…

Convinced that she wouldn't actually take him up on his offer, he'd put out some feelers to the bigger accounting and finance companies in Sydney, in case she didn't have the smarts, or the courage, to do the job.

He start to flip pages and whistled at the detail she'd gone into. He'd underestimated her, he quickly realised, and badly. There were SWOT analyses, alternative suggestions on how to set up his company legally, and a checklist of all the paperwork that needed to be submitted to the relevant authorities to become compliant. She'd gone above and beyond and— *Holy hell!* A paragraph caught his eye. He'd never thought of that. Neither, it seemed, had Patrick.

And if they set the company up as she suggested they would avoid some of the nasty and complicated regulations that governed foreign-owned entities.

'When I said that I wanted a list of what needed to be done I expected a page or two—not a doctoral thesis.'

Willa shrugged. 'What can I say? I'm an over-achiever and it was fun…putting my brain and training to work.'

Rob tapped the folder and held her eyes. 'Good job, Willa. I'm seriously impressed.'

Willa sucked in her breath, hope shining from her eyes. 'Impressed enough to give me the job?'

Rob, hoping that he wasn't making a huge mistake, slowly nodded. 'Yeah. I'm handing the paperwork over to you.'

Willa shot up so fast that she skidded backwards over the polished wooden floor and did a crazy dance on the spot. 'Yes! Yes, yes, yes, *yes*!'

Rob grinned and watched the years roll off her as she went a little silly. He sat back in his chair and placed his ankle on his knee, watching her twirl around. What a waste of her brain these last eight years had been, he thought. Her solution to his business's greatest stumbling block was simple and clear-thinking and neither he nor Patrick had even come close to thinking of it.

Hell, for that alone he would have hired her. But, although he'd only skimmed through the document, there was also a wad of information in there that he could use, as well as steps towards what they needed to achieve.

Whoomph!

Rob tensed as a bundle of warm, fragrant flesh fell into his lap and a feminine mouth started placing kisses all over his face.

'Gerrrrooofffff!' he muttered, gently placing his hand on her face and pushing her away. 'Stop doing that.'

Willa launched herself at him again, kissing his temple. 'I absolutely won't. Thank you—' kiss '—thank you—' kiss '—thank you.'

'Okay, enough already.' Rob leaned back out of her reach.

Willa, her legs straddling his thighs, grinned at him. 'Why? Shouldn't I be kissing my boss like that?'

She looked horrified, and Rob knew exactly what she was thinking.

'Oh, hell…maybe I shouldn't be kissing you at all!'

Rob chuckled. 'Don't be silly, Willa. Kiss me—just not like a sloppy puppy.'

Willa remained serious and he sighed. She was going to complicate this, he could just tell.

'Maybe we shouldn't if we're going to work together,' she said, gnawing on her bottom lip.

'Stop that.' He tapped her lip with his finger. 'That's my job.' He sighed. 'Don't worry, gorgeous. You're going to work for me and we're going to keep sleeping together until my company is up and running and I go back to South Africa. Work is work and everything else is fun…is that clear?'

Willa pursed her lips. 'S'pose.'

Rob flashed her a grin as his hands drifted over her stomach and then up to cup her breasts, his thumbs easily finding her nipples and rubbing them into hard points.

'You have the prettiest body,' he muttered, going to work on the buttons of her shirt, cursing as his big fingers battled to pull them through their tiny slits. 'To hell with this!'

He ripped her shirt open. Willa just looked at him, and then down at her transparent bra.

'I didn't like the shirt, but don't you *dare* rip this bra....' Willa retorted—and then stopped speaking as he sucked her, fabric and all, into his mouth.

Willa responded to the rasp of the fabric against her ultra-sensitised nipples and moaned, grinding into his hard erection, which was perfectly placed to give her the maximum pleasure.

Rob, not in the mood to wait, or to take orders from her, flashed her a naughty grin and with one twist detached a see-through triangle from its strap.

Willa's mouth dropped open as the material fluttered down. 'Dammit, Rob, I told you not to rip it! Now you're not getting the glasses!'

No sexy nerd glasses? *Oh, damn.* 'Couldn't you have told me that earlier?' he complained, his hand coming up to rest on her bare breast. 'Please? Pretty please?'

Willa tried to look annoyed—which she did well, considering that she was rotating her hips and sliding against the pipe in his pants.

'No.'

Rob grabbed her hips and lifted her off him, easily holding her in the air. 'Then you don't get to do *that*.'

Willa thought for a moment and then wriggled off his lap. Standing with her back to him, in between him and the desk, she stripped off her shirt and the broken bra and quickly shimmied her pants over her hips. Keeping her strappy sandals on, she stretched as Rob played with the beaded T of her G-string. His heart picked up pace as he traced the cleft of her buttocks, touching the skin under the gossamer band of her thong.

'These make men stupid,' he muttered, placing an open-mouthed kiss on one of the two dents above her butt cheeks.

Pulling the clip that kept her hair off her neck, Willa shook her head and her hair tumbled down, heavy and thick against her back. Leaning across the desk, she picked up her heavy glasses and slipped them onto her nose.

'Let's see you, numbers nerd,' Rob ordered and, his hands on her hips, spun her around.

She gripped the desk with her hands as she leaned back, her back arched provocatively, her hips tilted and her eyes lowered in passion.

Damn, she had no idea how sexy she was, Rob thought, looking up into those eyes that echoed the waters of the bay. He'd never quite understood the expression 'drowning in her eyes', and had thought that it was over-used by poets and posers until this very minute. They were deep and mysterious and held a million secrets...

She was such a contradiction, Rob thought, leaning forward and taking a moment to slow his heart down by resting his forehead on her fragrant stomach. Amazingly, shockingly bright, a little naïve, a lot innocent. Stronger than she realised and tougher than she gave herself credit for. In another life, if he was another guy, he'd be finding a way to make her his...

But he couldn't give her anything more—*be* her anything more. Apart from the fact that his time here was limited, relationships of any depth or length required trust—and that wasn't something he could do. *Ever.*

Still, this woman was the first in a very long time—okay, in for ever—who had made him even consider that possibility. And that was why he had to be doubly careful around her… They were sleeping together and now working together. The lines were getting blurred very fast indeed.

Slow it down, moron. Seriously. Because someone is going to get certain parts of his anatomy put through a grinder. His heart and his balls ran for cover at the thought…

All he had—all he *could* have—was right now, and he could suck the life out of every moment with this woman. And he intended to, he thought as he slowly stood up.

Instead of kissing her upturned mouth Rob dropped feather-light kisses on her collarbone, nibbled her neck, and sucked on that sweet spot between her neck and ear. Willa tipped her head to allow him better access and picked up his hand and placed it on her breast. To tease her he just held her in his palm, but she growled her disapproval and pushed her breast into his hand.

'I need you to touch me.'

Rob laughed lightly. 'Getting there,' he replied.

This was his fantasy and he wouldn't be rushed. So he teased and tormented; tasting the skin on the inside of her elbow, the top of her hip. He nuzzled the inside of her thighs, explored her knees, and tangled his tongue in the fine three-strand chain around her slim ankle. He feasted. And when he thought Willa couldn't stand another minute more he started the process all over again.

When he finally pulled her thong to one side and found her sweet spot with his tongue she orgasmed instantly, and he slid two fingers into her and nuzzled her to another high. As pliant as a doll, she let him spin her around. He laid her across the desk and unzipped his cargo shorts. Taking the condom from his back pocket—he'd taken to carrying one around for situations just like these—he rolled it on and, spreading her legs, slid into her wet wild warmth and rotated his hips. So hot, so deep, so *Willa*.

Happy to delay his pleasure, he lay across her back,

content to stay sheathed in her, running his hands up and down her sides before sliding them around to her front and stroking her nipples with his thumbs.

Willa, being Willa, slowly stirred, and he felt her push back against him, recognised the tension in her body that he'd come to know so well. She was up for another orgasm and he would give her one—slow and hot...

Except it didn't happen the way he'd intended. She pushed back and he hit her G-spot—and suddenly she was demanding more, and he was pumping, and if he had to stop he would just die...

He heard Willa scream and felt her clench around him and another burst of pure energy pulsed through him.

Yeah, Rob thought as he locked his knees to keep himself from collapsing. It wasn't love, or for ever, but it was still damned amazing.

He could live with that.

'Need coffee,' Willa muttered, her face in Rob's shoulder.

This was fair, because something of his was still buried in her as well.

Rob patted her butt. 'It's your turn. I made it yesterday morning.'

'You make better coffee.'

'This is true, but it's still your turn.' Rob pulled his head away to look into her face. *'Ack*...don't we sound domesticated?'

They did—and she liked it, Willa thought. Better watch that or else she would get accustomed to waking up to Rob and going to sleep with Rob as well as sleeping with Rob.

Willa rolled off him and sighed, pushing her tangled hair out of her face. Who was she trying to fool...? She was already getting used to all of the above. *And* his coffee.

No doing anything stupid, here, Willa—like falling for

him in any way, shape or form. She was not going to be moronic about this…

Rob walked to the en-suite bathroom. She heard the toilet flush and a burst of water suggesting that he was brushing his teeth or washing his hands. Probably both. Willa rolled onto her stomach, turned her head to the window and looked out onto the bay. It was a gorgeous summer's day, and if she and Rob weren't up to their ears in work she'd suggest that they take a canoe and snorkelling equipment into the reserve and have a picnic.

It was Saturday, after all.

'Guess I'm making coffee.'

She flicked her eyes to the free-standing mirror to her right and saw that Rob had pulled on a pair of shorts and was looking fit and hot and—more importantly—awake.

'How do you *do* that?' she grumbled.

Rob walked around the bed and sat on the edge, placing his hand on her hip. 'Do what?'

'Look all chipper and raring to go? Especially after sex?'

'Sex energises me.' The corners of that amazing mouth—so talented—tipped up. 'I've been feeling very energetic lately.'

Willa smiled. They had been going at it like muskrats— or whatever animal it was that bonked like crazy.

'And laziness, moving slow, is a habit,' Rob added. 'I've noticed that people who don't have to get moving quickly— to get to work on time, to make appointments—are perpetually lazy. *And* late.'

That was true; Willa admitted reluctantly. She had little sense of time and was nearly always late to everything.

Rob's expression turned serious. 'That's something that you're going to have to work on, Willa. I hate people not being punctual and I hate laziness.'

Willa slowly sat up and tried to ignore the flash of hurt annoyance coursing through her. 'I'm not lazy…'

Rob just looked at her, his face implacable. 'Yeah, you are. And why shouldn't you be? You spent the last eight years being told to look pretty, to do nothing, be ornamental. It doesn't work for me.'

Willa said the first thing that came to mind. 'Good thing you're not sticking around, then.'

Rob's hand gripped her thigh and squeezed. 'Except that you are now working for me…and I expect my pound of flesh. Work-wise. That's a solid eight, maybe a ten, sometimes twelve-hour day.'

Willa blinked at him. 'God!'

'I need to know that you can work until the job is done… If you don't think you can then maybe you should say so now, before we go any further. No hard feelings. I'll just find someone else.'

Like hell he would. Willa felt something swell in her throat and thought it might be pride—or something close to it. He was *not* going to dismiss her, think less of her, just because she'd sat on her backside for eight years…

'I wasn't given a choice to do anything else,' she protested.

Rob shook his head. 'I don't accept that, Willa. You *always* have a choice. The choices might be hard, but there is always something to choose between.'

'You don't know what it was like, living with him.'

'Probably not.' Rob agreed. 'But I believe that we live with the consequences of the choices we make. For years you lived with the consequences of staying with your husband and that was your choice. Now you're living with the consequences of divorcing him—which…' he looked around '…don't seem to be that bad. But none of that has anything to do with me…'

'Exactly,' Willa murmured, vastly irritated.

'But what *does* concern me is your work ethic and whether you can pull your weight with me. I run fast and

I run hard and I expect you to keep up. You don't—you're fired.'

Willa closed her eyes at his brutal statement. His bald honestly had the ability to scald skin, she thought. Yet, that being said, it was still a sweet pain. For the first time in her life she knew exactly where she stood, what was expected of her. And nobody was going to give her a head start because of who she was connected to. For the first time ever she was going to sink or swim and she was in control.

It was her choice...

She lifted her chin and looked Rob straight in the eye. 'I choose to work my ass off.'

'Good. I expect nothing less.'

Nobody had ever been this forthright with her, this honest. She'd always been handled with kid gloves and it was both enthralling and annoying, to be treated so... She wanted to say so carelessly, but that wasn't fair to Rob. He wasn't a careless man but he *was* demanding. He had a high set of expectations and he expected her to reach them. She didn't intend to let him down.

More importantly, she didn't intend to let herself down.

'Let's go out tonight,' Rob suggested, changing the subject adroitly.

Her lover was back and her boss had—temporarily, she was sure—left the building. She couldn't keep up with who she was dealing with and she didn't like it. And if she didn't put her foot down now... What was Kate's favourite saying? *You teach people how to treat you...*

'This isn't going to work for me,' she stated firmly.

'What? Having some dinner? Seeing a show?'

'That too, but no... You flipping between boss and lover.' Willa pushed her hair back and waved at the bed. 'I declare this a no work zone.'

'I've lost you. Explain.'

Willa made herself meet his eyes. 'You can't segue from

talking about sex and how it energises you into making a comment about my work habits and what you expect. And then switch back to lover mode and talk about where we should eat dinner. That's not fair. When you're in my bed, when we're naked, you don't get to say things like that.'

Willa held her breath as she saw the emotions run through Rob's eyes. She was starting to be able to read his eyes, she thought. Irritation, thoughtfulness...embarrassment?

Rob rubbed the back of his neck before reaching over to cup her face. 'You're right.'

You're right? That was it? No comeback? No long speech asking how she could possibly think that, that he had a right to say what he—?

'I'm sorry.'

He was *apologising*? Holy smokes! Seriously?

'That's okay.' Willa managed to get the words out despite her astonishment. A big, alpha man who wasn't afraid to admit he was wrong? She hadn't thought they made that type of man any more.

'So—new rule. We only talk business in the study... Everywhere else, especially the bedroom, is off bounds for work and business,' Rob reiterated. 'Okay, sorted. Now, about dinner...'

Willa took a moment to get with the programme, still amazed at how easily the issue had been resolved. She pulled a face. 'I would love to, but I can't. I have a fiftieth birthday party to attend.'

'I thought you said that you don't have any friends in Sydney?'

'Well, I don't...not really. Except for Misha and Vern. It's his fiftieth birthday party and they've begged me to come. I'm absolutely dreading it.'

'Because the douche will be there?' Rob guessed.

'Yeah.'

'So don't go. Life is too short to do things you don't want to. Blow it off. Let's go have some fun instead.'

She wanted to, but she couldn't. Misha and Vern had been her biggest allies and staunchest defenders when she'd been married to Wayne. They were one of the most influential and nice couples in that elevated social strata.

Unlike the wives and girlfriends of Wayne's friends and business cronies, Willa hadn't had children or a career, and she'd hovered on the outside of their group, rebuffed one too many times to make much of an effort to be included. The husbands had been a different story: to them she'd been fair game. She'd been groped, hassled and propositioned, and whenever she'd complained to Wayne he'd accused her of looking for attention.

Walking back into that den of vipers would stir up gossip, and she would have to endure not only seeing Wayne again but the nasty asides, the up and down looks, the sotto voce comments behind manicured hands.

'Misha and Vern were always nice to me—my social haven, if you will. They were always happy to include me in their conversations, at their table, welcoming my opinions. Attending Vern's birthday bash is my way of showing my appreciation,' Willa stated.

'Do you want me to come with you?'

Willa stared at Rob's hand on her thigh, broad and masculine. Of *course* she wanted him to come with her—what could be better than walking in with a super-sexy new man on her arm?—but she refused to ask him. She could— *would*—do this on her own if she had to. She wasn't the same person she'd been then; she was stronger, happier, confident.

'What's the dress code, where is the party, and what time do we have to be there?' Rob asked.

Willa imagined punching the air and doing a crazy happy dance but she kept her face straight. 'Black tie, on a yacht in Campbell's Cove, at eight. Thank you for offering to escort me.'

'Like those expressive eyes of yours weren't begging me to,' Rob scoffed, leaning forward to brush his mouth across hers briefly.

'It'll be staid and stuffy and Wayne will most definitely make an appearance.'

Rob raised an eyebrow. 'Are you trying to talk me out of going with you?'

'I just want to make sure you know what you're *volunteering* for. You don't have to come if you really don't want to.' Willa lifted her chin. 'I can and will go on my own. I'll be absolutely fine.'

'Sure you will—but you'll be a hell of a lot better with me,' Rob shot back, and shoved his hand through his messy hair.

Yeah. No arguing with that.

'Look, Willa, I'm not totally insensitive or emotionally stunted. I can see that you'd rather walk on broken glass than go, but I admire your sense of loyalty—and, trust me, I'm as surprised by my offer to go with you as anyone. It's not something I'd usually waste my time on, but you look like you could do with some support and it looks like I'm it. Why do I suspect that too few people have really been there for you when you needed them to be?'

Willa blinked her tears away and licked her lips. Wasn't that the truth? She knew that her father and brother loved her, but her father wanted her to have a perfect life, to be protected, and she and Luke had never been close. She'd allowed her friendships with the people she met at the Weeping Reef resort to fade away when she'd stepped into Wayne's world—only to find out that his world was a hard place and that her husband, so charming and charismatic on holiday, was the King of Cold and Cruel.

God, didn't she sound melodramatic? But it was only

now that she was standing in the sun she realised how frozen she'd been. She knew that she was being irrational, but she felt that the party tonight had the ability to flash-freeze her again.

Rob lifted her chin in order to make her look at him. She didn't know that her eyes were large and miserable and soul-deep scared.

'You don't have to go,' he reiterated.

'I do. For Misha and Vern and for my pride.'

'Okay, then. I'll be with you every minute, and to get to you Wayne will have to go through me,' Rob promised her. 'Trust me, I'm more than a match for him.'

Willa looped her arms around his neck and placed her face on his shoulder. 'Thanks.'

Rob's hand brushed over her hair, down her spine. 'I've got your back, Willa.'

CHAPTER SEVEN

LATER THAT MORNING Willa left Rob to work out in her gym and headed to Surry Hills for lunch with her girls. She now had 'girls', she thought as she spotted Kate's bright red head at the back of the restaurant. Kate and Amy and…Jessica.

Jessica—who seemed to collect people like some women collected shoes. And that was okay, Willa thought. It wasn't as if she had so many friends that she could refuse the offer of friendship from anyone.

Willa, dressed in a bright pink halterneck dress and peony-pink flip-flops, hair up in a tail, grinned at her friends as she slipped into the empty fourth chair.

'Dear God,' Amy murmured. 'You're *so* getting lucky.'

Willa grinned. 'I so am…' Turning to the waiter, she placed her order for a virgin mojito.

'What's the point?' Amy cried.

'The last time I drank with you I woke up to a stranger in my bed and a house full of guests,' Willa explained.

'The stranger is still there, bonking your brains out, and you told me that it was a fabby party,' Kate replied crisply. 'Add the booze,' she told the waitress.

When Kate used that tone of voice nobody argued.

The waitress snapped her chewing gum and grinned. 'Sure. Something to eat?'

'Later, honey, thanks—just bring the drinks, please,' Kate said, and waved her away. She leaned back in her chair and sent Willa a thoughtful look. 'This isn't just about sex…something else has happened.'

Kate, after spending so many hours with Willa hammering out her divorce, had become something of a big sister, and probably knew Willa better than any person alive. She'd held her hand, mopped up her tears and—metaphorically—slapped some sense into her. Kate had ripped the rose-coloured glasses off her eyes and had made her grow up, and for that Willa would be eternally grateful.

Willa's eyes sparkled with delight and she wiggled in her seat like a puppy waiting for a milk bone. 'I've got a job.'

Amy whooped her delight and Kate, far more controlled, squeezed her hand.

Leaning across the table, Jessica high-fived her. 'That's fantastic, Willa. I'm so happy for you…'

'With who? When do you start?' Kate demanded.

'Rob's accountant had to fly back home for a family emergency and Rob said that I can take over.' Willa's words bubbled like champagne. 'And there's so much to do… He's just handed everything financial over to—'

Willa looked around the suddenly sombre faces and frowned. It was as if someone had just tossed an icy bucket of water over her friends and they were less than amused.

'What's the matter?'

Amy looked at Kate, who lifted her eyebrows in response. Neither of them said anything.

'Okay, you guys are starting to scare me,' Willa said, her hand on her heart. 'Two seconds ago you were happy for me and now you're exchanging *what-the-hell-has-she-done?* looks across the table.'

Amy took a sip of her wine and waited until their perky waitress had placed Willa's mojito in front of her and left before speaking again. 'When you said you had a job we thought you meant a real job.'

Excuse me? What? 'A real job? Sorting out Rob's company finances is a hell of a job, thank you very much.'

'It's a job with someone you're sleeping with,' Amy murmured.

'Is he actually paying you?' Jessica asked baldly before Willa could respond.

'Uh…' They hadn't actually discussed that. She hoped so, but frankly she'd work for free to get the experience she so desperately needed.

Kate rolled her eyes. 'Hell, Willa, have I taught you nothing about protecting yourself?'

Willa frowned, not really understanding how she'd coloured outside the lines. 'I've lost you.'

'Rob is sleeping with you and you're now working for him as well? If you tell me that you're cooking for him and doing his laundry I will slap you,' Amy told her. 'Look, don't get me wrong, I like Rob—but he's not a keeper. What are *you* getting out of what looks to be a very one-sided relationship?'

'Good sex?' Willa quipped. 'Oh, lighten up, all of you, I'm not a complete idiot! Firstly, it's not a relationship… we're having fun together as long as he is in the country. There are no expectations on either side.'

Under the table, Willa crossed her legs.

'As for me working for him—even if it wasn't the most challenging work I've done…ever!…I'd be a fool not to do it because I am out of options. When Rob goes I can put working for him on my CV—show that I have the experience people keep telling me I need to get a decent job. That's golden, girls. I am not doing this to make him happy. I'm doing it because it benefits *me*.'

Amy still didn't look convinced. 'You're not the type to keep it light and fluffy, Wills.'

'Trust me—I've learnt. I'm not the naïve innocent you used to know, Amy. I'm a bit wiser, I hope. I'm not stupid enough to hand over my heart again for someone to stomp on it. Besides, Rob would tell me to put it away and stop looking for hearts and flowers.'

'Good girl.' Kate nodded. 'As long as you're thinking with your head and not your va-jay-jay.'

'God, Kate,' Jessica muttered, after choking on her sip of wine. 'What an expression!'

'My grandma heard it on TV and now she uses it all the time. She says it's only fair that if men think with their penises then woman think with their…you know. Good for goose and gander and all that,' Kate explained.

'Your grandma sounds like a hoot,' Willa said, glad to have the spotlight off her.

'She and my mother were the original bra-burner and hippy chick. They constantly give me stick because I'm not fighting for the cause…'

'You're a brilliant family lawyer,' Willa protested.

'That I am,' Kate agreed. 'And a better divorce lawyer.'

Divorce—nearly there. The Pain…the party… Willa remembered where she had to be tonight and winced.

'You're pulling a face,' Kate muttered. 'Why are you pulling a face? What's happened? What's the matter?'

'Geez, take a tranq, Kate,' Willa told her. 'It's just that I have to attend a party tonight and Wayne-the-Pain will be there. I so don't want to go.'

'So don't go,' Jessica said, looking at the menu.

'That's what Rob said.' She wished she could see the world in black and white, as they seemed to, but for some reason her world held every shade of grey.

'You said that you've broken ties with Wayne's group. Why this function?' Amy asked. 'And, more importantly, should I have a beef or chicken burrito?'

Willa waited while her friends placed their food orders before explaining why she felt she had to attend, stirring her untouched mojito with her finger. 'I said I'd go, Kate. I know that you didn't want me to have any contact with Wayne, but—'

'Willa, that was when we were first negotiating your

divorce. The divorce papers are signed and lodged with the court now. They just need to go through the process. There's no going back from what we've negotiated. You could sleep together again and nothing would change.'

Willa mimed shoving a finger down her throat.

'So, are you going to go on your own or are you going to take Hot and Sexy with you?' Amy asked.

'He offered to come with me. Thank God. Because while I'm still dreading going, I'm dreading it marginally less.'

Kate placed her hand on her shoulder and squeezed. 'Wayne is not worth a minute of your time. Go tonight, be fabulous, act confident and look happy.'

'I *am* happy,' Willa stated, and the truth of that knowledge resonated deep inside her. And not only because she had a sexy man rumpling her sheets but because she felt like Willa—like herself. Not her father's princess, or Wayne's wife, or Luke's sister…just Willa. Young, strong, healthy, smart.

Willa.

Maybe she was starting to like who she was now. No, she *did* like who she was now…and wasn't that the best feeling in the world? Ever?

Dressed in a black suit, white shirt and a black tie—the closest he was ever going to get to a monkey suit—Rob stood in the kitchen and waited for Willa to come downstairs, a glass of red wine in his hands.

Dickied up and looking fly was not the way he wanted to spend his Saturday night…and normally it would take a gun to his head to get him to do something he didn't want to do… Yet here he was, prepared to play Willa's protector, her knight in a sharp black suit.

What was with that? He was nobody's white knight. He didn't want to play the role. He'd failed once in that role before. Which begged the question…why her? Why now?

Willa had come back from lunch sounding chipper, but as the afternoon had worn on and evening had approached she'd got quieter and more distant and he'd become…annoyed.

'Why are you going if you're dreading it so much?' he'd demanded, fed up with her silences. 'Why do you want to put yourself in that position? Just to say thank you to some people who were once nice to you? Send them a card, for God's sake!'

Willa's eyes had met his and they'd blazed bright. 'Obviously you've never felt less than unnoticed, lacking. But I have. And I am going to that party and I am going to hold my head up high and show them that I am *not* the wimpy wife they all thought I was. I do not want their last impression of me to be that quiet, insecure woman who was so easily dismissed. And I'll do it with or without you.'

His annoyance had faded after that as he'd realised how much guts it was going to take for her to walk into that room, filled with people who'd always dismissed her. This party was more than just making an appearance. It was her way to say goodbye to her old life, to walk away from those people and her waste-of-space ex with her head held high. She needed to go for her own pride and self-respect. He understood pride and self-respect and he appreciated Willa's courage.

His girl would be fine, Rob thought. Just the fact that she was doing this when it would be a lot easier not to told him that she was a stronger character than she realised.

"Respect, Willa."

Rob heard the click-clack of Willa's heels against the tiles and turned to look at her. The saliva dried up in his mouth. Dear God, she looked amazing. Like her eyes, her dress was silver shot through with green, clinging to her slim frame like a second skin. Thin cords held the dress up, crossed over her shoulders.

Rob lifted his finger and traced their outline. Willa obediently turned and his blood rushed out of his brain as he saw that the cords criss-crossed her smooth bare back to hold the fabric on either side of those back dimples he loved to kiss.

'How the hell did you get into that?' he asked.

'With difficulty,' Willa answered on a smile. 'Like it?'

'Hell, no—I love it and I can't wait to get you out of it,' Rob replied, taking a big sip of wine to lubricate his throat and to rehydrate his mouth. It didn't work. 'Want a drink?'

'Do we have time?' Willa asked, placing her silver clutch on the kitchen counter.

'Some. Besides, a dress like that deserves a late entrance. You look stunning.'

'Thank you. You don't look too shabby yourself.'

Willa took the half-glass of wine he held out and took a small sip.

'Why am I doing this, Rob?'

'You're taking back your self-respect,' Rob told her. 'That's always a fight worth fighting. *Always*, Willa. I wish I could...'

Respect myself again. Like myself again.

That one decision so long ago had changed everything. *Shut up, Hanson.*

God! He'd never told anyone about his mother's disastrous second marriage, the part he'd played in it.

Willa cocked her head, her smoky eyes pinning him to the floor. 'You wish that you could...what?'

Rob rubbed the back of his neck, uncomfortable. 'Nothing—sorry. Thinking aloud.'

'I feel like you censor your words around me—that you start to tell me stuff and then you pull back.'

Rob couldn't lie to her. 'I do.'

'I'm a pretty good listener, Rob.'

'Honey, what's the point of listening if nothing can be

changed?' Rob replied, his tone low but resolute. 'Do you want some more wine?'

'If we don't get going I'm not going to go at all. I decided not to go to this party a hundred times today.' Willa tipped her head, staring at him with soul-searching eyes. 'I'd love to know one of your secrets, Rob, since you seem to be witnessing *all* of my little foibles, quirks and paranoias.'

Feeling like a butterfly pinned to a board, he shuffled his feet, torn between wanting to tell her about his past and wanting to run screaming into the night. In his head he opted for running and screaming.

He made a show of pushing back the cuff of his shirt to look at his watch. 'On second thoughts, leave the wine. I think we should get going.'

Willa slid off her chair and took the hand he held out. She picked up her clutch and hauled in a deep, deep breath.

Rob put his hand on her back. 'You okay?'

Willa managed a small smile. 'A hundred percent… If I tell you to turn the car around, just ignore me, okay?'

Rob, seeing the fine tremors that skittered through her body, pulled her in to his chest and wrapped his arms around her slight frame. Bending his head so that his mouth was on her ear, he spoke softly. 'You're not alone, Willa, not this time.'

Rob had attended his fair share of boring parties over the years—it was the price you paid when you did business with people who had money—but this one took 'boring' to new heights. The guests, around thirty in all, were either pompous, arrogant, annoying or all three at once, and no one tried to hide their curiosity about 'Willa's new man'.

'Willa's new man' couldn't give a rat's about what they thought of him, but he hated the up and down looks they gave Willa—as if any of the women here could hold a candle to her in the looks or brains department—and the insincere small talk they deigned to send her way.

Rob stood next to the bar on the enormous catamaran berthed in Campbell's Cove which, as Willa had told him, was one of the most picturesque super-yacht berths in the world. He could understand why. The marina was nestled between the Opera House and the Harbour Bridge and had outstanding views.

Sydney was a gorgeous city, Rob thought. He could see himself living here... He rubbed his eyes with his finger and thumb, wondering where that thought had come from. He loved his country, his home city, loved the energy and vibe of Jo'burg. Unlike many of his friends he'd never considered emigrating south. He was a born-and-bred African and he loved his South African life.

But, seriously, Oz wasn't that bad—and, he thought, looking at Willa's slim back as she spoke to their hosts, the girls weren't too shabby either. At least that one wasn't...

No one would believe that she'd spent the day as a bundle of nerves: she looked composed and dignified and super-hot.

'Willa *has* improved in the six months since we last saw her.'

Rob turned at the sound of a nasal voice at his elbow and met the calculating eyes of a brown-eyed brunette who'd spent far too much time in the sun—or, more likely, crisping herself on a sunbed. Eye-lift, boobs definitely fake and collagen lips. She was more plastic than cheap margarine.

And she was putting her bright red claws on his arm. *God*.

'So, where did our little Willa find *you*?' she drawled, empty martini glass in her hand. 'Or did she hire you?'

What. The. Hell.

'Excuse me?' he said, his voice low and containing a warning that she should be very, *very* careful.

She was either too stupid or too drunk to hear it. 'No offence, but Willa's not the type to find you on her own. She's a curious blend of timid and arrogant, shy and superior.'

Rob bit the inside of his lip to keep his words from stripping several layers of skin off her. He had a razor-sharp tongue and knew that he could inflict a cutting retort that would take her off at the knees. *Rein it in, bud. This isn't your fight and you don't need to make it worse for Willa than it already is.*

Tanned Plastic was trying to tap his mouth with her index finger and he yanked his head away just before she made contact.

'Anyway, I might have some use for your…*services*. Give me your mobile number so that I can contact you.'

Rob, his temper on a low simmer, sent her a bland look. 'Lady, I'd rather find a bathtub and chew my wrists off.'

Picking up his glass of whisky, he walked away from her fish face and walked up to Willa, who was still talking to their hosts.

'Nice friends you have,' he said to Misha, taking a sip of his whisky and welcoming its burn.

Willa gasped at his rudeness but, to his surprise, Misha just laughed.

'Dreadful aren't they? Especially Janice…that's who you were just talking to.'

Misha sent him a wide grin that he couldn't help returning.

'That's why we invited you, Willa. We wanted someone nice to talk to.'

So why have a fiftieth birthday party with people they didn't like? It didn't make sense, Rob thought—and then voiced his opinion out loud.

Instead of taking offence, Vern just shrugged. 'I believe in keeping my friends close and my enemies closer. So what do you do for a crust, Rob?'

'Janice thinks I'm a male escort,' Rob said blandly.

'Janice is a fool,' Misha replied. 'And desperately jealous of Willa.'

'She is not,' Willa protested.

'Of course she is,' Rob agreed. 'She's been throwing daggers at you all night. As are quite a few of the other women. You're at least twenty years younger than them, gorgeous, and most of the men here can't keep their eyes off you.'

'And why wouldn't they stare?' Vern said, lifting his glass to Willa. 'You look wonderful, my dear. Misha, there's the Thompsons—we should go say hello.' He looked at Rob. 'Enemies...'

'Do you have *any* friends here?' Rob asked.

Vern grinned. 'One or two. Look after Willa for us.'

'Will do.' Rob shook his head, puzzled, and looked down at Willa. 'What on earth does Vern do?'

'What doesn't he do?' Willa replied, lifting one bare shoulder. 'He's one of Australia's richest businessmen and he has interests in...well, literally everything. Hotels, mines, media, retail...'

Rob whistled his surprise. 'And your ex is a business associate of his?'

'Yeah.'

'Huh.'

So her ex swam in the same school as the big-boy fish? He'd be impressed but...he wasn't. Not by any of it. The yacht was swish, but the people were crappy, and the four-piece band playing in the corner was coma-inducing. The snacks were ordinary and he'd have more fun dodging taxi drivers in rush hour in downtown Jo'burg. He was bored, and when he was bored he tended to get into trouble by stirring up trouble.

'Can we go yet?' he asked, seeing that many eyes were still on them. He felt like an exhibit at a freak show.

Oh, well, might as well give them something they could really gossip about.

Rob bent his head and placed a long, sexy kiss on Willa's shoulder. When he lifted his head to look at her he saw that her eyes were smouldering with passion. Maybe they could find an empty bedroom—closet, bathroom—on this monstrous floating tub and have some fun.

'I want you,' he told her, sotto voce.

Willa licked her lips and he felt his blood rushing south.

'You always want me.'

'This is true.' He lifted her hand, opened her fingers and dropped an open-mouthed kiss on the centre of her palm. 'Is that a problem?'

'Yeah…kind of… Because when you look at me like that my knees go all wobbly and my vision blurs,' Willa admitted.

His ego puffed out its chest and did a high-five at the thought…

'And my panties get all wet.'

Okay, there went his knees. *Well-played, gorgeous.* 'Keep that up, honey, and I swear I'll give this room something more to talk about.'

Willa tipped her head. 'What would you do, Rob?'

Rob stepped up closer to her and his breath played with the hair at her ear. 'I'd run my hands up your stunning legs, pull that dress over your hips, push your thong aside and start moving.'

Willa kissed the side of his jaw. 'Panties now soaked—'

'You're making a spectacle of yourself, Willa. Stop it.'

Rob's hand fisted but he took his time moving away from Willa, dropping a brief but possessive kiss on her lips before pulling back and lifting his eyebrows at the balding blond man who was standing far too close to them, steam coming out of his ears. Okay, not literally, but still…

Rob didn't need his MBA to tell him that this was Wayne, Willa's soon-to-be ex-husband.

'Willa, do you *have* to embarrass me like this?' Wayne demanded. 'You're my *wife*, dammit!'

Rob opened his mouth to blast him but then remembered that Willa wanted to do this herself…recapture her pride and self-respect. He lifted an eyebrow at her but she wasn't looking at him. Her eyes were firmly on Wayne—a snake about to strike. She needed to handle this, he reminded himself. This was her party and he'd play bouncer—ready to step in if things got out of hand.

Wayne took a sip of whisky from his glass and his brows lifted to his receding hairline. 'What are you doing here anyway? These aren't *your* friends any more.'

Could he sound any more childish if he tried? God, what a moron. *Okay, Willa, any time now—blast him.* Rob placed a hand on her lower back and gave her an encouraging tap, but she just stood there, a fawn caught in the hunter's sights. He recognised that look. He had seen it on his mother's and sister's faces—probably on his own too.

'You've picked up some weight since I last saw you. You really should monitor your ice cream intake. Your backside is getting *huge*,' Wayne stated, his eyes glinting with malicious amusement.

Rob *so* wanted to punch him. For a moment he saw Stefan in Wayne's face and knew that he was dealing with the same type of character, the same need to control.

He rubbed his hand over his face. If he had to get involved with a woman, why couldn't it be with one who didn't make him feel as if he was reliving his past? Why did she have to be the one person he could thoroughly understand—who could probably understand him? He was already having problems keeping his emotional distance from her—how was he supposed to keep her at arm's length knowing just how miserable her last eight years must have been? Why couldn't she just have had an ex she'd fallen out of love with? Was that too much to ask?

The universe, he decided, had a sick sense of humour sometimes.

Rob noticed that they were attracting the attention of the rest of the room and decided that enough was enough. He couldn't stand here while the woman he…whatever he felt for Willa…was insulted and disparaged. He'd done that before and he'd never allow it to happen again.

'Back off, dude. Now,' he growled in Wayne's direction.

Wayne turned his attention to him and Rob held his shark-like eyes. Soft, mean and dangerous, he thought. But one punch to that jaw or a hook into his sternum would have him out cold or gasping like a fish. Lovely image, that.

'Who the hell are *you*? Did she hire you for the evening?' Wayne demanded.

Rob rolled his eyes at Misha and Vern who, obviously hoping to avoid blood on their expensive teak floors, had scuttled up to them. 'Nice to know that if the gyms and clothing line don't work out I have another option.'

Misha's eyes glinted with amusement. 'It's always good to have a Plan B. Wayne—really? Another scene?'

'We're still married, Michelle.'

Misha sent him a look to pin him to the floor. 'And where *is* your current lady-love, Wayne, darling? Oh, look.' She tapped the face of her disgustingly expensive diamond-studded bracelet watch and smiled brightly. 'It's after nine so it's probably past her curfew.'

'Not funny,' Wayne muttered.

Rob grinned at Misha. 'I thought it was. Didn't you, Willa?'

He sighed. Willa was still doing her 'see no evil, speak no evil and hear no evil' thing.

The rest of the room remained silent, Rob noticed, enthralled by the drama. Misha, obviously trying to rescue the situation, turned back to Wayne.

'Rob was telling me earlier that he owns a couple of fitness centres in South Africa as well as a chain of sports stores. He's expanding his business to Sydney, then Perth and Melbourne.'

'Interesting,' Vern murmured. 'A little risky when you have competition from Just Fit?'

Rob nodded. 'I've had two business consultants plus Willa look over the market research. They all agree that there's a gap in the market.'

'Like *Willa* knows anything about market research,' Wayne mocked. 'She's nothing but a pretty empty shell.'

'Careful,' Rob warned him. 'That's my accountant you're talking about.'

Wayne's eyes widened with astonishment and then he erupted into laughter. 'Oh, come on—you're kidding, right? You hired her as your *accountant*? You're stupider than you look!'

Rob flicked a glance at Willa, who still stood staring at Wayne, face ashen and eyes wide with hurt confusion. *Dammit, say something, Willa,* he urged her silently. *Take control, don't let this moron win.*

Rob squeezed her hand and she looked at him. He tipped his head in Wayne's direction, his eyes urging her to take a verbal swing. 'I've got your back,' he mouthed.

Willa took a deep breath, and he wondered if she knew that when she spoke her low, quiet, controlled voice had more power than shouting and screaming.

'I actually don't care what you think about me any more because you mean absolutely nothing to me. You didn't want a wife. You wanted a blow-up doll—someone who would feed your ego and tell you how wonderful you are. Except that you *aren't* wonderful...you're a sad man who gets his kicks from putting people down. And I am done with you.'

Yeah, you go, girl. Rob waited for her to say more but she just kept her eyes on Wayne's face, looking classy and strong and proud.

Rob couldn't help adding his two cents because—well, he wasn't going away without taking a couple of swings himself. Verbal only, of course. He looked Wayne in the eye and used his toughest, hardest, don't-mess-with-me voice.

'You must be a special kind of stupid not to realise how bright Willa actually is. She has a mind like a steel trap and she has the credentials to back it up. Smart and sexy… What kind of man would let *that* go?'

'I made her. I gave her everything!' Wayne spluttered, his face mottling instantly.

Typical bully—stand up to them and they back down… fast. The fact that he had six inches, ten years and twenty pounds of muscle on Wayne also helped.

'You gave her nothing of value.' Rob shook his head. 'She wasted far too much time on you…and now she's done.'

He deliberately turned his back to Wayne and stood in between him and Willa—a silent but, he hoped, an effective insult.

He winked at Willa and held out his hand. 'Ready to blow this joint, honey?'

'*So* ready.' Willa slid her much smaller hand into his.

He lifted his head at his hosts. 'Thanks, Misha and Vern… I wish I could say it's been fun.'

Vern grinned as he shook Rob's hand. 'I like you…come back.'

Rob shook his head. 'Nah, life is too short to spend my leisure time with people I don't like.'

Vern, instead of being insulted, just nodded. 'You may be right, son.'

'Happy birthday anyway.'

Rob tugged Willa and wrapped his arm around her slim waist. He bent his head to speak in her ear.

'So, where were we before we were so annoyingly in-interrupted...? Oh, I was sliding on in and your legs were wrapped around my hips...'

CHAPTER EIGHT

WILLA LOOKED ABSOLUTELY SHATTERED, and for that Rob wanted to go back onto that fancy yacht and pitch her waste-of-oxygen ex over the side. The funny, charming, sexy woman he'd spent the last few weeks with was gone and he was furious that the moron had wiped away her self-confidence, her happiness.

He looked sideways at her and thought that she looked like a 'roo in the headlights of a road train. Unfortunately he understood how deeply the scars of emotional abuse ran. He was proud of her, but she didn't seem to under-stand how far she'd come. Sure, she hadn't said much, but she'd said *something*.

It didn't matter that her words had just bounced off Wayne and that he'd only sat up and taken notice when Rob took him to task. None of that mattered because Willa had stood up for herself and he was proud of her. Yeah, he'd jumped in and got all he-man and protective, but he knew, deep down, that if hadn't been there Willa would have been just fine.

Eventually.

'So, on a scale of one to Chinese water torture, how much fun was *that*?' Rob asked as he opened the passen-ger door to her Mercedes, gesturing her inside.

Willa looked up at him, the sheen in her eyes suggest-ing tears. 'I'm so sorry.'

Rob slammed her car door shut and stalked around to the driver's seat, sliding inside and sending her a puzzled look. 'What exactly are you sorry for, Willa?'

'For everything. For even asking you to go.'

'You didn't ask me. I volunteered. Try again.' Rob started the car, pulled off, and flicked her another look. 'Put your seat belt on, honey.'

Willa just looked at him, so Rob leaned across her, pulled the strap from the harness across her body and snapped the lock into place.

'I put you in a silly situation and we had the attention of the entire room on us.'

As if he cared about that. 'I couldn't give a monkey's if all of Sydney was watching us,' Rob growled. Knowing that he'd sounded harsh, he placed a warm, large hand on her knee and tried to dial it down. 'Willa, I don't care what people think of me—I do not live my life wondering how to please other people and meet their expectations.'

'But you think I do,' Willa stated quietly.

'Actually, I think you were pretty amazing tonight.'

Willa snorted her disbelief. 'All I feel is humiliated. And stupid.'

'You don't have to feel that way.'

'I stood there with a mouth full of teeth and when I finally said something it was a couple of sentences that he hardly bothered to pay attention to.'

'That doesn't matter.'

'He didn't hear me or care!'

'And that's on him—not you. You did what you needed to do.'

Rob squeezed her knee again and wished he could pull over to take her in his arms, to offer the comfort he knew she so desperately needed. She was the only woman who had ever made him want to offer tenderness, to become involved. And it scared the hell out of him.

But worrying about how emotionally tied up he was becoming with this woman was for later... He was a man. He couldn't multitask.

He saw the stubborn tilt to her wobbly chin and gave it another shot. 'Where did you get this idea that you aren't entitled to express your feelings? Earlier you said that you didn't want them to remember you as a wimpy wife or as an easily dismissed insecure girl. You were talking about taking back your pride and self-respect.' Rob flicked her a glance. 'You did that.'

'Not very well,' Willa muttered. 'I got scared.'

'You didn't—don't—need to be. He's a wimpy moron in an expensive suit.' Rob kept his voice low and tried for soothing. He didn't know if he'd reached it…he'd never aimed for soothing before. 'I was standing right behind you. I wouldn't have allowed him to get close enough to touch you.'

Willa closed her eyes. 'I wasn't that type of scared. I felt myself sliding back into the person I was with Wayne—anxious to please, nervous, compliant—and that terrified me. What if this is who I actually am? Who, underneath it all, I'll always be?'

Yeah, he could understand that. He'd watched her sliding away tonight, back into a place where nothing and nobody could touch her. The person she was with him—cheeky, mischievous, confident—had disappeared at Wayne's first insult and she'd frozen, unable to get her vocal cords to move. Wayne had put her there, back in the life she'd hated, the state she'd hated, with a couple of well-placed barbs.

Seriously, he could still turn this car around and rearrange Wayne's face.

'I feel weak and foolish and sad.'

Rob placed his hand on her thigh and squeezed. 'You really don't need to.'

Willa looked out of the window as Rob turned into her driveway. He stopped the car, rested his arms on the steering wheel and looked out onto the dark night before reaching into his suit pocket to pull out his mobile.

'What are you doing?' she asked, her heart in her throat.

'Calling a taxi,' Rob answered quietly.

'You don't have to go.'

'Yeah, I think I do.' Rob looked at her with hot eyes. 'I think we should give each other a little space right now.' He shook his head as panic skittered across her face. 'Willa, get a grip!' *Tender, Hanson, remember to be tender.* He dropped his voice. 'I'm suggesting a night apart—that's it. Some time for me to work off the fact that I want to use your ex as a punchbag and some time for you to work through what happened tonight.'

Willa let out a long, relieved breath. 'Okay…but don't call a taxi. Take this car. I don't need it.'

'You sure?' Rob asked her.

'Yeah.' Willa opened the passenger door and looked at Rob, her battered heart in her eyes. 'I'm sorry I disappointed you.'

Rob rubbed his forehead with his fingers. 'Honey, that's just it. Either I'm not explaining this well or you're not hearing me but you damn well *didn't*.'

Rob let himself into Willa's house courtesy of the key he'd found in her sports car and wondered what he should do, say, to make things right. This was completely uncharted territory for him, he admitted, heading for the kitchen, where he could hear music playing from the retro radio on the long shelf next to the door.

He only ever dated, slept with, strong women, confident women—women who knew who they were and what they wanted. *How would you know what they wanted?* he asked himself mockingly. *You never stuck around long enough to ask or to find out whether their confidence was a shield or their strength was faked.*

Willa was strong, he admitted. You couldn't survive a controlling marriage, get your degree and then find the guts to leave if you weren't. If he had to judge only by last night's response, then he might have to say that she was weak and easily cowed, but last night she hadn't been the same person she was with him. With him she was sharper, funnier, stronger, chirpier.

Who was the real Willa? Maybe she was still too fragile? Maybe she needed someone…different? Better? He was impatient and gruff and forthright—too damn honest for most people, especially women, to handle. He was sometimes brutal, always clear-thinking and matter-of-fact; he called things as he saw them.

The thought of her being with anyone else made him want to put his hand through the wall, but despite his caveman response—and what was *that* about?—he knew that the right thing to do was to back away, to give her space. Which posed a problem since, A. She was working for him, and B. He didn't want to.

Rob poured two cups of coffee and took them to the office, where he'd expected Willa to be. Not finding her behind her desk, he stepped through the door of the study onto the veranda and found her sitting on the edge of the pool, her feet in the water.

Hearing his footsteps, she lifted her face. He wished that she wasn't wearing huge sunglasses that dominated her face; he wanted to see her eyes. Firstly because looking into Willa's eyes was always a pleasure, but mostly because then he could read, so clearly, what was troubling her.

'Take your shades off for a moment.'

'Why?'

'Please?'

Willa shrugged and pushed her glasses up into her hair. He scanned her face, her eyes, and, yep, there they were. Anger, humiliation, sadness.

'Here.'

Willa took the cup he held out with murmured thanks

and Rob lowered himself to sit next to her, taking the sunglasses off the top of his own head and sliding them onto his face. He slipped hers back onto her nose.

'You okay?' he asked, when she didn't say anything at all.

'Still feeling like a fool,' Willa admitted quietly.

'What for? For not saying more or for marrying that moron? Or for going to that party in the first place?' Rob asked. *Yeah, too honest.*

'All of the above,' Willa stated. 'God, this coffee is good—but it would've been better with a doughnut. I'm starving.'

'Well, you didn't eat anything on the yacht last night.'

'Catamaran.' Willa saw the look he sent her and shrugged. 'It was a catamaran…two hulls…not a yacht. Just being accurate.'

'I'm a city boy. I know Jack about yachts and boats,' Rob replied. 'So, are we going to talk about last night?'

'It's such a gorgeous day,' Willa said, looking past him to the harbour in the distance, the gentle waters of the bay below them. Rob was back and her world made sense again.

'Nice try, but we're not changing the subject.'

Willa sighed as she recognised the stubborn look in his eye. 'I've said, over and over, that I feel a fool! Especially since I know that he's a balding bully—a little man with a big ego that needs to be fed.' Willa put her cup down on the pavement, looking anguished. 'Why couldn't I say more?'

'Had you seen him since you separated?'

Willa shook her head. 'Only in meetings with Kate, and then she and his lawyer did most of the talking.' She sighed and leaned back. 'I suppose you think that's stupid?'

Rob tapped his finger against the mug he held. 'No, not stupid.'

'I'm so angry with myself because I've worked so hard over the last months to stop believing the crap he fed me about myself. I've been telling myself that I was young and impressionable, that I didn't have anyone in my life to counter his opinion, and that that time is over—*he* is over. I believed that. But then he was there and I went straight back into stupid mode.'

'Habit reaction. It's classic abuse-sufferer behaviour,' Rob murmured.

'He didn't abuse me…' Willa protested.

'Verbal abuse is still abuse and it's just as dangerous. Bet he also played the blame game and the silent game and the can't-please-me game as well.'

'You sound like you know what you're talking about.'

'I *do* know what I'm talking about,' Rob admitted reluctantly. 'My stepfather abused my mother and my sister for three years until my uncle put a stop to it.'

Willa bit her bottom lip in sympathy. 'I'm so sorry. How…?' Her heart bled for him, for the pain she could still see in his eyes, the bleakness in his voice. 'I'm not sure what to say…'

'Not a hell of a lot *to* say. We were weak, still reeling from the death of my dad a year before, and Stefan was our rock, our comfort, my dad's best friend. He and my mum grew closer and she asked me if I thought she should marry him.'

'And you said yes?'

'I wanted her to be happy again and—' Rob abruptly stopped speaking, taking a sip of his coffee instead.

'And?' Willa prodded.

Rob stared at the bright blue pool. 'And I wanted to go off across country to study at uni. I could do that without guilt if I knew that he was looking after my mum and sister. Then he moved in and took over their lives…he made me what I am.'

'Which is?' Willa asked crisply.

'Generally flawed. Mostly distrustful. Of myself and

of everyone around me. Impatient, closed-off, unwilling to commit.'

'Why?'

'After my dad, Stefan was my hero. I genuinely respected him—loved him, even. I would never have thought that he would turn into an abusive bully. I learnt the hard way that what you see is never what you actually get.'

'"Impatient, closed-off, unwilling to commit..."' Willa tipped her head. 'Sounds like somebody made a list.'

'Many somebodys—all female, all mad when I dumped them.' Rob shrugged, looking resigned and then resolute. 'They weren't wrong, Willa.'

They'd forgotten to tell him that he was hard-working and sexy, honourable and loyal, had a wicked sense of humour and a protective instinct a mile long.

Rob lifted a powerful shoulder in an agitated shrug. 'The thing is...because I don't—*can't* trust, I don't have relationships. I have flings. When it starts getting a bit too real, I bail.'

Willa pulled in a deep breath, feeling compelled to ask, to find out exactly where she stood with him. 'Is *this* getting a bit too real? Are you wanting to bail?'

Rob twisted his lips. 'I'm thinking that if you were in an abusive relationship then I am exactly the wrong type of guy you should be having a rebound fling with. You need someone gentle, compassionate, patient. I'm none of those things...'

Willa was quiet for a moment, thinking about what he'd said. It wasn't as if she hadn't had the same thoughts a couple of times during the long night. A nice man would be easier, calmer—wouldn't force her to confront her demons, would let her ease into her new life. A gentle man would give her time and compassion...

Except that she didn't need time and compassion. She

needed a boot up the backside. She needed someone to yank her out of her 'woe is me' attitude and tell her to get a grip and get a life. There was something about Rob that inspired her to be tougher, stronger. Rob, just by being Rob, made her want to step up to the plate and take her best shot. To be brave enough to try.

He wasn't easy, but his attitude was good for her.

He was perfect for her right now. Maybe for ever. He didn't let her coast or cruise…

Willa pulled her glasses off her face and tapped them against her knee. 'No, you're not patient or gentle, but I know that you can be compassionate. And I don't need someone to pussyfoot around me. I've been protected and cosseted my whole life. I need a man who doesn't want to treat me like china—a man who demands that I stand on my own two feet, that I be a woman and start acting like one.'

'I call it like I see it. I always have…it's just who I am.'

'And I need someone in my life like that.'

Willa saw him mentally retreat, saw him back-pedalling and knew that this conversation had gone too deep, too quickly. Rob was looking panicked, and she wouldn't be surprised if he broke out in hives some time soon.

Relax, Rob, it's all still good, she wanted to tell him. Despite this conversation she knew that it was just surface, just temporary between them.

Because he was looking faintly green, she gave him some breathing room. 'I'd like you to carry on being your gruff self for as long as you're here—even if it that is only for a couple more days, weeks… When *are* you heading back to South Africa?'

Relief loosened that tight, ticking muscle in his jaw, the tense cords of his neck, and she vaguely listened to him explain that he might be here for three more weeks, a month at the most, quickly understanding that this was still very much just a fling for him.

Willa bit the inside of her lip.

Unfortunately she was starting to feel that, for her, maybe it wasn't any more.

Willa looked around the dining table at her friends and wished Brodie had accepted her invitation to dinner, although she'd never expected him to. Seeing Rob and Scott deep in conversation about an architect she'd never heard of reminded her of how well Scott and Brodie had got along— how they'd have those same masculine, short-sentence conversations that went on for hours.

She liked having people around her table...liked being able to feed them, cook for them. A simple meal. Chicken pasta and salad. Garlic bread. Good wine from the cellar downstairs. Excellent company.

Talking of which, she wished Kate was here, but she, like Brodie, supposedly had to work. Amy was here, and Jessica had brought along the Weeping Reef ex-lifeguard she'd left with the other day and the six of them had laughed and chattered through dinner and more than a few bottles of wine from the cellar.

She had a lot to be grateful for...

She should be happy...

She was having explosive sex with a man who excelled at the art, she had reconnected with her friends and she had a job that challenged her on every level. So why was she feeling out of sorts, dissociated, unsettled?

Willa left her friends talking and picked up some empty plates and took them to the kitchen. Wanting a minute to herself, she looked out of the kitchen window as she held on to the granite edge of the counter. She'd come so far in eight months; she should be incredibly proud of herself...

Should be...should be...should be...

But what had she done, really? She'd walked away from her sucky marriage…big deal. That was nothing in the scheme of things; women defied governments, defended their countries, fought poverty and sexism and lack of education all over the world. Her leaving Wayne wasn't exactly behaviour worthy of admiration—especially since it had been about eight years overdue.

She was living in a mansion house that her ex had paid for, driving a car that her ex had paid for, and at the only opportunity she'd had to show Wayne—to show herself—that she was her own person, she'd blown it.

As for Rob…her one-night stand had turned into an affair with a sell-by date; she wasn't sure what that date was, but it would soon be over. And because she'd been desperate to work, and had begged him for the job, she'd landed her position as Rob's accountant by default too.

She was, basically, sleeping with her boss.

She hadn't pitted herself against any other applicants, she hadn't been measured against her peers. How could she be sure that she was as capable as them? That she had the job because she was actually good at it and not just good at the bedroom-based activities she engaged in with Rob?

Seeing an open bottle of red on the counter, she reached for a glass and poured herself a half-glass that she threw down her throat. He had an accountant and a lover…good deal for *him*.

Basically, she was still living her life according to other people's tenets: she'd been the good daughter, then the trophy wife, and now she was exactly what Rob wanted—his casual fling and his accountant.

What did she want, for God's sake? And was she ever going to start making decisions for herself?

Willa poured herself another glass of wine and sipped it slowly. Yeah, maybe it was about time she started doing exactly that.

* * *

Willa and Kate were lying on loungers in the late-afternoon sun, a pitcher of icy sangria between them, drying off after a refreshing swim. Kate pushed her designer sunglasses up on her face and rolled her head to look at Willa.

'Where's Hot and Spicy?'

Willa smiled at the moniker. 'He went to Brisbane for a couple of days. He's meeting with some people who want to buy into his franchise. Next week he's heading to Perth.'

'He looks too rough and ready to be such a hotshot businessman. He looks like he should be a rugby player or a surfer,' Kate stated idly.

'I know, right? But he's great at what he does. He's got brilliant instincts and great vision—though he's not wild about the accountancy side of the business,' Willa said, thinking that getting Rob to discuss VAT and tax was akin to pulling teeth.

'And that's why he hired you.' Kate rolled over onto her side and rested her head in her hand. 'How's that working for you?'

'I love it…' Willa replied. 'I love making numbers dance.'

Kate pulled a face. 'I'm with Rob on the hating accountancy part…I find it deeply boring. And are you managing to work together *and* sleep together?'

Willa looked out onto the harbour. 'Rob makes the transition a lot easier than I do. He flips a switch and instantly forgets that we've just had an argument about cash flow and staff benefits. I take a lot longer to…transition.'

'Rob understands that there's nothing personal in the argument but you don't seem to,' Kate commented. 'It's something that comes with experience. Give it time and you'll get there.'

Willa refilled their glasses with sangria and handed Kate hers. She tapped her nails against the icy glass… She needed to talk to somebody about Rob and since Kate was now her closest friend she was duly elected. 'I'm feeling really confused, Kate, and slightly at sea.'

Kate sat up straight and pulled her sunglasses off her face. She scanned Willa's face before asking, 'Okay…why?'

Willa took a sip of her drink before putting the glass on the table between them. The sun had started falling in the sky and was turning from gold to orange. 'When I got over the shock of living on my own, without Wayne, I promised myself that I would do what I wanted to do and what I felt was right—for me.'

Kate didn't respond, just cocked her head in interest.

'I was just getting to a point in my life when I felt like I was coming into my own, being me, and I fell into bed with Rob.'

'Mmm-hmm. And the problem is…?' Kate placed her elbows on her crossed knees and cupped her face in her hands.

Willa huffed out her breath. 'I'm not even sure if there is a problem or whether I'm just making problems…' she admitted, now wishing that she hadn't opened this can of worms.

'Just spit it out, Willa.'

'I still feel mortified that I clammed up when Wayne insulted me in front of all those people. Rob was there, but I just stood there and got…scared, stupid. It was like stepping back into being that downtrodden, subservient wife I had been and I hated it! My words dried up and all I wanted to do was run away from him, as far and as fast as I could. Rob had to stick up for me.'

'But you *did* speak.'

'I didn't say enough,' Willa stated.

'It's okay, Willa. Stop being so hard on yourself.'

Kate didn't look outraged or even disappointed. Easy for Kate to say, but Willa didn't want to be the subservient, meek, timid woman she was with Wayne; she wanted to be bold and fierce and confident—all the time!

'You've come a long, long way, Willa. Don't lose sight of that just because you had a setback with The Pain.'

But maybe she hadn't come as far as Kate thought—as far as she'd believed she had. Her life had changed so dramatically and she was having difficulty processing all the changes. She was still getting used to being on her own, coming to terms with the demise of her marriage and the part she'd played in it. Sure, Wayne was an idiot of extraordinary skill, but she'd *allowed* him to treat her like that; by not fully standing up to him she'd given him permission to treat her badly.

He'd called all the shots in her marriage and her life and... Willa rubbed her hands over her face. And she was scared that she was allowing history to repeat itself.

Rob was, to an extent, calling all the shots in this relationship. He was a force of nature and she was in danger of being swept away by the strength of his personality. He'd fallen into her bed and fallen into her life and now he was her boss.

Holy hell, what had she jumped into here? Had she gone straight from the frying pan into—well, the sixty-fourth level of hell? Had she been blinded by Rob's handsome face and luscious body and his ability to give her mind-blowing orgasms? Was she that weak, that shallow, that starved for attention?

What did she want? What did she deserve?

Surely it was more than this?

'Oh, fudge,' Kate said, scrunching up her eyes.

'What?' Willa asked.

'That look on your face—I recognise it as your Willa-digging-her-heels-in look.' Kate stood up and knotted her wrap on her right hip.

Willa smiled reluctantly. 'Am I that transparent?'

'Sorry…but, yes. What are you thinking about, honey?'

Willa adjusted the cups of her strapless pink bikini. 'I'm thinking that it's time I worked out exactly what I want from life and men…and Rob. I need to start deciding what is right for *me*.'

Kate placed a hand on her chest and wiped away an imaginary tear. 'My baby girl is finally growing up.'

Willa didn't have a verbal comeback so she placed her hands on Kate's shoulders and pushed her into the pool.

CHAPTER NINE

'YOU BITCH!'

Willa, barrelling up the steps to the front door after her early-morning run, jumped a foot in the air as Wayne stepped out of the shadows of the veranda, a menacing look on his face.

Recognising that he had a major temper brewing, she slapped a hand on her chest and closed her eyes. *Not now*, she prayed. She was so close to being free of him. Why was he here? What did he want?

'How dare you embarrass me in front of my friends, my business associates last week? Everyone was laughing at me behind my back!' Wayne hissed. 'Vern cancelled a deal with me yesterday—said that he didn't like the way I treated you. You stupid bitch.'

And this was *her* fault? How? Willa desperately wanted to tell him not to call her names, that he was no longer allowed to do that, but seeing the cold fury in his eyes had sent her words and her courage belting away. Again.

And she'd seen Wayne angry before, but she'd never seen that sadistic gleam in his eyes. 'You think you're so smart, with your hulk boyfriend protecting you, but I'm not done with you. I'm not done showing you how useless I think you are... *I'm not done.*'

Willa bit her lip and thought that she had to get away. She moved to the right but Wayne blocked her escape down the path to the road. She was trapped... God, why she had allowed Rob to go back to his flat last night? If Rob was here then Wayne wouldn't be doing this… Then again, Wayne was a coward. He had to know that Rob wasn't here…

Dear God, she was on her own.

'Calm down, Wayne.'

Wayne gripped the top parts of her arms and his fingers dug in. Willa winced, but didn't attempt to remove herself from his grasp.

'I will not calm down, bitch. I am so goddamn angry with you… You will not defy me; you will not make me look stupid. I will bloody teach you this lesson if it's the last thing I do. Open the door and get inside.'

Oh, crap, she was in bigger trouble here than she'd thought.

Willa fought down the urge to panic and ignored the pain of his fingers digging into her arms. If she let him into the house she would be at his mercy…but if she didn't he might just start hitting her here.

Because being hit was in her immediate future. She knew that as well as she knew her own name. He'd never done it before, but losing face with Vern would have pushed him over the edge. Wayne, being the narcissistic ass that he was, would always find someone else to blame.

Willa froze, every muscle in her body tensing. She wanted to fight him but she was so damn scared. She wanted to scream at him but knew that would just make him madder. She was trapped…

This was how Amy had felt, she thought. Terrified and alone… She remembered Amy's bruises and injuries and she shuddered. *Oh, Ames…*

'Open the bloody door or I swear I'll just make it worse.'

Wayne shook her and Willa reached for the key. Maybe if she just listened to him he would come to his senses and she'd escape with nothing more than a slap…

Don't go in the house, Willa. Fight.

Willa felt her anger swell and her courage return with

the force of a tidal wave. She was not doing this again—
she was not going to be Wayne's wimpy wife ever again!

Whirling around, she slapped both her hands on Wayne's
chest and, shoving as hard as she could, pushed him back a
couple of steps. She'd never, as long as she lived, forget the
astonished look on his face. It gave her even more courage.

'You want to take a swing at me? You do it right here,
you bastard!'

Wayne's eyes widened and Willa saw his fist clench.
Instead of retreating, Willa got in his face.

'But you should know that I'll fight back, I'll fight you
with everything I have! And if you touch me you'd better
kill me because I swear to God I will nail your saggy ass
to a wall when I charge you with assault,' she hissed.

Wayne stopped in his tracks and looked at her, hesitating. Willa felt her power surge again and she knew she
wasn't nearly done with him. She had no back-up but she
didn't need it...not this time.

She was Willa Moore, and she was going to take control of her life, dammit!

'You will never disparage me, insult me or put me down
again! You will never threaten me with violence, put your
hands on me or make me feel less than I am.' Willa's chest
heaved with anger and her eyes were laser-sharp.

'Willa, calm down...'

Willa actually growled at him. 'Don't you *dare* tell me
what to do! God *damn* you! You complete bastard moron!'

Wayne looked around and started inching his way towards the steps. 'I think that you should—'

He was still talking? Really? Well, it wasn't his time to
talk, it was hers. She had eight years' worth of anger needing an escape and he was in her target zone.

'I actually don't care what you think I should do, you
spineless, pathetic, shiny-headed weasel. I'm not a little girl
any more. Come to think of it, why can't you have relation-

ships with women who are women and not girls, Wayne? Are you that insecure?'

Willa gave him half a second to answer before storming in again.

'Are you threatened by women being smarter, older? Do you see young girls as women you can mould? Are you just sick? I had so much to give, dammit, and you stifled me at every turn—'

'I wanted to protect you!' Wayne protested.

'You wanted to control me and, well done, you succeeded...for a while.' Willa shoved her hands into her hair and tugged. 'But I've escaped your saggy clutches now, you horrible man, and I won't be made to feel bad about it—especially not by you.'

'Hey, Willa. Morning!'

They both whirled around and Willa saw her sprightly neighbours, Jerry and Luella, at the bottom of her driveway, their Alsatian Ben between them. She finally had Wayne on the back foot, she had so much more grief to give him, and she was being interrupted. Wayne, the soft, yellow-bellied coward, looked relieved.

Jerry frowned when Willa didn't respond, and he and Ben walked towards her up the path. Ben growled and Jerry looked from Willa to Wayne.

'Everything okay here?'

Wayne looked even more relieved. 'I'm just leaving.'

Willa saw the enquiring look Jerry sent her and shrugged. 'My revolting ex.'

Jerry, six two and still powerful, despite being in his sixties, crossed his tree trunk arms and glared at Wayne. 'We'll just wait until you do just that.'

Ben went to sit next to Willa's legs and growled when Wayne took a half-step towards her. Wayne muttered an obscenity, sent Willa a furious look, and when neither she nor Jerry—nor Ben—moved he whirled away and stomped down the driveway.

Jerry waited until he saw Wayne roar off in his Ferrari before he placed a meaty hand on Willa's shaking shoulder. 'You okay, hun? He looked like a nasty piece of work.'

Willa released the breath she was holding. 'He is. But today—' she grinned at him '—I was nastier. Thanks, Jerry.' She rubbed Ben between the ears. 'You too, Ben.'

Jerry took the key from her shaking hand, put it in the lock and pushed her door open for her. 'Lock it behind you and be careful. Where's that nice guy who's been hanging around?'

'Rob?' Willa pushed her hand through her hair. 'He'll be around later.'

'Good.' Jerry pushed her inside. 'Take care and call me if the other guy comes back.'

'Thanks, Jerry.'

Willa blew him a kiss, slipped inside her house, closed the door and locked it. Leaning against the door, she slid to the floor, wrapped her arms around her knees and cried.

She shouldn't be crying, Willa thought, brushing at her tears. She'd fought the monster under her bed, the one inside her head, and she'd won. She should be laughing, dancing, celebrating...

She had her self-respect back. She hadn't disappointed herself again. She'd fought back. So why was she crying?

Cleansing tears, she realised eventually. Facing Wayne down had been like removing a festering thorn: the irritant was out, but there was still some muck in the hole.

So Willa, her back to the door and her head on her knees, allowed herself to cry. To be cleansed.

When Rob got to Willa's at midday he had to wait while she answered the front door, which for once was locked. Silently, he followed her stiff back to the study. He had enough experience with women to realise that something was amiss, and he ran back through their last couple of conversations to see if he'd put his foot in it or forgotten something important… He couldn't think of anything in particular, but who knew?

Maybe it wasn't him… Maybe she'd had a fight with one of her girlfriends—or might she be getting sick? Did she look a little red? Rob shook his head at the urge to place the back of his hand against her forehead to see if she was running a temperature.

He was, he was humiliated to admit, a sap. Why did he care so much? He was just here, with her, for a little company, a lot of sex. Some laughs…

He wasn't here to fix her, protect her, look after her. That wasn't his job.

Willa, dressed in a pair of cut-off jeans and a long-sleeved tee—it was about a million degrees outside…why the long sleeves?—walked around her desk and sank into her chair.

'We need to go through the cost projections for the store and the cash-flow projections for the gym,' Willa said crisply, looking at her computer screen. 'Let me just print them out.'

Rob frowned, conscious of the fact that Willa hadn't yet met his eyes. He peered into her face, noticing that she looked a little pale. Hell, maybe she *was* getting sick…

'Hey, are you okay?'

'I'm fine,' she snapped.

Okay, then, bite my head off, why don't you?

'You're looking out of sorts and you're wearing sleeves on a steaming hot day. Are you getting sick?' Rob persisted.

'Maybe.' Willa gestured to her desk. 'Can we get to work, please?'

'No.' Rob walked around the desk, lifted her chin and

looked into her unhappy red-rimmed eyes. 'Have you been crying?'

'Rob, enough! I just want to get to work; we have so much to do!'

Rob placed his hands on the armrests of her chair and shook his head. 'Firstly, it's Sunday—and it's against my religion to work on a Sunday.'

Willa snorted. 'What religion is that? Paganism?'

'And secondly something big is bothering you.'

Rob placed his hands on her arms and his blood froze when she let out a smothered yelp of pain. Instinctively he recognised that sound: the sound of someone—a woman... *his* woman!—trying to hide an injury. Dropping her back into her chair, he swiftly reached for the hem of her T-shirt and tugged it up.

'What are you doing? I'm not getting naked right now!'

'Take the T-shirt off, Willa,' Rob stated, his voice low and hard. His tone suggested that she did not argue with him.

Willa's voice broke. 'Please, Rob, just let it go.'

Like hell. 'Off. Now.'

He tugged the hem of the shirt again and, feeling the resistance leave her, gently pulled the T-shirt over her head. His eyes scanned her torso and then he saw the purple, perfect bruises that indicated fingers holding her left arm far too tight. His eyes jumped to her other arm where she had a matching set.

'When was he here?' he growled, stepping back and looking at her through a red mist of temper. He had to control it this one time. He had to be better than he was.

'It's nothing—'

'It's something, Willa. Let's have it,' Rob said, struggling to keep his composure.

'Early this morning,' Willa admitted reluctantly. 'He was waiting for me when I came back from my run.'

Willa yanked her T-shirt out of his hands and pulled it over her head. Somewhere, in the place that wasn't all caveman, he realised that her voice radiated frustration and temper but no timidity.

'He said that I'd embarrassed him and he was going to teach me a lesson… I think if he'd got me into the house then he would've slapped me around.'

Rob felt his gut clench and nausea roil through him. He breathed through his nose and ordered his stomach to settle down. 'Dear God…'

The words were more of a plea than a blasphemy.

'For far too many minutes I just stood there…couldn't fight him. Couldn't say a damn thing… I've never seen him look like that… I was so scared.' Willa wrapped her arms around her middle and dropped her head.

Rob couldn't comfort her—he was too angry. Instead he pivoted on his heel and slammed his fist into a wooden cupboard behind him. Willa gasped, and fire rocketed up his arm, but it was worth it because for a moment—just a moment—he imagined that it was Wayne Fisher's face on the other side of his fist.

Then he rested his head against the cupboard as he pulled in deep breaths, grateful that the punch had taken the edge off. When he thought he could face her again with a measure of calm, he turned around.

Willa's mouth had dropped open and he was, on one level, pleased to see a spark back in her eyes.

'Was that necessary? Jeez—calm down, Rob.'

He was calm. Just… But he was still in the zone. To prove his point, if only to himself, he lowered his voice even further. 'He put his hands on you…he was going to beat you—terrorise you! I'm trying, very hard, to stop my-self from going caveman.'

'I *handled* him!' Willa cried. 'If you could pull your head out of your ass for five seconds and concentrate, you'd actually hear what is important here! I stood up to him—without you, I might add. I tore into him and it felt brilliant! This isn't your problem, Rob!' she stated, leaning forward. 'He's my ex-husband, my problem, my issue! He pushed and I pushed back harder! He left with his tail between his legs…'

Rob stared at a spot on the wall past her head, his back teeth grinding together. At this rate he might have to get them crowned. 'I should've been here…'

'I'm glad you weren't,' Willa admitted candidly, and rolled her eyes at his ferocious scowl. 'I needed to do that, Rob! I needed to take him on, to fight back—'

'You could've made it worse.'

'Coulda, woulda, shoulda… I *didn't*! He backed down and he'll never try that again.'

'You hope. Still, if I'd been here…'

'If you'd been here I might have let you handle him—but *I* needed to. Can't you understand that?' Willa sighed and rubbed her hands over her face.

'He put bruises on your arms and he made you cry,' Rob stated in a bleak voice.

'The bruises will fade and I cried because I felt like this huge weight was finally off my shoulders.' Willa stood up, took a step towards him and wrapped her arms around his neck, burying her face in his chest. 'I need you to let this go. I was getting there, and now I'm upset because *you're* upset. He's not worth it, Rob.'

Rob allowed himself to run his uninjured hand down her back. 'He can't be allowed to get away with threatening you; that's not acceptable, Wills.'

'I'll tell Kate. She'll know what to do,' Willa conceded and Rob felt his temper start to drain away.

'Call her now,' he insisted.

Willa nodded and dropped her arms. She lifted his hand

and winced at his scraped and swelling knuckles. 'Oh, Rob, dammit. This needs ice.'

Rob looked at his hand and shrugged. He couldn't feel anything at the moment—adrenalin was keeping the pain at bay—but he knew that in an hour or so he'd be feeling the effects of punching a solid oak cabinet.

He slid a glance to the cupboard, where a fist-sized dent was impossible to miss. 'Sorry, Willa, I've ruined it.'

'I don't give a damn about the cupboard; I'm just worried that you've broken some fingers!'

Rob wiggled his fingers and felt pain shooting up his hand. *Hellfire and all its demons.* 'Not broken.'

'You need an ice pack.' Willa dropped his hand and rested her forehead against his chest. 'Despite the fact that you went all Neanderthal on me, I'm so glad you're here now, Rob.'

Rob wrapped his arms around her cold body and pulled her into him, trying to get her as close as possible. 'I should have decked him the other night, Wills.'

'He went home today feeling terrible, Rob. He heard me—he finally heard me. That's all that matters right now.'

An hour later Kate paced Willa's kitchen, an untouched cup of coffee in her hands, her mouth pursed and her eyes flashing with anger. She looked from Willa to Rob, who was holding a bag of peas against his now swollen hand, and back again.

'The problem is that he didn't actually *do* anything,' Kate said, having listened to Willa telling the story of her encounter with Wayne.

'He threatened her, Kate! Bruised her!'

'Rob, if the police arrested people on threats our jails would be jam-packed. And he could easily claim the bruises weren't caused by him,' Kate retorted. 'I want to tell you that there's something we can do but there isn't! Dammit.'

Rob just growled his displeasure.

Willa looked at her dark knight and swallowed her smile. She really believed that he and Kate were both overreacting. She knew Wayne and he was a consummate bully. He'd scuttled away from her and he wouldn't try anything ever again. He'd cut her out of his life, wouldn't acknowledge her ever again and she was *so* okay with that.

Rob, however, was still vibrating with suppressed anger. For her.

'I hear what you're saying, Kate, and I understand. Wayne was in a temper. He was furious that he'd lost the deal with Vern and it's in his nature to look for a scapegoat. I was it. He won't try this again...he can't afford to get arrested on a charge of assault.'

Kate nodded, finally took a sip of her now cold coffee and grimaced. 'I agree. However, I *will* be making a call to his attorney in a minute and I *will* tell him what happened this morning. I will also tell him that if his client comes within a hundred metres of you, I will take out a restraining order on your behalf. Will your neighbour back up your claims?'

'He can tell you that he was holding me and acting crazy and threatening,' Willa said.

'Good.'

Rob pulled out his mobile from his pocket and fiddled with the buttons. 'Take your T-shirt off, Willa.'

'Haven't we sung this song already today?' Willa complained.

'Photo evidence,' Rob replied, impatient.

'It's a good idea, Willa,' Kate agreed. 'I'll attach it to the follow-up e-mail I'll be sending his lawyer.'

'Dammit...' Willa muttered, and took her shirt off for the second time.

Rob's lips firmed and his jaw clenched as he lifted his mobile to photograph her arm. Willa looked down and grimaced. What had been faint blue smudges this morning were now livid purple bruises.

'Don't punch anything,' she warned Rob, who looked ready to do that again.

Rob glared at her as the phone's camera did its thing, and when he was finished he pushed his chair back from the table, handed Kate his mobile and stalked from the room.

Willa started to go after him but Kate's hand on her arm halted her flight across the room. 'He needs some time on his own, Willa. Leave him. He needs to work through his anger—to process what's happened.'

'He's so angry, Kate.'

'Of course he is; he wasn't able to protect you, and to an alpha male like Rob that is like a massive kick in the nuts by a little girl. Give him time, Wills. He'll come back when he's worked through it.'

Willa looked at Rob's disappearing back and remembered what he'd said about his stepfather—that he'd been abusive towards his mother. Maybe Wayne's crazy stunt had pulled a whole lot of memories and angst to the surface.

She suspected it might be a long time before he came to her...

If at all.

Taking Kate's advice, Willa left the brooding Rob alone and, thinking she needed something to take her mind off her crazy morning, decided to tackle the cost projections and cash-flow spreadsheets herself. Soon she was lost in the numbers, carried away with her work. Here there were no mad ex-husbands wanting to teach her a lesson, nor brooding part time lovers, there were just the numbers; straightforward and simple.

Rob pulled her back to the present by knocking his good fist on her desk.

Willa jerked her head up, pulled her glasses off and rubbed her eyes. 'Hi.'

'Hi back. I've made lunch,' Rob said. 'Take a break—you've been at it for four hours.'

'Ah...okay.' She stretched her spine before climbing to her feet and following Rob out to the veranda. On the wooden table he'd placed a huge seafood salad, plates, and an icy bottle of white wine. Willa instantly began to salivate.

Sliding onto the wooden bench, she reached for a plate and dumped the avocado and prawn-rich salad onto her plate. 'This looks *so* good.'

Rob poured wine into the glasses, handed hers over and took a seat opposite her. Willa saw that he was only using one hand and grimaced in sympathy. His other hand was swollen, black and blue.

'Is it very painful?'

Rob looked at his fingers and shrugged. 'I'll live.'

Boy-speak for, *Hell, yeah, it's sore.*

'I'd like to move in here. Is that okay with you?' Rob asked, his tone sober. 'I'm worried he'll come back.'

'I really don't think that is likely. Besides, I'll be divorced in a couple of weeks,' Willa responded, looking at her heaped fork.

'Say yes, Wills. Please?'

Willa mentally debated what to do. Rob was spending most nights with her anyway, and it was stupid him renting an apartment that he rarely occupied. And there was no doubt that she'd feel safer with him around...not that she needed to feel safe. She now knew that she could handle Wayne—once a day and twice on Sundays.

But she wanted Rob with her not as a guard dog or a sleeping aid but as the man she wanted in her life—as someone she wanted to spend as much time with as possible.

She wanted him to see her as his equal, as someone strong and capable, not as a weakling who needed his protection. She wanted him to *want* to be with her—not because he had a misplaced white knight complex.

'I don't need your pity or your protection, Rob,' she told him, after she'd forthrightly explained her dilemma.

Rob sat back in his chair and a glint of amusement sparked in his eyes. 'I like the set of teeth you've suddenly grown, Willa.'

Willa stared him down, unwilling to be distracted from the matter at hand, and Rob eventually lifted a hand in resignation. 'I'm by nature a protector, and I can't and won't apologise for that. I will always jump in front of the bus, the bullet, the wild pack of hyenas. But I don't pity you. I don't believe in pity.' He flashed her his panty-melting grin. 'And I like the idea of being able to fool around whenever and wherever we please.'

'We're doing that already,' Willa pointed out, sure that he was trying to bamboozle her.

'Yeah, but occasionally I still drive to the flat at night—a danger to all road-users as my mind is usually still in bed with you.'

Willa narrowed her eyes at him as she fought a grin. 'You are *so* full of it. Okay,' she said, before she forked her salad into her mouth. 'Move in.' Her eyes twinkled for the first time that day. 'There are many guest bedrooms to choose from.'

'Ha-ha, funny girl.' Rob narrowed his eyes at her. 'The only place I am sleeping is next to you.'

'We won't get a lot of sleeping done,' Willa told him, her lips curving in anticipation.

Rob looked at her quizzically. 'And why,' he asked in that sexy drawl, 'would *that* be a problem?'

Rob, coming up from Willa's gym, rubbing his sweaty face and bare chest with a towel, stopped abruptly when he heard voices in the formal lounge.

Poking his head around the doorframe, he saw Willa, dressed in a pencil skirt that ended a couple of inches above her knees and a formal business jacket that he hated. Her fabulous hair was pulled into a tight knot at the back of her head and she was having an earnest discussion with two men in sharp suits. The younger held a tablet and was making notes in between sneaking looks at Willa's legs. Although Rob didn't like it, he couldn't blame him—he liked Willa's legs too…especially when they were wrapped around his hips.

'As I understand it, the house was custom-built about four years ago,' Willa was saying.

Intrigued, Rob slung the towel around his neck and pushed his shoulder into the doorframe. Willa hadn't mentioned that she had an appointment this morning and he was surprised to find himself vaguely irked about that. Why hadn't she told him? What was she planning? Why were these men in her house?

The older gentleman saw Rob leaning against the doorframe and lifted his head in acknowledgement. Willa turned, sent him a *go-away* smile and walked over to the wooden and glass doors that led onto the veranda.

'Let me show you the outdoor entertainment area and the garden—and obviously the view.'

Rob lifted his eyebrows at her unsubtle dismissal and wondered whether they were potential buyers. Her divorce would be final in a couple of weeks and the transfer of property should be a simple process, allowing her to dispose of the house as she saw fit.

Rob thought she was mad… The house was incredible, and she'd never be able to afford another property in such an exclusive area again. The views were awesome, and it only needed new furniture and decent art and it would be a fabulous family home…

Except that Willa didn't have a family. And it was ridiculously big for one or even two people. But she would have a family one day... Rob rubbed the back of his neck as he headed to the kitchen for some water. Why the hell was he thinking of Willa and her future family? And why was he irked at the thought of not being a founding member of that family?

He was a short-term option; he could *only* be a short-term option—nothing else.

The doorbell chimed and Rob cursed softly. It was like Grand-damn-Central Station around here this morning. He walked back into the lobby and yanked the front door open.

A fit-looking guy who looked to be a little older than him flashed a confident smile. 'Hey, I'm from Pearson's, the valuers.'

'Yeah? So?'

'Ms Moore here? I've come to do an evaluation on the gym equipment.'

Rob had hardly had any time to process that statement when he saw a thin blonde woman, older than him, walking up the driveway, the ubiquitous tablet in her hand. When she reached the steps she stopped and looked at Rob in approval. He felt like a prime roast in the supermarket, scared that she would pick him up and take him home...

'Well, hello. Who are *you*?' she drawled, her eyes on his bare abs.

For the first time in...well, for ever, he understood why women complained when men had conversations with a woman's chest.

'Who are *you*?' Rob shot back, thoroughly out of sorts and feeling a little left out. Oh, he knew it was childish, but why hadn't Willa discussed this with him?

The cougar introduced herself and laid a hand on his arm. 'I'm here to value the art and the furniture.' She looked past him and gasped.

Rob turned to see that she was gushing over the mas-

sive abstract on the wall—the one that both he and Willa
hated with a passion.

'Oh, my Gawd, is that a Johnno Davies? Holy mack-
erel, it *is*!'

'Looks like someone vomited green paint all over a canvas,' Mr Gym Valuer said in a low voice to Rob.

His type of guy, Rob thought. 'It so does.'

He stepped back so that Willa's guests could enter the
hall. He gestured to the couch along the opposite side of
the wall.

'Take a seat. Willa is busy with...someone else, but I'll
let her know that you are here.'

Rob left them in the hall and headed into the kitchen,
picking up his mobile from the counter, where it was charg-
ing, and firing Willa off a text message.

More people in your hall. What the hell are you doing? And
I thought that I was buying your gym equipment!

He growled when he saw that her response was just the
thumbs-up icon.

CHAPTER TEN

'YOU'RE LATE.'

Willa, walking into her study two hours later, frowned at his growly words and thundercloud face. Rob was sitting behind her desk and working on her laptop—in her house. Something was wrong with this picture, she thought.

Her desk, *her* laptop, *her* spreadsheets.

'Excuse me?' she said, giving him the opportunity to choose another greeting…to have a do-over.

'Last time I checked you were employed as my accountant, and I've been sitting here twiddling my thumbs waiting for you.'

Willa placed her hand on the back of the chair and looked at the grizzly bear who was occupying her space. Hmm, she didn't need this nonsense, this snarky attitude today.

'Might I remind you that I sat up for most of the night working through that franchise contract that you tossed my way yesterday afternoon? The one you said you needed to send off first thing this morning?'

The muscle in his cheek jumped and his eye twitched. 'That was business.'

'And those people today were *my* business. My world doesn't stop just because you're paying me.' Willa tipped her head. 'Oh, wait. *Are* you paying me? We never actually discussed my salary.'

Rob had the grace to look momentarily ashamed. 'Of course I'm bloody paying you. I just haven't got around to setting that up…' Rob twisted his lips. 'What's your hourly rate?'

Willa remembered the rate she'd seen in one of those advertisements for an accountant and, because she was irritated with him, doubled it.

Rob winced and then nodded. 'Okay.'

Hot damn. Okay, then.

Willa grabbed a pen and notepad and scribbled her bank account details down, before slapping the paper on the desk in front of him. 'And for the use of my home as your office? And my laptop and internet connection?'

He shoved his chair away from the desk and stood up, every inch of him masculine, powerful and angry. 'Why don't you give me an invoice for all the expenses you've incurred on my behalf and I'll do you a transfer right now?'

Willa flashed him a smile, nipped past him and sat in her chair, sighing at the heat in the fabric created by his delicious rear end. 'Okey-dokey—will do.'

Rob shoved his hands into the pockets of his chinos and scowled. 'Why are you acting like this?'

'Why did you change the formula on this spreadsheet? Don't mess with my numbers, dammit!' Willa lifted her eyes from her screen as his question made sense. 'Acting like what?'

'Acting weird.'

Willa's look suggested that he find another way to phrase that question and Rob took the hint. 'These last few days… You're different…'

'Different how?' Willa leaned back in her chair and placed her feet, encased in two-inch scarlet heels, on the corner of the desk, unaware that her skirt had ridden up and he could see most of her thigh.

'Assertive and…bossy. *And* you took the initiative in bed last night…'

Willa smiled slowly. 'You were moaning and panting and groaning… I thought you liked what I did.'

'I did…' Rob expelled his breath on an audible sigh,

looked frustrated and pinned her with hot eyes. 'But we're not allowed to talk about sex in this room, remember? So... Who were those people who were here?' he asked, suddenly changing the subject.

'Property, gym equipment art and furniture valuers.'

'*I* made you an offer on the gym equipment,' Rob pointed out.

'And it was a fair offer, apparently. But I didn't know that until I got an independent valuer in to tell me,' Willa explained.

She'd never believed for one minute that Rob would cheat her—if anything she'd thought that he might over-pay because he felt sorry for her. But this way, having a second opinion, had made her feel loads better. She also had a ball park figure for what she might expect for the modern minimalistic furniture and the awful art—which was a lot, *lot* more than she'd expected.

When she received their written quotes she would put their lowest estimates into a spreadsheet and work out her personal assets and liabilities, and from there she could make informed decisions.

Her decisions. About *her* life—financial and otherwise.

'Why didn't you tell me they were coming? That this was what you were going to do?'

Willa scratched her neck. So *that* was the bug that had climbed up Rob's ass and started chomping on it. He was annoyed because she hadn't asked his opinion or advice.

'Should I have? Was I expected to?' she asked quietly.

'I...well...yeah,' Rob replied. 'We're practically living together!'

'So? In a couple of weeks...a month...we *won't* be living together. You'll be onto your next short-term fling—' Willa kept her voice cool while her heart spluttered at that thought '—and I'll still be making my own decisions. So what's the point?'

'The point is—'

Willa lifted her eyebrows, waiting for him to finish his sentence.

When he didn't, Willa dropped her legs and leaned forward. 'Rob, you told me that this is a no-strings-attached fling. I'm just playing by the rules, and according to those rules you don't get to be huffy when they change. Do you *want* to change any of those rules?'

Rob, his eyes hot and frustrated on hers, took a long time to answer. 'No.'

Willa rested her folded arms on her desk and looked him in the eye. 'Your turn to ask me.'

'Ask me what?'

'Whether I want to change the rules,' Willa explained patiently.

Dear Lord, boys were bad at this give-and-take stuff.

When Rob didn't answer her, she gave him the stink-eye. 'Or don't I get to have a say in this situation? Am I just supposed to be grateful for what you give me and ignore what I want? What I'm feeling?'

'It would be...easier for me,' Rob admitted, honest as usual.

Except that she was no longer in the business of making decisions based on what was easier for other people. She'd been there—been the dumb girl in the wet T-shirt competition that had been her life.

She wasn't doing that any more.

Willa just held Rob's eyes, and he eventually sighed and said, in a resigned tone, 'I know that I'm going to regret not ending this conversation right here and now but...okay. What do *you* want, Willa?'

Willa rolled her eyes. 'There you go again.'

'Are you going to tell me what's bugging you or do I have to guess?' Rob demanded.

Willa could see that he was fast running out of patience. If she was going to do this, it was now or never.

Doormat Willa lifted up her head to whisper, *Preferably never...*

Willa took a deep breath. 'I want to change the rules... about us.'

'Meaning?'

Willa swallowed. 'Meaning that I don't just want an affair with you any more. Meaning that I want this to mean something, to go somewhere—to be more than me working for you and sleeping with you.'

Rob sat up, placed his forearms on his thighs and looked at her across the desk. He swore softly. 'Dammit, Willa, we weren't going to do this.'

'I can't help the way I feel,' Willa said. 'And I'm feeling more than I should.'

'I think you're confused. A lot has happened over a month.' Rob rubbed his jaw with his hand. 'We met, fell into bed, you got the job, you met your old friends... It's been a busy month. You're...'

Willa lifted her eyebrows in irritation. 'I'm...what?'

'Overwhelmed...you're overwhelmed.'

And wasn't *that* a verbal pat on the head? *God!* Willa looked at her desk and wondered if she could risk braining him with her stapler. It was big and heavy, and she only wanted to bash some sense into him, not kill him.

'I'm *overwhelmed*. Ah, now I understand.' She spoke softly. 'Thanks for clearing it up for me.'

'I hate your sarky quiet voice.'

'You once said you loved it,' Willa pointed out.

'Not when its directed at *me*!' Rob glared at her. 'God, where is this coming from? I don't recognise you any more!'

Willa felt her blood snap and crackle with temper. 'You mean you don't recognise the quiet, meek woman who asked *How high?* and *How far?* when you asked her to jump? You don't recognise this one, who can make her own decisions, who knows her own soul, who doesn't need your protection, your big badass attitude to keep her from harm?' Willa shouted. 'You talk a good talk about women being equal and strong and standing up for themselves, but you can't walk the walk!'

'That's not fair—'

'Isn't it?' Willa demanded as all her old insecurities bubbled to the surface. 'You wanted a one-night stand; I gave it to you. You wanted an affair: I said yes. You wanted to move in after Wayne was here and I said okay. But you're not happy when I get people in to value my art, my house, my possessions, because I didn't run it past you first. You wanted an accountant and I begged you to hire me—'

'Begged? What?'

'It's all about you. When I say that I want something—something more from you—you think that I'm asking you to handle a vial of Ebola. I'm good enough on your terms, but not for anything more!'

'We *both* agreed on nothing more!' Rob roared as he pushed his chair back so hard that it skittered over the dark shiny floor.

He loomed over her desk and Willa, feeling at a disadvantage, leaped to her feet.

'*You're* the one who is complicating this! I don't *do* complications! I fancy you, I adore your body, I enjoy your friendship and I think you are an excellent accountant—'

'Influenced by the fact that I give you sex at the end of the day,' Willa interrupted with a hot shout.

Rob's eyes hardened. 'That comment isn't worthy of you and it's an insult to me.'

Willa slapped a hand on her heart. 'Dear God, I've insulted you. I'm *so* sorry!' she fake gushed.

Rob raked both hands through his hair. 'Why can't you just take this for what it is? Why are you pushing for more?'

Willa slapped her hands on the desk. 'Because I *deserve* more, dammit! Because I deserve a man who will love me and trust me, who wants to be with me, who wants to complicate the hell out of his life *because* of me.'

Rob, his chest heaving, stared at her for a long time before slowly shaking his head. 'I'm not that man, Willa. I said I could never be that man. I've always been honest with you.'

Willa stepped back and folded her arms as her temper drained away. 'Okay, then. But I am not prepared to settle for less than I deserve.'

Rob looked astounded for a second, before his I-don't-care expression slid back into place. 'You're breaking it off?'

'Yes.'

'You're sure you want to do that? I don't go back...*ever.*'

Willa wanted to hyperventilate. This was a big step—a huge step...an irrevocable step. Was her self-respect worth it? Was not having more of Rob worth the pain of not having any of Rob? Was she just acting out of anger? Fear?

You deserve more...you deserve it all.

She did. She really did. She was no longer prepared to settle for the crumbs of life. She wanted the meat and potatoes *and* the sushi *and* the tiramisu of life. She wanted it all.

She sucked in a breath and nodded her head. 'The only thing I'm sure of is that I want more than this.'

Rob swore softly, stood up straight and jammed his hands in his pockets. A stranger took the place of her lover and she wanted to weep.

'And your job?' he asked.

Ah, her job. 'As you said, the one has nothing to do with the other. I'll carry on for as long as you need me.'

'That might not be for much longer,' Rob stated, his voice cool and his expression remote. 'Patrick will be back to work in a couple of weeks or so and he'll take over. However, I do need to go home anyway. We can correspond via email—at a push by phone.'

Behind her back Willa linked her hands, squeezing them so that she kept her tears at bay. This was it. He was walking out of her life and it was the most dreadful experience...*ever.*

Rob gestured to the door. 'I'll just go and pack my stuff.'

'Some of your clothes are in the laundry.' Willa managed to get the words out. 'Just lock the door when you leave.'

Taking my heart with you...

Rob flung his clothes into a duffel bag before stomping to the bathroom and, with one swipe, dropping his toiletries into the bag as well. What the hell had just happened? One moment he was irritated that Willa hadn't spoken to him about the valuers coming round and the next he was being booted out through the door like a bad smell.

And what was all that about it all being his way? He didn't understand this...*any* of this.

Except that wasn't true, he thought, sitting down on the bed where they had spent so much time laughing and loving and being together. For the first time in his life he'd tumbled into a woman's arms, into her life and world, and forgotten to put up barriers to keep her out and to keep his emotions tightly corralled.

He'd allowed them a little bit of freedom and in the process had totally forgotten that freedom always came with a price.

'I want more than this.'

He didn't have more to give her—he *couldn't*. He had responsibilities back home, a life he'd worked very hard to establish. He didn't want to let her go but he couldn't give her anything more than what they currently had.

Rob rubbed his hand over his face. Yes, he was establishing his company in Australia, but that didn't mean he'd be in the country for any length of time in the future; managers would be hired and he'd only be around occasionally.

Willa wouldn't settle for a man who dropped in and out of her life. She couldn't be his priority and she was right: she deserved to be. She deserved a man who could give his whole heart—someone who was willing to love her and be loved in return...someone who knew how to trust, to try.

Rob rubbed at his chest above his heart. It felt as if it was being put through a mincemeat machine.

Feeling ridiculous, he hauled in a deep breath. It was just a short fling, he told himself, happy for the first time ever to lie. There was nothing to feel hurt about. She'd just blindsided him with her talk of wanting more. He didn't do more—never had, never would. It was better that they were calling this quits now, before they got in too deep and too far and someone got hurt.

She'd asked, he'd answered, and now they were done.

Except that he didn't feel as if he was done...as if it was over. He wasn't quite sure how he was going to manage walking out of her door, out of her life.

His heart wanted to stay yet his brain insisted he go. And he always, *always* listened to his brain.

His heart was too vulnerable to make decisions like these.

A week later Willa's divorce, which she'd all but forgotten about, was finally granted. Kate, refusing to let her slink back to her house to lick her very wounded heart alone, dragged her off to Saints, where Amy and Jessica waited at a secluded table in the corner of the Surry Hills restaurant.

After accepting their hugs and congratulations on having The Pain officially removed from her life, Willa slipped into a chair and couldn't help the tears that slid down her face.

'Oh, dear God,' Amy said, grabbing her serviette and trying to dab Willa's eyes from across the table.

'Why are you crying?' Jessica demanded. 'I thought you *wanted* to get divorced?'

Kate smacked Jessica's hand with the back of a spoon. 'It's stress relief. It's a fairly natural reaction; I see it all the time.'

As if she would waste any of her tears on Wayne-the-Pain, Willa scoffed. He wasn't worth it. No, she didn't care about Wayne, or her divorce, or anything to do with her past.

Except Rob. That was the only part of her past she regretted. That she wanted back. Who would ever have thought she could miss someone she'd only known for a month so much? Her heart ached from morning to night and her house had never seemed bigger or emptier or lonelier before. Her fridge was empty, she'd made quite a dent in the contents of the wine cellar, and she spent hours looking out to sea, reliving her too-short time with him.

One minute she was cursing herself for not taking every minute he could give her, and then she felt that she'd done the right thing—that she'd been right to ask for more. She loved him, but she knew that he wasn't obligated to love her back. That wasn't in the rulebook of life.

These feelings would fade, she realised. The hurt and the despair would go away eventually. But his memory never would.

Another batch of fat tears rolled down her face.

'Hey,' Kate murmured, putting her arm around Willa. 'It'll be okay, honey. Let's get some cocktails into you and dry up your tears… Didn't you tell me that you and Rob were going to do something wild to celebrate your divorce?'

'If he was here… He's left.'

Three sets of eyes locked on to her face.

Willa sniffed, wiped her eyes and lifted her shoulders. 'It's over. He went back to South Africa a week ago.'

'Why didn't you call me?' Kate demanded.

'Or me?' Amy added.

Because she'd needed to be alone. Because she was used to being alone. Her friends would have come running, bringing ice cream and sympathy.

She'd done them a disservice, Willa realised. If they asked her for help she'd give it without hesitation…why did she assume they wouldn't?

'I'm sorry; I didn't think. I should've called you…'

Kate leaned forward. 'Are you *sort of* over or *over* over?'

'And why?' Jessica demanded.

Willa wondered how to answer that, and eventually decided she was too tired and too sad to sugar-coat the truth. Maybe Rob's honesty had rubbed off on her.

'There are a couple of reasons—the big one being that I am in love with him and I want more. And he doesn't. I'm tired of being in relationships that work for the men in my life and not for me. And Rob had it great—he had an accountant on tap, and when he was done with her he had a lover. All very nice and easy and uncomplicated.'

Amy looked from Willa to Kate and back to Willa. 'I understand the bit about you want more and he doesn't, but what are you on about with regard to your job?'

Willa shrugged. 'He needed someone to do the work. I was handy. It wasn't like he interviewed anyone else…he took the easy way out.'

'Willa, don't you remember how hard you fought him to get that job?' Amy cried, exasperated. 'It would have been a hell of a lot easier for him to hire an accountant with experience, and with no messy personal ties.'

'Not to mention cheaper,' Kate commented, her chin in the palm of her hand.

Willa frowned. 'What?'

'Do you remember that discussion we had about your future? I asked you about what income you could expect? You told me what rate Rob was paying you and I was slightly irked because it was more than *my* hourly rate. Then I looked it up and it's more than double what experienced CPAs are getting.'

Amy grinned, and Willa knew that she wasn't picking up the point Kate was trying to make. 'I don't understand what you're trying to say.'

'She's saying that Rob would never pay anybody double the going rate if he didn't think they were worth it,' Jessica stated.

'Not even *you* are that good, honey.' Kate patted her arm.

Willa's mouth opened and shut like a fish. 'But—'

'But what?' Amy demanded. 'Willa, how did you manage to forget that Rob is the most honest, direct, man you've ever met? Hell, *we've* ever met!'

'Um...'

'If he employed you, he thought you were worth that money. If he was with you, it was because he wanted to be with you. His honesty would demand nothing less,' Amy raged on. 'He could have just walked on out after that first night, but he didn't—he stuck around.'

'Um, I—'

'If you told him you loved him and he didn't return that love then that's one thing,' Kate added. 'But you can't accuse him of not being honest, Willa, of having ulterior motives.'

Willa looked past Jessica but didn't see the customers in the packed restaurant. She just saw Rob's face...confusion, hurt and panic in his eyes.

'I didn't actually tell him that I loved him.'

Amy dropped her face into her serviette and groaned. Willa thought she heard a muffled swear-word. 'This just gets worse and worse.'

'I just said that I needed more. He said not to complicate things and I ended it.'

Kate took a big sip from the glass of wine at her elbow.

'Dear God in heaven—you shouldn't be allowed out on your own. You said you wanted *more*…what does he think "more" means? Marriage? Living together? Donating a kidney?'

'Nothing like that. I just want to be with him—be able to know that he is mine, and I'm his…that we can give this… *thing* between us a chance,' Willa protested.

'Boys need to be told carefully and in short sentences, using small words, what you want,' Jessica told her, her face serious. 'Like Winnie-the-Pooh, big words baffle them, and an open-ended statement like "I want more" sends them into a tailspin.'

'Especially men who are as commitment-phobic and distrustful as Rob,' Amy added.

Willa sighed. 'Maybe I should give up on men and get me to a nunnery.'

'And never have any fantastic sex again? *Pfft*…' Kate muttered.

Willa cocked her head, happy to move the spotlight off her. 'Are you having fantastic sex that I don't know about?'

'Only with Big Burt—and his batteries are flat.' Kate sighed. 'I keep forgetting to replace the damn things.'

Jessica's eyes widened. 'Why would anyone name their vibrator Burt?'

'*From Here to Eternity*…Burt Lancaster?'

Jessica looked blank and Kate rolled her eyes. 'Seriously? You've never heard of either the film or the star?'

'As fascinating as your sex-life is or isn't…' Amy smiled at Kate but refused to be distracted '…we're talking about Willa and the utter cock-up she's made of her life.'

'Just for a change…' Willa murmured.

'Stop whining,' Amy said sharply.

Willa heard Rob's voice saying the same thing. Okay, no whining—even though she felt as if her life was falling apart.

'And tell me what you are going to do about Rob. And if you say *nothing*, I swear I will stab you with my butter knife.'

What *could* she do about Rob? Willa thought later that night, sitting at her desk in the study, the night inky black behind her. What did she *want* to do? What did she *want* from him?

Marriage? Kids? Fifty years of sharing beds and bathrooms and domesticity? Did she want to be someone's wife again? She'd just become Willa again, and she didn't think she was ready for such a drastic step—with Rob or anyone.

So what *was* she ready for? What did she *know*?

She knew that she missed Rob—that every day without him, instead of getting easier, just became more difficult. She knew that her house, when he was in it, became a home and not a collection of expensively furnished rooms.

Rob being gone was confirmation that she definitely didn't need a gentle man, as he'd once said. She didn't need someone to ease her into life again. She needed Rob's unflinching honesty, his way of making her see her surroundings and herself clearly. And maybe her friends were right—maybe she had been stupid to question his desire to be with her, to spend time with her. Rob, honest to the core, wouldn't do anything he didn't want to.

When he'd been with her it had been because he was exactly where he'd wanted to be. Even if it was as a temporary fling...for an affair that had an expiration date. He'd never promised or even suggested more...

It wasn't *his* fault that she wanted more than they'd had. She wanted love, obviously. And fidelity. And a level of commitment—not necessarily marriage. But mostly she just wanted him.

Gruff, honest, direct. Full of integrity.

And she wanted him to trust her. With his business, his

heart, his love, his life. That was non-negotiable—the line in the sand. She knew what it was like to live with a man who didn't respect her, didn't include her, who thought of her as a possession and not with pride. She wanted to be a fully invested partner in every way possible.

But to be that Rob would need to trust her. The one thing he couldn't do.

Willa leaned back in her chair and propped her bare feet on the desk. She couldn't accuse him of deceiving her… the opposite was true. Rob had always treated her fairly, with honesty. From the first time she'd suggested they sleep with each other he'd told her that they couldn't have anything but good sex. She was just a way to pass the time while he was in Oz. Then she'd said that she wanted more, and he'd said no.

Honest, direct, final.

Willa placed her forearm over her eyes and sighed. *But if you could make him change his mind, universe, that would be great.*

Any time you want to.

CHAPTER ELEVEN

BACK HOME IN Johannesburg, Rob was in the pool, two feminine arms looped around his shoulders and an exquisite face buried in the crook of his neck. He smiled when he heard low chuckles as his fingers tickled her ribcage.

Little Kiley, her chubby legs kicking against the water and narrowly missing his crotch, squirmed in his arms and he let her drop into the water. She fell like a stone and popped up a couple of seconds later, laughing. At four, Kiley was a fish, and she loved the water as much as he did.

Her hand clutched his arm and he looked down into her face, thinking that he'd like a little girl one day—or a little boy with greeny-silver eyes and dark hair, Willa's stubborn chin...

Not going there...

To distract himself he looked around and saw that his mum, on the veranda, was putting the last platter of food on the long wooden table and his Uncle Sid was taking a seat at the head of it.

'Grub's up,' he told his family.

Patrick was lying on a double lounger next to his wife Heather, under an umbrella at the shallow end of the pool, and his sister Gail was snuggled up in the colourful arms of the tattoo artist playing tonsil tennis.

Gack.

'Cut it out before I turn a hose on you two,' he called, and ignored Gail's rolling eyes when she surfaced for air. If he wasn't getting kissed then nobody else should be either.

Especially his baby sister, who surely wasn't old enough to be kissed like that!

Rob boosted Kiley out of the pool and climbed out himself, reaching for a towel and wrapping it around his hips. Pulling on a T-shirt, he walked towards the veranda and took the beer Sid held out to him.

It was a stunning day, and the people he cared most about, the ones he loved and trusted, were all here. All but one...

How weird that he felt that his group, his family, was missing an important element... Willa wasn't here and his family didn't feel complete.

Rob pulled out a chair and tried to ignore his feeling of discontent. It was what it was, he told himself. Nothing had changed...

He smiled as Kiley climbed up onto his lap, blithely ignoring the booster chair her father was urging her into.

'Hey, I'm your *dad*,' Patrick complained good-naturedly.

'But I'm her favourite person,' Rob replied as she wound her arms around his neck.

'Only because you bring her presents and sneak her ice cream when we're not looking.'

'Godparent privilege.'

'Bribery,' Patrick shot back, sitting down next to him. '*Now* I understand your success rate with women.'

Rob's smile was a bit forced. 'Heather's looking a lot better,' he said, changing the subject.

Rob pushed his hair back from his face as Kiley pretended his thigh was a horse, waiting impatiently for Heather to dish her up some food. God, he missed Willa—wanted her here. He'd never missed any of his short-term flings before; normally he wished them well and seldom thought of them again. Not the case with Willa, who was the first thing he thought of in the morning and the last thought he had at night. Then he dreamed about her—hot, *hot*, sensual dreams that woke him up with a hard-on from hell.

Such fun. *Not.*

'I deserve a man who will love me and trust me, who wants to be with me, who wants to complicate the hell out of his life because of me.'

He wanted to be that man. It was that simple and that complicated. Yet he couldn't be that man…

Gail and Tattoo sat opposite him and immediately leaned towards each other for another kiss.

'Give it a rest, for God's sake,' he muttered, and Gail, the witch, just laughed.

When they all had plates piled high in front of them, Gail leaned back in her chair and pushed her hair off her forehead. 'I have an announcement to make.'

Rob, his fork halfway to his mouth, gave her a hard stare. A sentence starting with those words could never be good. He lowered his fork and took a sip of his beer, his eyes not leaving his sister's face. Whatever she was thinking about doing, she could just forget it. She was *not* moving in with or marrying Tattoo, and if she said she was pregnant or that she was quitting uni he'd freak.

'As you all know, I'll be receiving my degree in three months.'

No, that wasn't possible. She hadn't been at university that long, Rob thought. Mentally rewinding, he realised that she had and wondered where the time had gone.

'I've decided to take a gap year,' Gail said, her voice serious. 'I'm going to London for a couple of months and then I'm going to travel.'

Oh, hell, no. How could he look after her if she was bouncing all over the world?

Rob shook his head. 'No, you're not.'

His mum leaned across Patrick to place a hand on his

forearm. 'Yeah, honey, she is.' Her voice was soft but determined, and it brooked no argument. 'I'm her parent, not you, and she has my full support.'

Gail sent him a mischievous look. 'Yeah, I'm cutting the umbilical cord. Jumping the nest. Spreading my—'

Rob held up his hand for her to be quiet. It didn't work. 'Spreading my wings. Flying the coop.'

Their mum's piercing look stopped Gail's crowing. 'I'm asking Rob to step away, but *I'm* still going to keep a very sharp eye on you, young lady. You have the impulse control of a two-year-old.'

Rob felt as if he'd dropped into a black hole. What was happening? He had to get this conversation—his life—back on track.

He placed his beer bottle on the table and folded his arms against his chest. 'Can we talk about this? It's a pretty big decision. We *need* to talk about this!'

Okay, that hadn't come out right. He'd sounded panicky and stressed and...*unhinged.*

His mum shook her head and he immediately recognised her stubborn expression. 'Talking about it won't change anything; she *is* going. You have to trust her—and me— enough to step away and let us deal with this. And while we're on the subject you need to stop mollycoddling us, darling. Enough now, okay?'

Rob knew that his mouth was open and that he was trying to speak, but no words were coming out. Taking his silence for permission, or acceptance, his family started a lively discussion about their plans for the future. A future he had no control over.

'You have to trust her—and me... Stop mollycoddling us.' Could he? Could he do that? He didn't think so. Standing guard over them had become a habit and...a shield. An excuse...

After a couple of minutes Patrick nudged him with his shoulder. 'So, *that* was a mighty kick up the jack, wasn't it?'

Rob turned to look at him, not realising that his eyes held fear and hope. And relief.

'Guess they just handed you a Get Out of Jail Free card, dude.'

'I have no idea what you are talking about,' Rob muttered.

Patrick chuckled, enjoying his cousin's predicament a little too much. 'Please… Everyone realises that you're trying to atone for leaving them with Stefan by hovering over them. But what you've never understood is that nobody ever blamed you for that…except you.' He grinned. 'And that's because you're an idiot. Now you have no excuse not to get your ass on the first plane out and go to Willa.'

Yes. No. Hell, maybe.

Rob stared down at his plate and lifted his broad shoulders. 'I hurt her, cuz.'

As a reasonable adult, and his best friend, Rob expected Patrick's support—a statement of wisdom, of thoughtful consideration. Instead Patrick just shook his head and placed his hand on his daughter's back.

'Kiley, honey?'

Kiley lifted her mouth from gnawing on a chicken bone to look his way. 'Mmmph?'

'What do we do when we do something bad or naughty?' Patrick asked in a gentle voice.

'Say sorry,' Kiley muttered, her mouth full of chicken.

Patrick's eyes laughed at Rob. 'See—even my four-year-old has a better handle on the situation than you,' he stated.

Rob narrowed his eyes at his cousin, his expression promising retribution. 'You think you are so damn smart, don't you?' He growled the words.

Patrick clinked his beer bottle against Rob's and shrugged. 'Nah, I don't think I am—I *know* I am.'

* * *

Willa, coming in from her morning run, heard her mobile ringing from where she'd left it on the hall table and fumbled her key into the lock of the front door. Thinking, hoping that it might be Rob, she barrelled through the door and snatched the phone up with a raspy, breathless, 'Hello?'

'Is that Willa Moore?'

Not Rob. Damn.

She almost replied that she was Willa Fisher-Moore, then remembered at the last minute that she was divorced and that she was reverting to her maiden name. 'Yes. Can I help you?'

'Hopefully.'

The caller gave his name and his company's name and Willa wrote them down on a notepad on the hall table. She'd heard of the company—a vitamin distribution company—and wondered why the CFO was calling her.

'Rob Hanson gave me your name. We're working together on a deal to supply his stores with our brand of supplements.'

'Okay…' Willa perched her bum on the edge of the hall table.

'In conversation, when he was raving about his superbright and intuitive Australian accountant, he told me how you'd found a creative way to work around an issue with foreign-owned entities.'

Say what? 'Please go on,' Willa said.

'Well, we have an issue that we have to solve before we launch our company on the Stock Exchange and we've had a dozen accountants look at it and tell us its irresolvable. Rob suggested that you take a look and that if *you* can't find a way around it then it *is* impossible. He said that you are bright and brilliant and that he'd trust you with his life.'

Willa felt the warm liquid rush of pleasure. God, could anything be sexier than an endorsement of her brain and

her skills? Oh, she knew that Rob loved her body, but this...
this was the best gift he could have given her.

Apart from his love and a happy-ever-after, obviously.

'Ms Moore?'

Willa pulled herself back to the conversation. 'I won't do
anything illegal or immoral, but if you'd like to e-mail me
your sticky problem I'll take a look. No guarantees, though.'

'Understood. I'm just grateful that you'll look at it. Obviously we'll compensate you for the hours you spend on it.'

Willa gave him her details, her hourly rate and her
e-mail address, and when she'd ended the call held her mobile to her chest.

If she'd been see-sawing between love and lust this one
action would have tipped her into love. Acceptance, valida-
tion, pride... By recommending her to his business cohorts
he'd shown her that he knew she wouldn't let him down,
that he was confident in her abilities, maybe that he trusted
her a little. In business, at least.

If only he could trust her with his heart and his love
and his time.

Universe...again? Please?

Rob turned off the ignition of his hired car and swallowed
at the 'For Sale' sign hammered into the grass next to the
kerb. So Willa had decided to sell. A pity, because he loved
this house. Loved the view, loved the openness...the access to the bay.

In a perfect world he could see him and Willa sharing
their time between this house and his house in Jo'burg, with
frequent visits to the family beach cottage in Knysna. If
they had kids one day then they would have to settle down
somewhere, maybe in Sydney, but really it didn't matter
where. Being together was important. Houses and things
not so much.

But he wasn't living in a perfect world. He was currently inhabiting a twilight world where nothing really made sense. Until he spoke to Willa and knew what course his future was taking then nothing would.

Heaven or hell. He would be experiencing one or the other fairly soon.

Rob pulled his keys out of the ignition and stepped out of the vehicle, his heart pounding in his chest. He walked up to the front door and thought about ringing the doorbell, but after all they'd shared that just made him feel stupid. Instead he tried the door, and—what a surprise—it opened to his touch.

Willa! God, how was he *ever* going to get her to take security seriously?

The first thing he noticed when he stepped into the hall was that the abstract painting on the wall was gone—and good riddance. Johnno Davies was one of the most famous artists around, but Rob didn't care what anyone said—green streaks on a white canvas could never be masterpiece.

Rob glanced at his watch; it was seven thirty and he wondered where she was. In the library-cum-office, working—Patrick kept tossing more work her way—or in the TV lounge? In bed reading?

In bed with someone else?

The thought popped into his head and his blood froze. *No damn way.*

Sprinting up to her bedroom, he flung her bedroom door open and found Willa on the bed, dressed in denim shorts and a sleeveless top, painting her toenails a fiery red. No lover to beat to a pulp.

At the sight of an intruder, Willa let out a blood-curdling scream.

A few moments later she felt her heart settle in her ribcage, slowed down her breathing and felt as if her world was realigning itself on its axis. He wasn't a murderer, he was Rob, and the cosmos was falling into sync again.

Unless he was here to tell her that there wasn't a chance in hell that they would ever be together?

Oh, hell...her heart had started bouncing again.

She made herself speak past whatever was blocking her throat. 'Um...why are you here?'

'Are you alone?' he demanded, his hands on his hips and looking fierce.

'Apart from the male strippers in my bathroom...'

Rob didn't look even vaguely amused at her quip, so she sighed and waved the nail polish brush around, not re-alising that she was flecking her white bed linen with red.

'Of course I'm alone.' Willa tacked an implied *moron* onto the end of that sentence.

Rob walked around the bed, took the nail polish from her and replaced the cap. Tossing it into the bedside drawer, he retreated a couple of steps and jammed his hands into the pockets of his Levi's, his eyes hooded...and wild.

Willa ignored the fact that only a couple of toes were painted and wrapped her arms around her knees, not hav-ing the foggiest idea what to say. She'd already asked once why he was here—should she ask again?

'Why—?'

'I—'

Their words collided and they both stopped speaking. Willa lifted her hands in a gesture for him to carry on talking.

'I want to change the rules,' he said, shocking her to the core.

Willa could hardly hear her own cool voice over the roar-ing in her ears. What did he mean? What *could* he mean? '*You* want to change them this time?'

A muscle ticked in Rob's jaw. 'Yeah. I want to totally rewrite them, in fact.'

'Ah. Um…'

Okay, it was official. He'd turned her into a blathering idiot. She swallowed, gripped her knees harder to keep them from knocking, and searched his face for a clue. It was there in the vulnerability in his eyes, in the tremor in his normally confident voice.

'I'm going to need a bit more of an explanation, here, Rob.'

Rob shoved his hand into his curls and tugged. 'I was at home and my family were all there but you weren't. The most important part of my family was missing and it didn't make any sense.'

Oh… Oh. Oh, my…Willa felt tears shimmer in her eyes as her mind started filling with possibilities. Did she dare hope?

'I missed you every minute,' Rob said, his voice hoarse. 'Me too.'

Rob kept his hands firmly in his pockets and Willa wished she could touch him, feel his heat, his hard body. But she knew that if they touched right now they would fall into lust and passion when they needed to talk through the emotion shimmering between them.

'I really meant it to be a fling, but you crawled under my skin and into my heart. You're smart and brave and wonderful and I—'

Willa held her breath.

'And I think that I'm in love with you.' Rob held up his hand as a delighted smile crossed her face. 'I've never been in love before, so I could be wrong.'

'Me neither.' Willa pulled a face when he looked sceptical. 'I haven't… Not as an adult with her eyes wide open.'

A smile finally touched the corners of Rob's mouth. 'So, what does love feel like?'

Willa tipped her head back to look at him, her face and her tone serious. 'It feels likes home—like my life suddenly makes sense with you in the room. It feels soft, but strong. I'm ecstatic that you're back and so, so grateful that you are. It feels...perfect.'

Rob just stared at her, a mix of naked emotion, hope and lust on his face.

Stepping towards her, he sat on the edge of the bed and lifted his hand to her face. 'It does feel perfect.' His thumb brushed her cheekbone.

'Missed you...' she murmured softly.

Rob groaned as his forehead touched hers. 'Missed you too, honey.'

'Rob?' Willa said, when he just stayed where he was, his body radiating tension.

Why wasn't he kissing her, holding her, ripping her clothes off her? Heat throbbed down below and she thought that if she didn't have his solid weight on her soon she would quite simply spontaneously combust.

'Mmm?'

'Are you going to kiss me some time soon?'

'If I do I'm going to be inside you so damn fast we'll go up in flames,' Rob retorted, licking his lips.

'And why would that be a problem?' Willa asked softly, draping her arms around his neck.

Rob's hand spanned her waist before moving over to her bottom. 'Another example of my idiocy... It's not a problem at all.'

Sex was different when love was involved, Willa thought, watching her naked man leave the bed and head into the bathroom. Always spectacular before, making love—and that was what it now was—was deeper, hotter, more thrilling. Her heart had orgasmed along with her happy place, and it was a feeling that she knew she'd never get enough of.

She wouldn't ever get enough of looking at Rob either—

naked, dressed…it didn't matter. Preferably naked, though, she thought as he walked out of the bathroom back to the bed.

Rob placed his hands on his hips, looked towards the bathroom, and then looked down at her. 'If we're going to be doing this for next fifty decades, at least, can I ask you a favour?'

Willa sat up and leaned back against the leather headboard, her soul singing at his reference to the rest of their lives. There wasn't anything she wouldn't do for him when he looked at her with love in his eyes.

'Sure…what?' she asked as he sat down next to her on the bed, facing her.

'Can you go on the pill? I want to be with you without the feeling of latex.'

Willa blinked at his prosaic statement, and then she laughed. Typical Rob, so damn forthright. 'I can do that. For you.'

'Well, since there won't *be* anyone else for you it had better be for me,' Rob growled, picking up her hand and placing a kiss on her wrist.

'So we are fully monogamous?' Willa asked.

'Hell, yes. Fully monogamous, fully involved, no half-measures.' Rob placed his hands on either side of her hips and leaned forward, his eyes demanding her full attention. 'I was wrong before.'

'For what?' Willa asked. 'For leaving me?'

'That too,' Rob admitted. 'I don't *think* I'm in love with you; I *am* in love with you. You okay with that?'

Willa sighed. 'Very.'

'I'm tough and tactless and honest—'

Willa placed her fingers on his mouth to stop him from talking. 'And you love me. But—'

He frowned. 'But?'

'Do you trust me?'

He swallowed as his eyes filled with emotion. 'I do, I promise. For me, I can't do one without the other.'

'Then that's the biggest gift you can give me. Along with the fact that you love me as I am…that you see me clearly. I love that—and I love you.'

Rob's eyes reflected the emotion that was brimming in hers. 'I never thought I needed to hear the words…hear a woman—*my* woman—speak them. I never realised the power, the…the hope for the future.'

Willa placed her face in the crook of his neck as he gathered her close. Their naked bodies tangled together, arms and legs and bits and bobs all finding their place, settling in, knowing that they were home. Her heart settled and sighed, and her soul curled up next to its warmth.

Willa yawned and Rob gently tugged her head back by her hair, so that he could see her face. 'You haven't been sleeping?'

'No, and neither have you,' Willa replied, before yawning again. 'Let's have a nap and then we'll find something for supper.'

But Rob's hand was cupping her bottom and his hardening erection told her that he had other plans.

'Or we can do that instead,' she said.

Rob pushed her back onto the bed and loomed over her, his erection nudging her entrance. He groaned. 'I just want to *feel* you…'

Willa surged up and he slipped inside, harder and hotter and so much better without a condom.

'Ah…hell…' Rob groaned and pulled out, cursing as he reached for a condom out of the box that lived in the bedside drawer. 'I'm not prepared to risk it. I'm too selfish to share you with a mini-me or mini-you just yet.'

Willa sighed her relief as she helped him roll on a condom. Kids were for the future—not for a while yet. She wanted to be selfish too, and concentrate on loving Rob. And having Rob love her…

As he was doing right now—and incredibly well too.

Much, much later they made it to the kitchen and Willa, feeling as if her legs had turned to Jello, slid onto a stool and placed her arms on the granite counter. She tucked Rob's T-shirt under her bare bottom and thought that Rob had never looked more sexy, wearing jeans and a satisfied, happy smile.

Except that the smile was now replaced with a frown as he pulled his face out of the fridge. 'Didn't you eat while I was gone? There's nothing in here!'

Willa lifted a shoulder. 'What was the point? I couldn't taste anything.'

Rob's eyes softened before he reached back into the fridge and pulled out a carton of eggs and a block of mouldy cheese. After hacking off the mould he beat the eggs and grated the cheese while Willa watched him.

'I'm sorry I hurt you,' he stated quietly. 'It was never my intention.'

'I know,' Willa replied, looking at her hands.

While she knew that she loved him, and he loved her, they still had a lot to work through.

'What now, Rob?'

Rob lifted an eyebrow at her.

'I don't want to push you into a corner, but where do we go from here?' Willa gabbled. 'Are you going to commute? How often will I see you? Can we *do* this?'

Rob reached across the counter and placed his hand on hers and squeezed. 'Willa…relax. We'll work it out… Let's eat first and then we'll chat.'

After polishing off cheese omelettes and toast and marmalade Willa made coffee and they walked onto the veranda to take advantage of the warm night.

Willa went to sit on one of the chairs, but Rob yanked her over to his chair and pulled her down onto his lap.

'I have no intention of letting you be more than a hair's breadth away from me for the foreseeable future.' He placed a kiss on her temple. 'Okay, let's thrash this out. I saw the "For Sale" sign outside—are you wanting to sell this house?'

Willa shrugged. 'It's so big...'

'For one person. For a couple too. But I like the space. It would be a wonderful family home later on.' Rob looked around. 'I'd buy it from you...for us.'

Willa looked at him in astonishment. 'Seriously? You'd live here?'

'In a heartbeat. I'd live in a tin shack if you were in it. But, that aside, if you want the cash in the bank I'll buy it. If you want to keep it as yours—as your asset—and share it with me, that's good too. If you want to sell it, that's your choice,' Rob said. 'I can't live here full-time, Wills. I have to go home regularly. My business needs me there and I like being around my family—even though half of them are going travelling. A long story,' he said at her quizzical look.

'Okay. So I'd see you every couple of months?' Willa swallowed. It wasn't ideal, but...

'Hell, no. Where I go, you go.' Rob twisted his lips as he realised what he'd said. 'That came out wrong. I'm hoping that you will continent-hop with me. Live with me here *and* there.'

Willa thought for a moment and sighed. 'I hate the thought of not being with you, but I do need to work, Rob. I don't want to be idle, useless—like I was. That means finding a job.'

'You *have* a job.'

Rob laughed at her shock.

'And this time it has nothing to do with me. Patrick wants you to carry on working with him... There's too much work and you've been taking a load off his shoulders. He said that even if I was idiotic enough to give you up *he* wasn't going to—you're too valuable to let go. So you'd report to him, not me, and it wouldn't matter if you worked here or there. Both.'

Willa couldn't believe his words and her stomach filled with warmth, with the thrill of knowing that her work was valued. 'That sounds amazing… I'd love to carry on working for…' she grinned at him '…for Patrick.'

Rob just shook his head and brushed his mouth against hers. 'Let me know what you want to do about this house, but the furniture has to go.'

'Okay,' Willa agreed, her head resting on his shoulder. She felt Rob take a deep breath and wondered what he was going to say next.

'Do you want to get married?'

Willa swallowed down the impulsive need to say yes and thought about his question. She could be honest, she reminded herself. Rob could take it.

'I love you, but no…not yet. I just got divorced—a week ago, to be precise—and I want to…*be*. Just be Willa for a while. Can you understand that?'

Rob yawned, and when he sank further down into the chair with her, utterly relaxed, she knew that he was fine with her answer.

'Let me know if that changes,' he said, his arms tightening around her. 'But, married or not, you're mine.'

'I *so* am,' Willa agreed, and allowed her eyes to drift closed.

EPILOGUE

WILLA LAY WITH her head on Rob's shoulder after they'd spent another day lazing around… AKA spending the day in bed, getting hot and steamy. It was her absolute favourite way to while away the hours.

Rob's hand stroked her spine and she listened to the reassuring thump of his heartbeat under her ear. This was love, she thought. Quiet, strong, tangible. Willa looked out of the huge window and sighed at the orange and pink sunset… Night was falling and she was starving.

Food…food would be good around about now.

'Rob…?' she wheedled.

She felt his grin. 'No.'

'You don't even know what I was about to ask…'

'Coffee, food, more sex… Actually, yes to more sex.'

She was utterly, crazily, besottedly in love with her man, but this house was run as a democracy—which meant that it was his turn to make supper. For about the fourth night in a row.

'No to everything but the sex,' Rob reiterated.

Willa turned her head and nipped his chest. 'You suck!' she muttered against his skin.

'No, actually, that was *you*…'

Rob's deep voice drifted over her and she laughed.

'By the way,' he said, 'I had the most amazing day planned for us today…'

Willa moved back slightly and tipped her head up to look at his rueful face. 'You did? What? And why?'

'Well, I owe you a day to celebrate your divorce.'

Willa wrinkled her nose, trying to keep up. Then she remembered asking Rob to do something wild with her to celebrate her freedom and she grinned. 'What were we going to do?'

'I hired a Ducati. We were going up the coast for lunch. Then we were booked to go sky-diving or bungee-jumping—and maybe abseiling.'

'Sounds like fun. And what happened to my day?'

Rob rubbed his hand over her butt. 'Well, we started making love and we didn't stop. Your fault.'

'Hey, you made something for me during the night and I had to use it!' Willa protested. 'We'll have to do all that another day…'

'Yeah…'

The strident peal of the doorbell had Willa bolting up in bed, her eyes as wide as saucers.

'The doorbell is ringing…are you expecting anyone?'

Rob looked at his watch. 'Oh, hell, yeah… Sort of forgot about that.'

Willa raised her eyebrows. 'Sort of forgot about what?'

'That would be the cocktail party in your honour.' Rob placed his hands behind his head and looked utterly relaxed. 'Kate and Amy and Jessica are throwing you a we're-so-happy-you're-divorced party.'

Willa placed her hand on her heart and her eyes looked suspiciously moist. 'Aw, that's so sweet. I hope they've organised food and drinks too…'

'Caterers. Hired bar. Hired music.' Rob shrugged.

Willa leaned over him and took his face in her hands. She kissed him before dropping her hands and sliding them over his chest, touching his hard, hot skin. 'I'd much rather call it my so-happy-to-have-found-you party.'

'I like that,' Rob growled.

Willa's fingers danced over his six-pack and slid under the waistband of his briefs.

Rob's eyes deepened with passion and he groaned. 'You keep doing that and we're not going anywhere.'

Willa smirked. 'Works for me.'

Then her mobile vibrated on her nightstand and she leaned across him to pick it up. She grinned and showed him the display with Amy's name on the screen.

Do not make me come and get you. You have fifteen minutes!!!!

Rob grinned and flipped her over. 'There is *so* much that I can do in fifteen minutes.'

He was true to his word—but they were still an hour late for her party.

* * * * *

HOW TO SLEEP
WITH THE BOSS

JANICE MAYNARD

For Caroline and Anna:
beautiful daughters,
dear friends,
exceptional women…

One

"I want you to push me to my limits. So I can prove to you that I can handle it."

Patrick stared across his paper-cluttered desk at the woman seated opposite him. Libby Parkhurst was not someone you would pick out of a crowd. Mousy brown hair, ordinary features and clothes at least one size too big for her slender frame added up to an unfortunate adjective. *Forgettable.*

Except for those eyes. Green. Moss, maybe. Not emerald. Emerald was too brilliant, too sharp. Libby's green eyes were the quiet, soothing shade of a summer forest.

Patrick cleared his throat, absolutely sure his companion hadn't intended her remark to sound provocative. Why would she? Patrick was nothing more to her than a family friend and a prospective employer. After all, Libby's mother had been his mother's best friend for decades.

"I appreciate your willingness to step outside your comfort zone, Libby," he said. "But I think we both know this

job is not for you. You don't understand what it involves."
Patrick's second in command, Charlise, was about to com-
mence six months of maternity leave. Patrick needed a replacement ASAP. Because he had dawdled in filling the
spot, his mother, Maeve Kavanagh, had rushed in to supply an interviewee.

Libby sat up straighter, her hands clenched in her lap,
her expression earnest and maybe a tad desperate. "I do,"
she said firmly. "Maeve described the position in detail.
All I'm asking is that you run me through the paces before
I have to welcome the first group."

Patrick's business, Silver Reflections, provided a quiet,
soothing setting for professionals experiencing burnout,
but also offered team-building activities for high-level
management executives. Ropes courses, hiking, overnight
survival treks. The experience was sometimes grueling
and always demanding.

The fill-in assistant would be involved in every aspect
of running Silver Reflections. While Patrick applauded
Libby's determination, he had serious doubts about her
ability to handle the physical aspects of the job.

"Libby…" He sighed, caught between his instincts about
filling the position and his obligation to play nice.

His unwanted guest leaned forward, gripping the edge
of his desk with both hands, her knuckles white. "I need
this job, Patrick. You know I do."

Libby had him there. He'd witnessed in painful detail
what the past year had been like for her—as had most of
the country, thanks to the tabloids. First, Libby's father had
been sent to prison for tax fraud to the tune of several million. Then eight weeks ago, after months of being hounded
by the press and forced to adopt a lifestyle far below her
usual standards, Libby's emotionally fragile mother had
committed suicide.

Quite simply, in the blink of an eye, Libby Parkhurst

had gone from being a sheltered heiress to a woman with virtually no resources. Her debutante education had qualified her to host her father's dinner parties when her mother was unable or unwilling to do so. But twenty-three-year-old Libby had no practical experience, no résumé and no money.

"You won't like it." He was running out of socially acceptable ways to say he didn't want her for the job.

Libby's chin lifted. She sat back in her chair, her spine straight. The disappointment in her gaze told him she anticipated his rejection. "I know your mother made you interview me," she said.

"I'm far past the age where my mother calls the shots in my life." It was only partly a lie. Maeve Kavanagh wielded maternal guilt like a sharp-edged sword.

"I don't have anything left to lose," Libby said quietly. "No home. No family. No trust fund. It's all gone. For the first time in my life, I'm going to have to stand on my own two feet. I'm willing and able to do that. But I need someone to give me a chance."

Damn it. Her dignified bravery tugged at heartstrings he hadn't tuned in ages. Why was Libby Parkhurst his problem? What was his mother thinking?

Outside his window, the late-January trees were barren and gray. Winter still had a firm hold on this corner of western North Carolina. It would be at least eight weeks before the first high-adventure group arrived. In the meantime, Libby would surely be able to handle the hotel aspects of the job. Taking reservations. Checking in guests. Making sure that all reasonable requests were accommodated.

But even if he split Charlise's job and gave Libby the less onerous part, he'd still be stuck looking for someone who could handle the outdoor stuff. Where was he going to find a candidate with the right qualifications willing to work temporarily and part-time?

If this had been an emotional standoff, Libby would have won. She never blinked as she looked at him with all the entreaty of a puppy begging to be fed. He decided to try a different tack. "Our clients are high-end," he said. "I need someone who can dress the part."

Though her cheeks flushed, Libby stood her ground. "I've planned and overseen social events in a penthouse apartment overlooking Central Park. I think I can handle the fashion requirements."

He eyed her frumpy clothing and lifted a brow...not saying a word.

For the first time, Libby lowered her gaze. "I suppose I hadn't realized how much I've come to rely on the disguise," she muttered. "I've dodged reporters for so long, my bag-lady routine has become second nature."

Now he was the one who fidgeted. His unspoken criticism had wounded her. He felt the taste of shame. And an urgent need to make her smile. "A trial period only," he said, conceding defeat. "I make no promises."

Libby's jaw dropped. "You'll hire me?"

The joy in her damp green eyes was his undoing. "Temporarily," he emphasized. "Charlise will be leaving in two weeks. In the meantime, she can show you how we run things here at the retreat center. When the weather gets a bit warmer, you and I will do a dry run with some of the outdoor activities. By the end of February, we'll see how things are going."

He had known "of" Libby for most of his life, though their paths seldom crossed. Patrick was thirty...Libby seven years younger. The last time he remembered seeing her was when Maeve had taken Patrick and his brothers to New York to see a hockey game. They had stopped by the Parkhurst home to say hello.

Libby had been a shy redheaded girl with braces and a ponytail. Patrick had been too cool at the time to do more than nod in her direction.

And now here they were.

Libby smiled at him, her radiance taking him by surprise. "You won't be sorry, I swear."

How had he thought she was plain? To conceal his surprise, he bent his head and scratched a series of numbers on a slip of paper. Sliding it across the desk, he made his tone flat…professional. "Here's the salary. You can start Monday."

When she saw the amount, Libby's chin wobbled.

He frowned. "It's not a lot, but I think it's fair."

She bit her lip. "Of course it's fair. I was just thinking about how much money my family used to spend."

"Is it hard?" he asked quietly. "Having to scrimp after a lifetime of luxury?"

"Yes." She tucked the paper in her pocket. "But not in the way you think. The difficult part has been finding out how little I knew about the real world. My parents sheltered me…spoiled me. I barely knew how to cook or how much a gallon of milk cost. I guess you could say I was basically useless."

Feeling his neck get hot, he reached for her hand, squeezing her fingers before releasing her. Something about Libby brought out his protective instincts. "No one is useless, Libby. You've had a hell of a year. I'm very sorry about your mother."

She grimaced, her expression stark. "Thank you. I suppose I should tell you it wasn't entirely a surprise. I'd been taking her back and forth to therapy sessions for weeks. She tried the suicide thing twice after my father's trial. I don't know if it was being without him that tormented her or the fact that she was no longer welcome in her social set, but either way, her pain was stronger than her need to be with me."

"Suicide never makes sense. I'm sure your mother loved you."

"Thank you for the vote of support."

Patrick was impressed. Libby had every right to feel sorry for herself. Many women in her situation would latch onto the first available meal ticket…anything to maintain appearances and hang on to the lifestyle of a wealthy, pampered young socialite.

Libby, though, was doing her best to be independent.

"My mother thinks the world of you, Libby. I think she always wanted a daughter."

"I don't know what I would have done without her."

Silence fell suddenly. Both of them knew that the only reason Patrick had agreed to interview Libby was because Maeve Kavanagh had insisted. Still, Patrick wasn't going to go back on his word. Not now.

It wouldn't take long for Libby to realize that she wasn't cut out for the rigorous physical challenges that awaited her at Silver Reflections. Where Charlise had been an athlete and outdoorswoman for most of her life, Libby was a pale, fragile flower, guaranteed to wilt under pressure.

Over the next two weeks, Patrick had cause to doubt his initial assessment. Libby dived into learning her new responsibilities with gusto. She and Charlise bonded almost immediately, despite the fact that they had little in common, or so it seemed.

Charlise raved about Libby's natural gifts for hospitality. And the fact that Libby was smart and focused and had little trouble learning the computer system and a host of other things Charlise considered vital to running Silver Reflections.

On the second Friday morning Libby was on his payroll,

Patrick cornered Charlise in her office and shut the door. "Well," he said, leaning against the wall. "Is she going to be able to handle it?"

Charlise reclined in her swivel chair, her amply rounded belly a match for her almost palpable aura of contentment. "The girl's a natural. We've already had four clients who have rebooked for future dates based on their interactions with Libby. I can honestly say that I'm going to be able to walk away from here without a single qualm."

"And the outdoor component?"

Charlise's glow dimmed. "Well, maybe a tiny qualm."

"It's one thing to run this place like a hotel. But you and I both know we work like dogs when we take a group out in the woods."

"True. But Libby has enthusiasm. That goes a long way."

"Up until a year ago I imagine she was enjoying pedicures at pricey Park Avenue salons. Hobnobbing with Fortune 500 executives who worked with her dad. It's a good bet she never had anyone steal her lunch money."

Charlise gave him a loaded look. "You're a Kavanagh, Patrick. Born with a silver spoon and everything that goes with it. Silver Reflections is your baby, but you could walk away from it tomorrow and never have to work another day in your life."

"Fair enough." He scratched his chin. "There's one other problem. I told Libby that she would have to dress the part if she planned to work here. But she's still wearing her deliberately frumpy skirts and sweaters. Is that some kind of declaration of independence? Did I make a faux pas in bringing up her clothing?"

"Oh, you poor, deluded man."

"Why does no one around here treat me with respect?"

Charlise ignored his question. "Your mother offered to buy Libby a suitable wardrobe, but your newest employee is independent to say the least. She's waiting to go shopping until this afternoon when she gets her first paycheck."

"Oh, hell."

"Exactly."

"Wait a minute," he said. "Why can't she wear the clothes she had when her dad went to prison? I'll bet she owned an entire couture wardrobe."

"She did," Charlise said, her expression sober. "And she sold all those designer items to pay for her mom's treatments. Apparently the sum total of what she owns can now fit into two suitcases."

Patrick seldom felt guilty about his life choices. He did his best to live by a code of honor Maeve had instilled in all her boys. Do the right thing. Be kind. Never let ambition trump human relationships.

He had hired Libby. Now it was time to let her know she had his support.

Libby was in heaven. After months of wallowing in uncertainty and despair, now having a concrete reason to get up every morning brought her something she hadn't found in a long time…confidence and peace.

For whatever reason, Patrick Kavanagh had made himself scarce during Libby's first two weeks. He'd left the training and orientation entirely up to Charlise. Which meant Libby didn't constantly have to be looking over her shoulder. With Charlise, Libby felt relaxed and comfortable.

They had hit it off immediately. So much so that Libby experienced a pang of regret to know Charlise wouldn't be coming back after today. Just before five, Libby went to Charlise's office holding a small package wrapped in blue paper printed with tiny airplanes. Charlise and her accountant husband were looking forward to welcoming a fat and healthy baby boy.

Libby knocked at the open door. "I wanted to give you this before you go."

Charlise looked up from her chore of packing personal items. Her eyes were shiny with tears. "You didn't have to do that."

"I wanted to. You've been so patient with me, and I appreciate it. Are you okay? Is anything wrong?"

Charlise reached for a tissue and blew her nose. "No. I don't know why I'm so emotional. I'm very excited about the baby, and I want to stay at home with him, but I love Silver Reflections. It's hard to imagine not coming here every day."

"I'll do my best to keep things running smoothly while you're gone."

"No doubts on that score. You're a smart cookie, Libby. I feel completely confident about leaving things in your hands."

"I hope you'll bring the baby to see us when the weather is nice."

"You can count on it." She opened the gift slowly, taking care not to rip the paper. "Oh, Libby, this is beautiful. But it must have been way too expensive."

Libby grimaced. She had been very honest with Charlise about her current financial situation. "It's an antique of sorts. A family friend gave it to my parents when I was born, engraved with the initial *L*. When I heard you say were going to name the baby Lander, after your father, I knew I wanted you to have it."

"But you've kept it all this time. Despite everything that's happened. It must have special meaning."

When Libby looked at the silver baby cup and bowl and spoon, her heart squeezed. "It does. It did. I think I held on to the set as a reminder of happier times. But the truth is, I don't need it anymore. I'm looking toward the future. It will make me feel good to know your little boy is using it."

Charlise hugged Libby tightly. "I'll treasure it."

Libby glanced at her watch. "I need to let you get out of here, but may I ask you one more thing before you go?"

"Of course."

"How did you get this job working with Patrick?"

"My husband and Patrick's brother Aidan are good friends. When Patrick put out the word that he was starting Silver Reflections, Aidan hooked us up."

"And the high-adventure stuff?"

Charlise shrugged. "I've always been a tomboy. Climbing trees. Racing go-karts. Broke both arms and legs before I made it to college. At different times, thank goodness."

"Good grief." Libby thought about her own cocoon-like adolescence. "Do you really think I can handle the team building and physical challenges in the outdoors?"

The other woman paused, her hand hovering over a potted begonia. "Let me put it this way…" She picked up the plant and put it in a box. "I think you'll be fine as long as you believe in yourself."

"What does that mean?"

"I've heard you talk about Patrick. He intimidates you."

"Well, I—" Libby stopped short, unable to come up with a believable lie. "Yes."

"Don't let him. He may come across as tough and intense at times, but underneath it all, he's a pussycat."

A broad-shouldered masculine frame filled the doorway. "I think I've just been insulted."

Two

Libby was mortified to be caught discussing her new boss. Charlise only laughed.

Patrick went to the pregnant woman and kissed her cheek, placing his hand lightly on her belly. "Tell that husband of yours to call me the minute you go to the hospital. And let me know if either of you needs anything... anything at all."

Charlise got all misty-eyed again. "Thanks, boss."

"It won't be the same without you," he said.

"Stop that or you'll make me cry again. Libby knows everything I know. She's exactly who you need... I swear."

Patrick smiled. "I believe you." He turned to Libby. "How about dinner tonight? I've tried to stay out of the way while Charlise showed you the ropes, but I think it would be good for the two of us to get to know each other better. What do you say?"

Libby felt herself flush from her toes to the top of her head. Not that this was a date. It wasn't. Not even close.

But Patrick Kavanagh was an imposing specimen. Despite his comfortably elegant appearance at the hotel, she had the distinct sense that beneath the dark suits and crisp ties lurked someone who was very much a man's man.

The kind of guy who made a woman's toes curl with just one look from his intense blue-gray eyes. He was tall and lean and had a headful of unruly black hair. The glossy, dark strands needed a comb. Or maybe the attention of a lover's fingers.

Her heart thumped hard, even as her stomach tumbled in a free fall. "That would be nice," she said. *Great*. Now she sounded like a child going to a tea party at her grandma's house.

Charlise picked up her purse and a small box. Patrick hefted the larger carton and followed her out of the room, leaving Libby to trail behind. Outside, the air was crisp and cold. She shivered and pulled her sweater more tightly across her chest.

Patrick stowed Charlise's things and hugged her. The affection between the two was palpable. Libby wondered what Charlise's husband was like. Obviously, he must be quite a guy if he let his wife work day after day with the darkly handsome Patrick Kavanagh.

Charlise eased behind the wheel, closed the car door and motioned for Libby to come closer. Patrick's phone had rung, and he was deep in conversation with whoever was on the other end.

Libby rested a hand in the open window and leaned down. "You're going to freeze," she said.

The pregnant woman lowered her voice. "Don't let him ride roughshod over you. You're almost too nice sometimes. Stand up to him if the occasion warrants it."

"Why would I do that? He's the boss."

Charlise grinned and started the engine. "Because he's too damned arrogant for his own good. All the Kavanagh men are. They're outrageously sexy, too, but we women have to draw a line in the sand. Trust me, Libby. Alpha males are like dangerous animals. They can smell fear. You need to project confidence even when you don't feel it."

"Now you're scaring me," Libby said, only half joking.

"I've known Patrick a long time. He admires grit and determination. You'll win his respect. I have no doubt. And don't worry about the survival training. What's the worst that could happen?"

Libby watched the car drive away, burdened with an inescapable feeling that her only friend in the world was leaving her behind in the scary forest. When she turned around, the lights from the main lodge of Silver Reflections cast a warm glow against the gathering darkness.

Since Patrick was still tied up on the phone, she went back to Charlise's office—now Libby's—and printed out the staff directory. She planned to study it this weekend. Facts and figures about everyone from the housekeeping staff to the guy who kept the internet up and running. Even at an executive retreat center famed for creating an atmosphere of solitude and introspection, no one at the level of these guests was going to be happy without a connection to the outside world.

Patrick found her twenty minutes later. "You ready to go? I guess it makes sense to take two cars."

Silver Reflections was tucked away in the mountains ten miles outside of town. In the complete opposite direction stood the magnificent Silver Beeches Lodge. Perched on a mountaintop overlooking Silver Glen, it was owned and operated by Maeve Kavanagh and her eldest son, Liam. Libby hesitated before answering, having second thoughts. "I'm sure you must have better things to do with your weekend. I'm not really dressed for dinner out."

Patrick's eyes darkened with a hint of displeasure. "If it

will make you feel better, I'll include these hours in your paycheck. And dinner doesn't have to be fancy. We can go to the Silver Dollar."

Patrick's brother, Dylan, owned a popular watering hole in town. The saloon was definitely low-key. Certainly Libby's clothing would not make her stand out there. "All right," she said, realizing for the first time that Patrick's invitation was more like an order. "I'll meet you there."

During the twenty-minute drive, she had time to calm her nerves. She already had the job. Patrick wasn't going to fire her yet. All she had to do was stick it out until they did some of the outdoor stuff, and she could prove to him that she was adaptable and confident in the face of challenges.

That pep talk carried her all the way into the parking lot of the Silver Dollar. The requisite pickup trucks were definitely in evidence, but they were interspersed with Lexus and Mercedes and the occasional fancy sports car.

Libby had visited this corner of North Carolina a time or two over the years with her mother. Silver Glen was a high-end tourist town with a nod to alpine flavor and an unspoken guarantee that the paparazzi were not allowed. It wasn't unusual to see movie stars and famous musicians wandering the streets in jeans and baseball caps.

Most of them eventually showed up at the Silver Dollar, where the beer was cold, the Angus burgers prime and the crowd comfortably raucous. Libby hovered on the porch, waiting for Patrick to arrive. The noise and color and atmosphere were worlds away from her native habitat in Manhattan, but she loved it here.

At Maeve's urging, Libby had given up the New York apartment she could scarcely afford and had come to North Carolina for a new start. Truth be told, her native habitat was feeling more and more distant every day.

Patrick strolled into view, jingling his car keys. "Let's

grab a table," he said. "I called Dylan and told him we were on our way."

In no time, they were seated. Libby ordered a Coke… Patrick, an imported ale. Dylan stopped by to say hello. The smiling, very handsome bar owner was the second oldest in the seven-boy Kavanagh lineup. Patrick was the second youngest.

Patrick waved a hand at Libby. "Do you remember Libby Parkhurst? She's going to fill in for part of Charlise's maternity leave."

Dylan shook Libby's hand. "I do remember you." He sobered. "I was sorry to hear about your mother. We have an apartment upstairs here at the Silver Dollar. I'd be happy to give it to you rent-free until you've had a chance to get back on your feet."

Libby narrowed her gaze. "Did your mother guilt you into making me an offer?"

Dylan's neck turned red. "Why would you say that? Can't a man do something nice without getting an inquisition?"

Libby stared from one brother to the other. Apparently, down-on-her-luck Libby had become the family *project*. "If you're positive it won't be an imposition," she said slowly. "I'm taking up a very nice guest room at Maeve's fancy hotel, so I'm sure she'd rather have me here."

Dylan shook his head. "Maeve is delighted to have you *anywhere*. Trust me. But she thought you'd like some privacy."

Patrick studied Libby's face as she pondered the implications of living above the bar. It was hardly what she was used to…but then again, he had no idea what her life had been like after the tax guys had swooped in and claimed their due.

Dylan wandered away to deal with a bar-related problem, and on impulse, Patrick asked the question on his mind. "Will you tell me about this past year? Where you've been? How things unfolded? Sometimes it helps to talk to a neutral third party."

Libby sipped her Coke, her gaze on the crowd. Friday nights were always popular at the Silver Dollar. He studied her profile. She had a stubborn chin, but everything else about her was soft and feminine. He would bet money that after one night in the woods, Libby was going to admit she was in over her head.

When she looked at him, those beautiful eyes gave him a jolt—awareness laced with the tiniest bit of sexual interest. He shut down that idea quickly. Maeve would have his head on a platter if he messed with her protégé. And besides, Libby wasn't his type. Not at all.

Libby's lips curved in a rueful half smile. "It was frightening and traumatic and definitely educational. Fortunately, my mother had a few stocks and bonds that were in her name only. We managed to find an apartment we could afford, but it was pretty dismal. I wanted to go out and look for work, but she insisted she needed me close. I think losing the buffer of wealth and privilege made her feel painfully vulnerable."

"What about your father?"

"We had some minimal contact with him. But Mama and I both felt betrayed, so we didn't go out of our way to visit. I suppose that makes me sound hard and selfish."

Patrick shook his head. "Not at all. A man's duty is to care for his family. Your father deceived you, broke your trust and failed to provide for you. It's understandable that you have issues."

She stared at him. "You speak from experience, don't you? My mother told me about what happened years ago."

Patrick hadn't expected her to be so quick on the uptake. Now he was rather sorry he'd raised the subject. His own father, Reggie Kavanagh, had been determined to find the lost silver mine that had made the first Kavanaghs in North Carolina extremely wealthy. Reggie had spent months, years…looking, always looking.

His obsession cost him his family.

"I was just a little kid," Patrick said. "My brother Liam has the worst memories. But yeah…I understand. My mother had every right to be bitter and angry, but somehow she pulled herself together and kept tabs on seven boys."

Libby paled, her eyes haunted. "I wish I could say the same. But not all of us are as strong as Maeve."

He cursed inwardly. He hadn't meant to sound critical of Libby's mother. "My mother wasn't left destitute."

"True. But she's made of tough stock. Mama was never really a strong person, even in the best of times."

"I'm sorry, Libby."

Her lips twisted, her eyes bleak. "We can't choose our families."

In an instant he saw that this job idea was laden with emotional peril for Libby Parkhurst. When it became glaringly obvious that she couldn't handle the physically demanding nature of Charlise's role as his assistant, Libby would be crushed. Surely it would be better to find that out sooner than later. Then she could move on and look for employment more suited to her skill set. Libby was smart and organized and intuitive.

There was a place for her out there somewhere. Just not at Silver Reflections.

He drummed his fingers on the table. "I looked at the weather forecast. We're due to have a warm spell in a couple of days."

"I saw that, too. Maeve says you almost always get an early taste of spring here in the mountains, even if it doesn't last long."

"She's right. And in light of that, why don't you and

I go ahead and take an overnight trip, so I can show you what's involved."

Libby went from wistful to deer in the headlights. "You mean now?"

"Yes. We could head out Monday morning and be back Tuesday afternoon." Part of him felt guilty for pushing her, but they had to get past this hurdle so she could see the truth.

He saw her throat move as she swallowed. "I don't have any outdoor gear."

"Mom can cover you there. And my sisters-in-law can loan you some stuff, too. No sense in buying anything now."

"Because you think I'll fail."

She stared him down, but he wasn't going to sugarcoat it. "I think there is a good chance you'll discover that working for me isn't what you really want."

"You've made up your mind already, haven't you?" He was surprised to see that she had a temper.

"No." Was he being entirely honest? "I promised you a trial run. I've merely moved up the timetable, thanks to the weather."

Libby's gaze skewered him. "Do I need a list from you, or will your mother know everything I need?"

"I'll email you the list, but Mom has a pretty good idea."

Libby stood up abruptly. "I don't think I'm that hungry, after all. Thank you for the Coke, *Mr. Kavanagh*. If you'll excuse me, it sounds like I have a lot to do this weekend."

And with that, she turned her back on him and walked out of the room.

Dylan commandeered the chair Libby had vacated, his broad smirk designed to be irritating. "I haven't seen you crash and burn in a long time, baby brother. What did you say to make her so mad?"

"It wasn't a date," Patrick said, his voice curt. "Mind your own damned business."

"She could do better than you, no doubt. Great body, I'm guessing, even though her clothes are a tad on the eccentric side. Excellent bone structure. Upper-crust accent. And those eyes… Hell, if I weren't a married man, I'd try my luck."

Patrick reined in his temper, well aware that Dylan was yanking his chain. "That's not funny."

"Seriously. What did you say to run her off?"

"It's complicated."

"I've got all night."

Patrick stared at him. "If you must know, Mom shoved her down my throat as a replacement for Charlise. Libby can handle the retreat center details, but there is no way in hell she's going to be able to do all the outdoor, back-country stuff. When I hired her, she asked me to give her a chance to prove herself. I merely pointed out that the weather's going to be warm the first of the week, so we might as well go for it."

"And that made her mad?"

"Well, she might possibly have assumed that I expect her to fail."

"Smart lady."

"How am I the bad guy here? I run a multilayered business. I can't afford to babysit Mom's misfits."

Dylan's expression went from amused to horrified in the space of an instant.

Libby's soft, well-modulated voice broke the deadly silence. "I left my sweater. Sorry to interrupt."

And then she was gone. Again.

Patrick swallowed hard. "Did she hear what I said?"

Dylan winced. "Yeah. Sorry. I didn't have time to warn you. I didn't see her coming."

"Well, that's just peachy."

The waitress appeared, notepad in hand, to take Patrick's order. "What'll you have?" she asked.

Dylan shook his head in regret. "Bring us a couple of burgers, all the way. My baby brother needs some cheering up. It's gonna be a long night."

Three

Not since the wretched aftermath of her father's arrest had Libby felt so small and so humiliated. She'd thought Patrick liked her...that he was pleased with her work to date. But in truth, Libby had been foisted on him, and he resented her intrusion.

Her chest hurt, almost as if someone had actually sucker punched her. When she made it back to her room on the third floor of Maeve's luxurious hotel, Libby threw herself on the bed and cried. Then she cussed awhile and cried some more. Part of her never wanted to see Patrick Kavanagh again. The other part wanted to make him ashamed for having doubted her. She wanted to be the best damn outdoorswoman he had ever seen.

But since that was highly unlikely to be the actual scenario come Monday, perhaps the best course was to explain to Maeve that the job hadn't worked out.

There would be questions, of course, lots of them. And although there might be other jobs in Silver Glen, perhaps as a shop assistant making minimum wage, it would be difficult to find a place to live on that kind of paycheck. She owed Maeve a huge debt of gratitude. Not for anything in the world did she want to seem ungrateful.

Which left Libby neatly boxed into an untenable situation.

Saturday morning she awoke with puffy eyes and a headache. It was only after her third cup of coffee that she even began to feel normal. Breakfast was out of the question. She felt too raw, too bruised. There was no reason to think Patrick would be anywhere near the Silver Beeches Lodge, but she wasn't taking any chances.

After showering and dressing in jeans and a baggy sweater, Libby sent a text to Maeve, asking her to drop by when she had a minute. In the meantime, Libby studied her paycheck. She had planned to buy the first pieces of her professional wardrobe this weekend. But if she was going to be fired Tuesday night, it made no sense to pay for clothes she might not need.

One step at a time.

When Maeve knocked on the door around eleven, Libby took a deep breath and let her in.

Maeve hugged her immediately. "I want to hear all about the job," she said, beaming. "I saw Charlise in town Wednesday, and she said you were amazing."

Libby managed a weak chuckle. "Charlise is being kind."

The two of them sat down in armchairs beside the gas log fireplace. Although now Libby could barely afford the soap in the bathroom, the upscale accommodations were familiar in their amenities. Growing up, she had traveled widely with her parents.

Maeve smoothed a nonexistent wrinkle from her neatly pressed black slacks. Wearing a matching blazer and a fuchsia silk blouse, she looked far younger than her age, certainly too young to have seven adult sons. "So tell me," she said. "How do you like working for Patrick?"

"Well…" Libby hesitated. She'd never been a good liar, so she had to tiptoe through this minefield. "I've spent most of my time with Charlise. But everyone on the staff speaks very highly of your son."

"But what do *you* think? He's a good-looking boy, isn't he?"

At last Libby's smile felt genuine. "Yes, ma'am. Patrick is a hottie."

"I know I'm prejudiced, but I think all my sons turned out extremely well."

"I know you're proud, and rightfully so."

"Five of them already married off to wonderful women. I think I'm doing pretty well."

Uh-oh. "Maeve, surely you're not thinking about playing matchmaker. That would be extremely uncomfortable for me."

Maeve's face fell. "What do you mean?"

"I'm starting my life from scratch," Libby said. "I have to know I can be an independent person. Although I was too naive to realize it at the time, my parents sheltered me and coddled me. I want to learn how to negotiate the world on my own. Romance is way down the list. And besides, even I know it's not a good idea to mix business with pleasure."

If a mature, extremely sophisticated woman could sulk, that's what Maeve did. "I thought you'd appreciate my help."

"I *do*," Libby said, leaning forward and speaking earnestly. "You looked out for me at the lowest point in my life. You helped me through Mama's death and took me in. I'll never be able to thank you enough. But at some point, you have to let me make my own choices, my own mistakes. Otherwise, I'll never be sure I can survive on my own."

"I suppose you're right. Is that why you wanted to see me this morning? To tell me to butt out?"

Libby grinned, relieved that Maeve had not taken offense. "No. Actually, I need your help in rounding up some hiking gear. Patrick wants to take advantage of the warm weather coming up to teach me what I'll need to know for the team-building, outdoor-adventure expeditions."

"So soon? Those usually don't begin until early April."

"I think he wants to be sure I can handle the physical part of the job." Libby spoke calmly, but inwardly she cringed, Patrick's words still ringing in her ears. *I can't afford to babysit Mom's misfits.*

Maeve stared at her intently. Almost as if she could tell something else was going on. "Write down all your sizes," she said. "I'll gather everything you need and meet you here tomorrow around one."

"I really appreciate it."

Maeve stood. "I have a lunch appointment, so I need to run. You'll get through this, Libby. I know how strong you are."

"Mentally or physically?"

"They go hand in hand. You may surprise yourself this week, my dear. And you may surprise Patrick, as well."

Patrick's mood hovered somewhere between injured grizzly and teething toddler. He was ashamed of himself for letting his aggravation make him say something stupid. But damn it, he'd been talking to his brother…letting off steam. He didn't go around kicking puppies and plucking the heads off flowers.

He was a nice guy.

Unfortunately for him, he could think of at least one person who didn't think so.

During the weekend, he gathered the equipment he would need to put Libby through her paces. Normally, he and Charlise shared the load: supervising the employees who organized the meals, interacting with the executives, teaching skills, coaching the group through difficult activities.

But Charlise was not only accustomed to being outdoors, she also had a great deal of experience in living off the land.

Libby didn't. It was as simple as that.

Patrick tried to juggle things in his mind, ways for him to take over some of Charlise's duties so that Libby could handle a lighter load. But that would only postpone the inevitable. This first experience had to play out as closely as possible to the real thing, so Libby would understand fully what was involved and what she could expect.

By Monday morning, his mood hadn't improved. He'd gone through his checklist on autopilot, but of course, he'd had to cover Charlise's prep, as well. He arrived at Silver Reflections several minutes before eight so he would have some time to mentally gear up for the day's events.

Libby's car was already parked in the small wooded lot adjacent to the building. It was an old-model Mercedes with a badly dented fender. Suddenly Patrick remembered where he had seen the car before. Liam's wife had driven it a couple of years ago until a teenage kid backed into her at the gas station.

Liam had decided it wasn't worth fixing and bought Zoe a brand-new mommy van. The damaged car had been in Liam's garage the last time Patrick saw it. Apparently, Maeve wasn't opposed to getting the whole family in the act when it came to her "rescue Libby" plan.

Patrick headed inside, greeted the receptionist with an absent wave and holed up in his office. Taking a deep breath, he leaned a hip against his desk, pulled his phone out and sent a text.

We'll leave at nine if that works for you...

Libby's response was immediate: I'll be ready.

Meet me out front.

He wondered if Libby was nervous. Surely so. But he knew her well enough already to be damned sure she wouldn't let the nerves show.

At 8:55 he hefted all their gear and headed outside, only to get his first shock of the day. Libby leaned against a tree, head back, eyes closed. On the ground at her feet lay a waterproof jacket. From head to toe, she was outfitted appropriately. Sturdy boots, lightweight quick-dry pants, a white shirt made of the same fabric and an aluminum hiking pole. He came do a dead stop and swallowed hard.

Every bit of what she was wearing was borrowed. Yet inexplicably she managed to look like a model for some weird amalgam of *Vogue* and L.L.Bean. The clothing fit her better than anything she had worn so far in his employ. Suddenly, he realized that Dylan was correct. Libby Parkhurst had a kick-ass body.

When he shifted from one foot to the other, he dislodged a piece of gravel. Libby's eyes snapped open, her expression guarded. "Good morning," she said.

He hated the guilt that choked him. "Libby, I—"

She held up a hand. "I don't want to talk about it."

They stared at each other for several long seconds. He couldn't get a read on her emotions. So he shoved aside the memory of her face in Dylan's bar and forced himself to zero in on basics.

"Three things," he said tersely. "The moment you feel

anything on your foot begin to rub, we stop and deal with it. A major key to hiking in the mountains is taking care of your feet. Blisters can be incapacitating. Understood?"

"Yes, sir."

Her smart-ass tone was designed to annoy him, but he didn't take the bait. "Secondly, if I'm walking too fast for you, you have to say so. There's no need to play the martyr."

"Understood."

"Lastly, you have to drink water. All day. All the time. Women don't like the idea of peeing in the woods, so they tend to get dehydrated. That's also dangerous."

The look on Libby's face was priceless. "Got it," she mumbled.

"Am I being too blunt?" he asked.

She gnawed her lip. "No. I suppose I hadn't thought through all the ramifications."

"That's what this trip is about."

He slid one of two backpacks off his shoulder. "I need to make sure the straps are adjusted correctly for you." Without asking, he stepped behind her and helped settled the pack into position. With a few quick tugs, he was satisfied. Finally, he moved in front of her and fiddled with the strap at her chest.

Libby made some kind of squawk or gasp. It was only then that he realized his fingers were practically caressing her breasts. He stepped back quickly. "I'm sure you can manage the waistband," he muttered.

"Uh-huh." She kept her head down while she dealt with the plastic locking mechanism. After a moment, she stared off into the woods. "I'm good."

"Then follow me."

Libby had taken yoga classes from the time she was fourteen, although during the past year, she'd had to keep up the discipline on her own. She was limber and more than moderately fit. But Patrick's punishing pace had her gasping for breath by the third mile.

His legs were longer than hers. He knew the rhythm of walking over rough terrain. And she was pretty sure he had loaded her pack with concrete blocks. But if Charlise could do this, so could she.

Fortunately, the boots Maeve had found for Libby were extremely comfortable and already broken in. Given Patrick's warning, Libby paid close attention to her feet. So far, no sign of problems.

It helped that the view from behind was entertaining. Patrick's tight butt and long legs ate up the miles. She had long since given up estimating how far they had come or what time it was. Since her phone was turned off to save the battery, she was dependent upon Patrick's knowledge of the forest to get them where they needed to go.

At one point when her legs ached and her lungs burned, she shouted out a request. "Water, please." That was more acceptable to her pride than admitting she couldn't keep up.

Patrick had a fancy water-thingy that rested inside his pack and allowed him to suck from a thin hose that protruded. Not the kind of item a person borrows. So he had tucked plastic pouches of water for Libby in the side pockets of her pack. She opened one and took a long, satisfying gulp. It took everything she had not to ask how much farther it was to their destination.

The two of them were completely alone…miles away from the nearest human. The wind soughed through the trees. Birds tweeted. The peace and solitude were beautifully soothing. But a chasm existed between Patrick and her. At the moment, she had no desire to breach it.

As forecasted, the warming trend had arrived with a

vengeance. Temperatures must already be in the upper sixties, because Libby's skin was damp with perspiration.

Patrick hadn't said a word during their stop. He merely stood in silence, his attention focused on the scenery. The trail had ascended a small ridgeline, and through a break in the trees, they could see the town of Silver Glen in the distance.

"I'm good," she said, stashing the water container. "Lead on."

Her body hurt and her lungs hurt, but eventually, she fell into a rhythm that was almost natural. *One foot in front of the other. Zen-like state of being. Embrace the now.*

It almost worked.

When they stopped for lunch, she could have sworn it was at least seven in the evening. But the sun was still high in the sky. Patrick had a more sophisticated standard for trail food than she had anticipated. Perhaps a certain level of cuisine was de rigueur for his Fortune 500 clients. Instead of the peanut butter and jelly she had expected, they enjoyed baked-ham sandwiches on homemade bread.

When the meal was done and Patrick shoved their minimal trash into his pack, she finally asked a question. "What do you do if you have someone who can't handle the hiking?"

He zipped his pack and shouldered it. "Companies apply to come to Silver Reflections. We have a long waiting list. Most of the elite businesses institute some kind of wellness programs beforehand. They'll include weight loss, stress management, regular exercise…that kind of thing. So by the time they come to North Carolina, most of the participants are mentally and physically prepared for the adventure rather than dreading it."

"I see." But she didn't really. Patrick was already walking, so she stumbled after him. "But what about people that aren't prepared? Do they make them come anyway?"

Patrick didn't turn around, but his voice carried. "A lot of top corporations are beginning to realize the importance of physical well-being for their employees as a means to increase the bottom line. If an executive has a physical limitation, then of course he or she isn't forced to come. But if an otherwise physically capable person chooses not to attend to his or her health and fitness, then it might be a sign that a top-shelf promotion isn't in the cards."

With that, the conversation ended. Patrick was walking as quickly as ever, making it look easy. Maybe Libby had slipped into the numb stage, or maybe she was actually getting used to this, but her aches and pains had receded. Perhaps this was the "runner's high" people talked about. Endorphins at work, masking the physical discomfort.

At long last, Patrick stopped and took off his pack to stretch. Libby followed suit, looking around curiously. It was obvious they had reached their destination. Patrick stood on the edge of a large clearing. The area was mostly flat. About thirty feet away, a narrow creek slid and tumbled over rocks, the sound of the water as soothing as the prospect of wetting tired feet in the chilly brook.

Patrick shot her a look, clearly assessing her physical state. "This is base camp."

"There's not much to it," she blurted out.

"Were you expecting a five-star hotel?"

His sarcasm on top of everything else made her angry, but she didn't want him to get the best of her. So she kept her mouth shut. If he wanted her to talk, he was going to have to initiate the conversation.

Somehow, it seemed almost obscene to be at odds with another human in the midst of such surroundings. Though it would be several more weeks until the new green of spring began to make its way through the sun-kissed glades, even now the forest was beautiful.

She dropped her pack and managed not to whimper.

Though it galled her to admit it, maybe Patrick was right. Maybe this job was not for her. It was one thing to come out here alone with him. But in the midst of an "official" expedition, Libby would be expected to pull her weight. Her new boss wouldn't be free to coach her if she got in over her head.

He knelt and began pulling things from his pack. "The first thing Charlise usually does is put up our tents. I'll be teaching the group how to do theirs."

"Okay." How hard could it be? The one-man tents were small.

"First you'll want the ground cover. It's the thing that's silver on one side and red on the other. Silver side up to preserve body heat."

Libby was a fast learner. And she was determined to acquit herself well. "Got it."

Patrick pointed. "Leader tents go over there." He stood, hands on hips, while she struggled to spread the ground tarps and smooth them out.

Next came the actual tents. Claustrophobically small and vulnerably thin, they were actually not that difficult to set up. Lightweight poles snapped together in pieces and threaded through a nylon sleeve from one corner of the tent to the opposite side. Repeat once, and it was done. The only thing left was to secure the four corners to the ground with plastic stakes.

All in all, not a bad effort for her first time. Even Patrick seemed reluctantly impressed. He handed her a rolled-up bundle that was about eighteen inches wide. "Look for a valve on one corner. It's not difficult to blow up. And it won't look like much when you're done. But having this pad underneath your upper body and hips makes for a much more comfortable night."

He was right. Even when she inflated the thin *mat-*

tress, it didn't seem like much of a cushion. But she wasn't about to say so.

To give Patrick his due, he didn't go out of his way to make her feel nervous or clumsy. Still, having someone watch while she learned new skills was stressful.

At last, both tents were up, pads and sleeping bags inside. The full realization that she and Patrick were going to spend the night together hit her hard. No television. No computers. Nothing at all for a distraction. He was gorgeous and unavailable. She was lonely and susceptible.

Nevertheless, the job was what she needed. Not the man. She couldn't let him see that she was seriously attracted to him. Cool and casual was the plan.

She stood and arched her back. "What next?"

Four

Patrick hadn't expected much from a young, pampered, New York socialite. But perhaps he was going to have to eat his words. During the morning, he had set an intentionally punishing pace as they made their way through the woods. Libby stayed on his heels and never once complained.

Was it the past year that had made her resilient, or was she naturally spunky and stubborn? That would remain to be seen.

He glanced at his watch. Even with this current spring-like spell, it was still February, which meant far less daylight than in two months when he traditionally scheduled his first team-building treks. Kneeling, he pulled a small camp stove from his pack. "I'll show you how to use this," he said. "The chef at the retreat center has a couple of part-time assistants who prepare our camping meals the day before."

"I assumed the execs would have to cook for themselves. Isn't that part of the outdoor experience?"

"In theory, yes. But so far, we've only done short trips… two days, one night. So our time frame is limited. Since we want them to do a lot of other activities, we preprepare the food and all they have to do is warm it up. We don't spend too much time on meals."

Once Libby had mastered the stove, she glanced up at him. "Surely you don't expect the entire group to use something this small."

"No. I have a group of local guys who come along to carry the food, extra stoves and extra water."

He stared at her, disconcerted by feelings that caught him unawares. He was *enjoying* himself. Libby was a very soothing person to be around. When she stood up, he walked away, ostensibly picking up some fallen limbs that had littered the campsite.

Grappling with an unexpected attraction, he cursed inwardly. With Charlise, he never felt like he was interacting with a woman. He treated her the same way he did his brothers. Charlise was almost part of his family. While he was delighted that she and her husband were so happy about the upcoming birth, he would be lying if he didn't admit he was feeling a little bit sorry for himself. Silver Reflections had been going so well. He had honed these outdoor events down to the finest detail. Then Charlise had to go and get pregnant. And his mother had saddled him with Libby. A remarkably appealing woman who'd already managed to get under his skin.

What was he going to do about it? Nothing. It would be a really bad idea to get involved personally with his mother's beloved Libby. Not only that, but with Charlise out of commission, he had no choice but to work twice as hard. And ignore his libido.

Surely he could be excused for being a little grumpy.

Libby called out to him. "What now?"

He turned around and caught her rolling her shoulders. She'd be sore tomorrow. Backpacking used a set of muscles most people didn't employ on a daily basis.

"I'll show you how we string our packs up in the trees," he said.

"Excuse me?"

He sighed, the look of befuddlement on her face the sign of an outdoor newbie. "Once we set up camp, we won't be hauling our backpacks everywhere. We'll use this as home base and range around the area."

"Why can't we leave the packs in our tents?"

"Bears," he said simply.

Up until that point, Libby had done an admirable job keeping her cool, but now she paled. "What do you mean, *bears*?"

"Black bears have an incredible sense of smell. And they're omnivorous. Anytime we're away from camp—and at night when we're sleeping—we'll hang our packs from a high tree limb to discourage unwanted visitors. Don't keep any food in your tent at all, not even a pack of crackers or scented lip balm or toothpaste."

"I washed my hair with apple shampoo this morning." Her expression was priceless.

"Not to worry. I should have told you. But the scent won't be strong enough by the end of the day to make a difference."

"Easy for you to say," she grumbled as she glanced over her shoulder, perhaps expecting a bear to lumber into sight any moment.

Patrick unearthed a packet of nylon rope. "There will be plenty of tall men around to do this part, but it never hurts to gain a new life skill. Watch me, and then you can try."

"If you say so."

He found a rock that was maybe four inches around

and tied it to the end of the rope. "Stand back," he said. Fortunately for his male pride, his first shot sailed over the branch. He reached for the rock again and removed it. "Now all you have to do is attach one end to your pack, send it up, and tie it off." When Libby seemed skeptical, he laughed, his good humor restored for the moment. "Never mind. I won't make you practice this right now. We have better things to do."

"Like what?"

He grabbed a couple of water pouches and a zippered nylon case, then hefted both packs toward the treetops, securing them. "I'm going to show you where I teach the groups how to rappel."

Libby's expression was dubious. "Does Charlise do the rappelling thing?"

It was the first time she had seemed at all reluctant to approach something new. "No. Not usually. So if you don't want to try it, you can watch me. But I do want you to get a feel for the whole range of activities we offer. C'mon… it's not far."

As they passed the two tents, neatly in place for the upcoming night, he felt his pulse thud. He'd never thought of camping out as sexual or even sensual. When he spent time with a woman, it was in fine restaurants or at the theater. Perhaps later on soft sheets in her bedroom. But certainly not when both parties were sweaty—and without a luxurious bathroom at hand.

He stumbled. Damn it. Libby was messing with his head.

The large rock outcropping was barely half a mile away. He strode automatically, only slowing down when he realized that Libby was lagging behind. When she caught up, he moved on without speaking.

Though she had been cooperative and pleasant all day, his inadvertent insult from Friday hung between them like a cloud. He would have to address it sooner or later, whether she liked it or not.

When they arrived at their destination, he unzipped the bag and pulled out a mass of tightly woven mesh straps. "Sometimes, if we have women along, I might ask you to help them get into their gear. If a female seems extremely modest or uneasy, it can be difficult for me or one of the guys to help with the harness…you know…too much touching."

Libby nodded. "I understand."

She stared at him intently as he prepared the equipment. Something about her steady regard made the back of his neck tingle. "I'm going to go around the side of that ridge and come out on top," he said. "That cliff is only about thirty feet high, but it looks really far off the ground when you're standing up there, particularly if you've never done anything like this before."

"I can imagine."

He tossed her a thin ground cloth to sit on. "Feel free to relax while I get up there. And you don't have to worry about ticks or other bugs. It's still too early for a lot of creepy crawlies."

Libby *hadn't* been worrying about creepy crawlies, but she was now. Ick. Her legs itched already from the power of suggestion.

If her companion had been any man other than Patrick Kavanagh, she might have assumed he was showing off. He could have explained how the rappelling worked without a demonstration. Maybe he just liked doing it. It was a sure bet he didn't have any interest in impressing her.

Without Libby to slow him down, he appeared at the top of the small cliff in no time at all. She shaded her eyes and watched as he secured himself to a nearby tree. He checked all of his connections and waved. Then, looking like an extremely handsome and nimble spiderish super-hero, he stepped backward off the rock shelf and danced his way to the bottom.

His skill was striking.

Something about a man so physically powerful and at ease with his body was very appealing. For a moment, she thought about other, more primal things he might do exceedingly well...but no. She wouldn't go there.

Once before when she was young and immature, she'd fallen under the spell of a magnetic, powerful man—with disastrous results. History would not be repeating itself. She was older now, old enough to be tempted. But sex and romance were off the table. Keeping this job had to be her focus.

The demonstration took some time. Once Patrick reached the bottom, he had to go back to the top and untie his ropes.

Finally, he reappeared, striding toward her. She handed him his water. He dropped down beside her, barely breathing heavily, and took long gulps. Already, the sun was sliding lower in the sky, and a chill began to linger in the shadows.

Libby pulled her knees to her chest and linked her arms around her legs. "That was pretty cool. Have you always been fond of the outdoors?"

Patrick wiped the back of his arm across his forehead. "Would you be surprised to know that I worked in advertising for several years in Chicago?"

She gaped at him. "Seriously?"

His smile was self-mocking. "Yes. I loved the competitive atmosphere—stealing big accounts, coming up with the next great ad campaign. Brainstorming with smart, focused, energetic colleagues. It was a great environment for a young man."

She snorted. "You're still young."

"Well, you know what I mean."

"Then what changed?"

He shrugged. "I missed the mountains. I missed Silver Glen. I didn't know how deeply this place was imprinted on my DNA until I left. So one day, I turned in my notice, and I came home."

"And started Silver Reflections."

"It took a couple of years, but yeah...it's been a pretty exciting time."

"So who's the real Patrick Kavanagh? The man I just watched scramble down a cliff? Or the sophisticated guy who roams the halls of his übersuccessful, private, luxurious executive getaway?"

His quick grin startled her. "Wow, Libby...was that a compliment?" Without waiting for an answer to his teasing question, he continued. "Both, I guess. Without the time in Chicago, I doubt I would have understood the needs of the type A men and women who eat, sleep and breathe work. I was one of them...at least for a few years. But I realized my life was missing balance. For me, the balance is here. So if I can offer rest and recovery to other people, then I'm satisfied."

"And your personal life?" Oops. That popped out uncensored. "Never mind. I don't want to know."

He chuckled but kept silent.

They were sitting so close, she could smell his warm skin and the hint of whatever soap he had used that morning. Not aftershave. That would be the equivalent of inviting bears to munch on his toes. Even mentally joking about it gave her a shiver of unease.

Not long from now, it was going to get dark. Very dark. Her nemesis, Patrick Kavanagh, was the only person metaphorically standing between her and the wildness of nature.

To keep her mind off the upcoming night, she asked another question. "Do you have any regrets?"

"Yes," he said quietly. "I'm sorry I said something so stupid and unkind, and I'm sorry you heard it."

She flushed, though in the fading light, maybe he couldn't see. "I told you I don't want to talk about it. You're entitled to your opinion."

He touched her knee. Briefly. As if to establish some kind of connection. "I admire the hell out of you, Libby. I didn't mean what I said on Friday night. My mother is one of the best people I know. Her instincts are always spot-on. Her compassion and genuine love for people have influenced my brothers and me more than we'll ever know."

"You called me a misfit."

Patrick cursed beneath his breath. "Don't remind me, damn it. I'm sorry. It was a crappy thing to do."

"I think the reason it hurt me was because it's the truth."

Patrick leaped to his feet and dragged her with him, his hands on her shoulders. "Don't be ridiculous."

He looked down at her, his jaw tight. He was big and strong and absolutely confident in everything he did. With the five-inch difference in their heights, it would be easy to rest her head on his shoulder. She was tired of being strong all the time. She was tired of not knowing who she was anymore. And she really wanted the luxury of having a man like Patrick in her life. But survival trumped romance right now.

"You've been a trouper today," he said quietly.

"But I'm not Charlise."

One beat of silence passed. Then two.

"No. You're not. But that doesn't mean you aren't capable in your own way."

He wasn't dodging the truth. Where she came from they called that *damning with faint praise*.

"I can learn," she said firmly. Was she trying to convince Patrick or herself?

His small grin curled her toes in her boots. "I know that. And I'm sorry I hurt your feelings. I'm not usually such an animal. Please forgive me."

She wasn't sure who was more surprised when he bent his head and kissed her. When either or both of them should have pulled away, some spark of longing kept them together. At least it felt like longing on her part. She didn't know *what* Patrick was thinking.

His lips pressed hers firmly, his tongue teasing ever so gently, asking permission to slide inside her mouth and destroy her with the taste of him. Her arms went around his neck. Clinging. Her body leaned into his. Yearning. It had been well over a year since she had been kissed. Echoes of past mistakes set off alarms, but she ignored them.

The moment of rash insanity set her senses on fire, helping her forget that she'd walked through her own kind of purgatory. It felt so good to be held. So safe. So warm. She trembled in his embrace.

"Patrick…" She whispered his name, not wanting to stop, but knowing they were surely going to regret whatever madness had overtaken them.

He jerked as if he had been shot. Staggered backward. "Libby. Hell…"

The exclamation encompassed mortification. Shock. Regret.

It was the last one that stung, despite knowing that keeping distance between them was for the best.

She managed a smile, though it cost her. "We'd better get back to camp. I'm starving, and it's going to be dark soon."

His apology should have erased the friction, yet they faced each other almost as adversaries.

He nodded, his expression brusque. "You're right."

This time, following him through the forest came naturally. No matter the strained atmosphere between them, in this environment, she trusted him implicitly to take them wherever they needed to go.

Dinner was homemade vegetable soup warmed on the camp stove. The chef had made the entrée and added fresh Italian rolls to go with it. While Libby tended to the relatively foolproof job of preparing the meal, Patrick started a campfire and rolled a log near the flames so they would have a comfy place to sit.

With the cup from a thermos, Patrick ladled soup into paper bowls that would later be burned in the fire. He'd explained that the aluminum spoons they used were light in a pack and good for the environment.

Libby ate hungrily. It was amazing how many calories one consumed by walking in the mountains. Neither she nor Patrick spoke. What was there to say? He didn't really want her here. Not to replace Charlise. And beyond that, they were nothing to each other. Virtual strangers. Except she normally didn't go around kissing strangers. She jumped when an owl hooted nearby. Though she was wearing a long-sleeved shirt and the day had been warm, she scrambled to find her jacket. Huddling into the welcome warmth, she stared into the fire and tried not to think about the night to come.

If she had any hope of convincing Patrick that she was capable of filling Charlise's shoes, she had to act as if spending a night in the dark, scary woods was no big deal.

She stared into the mesmerizing red and gold flames, listening to the pop and crackle of the burning wood. The scent of wood smoke was pleasant…a connection, perhaps, to her ancestors who had lived closer to the land.

She and Patrick had eaten their meal in complete silence. Libby was okay with that. All she wanted to do now was get through this overnight endurance test without embarrassing herself.

She cleared her throat. "So, it's already dark. And it's awfully early to go to bed. What do people do in the woods when they camp out during the winter?"

Patrick's face was all planes and angles in the glow of the fire. He was a chameleon—dashing and elegant as a Kavanagh millionaire, but now, a ruggedly masculine man with unlimited physical power and capability. Looking at him gave her a funny feeling in the pit of her stomach.

The sensation was no secret. She was seriously in lust with her reluctant boss, despite his arrogance and his refusal to take her seriously. He could be funny and charming. He had been remarkably patient, even when saddled with his mother's charity case.

But the truth was, he didn't want her on his team. And when it came to the attraction that simmered between them? Well, that was never going to amount to anything, no matter how many hours they spent alone in the woods. She pressed her knees together, her heart beating a ragged tempo as she waited for an answer to what was one part rhetorical question and the other part a need to break the intimate quiet.

If she had a tad more experience, or if she honestly believed that Patrick felt a fraction of the sexual tension that was making her jumpy, she might make a move on him. But despite his kiss—which was really more of a hands-on apology—she didn't delude herself that he had any real interest in her.

Women like Charlise were more his type. Athletic superwomen. Not timid females afraid of the shadows.

Besides, she had to stay focused on starting her life over. She was on her own. She had to be strong.

She had almost forgotten her question when he finally answered.

Five

"Speaking for myself, I suppose it depends on who I'm with."

Patrick wasn't immune to the intimacy of the moment. He still reeled from the impact of the kiss. But all else aside, his mother would kill him if he played around with Libby. Libby was emotionally fragile and just coming out of a very rough period in her life. He couldn't take advantage of her vulnerability, even if she was already worming her way into his heart.

A part of him wanted to tell her how much fun sleeping-bag sex could be. But that would be crossing the line, and Libby Parkhurst was off-limits. He'd be exaggerating anyway. Most of the women he'd been serious about would run for the hills if he suggested anything of the sort.

It occurred to him suddenly that his love of outdoor adventure had largely been segregated from his romantic life. He hiked with his brothers. He took clients out in the woods with Charlise. But he'd never really wanted to bring a woman along in a personal, *intimate* sense.

Yet with Libby, he was tempted. Unfortunately, temptation was as far as it went. He had to keep her at a distance or this whole scenario might blow up in his face. Particularly when he had to fire her.

He picked up a tiny twig and tossed it into the fire. "You can always listen to music. Did you bring an iPod? It was on the list."

Libby nodded, her profile disarmingly feminine in the firelight. "I did. But if I have earbuds in, I won't be able to hear the wild animals when they come to rip me limb from limb."

Patrick chuckled. Despite Libby's lack of qualifications for the job as his assistant, he enjoyed her wry take on life. He also respected the fact that she acknowledged her fears without being crippled by them. As if he needed more reasons to be intrigued by her. But that didn't make her an outdoorswoman.

"I won't let anything happen to you, I swear." It was true. Libby might not be the one to cover the maternity leave, but he felt an overwhelming urge to protect her.

Eventually, Libby needed a moment of privacy in the woods. He had known it was coming. But he was pretty sure she wasn't comfortable about the dark.

When she stood up, she hedged. "I, uh…"

"You need to go to the bathroom before we call it a night."

"Yes."

He'd seen her blush before. Right now her face was probably poppy red. But he couldn't tell in the gloom. He handed her a flashlight. "Do you want me to go with you, or shall I stay here and face the fire?"

Long silence.

"Face the fire. But if I'm not back in ten minutes, send out the rescue squad."

Again, that easy humor. He sat and concentrated on the flames, feeling the heat on his face. His libido thrummed on high alert. It had never occurred to him that spending a night in the woods with Libby Parkhurst would test his self-control.

He had forgotten to glance at his watch when she left. How long had she been gone? Now she had *him* hearing all sorts of menacing sounds in the forest. "Libby," he called out. "You okay?"

He held his breath until she answered.

"I'm fine." Her voice echoed from a distance, so he stayed put.

At last she reappeared. "What time do we need to be up in the morning?" she asked.

"I'll get breakfast going…most importantly, a pot of coffee. You can pop out of your tent whenever you're ready."

"What about our packs?"

"I'll take care of it. When you get in your tent, make sure to take your boots off and put them by the exit. That way you won't get your sleeping bag muddy. The bedding I brought is warmer than the type we use in April. I hope you'll be comfortable."

"I'll be fine. Good night, Patrick."

He wished he could say the same. He was wired and horny. That was a dangerous combination.

With moves he had practiced a million times, he scattered the coals and made sure the fire was not in danger of spreading while they slept. Then he took both packs and hung them from a nearby treetop.

After crawling into his own tent and taking off his boots, he zipped the nylon flap and got settled for the night. His sleeping bag was high-tech and very comfortable. The temperature outside was perfect for snuggling into his down cocoon and sleeping.

Which didn't explain why he lay on his back and stared into the dark. The noises of the night were familiar to him. Hooting owls. Sighing wind. The *click-clack* of bare winter branches rubbing together.

Libby's tent was no more than four or five feet away from his. If he concentrated, he thought he might be able to hear her breathing.

He was almost asleep, when a female whisper roused him.

"Patrick. Are you awake?"

"I am now." He pretended to be gruff.

"What am I supposed to do if a bear tries to eat my tent?"

He grinned, even though she couldn't see. "Libby. People camp out in this part of the country all the time. We're not far from the Smoky Mountains. It's perfectly safe, I swear."

"I was kidding. Mostly. And I'm not being a wimp. I just want to be prepared for anything. But people *do* get attacked by bears. I went online and did a search."

"Are you sure you weren't reading stories about grizzlies? We don't have those in North Carolina."

"No. It was black bears. A woman died. They found her camera and she had been taking pictures."

"I remember the story you're talking about. But that was a long time ago and the woman, unfortunately, got too close to the bear."

"But what if the bear gets too close to me?"

He laughed. "Would you like to come sleep in my tent?" As soon as the words left his mouth, he regretted them. He hadn't consciously meant to flirt with her, but the feelings were there.

Long silence. "You mean with you?"

"Well, it doesn't make much sense just to swap places. If it will help you be more comfortable, I'm sure we can manage to squeeze you in here if we try."

Another, longer silence. "No, thank you. I'm fine. Really."

"Your choice." He paused. "Tell me, Libby. Did your family never vacation outdoors? National parks? Boating adventures? Anything like that?"

He heard the sound of rustling nylon as she squirmed to get comfortable.

"No. But I have a working knowledge of all the major museums in Europe, and I can order a meal at a Michelin-starred restaurant in three languages. I've summered in the Swiss Alps and wintered in Saint Lucia. Still, I've never cooked a hot dog over a campfire."

"Poor little rich girl."

"Not funny, Patrick. I happen to know the Kavanaghs are loaded. So you can't make fun of me."

"*Can't* or shouldn't?"

She laughed, the warm sound sneaking down inside him and making him feel something both arousing and uncomfortable.

"I'm going to sleep now," she said.

"See you in the morning."

Aeons later, Libby groaned. Morning light meant the dawn of a new day, but she was too warm and comfortable to care. For the past hour, she had actually been sleeping peacefully. Now, however, she had to go to the bathroom. And unlike any normal morning, she couldn't crawl back into bed afterward, because she would be completely awake.

She felt as if she had barely slept all night. Every noise was magnified in her imagination. She would doze off finally, and then minutes later some ominous sound would wake her up. It was an endless cycle.

To make matters worse, Patrick had fallen asleep almost instantly after their "bear" conversation. She knew this, because he'd snored. Not an obnoxious, chain-saw sound, but a quiet masculine rumble.

How did he do it? How did he sleep like a baby in the middle of the woods? Her hips were sore from lying on the ground, even with the pad, and she didn't know how *anyone* could manage restful slumber without some white noise.

Hiking enthusiasts talked about the peace and quiet of nature. Clearly they had never actually spent a night in the outdoors. The forest was *not* a silent place.

Though the temperatures were supposed to hit the sixties again this afternoon as the February warm spell lingered, this morning, there was a definite nip in the air. She shivered as she sat up and fumbled her way into her jacket. She could already smell the coffee Patrick had promised.

She rummaged in her pocket for the small cosmetic case she'd brought with her. A comb and a mirror and some unscented lip balm. That was it. Fortunately, the mirror was tiny, because she didn't really want to see her reflection. She had a feeling that her appearance fell somewhere between "dragged through a bush backward" and "one step away from zombie."

Putting on boots was her first challenge. Then, after struggling to tame her hair and redo her ponytail, she shook her head in defeat. She didn't need to impress Patrick with her looks. Why did it matter?

When she unzipped her tent and climbed out, she didn't glance in Patrick's direction. Instead, she headed off into the relative privacy of the forest. After taking care of her most urgent need, she returned to the campsite. Patrick looked rested, but his hair was rumpled and his jaw was shadowed with dark stubble.

Still, he looked gorgeous and sexy. Life wasn't fair at all.

He looked up from his contemplation of the fire when she sat down. "Mornin'," he said. The word was gruff.

She nodded, unable to come up with a scintillating response. The mood between them was undeniably awkward.

He poured her a cup of coffee. "Careful, it's hot."

"Thanks." Adding sugar and a packet of artificial creamer, she inhaled the steam, hoping the diffused caffeine would jump-start her sluggish brain. So far, the five-word conversation between her and her boss was taxing her will to live.

Two cups later, she began to feel slightly human. Even so, the fact that she had been wearing the same clothes for twenty-four hours made her long for a hot shower.

"What next?" she asked. The sooner Patrick taught her the drill, the sooner they could go home.

"We break down camp. With a group event, we'll have the camp stoves set up right over there. The guys that packed in the food and supplies will be your assistants. The meal is simple, homemade oatmeal with cinnamon and brown sugar for those who want it. Precooked bacon that we crisp up in a skillet. Whole oranges. And of course, coffee."

"Will I have to cook the oatmeal?"

"No. Only warm it. It's mostly a matter of being organized and making sure everyone gets served quickly. They're always eager to get started on the rest of the day, so we try not to drag out the meal process."

"I can handle that."

"You ready to head out?"

Gulp. Of course. She noticed he didn't say "head home." Clearly there was more to be learned.

She paid close attention as Patrick showed her how to

break down the tents and put out the fire. Once they re-loaded their packs, the site was pristine. It went without saying that a company like Silver Reflections would respect the sanctity of the natural world.

Patrick wasn't very talkative this morning. Perhaps he was regretting their momentary lapse. Or maybe he had other issues on his mind. Losing Charlise's expertise for six months had to be frustrating for him. Maybe everyone would have been a lot happier if Patrick had simply stood up to Maeve and told her he would find his own, far more qualified, temporary employee.

Still, even given the circumstances far beyond her comfort zone, Libby realized she really wanted this job. Beneath the physical challenges she was experiencing lurked exhilaration that she was facing her fears and conquering them…or at least trying to…

This morning's hike was shorter, no more than three or four miles. And Patrick's pace was more of a stroll than a death march. With the sun shining and the birds singing, it was almost easy to dismiss her sleepless night.

When they stopped for a snack, Patrick didn't take the time to unpack any kind of seating tarp. Instead, they leaned against trees. Recent rains had left the ground damp, particularly beneath the top layer of rotting leaves. He fished salted peanuts and beef jerky from his pocket. "This will give you energy," he said.

"Do I look that bad?"

His lips quirked. "Maybe a little frayed around the edges. Nothing to worry about. But it will be several hours before we get home, so you have to keep up your strength."

She bit off a piece of jerky, grimacing at the taste. "That sounds ominous. What's next? Building a canoe from a tree? Making blow darts from poison berries? Killing and skinning a wild animal with my bare hands?"

Patrick chuckled. "You've been watching too many movies."

"Then what?"

"We're going underground."

Her stomach fell somewhere in the vicinity of her boots. "Um, no. I don't think so. I got locked in a closet for several hours when I was a little kid and I've been claustrophobic ever since. I don't do caves."

It seemed as if he were baiting her, but she couldn't be sure.

"No caves in these mountains," he said. "It's the wrong kind of geology. You might find some large rock overhangs that provide shelter…but not the places where spelunkers investigate tunnels deep into the earth."

"Then what?"

"A mine." He didn't smile. In fact, his face was carefully expressionless.

Was this the part where she was supposed to throw up her hands and say "I quit"? "What kind of mine?" she asked, thinking about every Appalachian horror story she had heard about shafts collapsing and miners being buried alive.

"Years ago, it was one of hundreds of silver mines in the area, but it's long since been tapped out."

"Then why go in?"

"The claustrophobia you mentioned is a very real fear for many people. When we bring groups out, I go down into the mine with three at a time. Usually, the participants have been prepped in advance about what to discuss. Something simple, but work-related. We sit in the dark as they try to carry on a conversation without panicking."

"And if someone *does* freak out?"

"Their colleagues talk them through it…part of the team-building aspect. You'd be surprised. Sometimes it's the tough macho guys who can't handle it. It's an eye-opener all the way around."

"Well, thanks for telling me about it," she said, her voice high-pitched and squeaky. "I'll do absolutely every-thing you want me to do *above*ground, no questions asked. But I think I'll take a pass on the mine thing. I hope that's not a deal breaker."

Patrick took her hands, staring into her eyes like a hyp-notist. "You can trust me, Libby, I swear."

She exhaled, an audibly jerky sigh. "This might be a good time to mention that my childhood was spent learn-ing how to be scared of everything. My mom wouldn't take me into Central Park because of muggers. No Macy's Thanksgiving Parade because of lurking kidnap-pers in the crowd. If a spider ever had the temerity to in-vade our apartment, things went to DEFCON 1 in a hurry. She didn't want me to have a boyfriend, so she told me I could get pregnant from kissing."

"You and I are in trouble, then."

She ignored his attempt at levity. "I was afraid of drowning in the bathtub and being exposed to radioac-tivity from the microwave. My Halloween candy had to be checked for razor blades, even though it was all a gift from our neighbors across the hall, people we had known for years. I could go on, but you get the idea."

"You know that your mother had serious issues."

"Yes." It was hard to admit it out loud.

"People don't commit suicide for no reason. Your fa-ther's fall from grace may have devastated her, but surely it was more than that."

"I know." She swallowed hard, chagrined to feel hot tears threaten her composure. "I also learned to be afraid that I might be like her."

"Bullshit."

Patrick's forceful curse shocked her.

He squeezed her hands, and released her only to pull her against his chest for a brief hug. Then he stepped back and brushed a damp strand of hair from her forehead. The compassion in his gray-blue eyes stripped her raw.

"Libby," he said quietly, "you may not be the right person for this job, but you're strong and independent and amazingly resilient. Not once have you whined about what the last year has been like for you. During terrible, tragic circumstances, you cared for your mother when she couldn't care for herself. You did everything a loving daughter could do. And even though it may seem like it wasn't enough, that's not true."

"I tried to get help for her."

"By selling all your clothes and jewelry to pay for treatment."

"How did you know that?"

He shrugged. "Charlise told me."

Of course. "It wasn't like I had a use for all that stuff," she said.

"Doesn't matter. You gave everything you had. You walked a hard road. You're nothing like her, I promise. Nothing at all. And you don't have to go down into a mine to prove it."

Six

Patrick felt out of his depth. He was neither a grief counselor nor a psychiatrist. All he could do was make sure Libby knew how much he respected and admired her. And better yet, he could resist the urge to muddy the waters with sex.

She stared at him, her expression impossible to decipher. "I've changed my mind," she said quietly. "I want to do it. Not to impress you or to convince you to let me keep the job, but to prove something to myself."

"There are other ways," he said quietly, now suddenly positive that he had made a mistake in bringing her.

"But we're here. And the time is right. Let's go."

She took off down the clearly marked trail, forcing him to follow along behind. Their destination was a little over two miles away. With Libby setting the pace, they made it to the mine's entrance in forty-five minutes. She stopped dead when he called out to her.

The mine was unmarked for obvious reasons. No reason to tempt kids and reckless adults into doing something stupid.

He caught Libby's arm. "We've had engineers reinforce the first quarter mile. Enough to withstand even a mild earthquake. We do get those around here. I wouldn't take clients in there if it was dangerous."

"I know." She bit her lip. "How do we do this?"

"We'll carry our packs in our arms. I'll go first, using a headlamp. You stay on my heels. When we get to a certain spot, I'll spread something on the ground and we'll sit. At any moment if you change your mind, all you have to do is say so."

"How long do you normally stay underground?"

"An hour."

When she paled, he backpedaled quickly. "But we can always walk in and simply turn around and walk out." He hesitated. Was his role to encourage her or to talk her out of this? "Are you sure, Libby?"

She nodded, her pupils dilated. "I'm sure. But since I'm pretty nervous, you won't mind if I disappear into the woods for a minute?"

He looked at her blankly.

"To relieve myself."

"Ah." While she was gone, he followed suit and then waited for her return.

Though the day was bright and sunny, Libby's skin was clammy when she reappeared. He touched her shoulder. "You might want to roll down your sleeves and put on your jacket. It will be cool in the mine." They had shed layers as they walked and the air grew warmer.

Libby did as he suggested and then stared at him. "What now?"

"Let's do this." He pushed aside the undergrowth that had taken over the mine's entrance since last year. Facing him was a wooden door set into the dirt. He wrestled it loose and pushed it aside. "Door stays open," he said. "No getting locked inside, I swear."

"Is that supposed to make me feel better?"

He shot her a glance over his shoulder. She was smiling, but in her eyes he saw apprehension. Even so, her jaw was set, her resolve visible.

"Follow me," he said.

Libby put one foot in front of the other, blindly trusting Patrick Kavanagh to lead her into the bowels of the earth. Months ago when she and her mother were grief stricken and displaced, trying to start a new life, Libby had been anxious and stressed and worried.

But not like this. Her skin crawled with unease. People were meant to exist in the light. Her heartbeat deafened her. "Patrick!" She called out to him, her stomach churning.

He stopped immediately, dropping his pack and turning to face her. The beam of his headlamp blinded her. They weren't far into the mine. Daylight still filtered in behind them.

"Steady," he said. Knowing his eyes were on her only amplified her embarrassment.

She held up a hand. "Don't touch me. I'm fine."

Patrick nodded slowly. "Okay."

Suddenly, she wanted to throw herself into his arms. He was strong and self-assured and utterly calm. She was a mess. No wonder he thought she couldn't handle Charlise's job.

Slowly, they advanced into the mine. A quarter of a mile sounded like nothing at all. But in reality, it felt like a marathon.

Her panic mounted. No matter how slowly she breathed and how much she told herself she could do this, her chest tightened and her stomach curled. "Wait," she said. Frustration ate at her resolve. Mind over matter wasn't working.

She dropped her pack and wrapped her arms around her waist. "Give me a couple of minutes. I can make it."

Patrick dumped his pack as well and removed his headlamp so that the light pointed at their feet. "It speaks volumes that you even tried this, Libby."

Wiping her nose with her sleeve, she shook her head. "I hate being so stupid." Now would be a good time for him to hold her and distract her with his incredibly hot and sexy body. But apparently, that wasn't going to happen anytime soon. Or ever.

"You're not stupid. Lots of people have fears…heights, spiders, clowns."

His droll comment made her laugh. "Clowns? Seriously?"

"Coulrophobia. It's a real thing."

"You're making that up."

She heard him chuckle.

"I wouldn't lie to you."

"What are you afraid of, Patrick?"

Before he could answer, a muted rumble sounded in the distance.

"Hang on, Libby," he said.

Before she could ask what or why, a roaring crash reverberated in the tunnel. Debris rained down on them, first in a gentle fall, and then in a heavy shower that choked them and pelted their heads.

She heard Patrick curse. And then she stumbled.

Patrick fumbled in total darkness for Libby's arm. They had both gone down in the chaos. His brain looked for answers even as he searched frantically for his companion. He latched onto her shoulders and shook her. "Say something, damn it. Are you hurt?"

Dragging her into his lap he ran his hands over her head and limbs, checking for injuries. When he found none, he sighed in relief. He chafed her hands and rubbed her face until she stirred.

"Patrick?" she muttered.

"I'm here." Just then, her entire body went rigid and she cried out.

"We're okay," he said firmly. "There's no need to panic."

She was silent, telling him louder than words she thought he was crazy. After a moment she tried to sit up. "What happened?"

He kept an arm around her, feeling the shudders that racked her body. Though he would walk through hot coals before admitting it, the infinite, crushing darkness was pretty damn terrifying. "I'm not exactly sure, but I can make a guess. The mine hasn't caved in. I told you we've had it checked and reinforced."

"Then what?" Her head was tucked against his shoulder, her hands curled against his chest, her fingernails digging into his shirt, as if she wanted to climb inside his skin.

"I think it was a quick tremor…a small earthquake."

"In North Carolina?"

"I told you. It happens. And we've had so damn much rain in the last three weeks, it's possible there was a landslide that blocked the entrance."

Nothing he could say was going to make the facts any more palatable. Libby's skin, at least the exposed part, was icy cold, far colder than warranted by the temperature in the mine. He worried she might be going into shock. So they had to take action…anything to break the cycle of panic and disbelief.

"I need to walk back to the entrance and see what it looks like."

Her grip on his shirtfront tightened. "Not without me."

He smiled in the dark. "Okay. But first we have to find the headlamp."

He let go of his precious cargo with one hand and sifted through the debris.

Libby was pressed so close to his chest he could feel the runaway beat of her heart. "Is it there?"

He found the elastic strap and lifted it out of the pile of dust and twigs and small stones. But when he flicked the switch, nothing happened. Feeling carefully around the outer portion of the LED lamp, he realized that the whole lens had shattered.

"It's here," he muttered. "But it's broken."

"What about our phones?"

How exactly was he supposed to answer that? Did he need to tell her they could be stranded for days and needed to preserve the batteries? On the other hand, if they were going to be rescued, it made sense to get as close to the entrance of the mine as possible. Unless, of course, there was another landslide. Highly unlikely, but possible.

"I have a couple of backup flashlights," he said. "All I have to do is locate my pack and get them. Will you be okay for a minute if I let go of you?"

"Of course."

The right words, wrong tone. She was perilously close to the breaking point.

Cursing himself for bringing her down into this hell-hole, he set her aside and reached out his hands like a blind man. The first pack he found was Libby's. Since he had loaded it himself, he knew the exact contents. But he had put the flashlights in his pack, because they were heavy.

Moments later, he found his own equipment. When he located the item he wanted and flicked the switch, the small beam of light was as welcome as fresh water in the desert.

Libby stared at him owlishly. "Thank God," she said simply.

"You have stuff in your hair," he said. "Not insects," he

added quickly. Leaning forward, he combed his fingers through the ends of her ponytail and picked tiny debris from the rest of her head. "There," he said. "All better."

His conversation was nonsensical. He freely admitted that. But what in the hell were you supposed to say to the beautiful woman you were buried alive with—the very one you were hoping to keep at arms' length because she was vulnerable and trusting and not the woman you needed in your life either personally or professionally?

"It's not my real color," Libby said.

"Excuse me?" He was befuddled, maybe a little bit in shock himself.

"The color," she said. "I'm a redhead. Maybe you remember from when I was a kid. But after the mess with my father, I started dying my hair so I would blend into the crowd. Now I'm afraid to change it back."

"Tomorrow," he said firmly. "Tomorrow you should make an appointment with a stylist and go back to being you."

At last, she smiled. A weak smile, but a smile. "You are so full of it."

"I'm serious. Men love redheads."

"You know what I mean. I'm not an idiot. The chances of us getting out of here anytime soon are pretty slim. No one is expecting us back until dinnertime. That's several hours from now. And by the time they start to wonder where we are, it will be dark."

"So we'll wait," he said. "We have a decent amount of food and water. If we're careful, it will last."

"How long?" The question was stark.

"Long enough."

He got to his feet, ignoring the lash of pain in his left calf. "Come on, woman. Let's see what happened. We'll take our gear with us."

They hadn't really come all that far. It didn't take long

to retrace their steps. Unfortunately, his guess was spot-on. With or without a tremor as the inciting incident, a goodly portion of the hillside had come sliding down on top of the mine opening. Wet, sludgy earth filled the entrance. Trying to burrow out would only make the whole pile shift and slither, much like digging a hole at the beach.

But Libby looked at him with such naked hope he had to do something. "Stand back," he said. "Maybe it's not as bad as it looks."

"May I hold a flashlight, too?"

It wasn't a good idea. Batteries were like gold in their situation. Still, she needed the reassurance of sight. Later on they could sit in darkness.

He reached into his pocket for the spare flashlight and handed it to her. "I'm serious," he said. "Don't get too close."

For a moment, he was stymied. Using his bare hands to dig seemed ineffective at best, but even mentally cataloging the contents of his backpack, he couldn't think of a damn thing that might serve as a shovel.

In the end, he tucked the flashlight under his armpit and awkwardly began to gouge his fingers into the wet mess. Dry dirt wouldn't have been so bad, but the mud was a frustrating opponent.

After ten minutes of concerted effort, he had made no headway at all. Not only that, he was starting to feel dizzy. He stumbled backward, his filthy arms outstretched. "This isn't going to work. I'm sorry, Libby."

"You're hurt," she said, alarm in her voice. "You're bleeding below the knee."

He blinked, trying to focus his thoughts. Maybe adrenaline had masked his injury, because now his leg hurt like hell. "I don't want to touch the flashlight with all this gunk on my hands. Can you look at my leg?"

Libby squatted and touched his shin. "Whatever it was cut all the way through the cloth."

"Probably a piece of glass. We've found all kinds of broken bottles and crockery down here over the years."

He flinched when she carefully rolled up the leg of his pants.

"Oh, God, Patrick," she gasped. "You need stitches. Sit down so I can look at it."

"Wait. Find the tarp in my pack. We're going to have to make a place to get comfortable." *Comfortable* wasn't even on the map of where they were located. But they would take what they could get.

Libby moved quickly, locating the large tarp and spreading it with one side tucked up against the wall of the mine so they could lean against something. When she was done, he pointed to an outside zip pocket of his pack. "There's a small, thin towel in there. Can you wet it, just barely, so I can get the worst of this off?"

Libby did as he asked, but instead of giving him the towel, she took his hands in hers and began wiping his fingers clean. It was a difficult chore, especially given the lack of water.

He still held the flashlight under his arm. Though he couldn't see Libby's face, there was enough illumination for him to watch as she removed the muck. It was an intimate act…and an unselfish one…because the process dirtied her skin, as well.

But finally he was more or less back to normal.

"Sit down now," she urged.

He was happy to comply.

With his back against the wall of the mine, he took a deep breath. He felt like hell, and his leg had begun to throb viciously. There's a first aid kit," he said gruffly. "Big outer pocket. Antiseptic wipes."

Libby put a hand on his thigh, perhaps to get his attention. "You've lost a lot of blood, Patrick. A lot. The cut is four inches long and gaping."

"Clean it the best you can. We'll use butterfly bandages." The words were an effort. "I'll hold the flashlight."

It occurred to him that he could reach his own leg...do his own medical care. But he couldn't seem to work up the energy to try.

Libby's touch was deft but gentle. Wisely, she didn't waste time getting rid of all the blood. He watched her concentrate on the cut, making sure the edges were clean, dabbing at tiny bits of dirt that might cause infection later. When she was satisfied, she sat back on her heels. "I'll let it dry a minute," she said, "before I use the butterfly thingies."

"Can you get me a couple of painkillers?" he asked, hurting too much to act macho at this particular moment.

"Of course."

He took them with a sip of water and sighed. "Is the skin dry?"

Libby traced around the wound with a fingertip. "Yes." She tore open a small packet and gently affixed the Band-Aid, pulling the open edges of the cut together. It took two more before she was satisfied. "The bleeding has stopped."

"Good." He closed his eyes. "Sit between my legs," he said. "It will keep us both warm."

He needed the human contact, but more than that, he needed a connection to Libby specifically. She might be completely wrong for him on far too many levels, but right now, they had each other and no one else. He wanted to feel her and know she was okay.

Seven

Libby felt like she was in a dream. But when she settled between Patrick's thighs, her legs outstretched, her back against his chest, the situation got a whole lot more real.

Strong arms wrapped around her waist. Big masculine hands clasped beneath her breasts. Patrick's breath warmed the side of her neck. "Are you going to be okay?" she asked. The tenor of his breathing alarmed her. That and his silence.

"It's just a cut. Don't worry about it."

She might be inexperienced when it came to medical care, but she wasn't stupid. Patrick needed a proper hospital, an IV of fluids and red meat. Instead, he was stuck down here with her.

"What time is it?" she asked, feeling her anxiety rise again now that the immediate crisis was past.

"We have to turn off the flashlights," he said quietly, the words ruffling her hair.

She didn't know which part worried her the most—the

fact that he deliberately ignored her question, or the regression to pitch-black darkness. Without vision, the world seemed ominous.

"Do you sing?" she asked.

He groaned. "You don't want to hear that, I promise."

"I'm sorry, Patrick, but if you don't talk to me, I might go bonkers."

"Okay, okay." The words held amusement.

"Tell me about your family. My mother used to keep in touch with Maeve all the time, but I don't really know much about the Kavanagh clan. What are your brothers up to these days?"

"Liam is the oldest. He married a woman named Zoe who is sort of a free spirit. We love her, and she's a perfect match for my stick-in-the-mud brother."

"Go on."

"You saw Dylan at the pub. His wife is Mia. Dylan adopted her little girl."

"Next is Aidan?"

"That's right. He and Emma divide their time between New York and Silver Glen. Then comes Gavin. He runs a cybersecurity firm here in Silver Glen. His wife is Cassidy, and they have twin baby girls."

"What about Conor? Wasn't he the big skier in the family?"

"Still is. He ended up marrying a girl he knew way back in high school. Her name is Ellie."

"Which leaves you and James…is that his name?"

"Yep. My baby brother…who happens to be four inches taller than I am and thirty pounds heavier. We call him the gentle giant."

"You love him. I hear it in your voice."

"Well, when you're the last two in a string of seven, you end up bonding. It was either that or be terrorized by our siblings on a regular basis. With James on my side, I had a tactical advantage."

"Your mother takes credit for marrying off the first five. I suppose you and James are next in her sights."

"Not gonna happen."

The blunt, flat-toned response shocked her. "Oh?"

"Let me rephrase that. I can't speak for my brother, but I'm not interested in tying the knot. Earlier, you asked me what I was afraid of and I never got a chance to answer you. The truth is, it's marriage. I tried it once and it didn't pan out. So I plan on being happily single."

She turned toward him, which was dumb, because she couldn't see his face. "You're divorced?"

"Worse than that."

"She died?" Libby gaped in the darkness, horrified, feeling as if she had stepped in the middle of a painful past Patrick didn't want to share. But now that the door was open, she couldn't ignore the peek inside this complicated man.

Patrick sighed, his chest rising and falling. He pulled her back against him. "No. The marriage was annulled."

It was a good thing Patrick was willing to talk about his past, because the only thing keeping Libby from climbing the walls was concentrating on the sound of his voice. All around her, the dark encroached. Would they have to sleep here and wake up here and slowly starve to death?

Panic fluttered in her chest. "What happened?" she asked.

Patrick wasn't a fan of rehashing his youthful mistakes, but he and Libby had to do something to maintain a sense of normalcy. The medicine had dulled the pain in his leg, though he still felt alarmingly weak.

He rested his chin on her head, inhaling the faint scent of her skin. Her upper-class upbringing meant she'd been taught the rules of polite behavior at an early age. He was sure Libby would never ask that kind of personal question under different circumstances.

But here in the mine, such considerations were less important than the need to feel connected.

He played with the fingers of her right hand, fingers that were bare. Where were the diamonds, the pearls, the precious gems this young, wealthy woman had worn? All sold for her mother's treatment. Libby's mom had betrayed that sacrifice by killing herself.

The picture of Libby he'd had in the beginning was fading rapidly, the colors blurred by the reality of who she was. She'd been a Madison Avenue heiress…no doubt about that. But Libby Parkhurst was so much more than the sum of what she had lost.

His feelings toward her were confusing. He wanted to protect her, both physically and emotionally. And though it was disconcerting as hell, he was beginning to *want* her. In the way a man wants a woman.

Even here in this dank, dark mine shaft—and even though he had a throbbing wound in his leg—his body reacted to the feel of her in his arms. Their relationship had been thrown into fast-forward. He was bombarded with emotions—tenderness, affection and definitely admiration. For a woman who had barely been able to contemplate walking into the mine shaft and back out again, it was nothing short of remarkable that she was still able to function, considering what had happened.

He realized she was still waiting for an answer about his marriage. "My girlfriend got pregnant," he said. "One of those terrible clichés that turns out to be true. I'd been careful to protect both of us, but…"

"Accidents happen."

"Yes. My brothers and I had been brought up with a very strict code of honor. Her parents wanted us to get married, so I agreed. In hindsight, I doubt my mother was thrilled, but what could she do?"

"And the annulment?"

"When the little boy was born, he was dark-skinned... African-American. Even for a girl who was terrified to tell her parents she was involved in a mixed-race relationship and even though she was embarrassed to admit she'd been cheating on her boyfriend, it was clear that the gig was up. We didn't need to have a paternity test done. The truth stared us in the face."

"Oh, Patrick. You must have been devastated."

He winced, even now reacting to a painful, fleeting memory of what that day had done to him. "We'd been living together as husband and wife. We had both graduated from high school...rented a small house. Even though I'd been upset and angry and not at all ready to become a father, after nine months, I'd finally come around to the idea. I was so excited about that little boy."

"And then you lost him."

"Yes. I walked out of the hospital and never looked back. I went home. Slept in the bed where I'd grown up. But nothing was the same. You can't rewrite history and undo your mistakes. All you can do is move forward and not make those same mistakes again."

He wanted to know what Libby was thinking, but he kept on talking. It was cathartic to rehash what had been a chaotic, deeply painful time in his life. It was a subject never broached by the Kavanagh clan. They had swept it under the rug and moved on.

"I didn't abandon the baby," he said, remembering the infant's tiny face. "I want you to know that. His father stepped up. As soon as the annulment was final, he married the mother of his child and they made a family."

"You must have been so hurt."

It was true. He'd been crushed. But he had never let on how much it affected him.

"Adolescence is tough for everybody," he muttered.

Libby turned on her side, nestling her cheek against his chest and drawing up her knees until they threatened his manhood. "You're a good man, Patrick Kavanagh."

He stroked her hair. "I'm sorry about this," he said.

Libby sighed audibly. "It will be something to tell our children one day." She stopped dead, realizing what she had said.

"Don't worry about it, Libby. I'm a very popular uncle, and I like it that way."

"Have you told Maeve how you feel?"

"I think she guesses. She hasn't quite put the marital screws on me like she has the others."

"I'm warning you, it's only a matter of time. You'd better watch your step around her. She's wonderful, but sneaky."

After that, they dozed. Patrick dreamed restlessly, always fighting an ominous foe. Each time he awoke, his arms tightened around Libby. She was his charge, his responsibility. He would do everything in his power to make sure she got out of this mess in one piece.

At last, they couldn't ignore the rumbles of hungry stomachs. "What do you want?" he asked. "Beef jerky or peanuts?"

"I'll take the nuts, I guess."

He handed her the water. "Three sips, no more. We have to be smart about rationing."

"Can we please turn on one of the phones and find out what time it is? Do you think there's any hope of getting a signal down here? We're near the surface."

"I'll look. And no. I don't think there's a chance at all of having a signal."

"You really suck at this cheering up thing."

He checked the time, oddly comforted by the familiar glow of the phone screen. "Seven fifteen."

"So it's dark outside."

"Yes." He turned off the electronic device and stowed it. "It doesn't really matter, though, does it? Not to us?"

"I suppose not." She sighed. "Tell me something else. Do you have big plans for the weekend?"

"I'm flying up to New York Friday morning to do an orientation for one of the teams coming in April. Peabody Rushford is a world-renowned accounting firm with A-list clients. We'll sit around a big conference table, and I'll go over the checklist with all of them. They'll ask questions…"

"May I go with you?"

He paused, taken aback. Maybe Libby was simply trying to convince herself she wouldn't still be trapped underground come Friday. "I'm not sure there's any reason for you to be there," he said. "I don't want to hurt your feelings, but this job is not the one for you. I think you know that."

"Maybe so. But I was thinking of a more personal agenda."

His mind raced, already inventing sexual scenarios where he and Libby ended up naked on soft sheets. "What kind of agenda?"

"I haven't been back to my building since the day my mother and I had to leave. I thought I could go see it. I can't get inside the apartment, of course. Someone else lives there now. But I think even standing on the street would give me some closure."

"Then of course you can come with me," he said. "I wish I could fly us up there in my new toy. I bought a used Cessna recently, but it's still being overhauled. So we'll have to take the jet."

"*Now* who sounds like the poor little rich kid?" she teased.

"You've got me. But to be fair, the Kavanaghs share the jet with several others owners."

"Well, that makes it okay, of course."

"If I were you, I don't think I would alienate the only human being standing between me and solitary confinement."

"Not funny, Patrick."

"Sorry."

They sat in silence. The teasing had kept the darkness at bay for a few moments, but the truth returned. They were trapped…with no hope of rescue until morning at least, and maybe not even then.

Libby stood up, accidentally elbowing him in the ribs. "I have to stretch," she said.

"Don't go far."

"Hilarious, Kavanagh."

He might as well stand up, too. But when he moved, he cursed as pain shot up his leg, hot and vicious.

Libby crouched beside him. "Give me the flashlight."

"Why? We need to save the battery."

"I'm going to look at your leg. Don't argue with me."

She was cute when she was indignant. He surrendered the flashlight wordlessly.

In a brightly lit room, he would have been able to examine his own leg. With nothing but the thin beam of the flashlight, though, he had to rely on Libby for an up-close diagnosis. "How does it look?"

"Bad."

"Bad as in 'needs an antibiotic,' or bad as in 'heading for amputation'?"

She turned the flashlight toward his face, blinding him. "That isn't funny. If we stay in here much longer, you could be in serious trouble."

He covered his eyes. "I choose to laugh instead of cry."

"I'll bet you've never cried in your life. Alpha males don't do that."

"I cried when my father disappeared."

Eight

"Oh, Patrick." Libby's heart turned over. She would bet every dollar of her first paycheck that he hadn't meant to say something so revealing. She sat back down, feeling warm and almost secure when he enfolded her in his arms again. "I know we touched on this during my interview, and I'm sorry to open up old wounds... Did he really just go away?"

"I was a little kid, so some of my memories are fuzzy... but I've heard the story a hundred times. My father was obsessed with finding the silver mine that launched the Kavanagh fortunes generations ago. He would go out for days at a time...and then one weekend, he simply never came back."

"I'm sorry."

"It was a long time ago."

Libby had a blinding revelation, which was really pretty funny considering she was sitting in total darkness. She and Patrick had both been betrayed by their fathers. But luckily for Patrick, *his* mother was a rock.

"Did anyone have a valid theory about what happened?"

"In the beginning, there were lots of possibilities. The police posed the idea that he might have simply abandoned us, started a new life. But his passport was in the safe at home and none of his clothes or prized possessions were missing. He couldn't have left the country, and since none of the family vehicles had been taken, the final conclusion was that he had been killed somewhere in the mountains."

"You mean by wild animals?"

"It's possible. Or he could have fallen."

"But his body was never found."

"Exactly. Which meant that everyone's best educated guess was that my dad went down inside a mine—looking for remnants of a silver vein—and the mine collapsed."

"Oh."

Patrick's arms tightened around her. "This probably isn't the best conversation for us to be having at the moment."

"It does have a certain macabre theme."

"Remember, Libby…this mine we're in *didn't* collapse. It's just that the entrance has been blocked."

"A fine distinction that I'm sorry to say is not very comforting."

"You have *me*. That's something."

Actually, that was a lot. Patrick's reassuring presence was keeping most of her panic at bay…at least for stretches at a time. But their enforced intimacy had created another problem.

In the two weeks she had worked for him, she'd done her best to ignore the fact that he was a handsome, funny, intellectually stimulating man on whom she had a perfectly understandable crush. She'd kept her distance and been a model employee.

But now, with his strong arms holding her tight and his rumbly voice giving her goose bumps when his warm breath tickled her neck and cheek, she was suddenly, madly infatuated. That's all it was. An adrenaline-born rush of arousal. Part of the fight-or-flight response.

The same thing would have happened if she and Patrick had been cave people fleeing from a saber-toothed tiger. Of course later, once they were safe, they might have had wild monkey sex on a fur pelt by the roaring fire.

Her mouth went dry, and the pit of her stomach felt funny. "Patrick?" Clearly her brain cells were being starved of oxygen. Or maybe she was truly losing it, because the next words that came out of her mouth were totally inappropriate. "Will you kiss me?"

She felt his whole body stiffen. "Never mind," she said quickly. "That was just the claustrophobia talking."

"We're not going to die. I promise." His voice sounded funny…as if he had swallowed something down his windpipe.

"And by extrapolation I'm supposed to understand that imminent death is the only situation in which you could see yourself kissing me? Because I'm *one of your mother's misfits*, and a general pain in the ass?"

"You're not playing fair, Libby."

She turned in his embrace, her hands finding his face in the dark. His jaw was stubbly. She rubbed her thumbs over his strong chin. "Kiss me, Patrick," she whispered. "I know I'm taking advantage of you in your weakened state, but please. I've wondered for days what kind of woman you want. I know it's not me. Under the circumstances, though, you could bend the rules…right?"

"Libby, darlin'…"

The way he said her name was pure magic. "I'm listening."

He made a noise that sounded like choked laughter. "You were never spanked as a child, were you?"

She shrugged. "My nannies loved me. So, no. Is that an offer?"

"What about the spiders and the mud and the dungeon ambience?"

"Are you stalling?"

"I don't want you to be embarrassed when we get out of here."

"Embarrassed that I asked for a kiss, or embarrassed that I kissed my boss? I don't think that last one is a problem. You've pretty well admitted that my days are numbered when it comes to working for Silver Reflections."

His hands tangled in her hair, his lips brushing her forehead. "For the record, I haven't completely made up my mind about your status at Silver Reflections. Plus, kissing will make us want other things."

"Too late," she said, breathless...longing. "I already want those other things, but I'm willing to settle for a kiss."

"God, you're a brat."

Somehow, the way he said it turned the words into a husky compliment. "Shall I leave you alone, Patrick?"

His fingers tightened on her skull. "No. That's not what I want at all."

Before she could respond, he angled her head and found her mouth with his. The first kiss was barely perceptible... no more than a faint brush of lips to lips. Even so, she melted into him, stung by a wild burst of hunger that couldn't be satisfied by anything less than full body contact.

The kiss deepened. Patrick muttered something, but she was too lost to translate it. They had done this once before. That "sort of an apology" kiss they had shared in the woods. But she hadn't taken him seriously at the time. She'd thought he was just being nice. Charming. Offering sophisticated reparation for a thoughtless, hurtful mistake.

This was different. This was desperation. Need. Raw, unscripted masculine hunger.

Her fingers fumbled with his shirt buttons, tearing at them until she could rest her cheek against hot male skin. She nipped a flat nipple with her teeth. "I'm getting used to the dark," she whispered.

He groaned. "I'm not." He did his own version of seek-and-find, palming her breasts and squeezing them gently. "I want to see you…all of you."

There were no words to describe the feel of his hands on her bare flesh. It didn't matter that his fingers were probably still mud streaked…or that she shivered with her shirt unbuttoned. She was drowning in pleasure.

Need became a demanding beast, telling her there was a way…insisting that the less-than-perfect circumstances weren't as important as the yearning to take Patrick Kavanagh and make him hers. Her brain made a bid for common sense, reminding her that getting involved sexually with Patrick Kavanagh was a really bad idea.

But other parts of her body spoke more loudly. "How big is this tarp?" she asked, her fingers trembling as she unbuckled his belt.

Patrick found himself in uncharted territory. At any given moment he could find his way through a dense forest on a moonless night with no more than a compass and his knowledge of the mountains. Right now, however, he was a blind man struggling in quicksand.

This was insanity. Complete and utter disregard for the seriousness of their situation. He had to call a halt…

"Touch me," he begged.

When Libby's fingers closed around his erection, he sucked in a sharp breath.

"You fascinate me, Patrick," she said softly, her firm

touch on his body perfect in every way...as if they had been lovers forever and knew exactly what the other liked.

"I'm no different from any other guy," he croaked, feeling his temperature rise as sweat broke out on his brow. "We see, we want, we take."

"And what if *I* take *you*?"

His heart stopped. He tried to remember all the reasons why he was supposed to be a gentleman. The family connection. Libby's recent losses. His mother's disapproval.

Nothing worked. He wanted Libby. Badly. Enough to ignore his better judgment.

After that, it was only a matter of logistics. It could work. Not ideal, but doable. He fumbled with his pants, trying to lower them, but Libby was plastered against his chest, and he couldn't bear to shove her away, even for a moment.

"Wait," she cried. "Stop."

"Damn it, woman, this was *your* idea." He would stop if he had to, but why in the hell was she blowing hot and cold?

She put her hand over his mouth. "Listen," she said, urgency in her tone. "I heard something."

Patrick heard something, too. But it was the sound of his libido crying out in frustrated disbelief. "What are you talking about?"

"Shut up and listen."

Now she was making him mad.

And then he heard it. A scraping sound. And something else. Something human. *Holy hell.* "Button your blouse."

He struggled with his own clothing, and then cursed when he needed her help to stand up. The pain meds had worn off, and his leg was one big ache. Funny how lust was a stunningly effective narcotic. Fumbling for the flashlight, he took Libby's hand and they moved forward.

"We can't get too close," she whispered.

He squeezed her hand. "Cover your ears. I'm going to yell. *"We're down here!"* His plea echoed in their prison.

But from the other side of the mud and rock, a garbled response told him someone had heard the three simple words.

Libby's fingernails dug into his palm. "Who do you think it is?"

"Does it matter? As long as it's not the Grim Reaper, I'm a fan."

They clung to each other, barely breathing.

Suddenly, an unwelcome sensation intruded. "Libby," he said hoarsely. "My ankle is wet."

She reached inside his jacket. "Is that a flashlight in your pocket, or are you glad to see me?" Dropping to her knees, she shone the light on his leg. "Oh, hell, Patrick. The butterfly strips came loose. You're bleeding like a stuck pig. We have to sit you down. Let me find the tarp."

"No," he muttered, feeling woozy. "A little dirt won't hurt me." Leaning on Libby with a death grip, he bent his knees and stumbled onto his butt, cursing when his leg cried out in agony.

She hovered at his side, crouching and combing her fingers through his hair. "Are you okay?"

"Never better."

Without fanfare, a hole opened up in the mud. The unmistakable sounds of shoveling reverberated off the tunnel walls.

A voice, oddly disembodied, floated through the twelve-inch opening. "Patrick! You okay, man?"

Patrick swallowed. "I'm fine."

He licked his lips, shaking all over. "That's James, my brother. How did he know we were here?"

Libby put her arms around him, holding him close. "To quote a man I know, does it matter? Hang on, Patrick. It won't be much longer."

At last, the opening was large enough so they could

lean through and allow themselves to be tugged out like bears from honey pots. Patrick staggered but made it to his feet. He blinked, seeing four of his brothers staring at him. He must look worse than he thought. "Thanks for coming, guys."

And then his world went black.

Libby had her arm around Patrick's waist, but she was no match for his deadweight when he lost consciousness. They both went down hard, despite the fact that James reached for his brother.

"What's wrong with him?" James asked, alarm and consternation in his voice. Then he eased Patrick onto his back and saw the injury for himself.

Libby disentangled herself but stayed seated. "He's lost a lot of blood. The cut will need stitches."

After hasty introductions, Liam Kavanagh rescued the two backpacks from the mine. James and Dylan hoisted their injured sibling onto a portable litter and started back. Gavin gave her a weary smile. "I'm gonna piggyback you," he said. "It will be faster that way."

In the end, the trip through the forest took over two hours. The Kavanagh men had to be exhausted. It was four in the morning by the time they walked out of the woods and into the main lodge of Silver Reflections. Maeve was waiting for them, her face creased with worry.

The only brothers missing were Aidan, who, she learned, was out of town, and Conor who had gone to summon an ambulance. He'd kept his mother company during the rescue operation.

Maeve grabbed Libby into a huge hug. "Oh, my God. We've been out of our minds with worry." She bit her lip, eyeing Patrick's pale face as his brothers set the litter on a padded bench seat. "The ambulance is waiting."

Liam had radioed ahead to let Maeve know they were on the way.

In the hustle and bustle that followed, Libby found herself curled into a deep, comfy armchair by a fire someone had been kind enough to build in the middle of the night. When all the men disappeared, Maeve touched her arm. "Come on, sweetheart. I'll take you back to the hotel before I follow them to the emergency room. Are you sure you don't need medical attention?"

"No, ma'am. I'm fine."

Libby dozed in the car, waking up only as Maeve pulled up in front of Silver Beeches.

Maeve gazed at her, exhaustion on her face. "Do you need help getting upstairs?"

Libby knew her older friend was anxious to check on her son. "I'm fine, Maeve. Go see to Patrick. I'm going to bed as soon as I can get there."

Looking at her reflection in the bathroom mirror a short time later was a lesson in humility. Libby had seen corpses who had more color…and more fashion sense for that matter. Her clothes were filthy and torn, her hair was a tangled mess and, as an added indignity, her stomach rumbled loudly, making it known that sleep was going to have to wait.

The shower felt so good, she almost cried. After shampooing her hair three times and slathering it with conditioner, she used a washcloth to scrub away the grime from the rest of her body. She wove on her feet, fatigue weighting her limbs.

When she was clean and dry, she ordered room service. Six in the morning wasn't too early for bacon and eggs. She had every intention of cleaning her plate, but she managed only half of the bounty before she shoved the tray aside and fell facedown onto the soft, welcoming bed.

Nine

Patrick wolfed down half of a sausage biscuit and watched as the female doc stitched up his leg. Thanks to several shots of numbing medicine, he was feeling no pain.

James leaned against the wall, as if guarding the room from unwanted intruders. Since they were the last people in the ER, Patrick was pretty sure any danger had been left behind at the mine. He and James had finally convinced all the others to go home and get some rest.

Patrick looked at his brother over the doctor's head. "Thanks, bro. You want to explain to me how you knew where I was?"

James's grin was tired but cocky. "I came up to Reflections yesterday to grab one of your gourmet lunches and see if you wanted to hike with me. The people at the front desk said you were in the forest teaching a new recruit the ropes. I set out around the mountain to catch up with you."

"You know where the campsite is…but have you ever even *been* to the mine?"

"No...but I've heard you talk about it. So I used my Boy Scout tracker skills and followed your trail. I eventually stumbled across the landslide. The mud was thick and slimy and fresh. It was then I realized you might be in trouble."

"Me and Libby..."

"Yeah. Since when do you camp out with pretty ladies?"

"It wasn't like that."

"I saw how she looked at you."

"We'd been through a tough time. It was a bonding experience." Patrick managed to keep his expression impassive, but his body was another story. "How did you dig us out?"

James grimaced. "That was the bad part. After I discovered I had *nothing* that was going to do the job, I ran back several miles to the knoll where we can usually get a phone signal and called Conor. He alerted everyone else. We all met up and brought the proper supplies."

"I owe you one, baby brother."

"Don't worry. I'll collect sooner or later. Like maybe an introduction to your newest employee?"

"I don't think so," Patrick snapped.

James raised an eyebrow. "Feeling a little territorial, are we?"

"She's not your type."

"Mom told me her story. She sounds like an amazing woman."

"She is. But she's had a tough time, and she doesn't need strange guys sniffing around."

"I'm not a strange guy... I'm your brother."

The doctor looked up from her work and smiled. "Do I need to referee this squabble?"

Patrick looked down at the long, red, angry wound on his leg. He hadn't needed a transfusion, but it was a close call. "No, Doc," he said, shooting his brother a glare.

Fortunately, Patrick's medical care wrapped up pretty quickly. In the car, James lifted an inquiring eyebrow. "Am I taking you home?"

Patrick gazed out the window, feeling exhausted and surly. "I want to go up to the hotel and make sure Libby is okay."

"She'll be asleep by now."

"Mom would give me a key."

James drummed his fingers on the steering wheel. "I know the two of you just spent the night together in a creepy, dark tunnel, but that doesn't give you the right to act like a stalker. Think, man. You can't open her door and peek in on her. That's way over the line."

Patrick slumped into his seat. His selfish need to see her would have to wait. "I guess you're right. Take me home."

After a shower, a light meal and five hours of sleep, Patrick found himself awake and antsy. The cut was on his left leg, so he wasn't limited as far as driving. When he couldn't stand being inside his house for another minute, he drove to Silver Reflections. His employees seemed perplexed to see him after his ordeal, so he holed up in his office.

Liam had left the two backpacks inside Patrick's door. Patrick dumped them out and started putting things away. One of the staff would take care of cleaning the tarps and other items. The rest Patrick stowed in specially labeled drawers along one wall of his suite.

When all of that was done, he couldn't wait any longer. He sent a text to Libby.

Hope you're feeling okay. You don't have to go Friday if you're not up to it. And stay home tomorrow...you deserve a rest...

He didn't dare say what he was really thinking…that he needed time to figure out what to do about her.

He hit Send and spun around in his leather chair. Maybe he'd been more affected by the experience in the mine than he realized, because his concentration was shot. When someone knocked at his door, he frowned, tempted to pretend he wasn't there.

But, after all, he was the boss. "Come in. It's open."

Libby was the last person he expected to see. She smiled. "I just got your text. Thanks for the consideration, but I couldn't sleep all day. I've been in my office talking to a guest who's disgruntled because he came here to relax and it's too peaceful to sleep. Apparently he lives in a brownstone walk-up across the street from a fire station."

"Ah. Maybe he needs more help than we can give."

"Maybe."

"I'm serious, Libby. Take tomorrow off. And do you still want to go to New York?"

"If you'll have me."

He would be damned glad to have her six ways to Sunday, but that wasn't what she meant. "You're welcome to come with me. As long as you know this isn't a nod from me about the job. I'll book you a hotel room this evening."

"Are you sure you want to do that? I've been learning how to manage on a budget. One room is definitely cheaper than two."

The challenging look in her eyes sent an unmistakable message. He stood up slowly and backed her against the door. "Are you sure it wasn't the adrenaline rush of certain death that sent you into my arms?" He kissed the side of her neck to test his hypothesis. His hips nudged hers. She was soft where he was hard.

Libby sighed as their bodies aligned with satisfying perfection. Her green eyes sparkled with excitement. "Perhaps it has escaped your notice, but you're a very sexy man."

"It was the bloody leg, right? Women can't resist a wounded hero."

"To be exact, I believe James was the hero."

She was taunting him deliberately. He knew that. And still, it pissed him off. "My brother is a great guy, but I doubt the two of you would get along."

"And why is that? I found him quite charming."

"If any Kavanagh is going to end up in your bed, it's going to be me." The declaration ended only a few decibels below a shout.

"Ooh…so intense. I have goose bumps. Still," she said, drawing the single syllable out to make a point. "I'm not sure it's a good idea to sleep with the boss."

"Then we won't sleep," he said. He kissed her wildly, feeling the press of her generous breasts against his chest. How had he ever thought she was meek and mousy?

Libby leaned into him, moaning when he deepened the kiss. "Your mother feels bad about our ordeal. She's treating me to a spa day and a shopping trip tomorrow. But I'll tell her no if you want me here. I'm not going to parlay this whole 'stuck in a mine' thing into special privileges."

"I *want* you to stay away," he said, entirely truthful. "I can't concentrate when you're around."

"How nice of you to say so."

He cupped her cheeks in his hands. "Be sure about this, sweet thing. If I do anything to hurt you, my mother will string me up by my ba—"

Libby clapped a hand over his mouth. "Watch your language, Mr. Kavanagh." She rubbed her thumb over his bottom lip. The simple caress sent fire streaking to his groin. "Are you *planning* on hurting me?"

He shifted from one foot to the other. "Of course not."

"Then relax and go with the flow. If nothing else in the last year, I've learned that's the only way to live…"

* * *

Libby took Patrick at his word about staying home the next day. She'd suffered no lasting physical effects from their unfortunate incarceration, but she *had* been tormented by dark dreams Wednesday night. She *needed* employment. But she *wanted* Patrick. Climbing into bed with him was not going to be in her best interests. The conflicting desires went around and around in her head. She woke up feeling groggy and vaguely depressed.

Maeve, however, refused to let any notion of gloom overshadow their day. When she met Libby in the lobby, she clapped her hands, practically dancing around like a child. "I'm so glad you're finally going to put your hair back to rights. I know your mother disliked that boring brown."

Libby raised her eyebrows. "Has anyone ever accused you of being overly tactful?"

Maeve chuckled, heading out to the large flagstone driveway where her silver Mercedes was parked. "I consider you family, my dear. And as your honorary aunt or stepmother or whatever you want to call me, I'm only doing my duty when I tell you that you have taken a beautiful young woman and turned her into a drudge."

Libby couldn't take offense. Maeve was absolutely too gleeful about restoring Libby's original looks. For a moment, Libby felt a surge of panic. She'd hidden behind her ill-fitting clothes and her nondescript hair color for the better part of a year. What if someone in New York recognized her?

As Maeve navigated the curvy road down the mountain, Libby took several deep breaths. She had started a new life. Did it matter if people knew who she was? *Libby* hadn't committed tax fraud.

Besides, most of the friends in her immediate social circle had melted away when the Parkhurst fortunes began to shatter. It was doubtful anyone would even want to acknowledge her. And as far as reporters were concerned, Libby Parkhurst was old news.

When Maeve found a parking spot in Silver Glen, the day of pampering began. First it was private massages, then manicures and pedicures at an upscale spa. Of course, most everything in Silver Glen was upscale. The beautiful alpine-themed town catered to the rich and famous.

An hour and a half later, once her Tahitian Sunset polish had dried, Libby admired her fingers and toes. This kind of self-indulgence had been one of the first things to go when she and her mother had been put out on the street.

It was amazing that something so simple could make a woman feel like she was ready to take on the world.

Next was the hair salon. Libby pulled a photo out of her wallet, one from her college graduation, and showed the stylist her original color. The woman was horrified. "Why would you ruin such an amazing head of hair? Never mind," she said quickly. "I don't even want to know. But before you leave here, young lady, I'm going to remind you what the good Lord intended you to look like."

Libby allowed the woman to whack three inches, since it had been ages since her last cut. Not only had Libby dyed her hair as part of her plan to go incognito, she had straightened it, as well. Little by little, the real Libby returned.

The stylist kept her promise. When it was done, Libby gazed in the mirror with tears in her eyes. Her natural hair was a curly, vibrant red that complemented her pale skin, unlike the dull brown that had washed her out and made her seem tired.

Now, the bouncy chin-length do put color in her cheeks. Parted on one side and tucked behind her ear on the other, the fun, youthful style framed her face and took years off her age.

Maeve beamed. "Beautiful. Absolutely beautiful."

Next stop was a charming boutique with an array of trendily clad mannequins in the window. Libby put her foot down. "I have money, Maeve. My first paycheck went in the bank this morning."

Patrick's mother frowned. "You nearly died in the service of a Kavanagh business. If I want to buy you a few things as a thank-you for not suing us, that is my prerogative."

Libby gaped. "You know I would never sue you. That's ridiculous."

But Maeve had already crossed the store and engaged the services of a young woman about Libby's own age. The clerk assessed Libby with a smile. "What kinds of things are we looking for today?"

Maeve shushed Libby when she tried to speak. The older woman steamrollered the conversation. "A little of everything. Casual chic. Business attire…not a suit, I think, but a little black dress. And a very dressy something for dinner…perhaps in ivory or even green if that's not too obvious with her fabulous hair."

The couture makeover became a whirlwind. Libby tried on so many garments, she lost count. When the frenzy was done, Maeve plunked down a credit card. "She'll wear the jeans and stilettos home…plus the peasant blouse. We'll take all the rest in garment bags."

Libby gave up trying to protest. In the months ahead, when she was able, she would do her best to repay Maeve. In the meantime, it was exciting to know that she would be able to accompany Patrick to New York looking her best.

Maeve declared herself exhausted when they returned to the Silver Beeches Lodge. "I'm going to see if Liam needs me," she said. "And if not, I'm headed home to put my feet up."

Libby hugged her impulsively. "Thank you, dear Maeve. I love you."

This time it was Maeve who had tears in her eyes. She took Libby's hands, her expression earnest. "Your mother was a precious woman…fragile, but precious. I still remember how proud she was when you were born. You were the light of her life. When you remember her, Libby, try not to think of the woman she became at the end, but instead, the woman she was at her best…the friend I knew so well."

Libby managed a smile. "It's no wonder your sons adore you."

Maeve waved a dismissive hand. "They think I'm a meddling pain in the ass. But then again, they know I'm always right."

Libby said her goodbyes and wandered upstairs to her room. She was determined to move to the apartment over the Silver Dollar saloon very soon. How many paychecks would it take before she could afford a rent payment? She chafed at the idea of living on Kavanagh charity, even if it was extremely luxurious and comfortable charity.

She and Maeve had lunched out before their appointments, so tonight, the only thing Libby ordered from room service was a chef salad. Often she ate downstairs in the dining room, but it had been a long, though pleasant, day. Sometimes it was nice to be alone and contemplate the future.

After her modest dinner, she packed the suitcase Maeve had loaned her. At one time, Libby had owned a wide array of expensive toiletries. Now she was accustomed to nothing more than discount-store moisturizer, an inexpensive tube of mascara and a couple of lipsticks for dressing up.

Her lace-and-silk nightgown and robe were remnants of the past. As were the several sets of bras and undies she possessed. It was one thing to sell haute couture at a resale shop. No one wanted underwear.

As she crawled into bed, she checked her phone. Patrick had messaged her earlier to let her know he would be sending a taxi to pick her up at seven o'clock tomorrow morning. They would rendezvous at the brand-new airstrip on the other end of the valley.

Patrick's brief text—and her equally brief response—was the only communication Libby had shared with him since she'd walked out of his office Wednesday afternoon. She missed him. And she had gone back and forth a dozen times about whether or not she was doing the right thing.

Their flirtatious conversation had left the status quo up in the air. What was going to happen when they got to New York?

She could tell herself it was all about finding closure… a bid for saying goodbye to her old life. And maybe trying one more time to convince Patrick she could do the job at Silver Reflections.

But she had a weak spot when it came to her fascinating boss. The possibility of sharing his bed made her shiver with anticipation. Right now, that agenda was winning.

Ten

Patrick had decided to bring in one of the standby pilots the Kavanaghs sometimes used instead of flying himself. For one thing, the deep cut in his leg was still sore as hell. And for another, he liked the idea of sitting in the back of the jet with Libby. She was no stranger to luxury travel… so it wasn't that he wanted to see her reaction when he dazzled her with sophistication and pampering.

It was far simpler than that. He wanted to spend time with her.

He arrived at the airstrip thirty minutes early. The past two nights, he hadn't slept worth a damn. He kept reliving the moment the landslide happened. The instant Libby faced one of her worst fears. Because of him. Residual guilt tied his gut in a knot.

Not that she had suffered any lasting harm. Nevertheless, the experience in the mine was unpleasant to say the least. He never should have let her go down there.

He was already on the jet when the taxi pulled up. Peeking through the small window of the plane, he saw Libby get out. The day was drizzly and cold. She was wearing a black wool coat and carried a red-and-black umbrella, her face hidden. All he could see was long legs and sexy shoes.

The pilot was already in the cockpit preparing for take-off. Patrick went to the open cabin door and stood, ready to lend a hand if Libby needed help on the wet stairs. She hovered on the tarmac as the cabdriver handed a suitcase and matching carry-on to Patrick. Then she came up the steps.

Patrick moved back. "Hand me your umbrella." He'd been wrong about the coat. It wasn't wool at all, but instead, a fashionable all-weather trench-style, presumably heavily lined to deal with the cold weather in New York. A hood, edged in faux fur, framed her face.

For some reason, he couldn't look her in the eyes...not yet. "Make yourself comfortable," he said over his shoulder. After shaking the worst of the water from the umbrella, he closed it and stored it in a small closet. Then he retracted the jet's folding steps and turned the locking mechanisms on the cabin door.

"We'll be taking off in about five minutes."

At last, he turned around. Libby stood in the center of the cabin, her purse and coat on a seat beside her.

His heart punched once in his chest. Hard. His lungs forgot how to function. "Libby?" Incredulous, he stared at her. She was wearing a long-sleeve, scoop-necked black dress with a chunky silver necklace and matching earrings. The dress was completely plain. But the slubbed-knit fabric fit her body perfectly, emphasizing every sexy curve.

Even so, the dress wasn't what made the greatest impact. Nor was it the extremely fashionable but wildly impractical high heels that made her legs seem a million miles long. The dramatic jolt wasn't even a result of her darkly lashed green eyes or her soft crimson lips. It was her hair. God, her hair...

His mouth was probably hanging open, but he couldn't help it. He cleared his throat, shoving his hands in the pocket of his suit jacket to keep from grabbing her. "Whoever talked you into changing your color back to normal is a genius. It suits you perfectly." The deep red curls with gold highlights made her skin glow. The new cut framed her face and drew attention to high cheekbones and a slightly pointed chin.

Libby shrugged, seeming both pleased by and uncomfortable with his reaction. She and her mother had been harassed by reporters for months. Looking the way she did right now, it would have been impossible for her to fade into a crowd. Hence the metamorphosis from gorgeous socialite to little brown mouse.

She nodded, her eyes shadowed. "I've been hiding for a long time. But that's over, Patrick. I'm ready to move on."

He couldn't help himself. He closed the distance between them. "You're more than the sum of your looks, Libby."

"Thank you."

He winnowed his fingers through her hair. "It's so light…and fluffy…and *red*." He lowered his voice to a rough whisper. "I want to take you right here, right now. In that big overstuffed captain's chair. You make me crazy."

She looked at him, her soft green eyes roving his face, perhaps seeking assurance of his sincerity. "I want you, too, Patrick. Perhaps I shouldn't. My life is complicated enough already. But when I'm with you, I forget about all the bad stuff."

He frowned. "I'm not sure I want to be used as an amnesiac device."

"Don't think of it that way. You're like a drug. But the good kind. One that makes me feel alive in the best possible way. When I'm with you, I'm happy. It's as simple as that."

Her explanation mollified him somewhat, but he still wasn't entirely satisfied. He wanted to kiss her, but the pilot used the intercom to notify them of imminent take-off. "This discussion isn't over," he said.

They strapped into adjacent seats and prepared to be airborne. Libby turned to look out the window. Her profile was as familiar to him now as was his own. He struggled with a hodgepodge of emotions that left him feeling out of sorts.

He liked being Libby Parkhurst's savior. In the beginning he had resented his mother's interference. But once Libby was installed at Silver Reflections, it made him feel good to know he was helping make her life easier. Now that she had acquitted herself reasonably well in the woods, there was really no reason not to let her finish out Charlise's maternity leave.

But did he honestly want Libby under his nose 24/7? The situation would be perfect fodder for his mother's wedding-obsessed machinations behind the scenes. Patrick, however, was more worried about becoming a slobbering sex-starved idiot.

He had a business to run. Silver Reflections was doing very well, but any relatively new business had to keep on its toes. He couldn't afford to let his focus be drawn away by a woman, no matter how appealing.

The flight to New York was uneventful. Patrick worked on his presentation. Libby read a novel. They spoke occasionally, but it was stilted conversation. Was he the only one feeling shaken by what might happen during the night to come?

Libby felt like a girl in a fairy tale. Except this was backward. She had already been the princess with the world at her feet. Now she was an ordinary woman trying to embrace her new life.

It didn't hurt that Maeve had spoiled her with a suitcase full of new clothes. When Libby was growing up, her mother had bought Libby an entire new wardrobe every spring and fall. The castoffs were given to charity. They were always good clothes, some of them barely worn. Libby had never thought twice about it...other than the few times she had begged to keep a favorite sweater or pair of jeans.

Such excess seemed dreadful now. The clothes she'd brought with her this weekend would have to last several years. They were quality items, well made and classic in style. Perhaps Maeve was more perceptive than Libby realized, because during their wild shopping spree, Maeve had never once suggested anything that was faddish, nothing that would be dated by the next season.

On the other hand, Libby knew it wasn't the clothing that defined her new maturity. The past year had been a trial by fire. She had struggled with the emotional loss of her father, grieved the physical loss of her mother and juggled all of that alongside the almost inexplicable loss of her own identity.

And now there was Patrick. What to do about Patrick?

He disturbed her introspection. "Do you have any current plans to see your father?"

"Will you think I'm a terrible person if I say *no*?"

His smile was gentle and encompassed an understanding that threatened her composure. "Of course not. No one can make that decision for you."

She picked at the armrest. "I've sent him the occasional note. And of course, I called him after Mother, well...you know."

"Was he able to attend the funeral?"

"No. The request to the prison would have had to come from me, and I didn't think I could handle it. I was pretty much a mess. Fortunately, my parents had actually bought plots where my father grew up in Connecticut. They even prepaid for funerals. So at least I didn't have to worry about that."

"Has he written to you?"

"Only twice. I think he's ashamed. And embarrassed. But mostly angry he got caught. My father apparently subscribed to the theory that tax fraud isn't actually a crime unless someone finds out what you've done."

"He's not alone in that view."

"Doesn't make it right."

"How long does he have to serve?"

"Seven to ten. It was a lot of money. And apparently he was not exactly repentant in front of the judge."

"Time in prison can change people. Maybe it will show him what matters."

"I suppose…" But she was dubious. Her father was accustomed to throwing his weight around. His money had made it possible for him to demand *what* he wanted *when* he wanted. She had tried to find it in her heart to have sympathy for him. But she was still too shattered about the whole experience.

Patrick leaned forward and pointed out her window. "There's the skyline."

Libby took in the familiar sight and felt a stab of grief so raw and deep it caught her off guard. Patrick didn't say a word. But he used his finger to catch a tear that rolled down her cheek, and he finally offered her a pristine handkerchief to blow her nose.

"It's not my home anymore," she said, her throat so tight she could barely speak.

Patrick slid an arm around her shoulders. "It will always be your *first* home. And at some point, the trauma of what happened will become part of your past. Not so devastating that you think of it every day."

"I hope so."

"Silver Glen is a pretty good place for a fresh start. I know you came to the mountains to heal and to get back on your feet financially. My mother would be over the moon if you decided to stay forever."

"What about you, Patrick?"

The impulsive query came from her own lips, but shocked her nevertheless. It was the kind of needy leading question an insecure woman asks. "Don't answer that," she said quickly. "I don't know why I said it."

His expression was impassive, his thoughts impossible to decipher. "I have nothing to hide. I've already told you how I feel about marriage. I get the impression you're the kind of woman who will want a permanent relationship eventually. Maybe you can find that in Silver Glen. I don't know. But in the meantime, we've come very close to a line you may not want to cross when you're no longer in fear for your life."

"Don't patronize me," she said slowly. "I mentioned the one-hotel-room thing when I was safely out of the mine and standing in your office. Did you forget about that?"

"A relationship forged under duress doesn't usually stand the test of time."

She scowled, even as the plane bumped down on the runway at LaGuardia. "For a guy who's barely thirty, you pontificate like someone's grandmother."

He sighed, his jaw tight. "Are we having our first fight?"

"No," she snapped. "That happened when you called me a *misfit*."

"So many things are clear now," he muttered, his hot gaze skating from her lips to her breasts. "It's the red hair. I could have saved myself a lot of heartache if I'd known that the woman I interviewed in the beginning was not a mouse, but instead an exotic, hotheaded spitfire."

"Patronizing *and* chauvinistic."

A deep voice interrupted their quarrel. "Um, excuse me…Mr. Kavanagh? We have to deplane now."

Libby groaned inwardly, embarrassed beyond belief. How much had the pilot overheard? Grabbing her coat and shoving her arms into the sleeves, she scooped up her purse and climbed over Patrick's legs to head for the exit. He let her go, presumably lingering to deal with their luggage.

A private limo awaited them, a uniformed driver at the ready. When Patrick climbed in to the backseat with her, she ignored him pointedly, her face still hot with mortification.

How was a woman supposed to deal with a man who was both brutally honest and ridiculously appealing? Was she seriously going to settle for a temporary fling? And what was the time limit? When Charlise came back in six months, did the affair and the job end on the same day?

Patrick took her hand. "Quit sulking."

Her temper shot up several notches. She gave him a look that should have melted the door frame. "I've changed my mind. I want my own hotel room. I need a job more than I need you."

He stroked the inside of her wrist with his thumb. "Don't be mad, my beautiful girl. We're in New York. Alone. Away from my meddling family. We can do anything we want…anything at all."

His voice threatened to mesmerize her. Deep and husky with arousal, his words had the smooth cadence of a snake charmer. She shivered inwardly. "How easy do you think I am?" Her indignation dwindled rapidly in inverse proportion to the increase in her shaky breathing and the acceleration of her rushing pulse.

Patrick lifted her wrist and kissed the back of her hand. "You're not easy at all, Libby. You're damned difficult. Every time I think I have you figured out, you surprise me all over again."

She caught the chauffeur's gaze in the rearview mirror. The man lifted an eyebrow. Libby blushed again and stared out the window. "Not now, Patrick. We're almost there."

Patrick settled back in his seat, but the enigmatic smile on his face made Libby want to kiss the smirk off his face. Fortunately for her self-control, the car pulled up in front of their destination. While Patrick swiped his credit card, Libby slid out of the vehicle, shivering when a blast of cold air flipped up the tail of her coat.

"Where's our luggage?" she asked, suddenly anxious about Maeve's nice suitcases and Libby's new clothes.

"The driver is taking them on to the Carlyle. They'll hold them for us until check-in time."

He took her arm. "C'mon. We're early, but I want to make sure they're ready for us." Ushering her through sleek revolving doors, he hurried her into the building and onto the elevator. Fortunately for Libby, the small space was crowded, meaning she didn't have to talk to Patrick at all.

On the twenty-seventh floor, they exited. An eerily perfect receptionist greeted them. Behind her in platinum letters were the words *Peabody Rushford*. Libby took off her coat, using the opportunity to look around with curiosity. It was difficult to imagine anyone from this upscale environment insisting that executives participate in one of Patrick's field experiences.

Moments later, after a hushed communication via a high-tech intercom system, they were escorted to the boardroom where Patrick would do his presentation. Every chair at the glossy conference table was situated at an exact ninety-degree angle. Crystal tumblers filled with ice water sat on folded linen napkins.

Not a single item in the room was out of place. Except Libby. She felt ill at ease. Why had she agreed to accompany Patrick? Oh, wait. Tagging along had been her idea.

She was still holding out hope that she could convince him to give her the job.

The executives trickled into the room, first one or two, and then three or four, until finally, the entire team was assembled. Eight men, four women. Plus the graying boss. She guessed his *underlings* ranged in age from early thirties to late forties. Libby was easily the youngest person in the room.

Patrick greeted each participant warmly, introducing himself with the self-deprecatory charm she had come to expect from him. He was confident and humorous, and he interacted with both men and women equally well. When everyone was seated, there were three chairs remaining at one end of the table. Libby took the middle one, leaving a buffer on either side.

She was here as an interested observer. No need to get chummy. Not now at least. The future remained to be seen. If she continued to work for Patrick—and it was possible he might decide to let her stay on—then no doubt, she would be meeting these people in April.

Honestly, it was hard to imagine any of this crew getting dirty in the woods. The women wore similar quasi uniforms. Dark formfitting blazers with matching pencil skirts and white silk blouses. Their hairstyles fell into two camps…either sophisticated chignons or sharply modern pixie cuts.

The men were equally polished. Their dark suits resembled Patrick's. Though he wore a red power tie, the executives' neckwear was more conservative. Finally, the room settled, and Patrick began his spiel.

Libby knew Patrick was smart. But seeing him operate in this environment was eye-opening. He spoke to the group as an equal…a man with experience in their world as well as the master of his own domain, Silver Reflections.

As the orientation proceeded, Libby watched the faces

around the table. One of the women and several of the men were actively engaged, frequently asking questions… demonstrating enthusiasm and anticipation. Others exhibited veiled anxiety, and some were almost hostile.

Patrick had shared with Libby that the CEO was an ex-marine…a man both hard in business and in his physical demands on himself. For him to insist that his top management people participate in Patrick's program was asking a lot. Libby wondered if anyone would bail out, even if it might mean losing their jobs.

During the official Q and A time at the end, one of the quieter women who hadn't said a word so far raised her hand. When Patrick acknowledged her, she pointed at Libby. "Does she work for you? I'd like to hear what she has to say."

Patrick gave Libby a wry glance and shrugged. "Libby?"

All eyes in the room focused on her. She cleared her throat, scrambling for the right words. She would never forgive herself if she botched this for Patrick. "Well, um…"

The woman stared at her with naked apprehension. Clearly she wanted some kind of reassurance and saw Libby as a kindred spirit.

Libby smiled. "I certainly understand if anyone in this room, male or female, has reservations about spending a night or two in the woods, particularly if your personal history doesn't include campouts and bonfires. To be honest, I was the same way. But when I came to work for Patrick, it was important for me to try this *immersion* experience. I had to prove to myself that I could step outside my comfort zone."

The woman blanched. "And how did that go?"

Libby laughed softly. "I'll be honest. There were good parts and bad." No reason to go into the mine-shaft fiasco. "On the plus side, the setting is pristine and beautiful and serene. If you haven't been much of a nature lover in the past, I think you'll be one when the weekend is over."

"And the less wonderful parts?"

Though only one woman was doing the interrogation, Libby had a strong suspicion that others around the table were hanging on Libby's comments, looking for reassurance.

"Spending the night on the ground was a challenge, even with a comfy sleeping bag and a small pad. I'm a light sleeper to start with, so I found it difficult to relax enough to sleep deeply, even though I was tired."

"Anything else?"

Libby hesitated. Patrick grinned and nodded, as if not perturbed at all by anything she might have to say. "Well," she said, "there's the issue of using the bathroom in the woods. Women are always at a disadvantage there."

A titter of laughter circled the table.

Libby continued. "But all of this is minor stuff compared to the big picture. You'll learn to rely on teamwork to get simple tasks done like meals and setting up camp and taking it down. I think you'll see your coworkers in a new light. And I promise you that you'll find skills and talents you never knew you had. Patrick is not a drill sergeant. He's a facilitator. His knowledge is formidable. You can feel entirely safe with him in charge."

For a split second, the room was silent. Patrick was no longer smiling. If anything, he looked as if someone had punched him in the stomach. What was he thinking?

The woman asking the questions breathed an audible sigh of relief. "Thank you, Libby. I feel much better about this now."

The boss nodded. "I encourage my people to ask questions. It's the only way to learn."

Now some of the men seemed chagrined. Suddenly the woman in the group who had seemed like the weakest link had earned the boss's respect. Libby was pleased that her own small contribution had helped.

After the session adjourned, most of the staff returned to their offices. The boss lingered to speak with Patrick, expressing his opinion that the orientation had gone extremely well.

Then it was time to go. Patrick and Libby retraced their steps to the lobby, both of them quiet. Libby stood on the sidewalk, huddled into her coat. "Do we split up now? And meet at the hotel later?"

Patrick pulled up her hood and tucked a stray strand of hair inside. "Is it important for you to be alone when you revisit your old building?"

She searched his face. "No. Not really. But I assumed you had other things to do."

He kissed the tip of her nose. "My business is done. I'd like to take you to lunch, and then we'll face your past together."

"I might cry."

Patrick chuckled. "I think I can handle it. C'mon, I'm starving."

Eleven

Patrick hailed a cab and helped Libby in, then ran around
to the other side and joined her. Heavy clouds had rolled
in. The sky overhead was gray and menacing. He gave the
driver an address and sat back. "If you don't mind, Libby,
I thought we would try a new place Aidan recommended.
It's tucked away in the theater district, off the beaten path
for tourists. He says they have the best homemade soups
this side of North Carolina."

Libby smoothed the hem of her coat over her knees,
unwittingly drawing attention to her legs. He had plans
for those legs.

She nodded. "Sounds good, but I'm surprised. I thought
men needed more than soup to consider it a meal."

"I might have forgotten to mention the gyros and tur-
key legs." His stomach growled on cue.

Libby laughed. "Now I get it."

"You were amazing back there," he said. "I never realized how much better these weekend trips would be if all

the participants have the opportunity to calm their fears beforehand. Everything you said was perfect."

"But you've always done orientations…right?" She frowned.

"I have. Yes. But the dynamics of these high-powered firms are interesting. No one wants to appear weak in front of the boss."

"Then how was today different?"

"I think your presence at the table connected with that woman. She saw you as an ally. And perceived you to be truthful and sincere. So that gave her the courage to speak out. Truthfully, I think there were others in the room who shared some of the same anxieties. So even though they didn't *ask*, they also wanted to know what you had to say."

"I'm glad I could help."

Patrick glanced at his watch. "Now, we're officially off the clock…business concluded."

"There's a lot of the day still ahead."

He leaned over, took her chin in his hand and kissed her full on the lips. "I'm sure we can find some way to fill the time."

"I'll leave the planning up to you." Her demure answer was accompanied by a teasing smile that made him wish he could ditch the rest of the day's agenda and take her back to their room right now. Unfortunately, waiting wasn't his strong suit.

The change in her appearance still threw him off his stride. The Libby with whom he had communed out in the woods and down in the mine was spunky and cute and fun. He'd been aroused by her and interested in bedding her.

This newly revamped Libby was something else again. She made him feel like an overeager adolescent caught up in a surge of hormones that were probably killing off his brain cells in droves. His libido was louder than ever. *Take Libby. Take Libby. Man want woman.*

To disguise his increasing agitation, he pulled out his phone. With a muttered "excuse me," he pretended to check important emails. Libby was neither insulted nor overly perturbed by his distraction. She stared out the window of the cab, perhaps both pleased and yet anxious about re-visiting her old stomping grounds.

That was one thing he loved about her. She wasn't jaded, even though a woman from her background certainly could be. Perhaps she had always been so fresh and open to life's surprises. Or maybe the places she and her mother had lived after being kicked out of their lavish home had taught Libby to appreciate her past.

The café where they had lunch was noisy and crowded. Patrick was glad. He wasn't in the mood for intimate con-versation. His need to make love to Libby drowned out every other thought in his head.

Libby, on the other hand, chatted happily, her mood upbeat despite the fact that she was facing an emotional hurdle this afternoon.

He drank his coffee slowly, absently listening as his luncheon date conversed with the waitress about what it was like to be an understudy for an off-Broadway play. At last, the server walked away and Libby smiled at Patrick. "Sorry. I love hearing people's stories."

He raised an eyebrow. "Yet I haven't heard all of yours. What did you study in college? Who did you want to be when you grew up? How many boyfriends did you have along the way?"

A shadow flitted across her face. "I was an English major."

"Did you want to teach?"

"No. Not really. My parents wouldn't have approved."

"Too plebeian?" he asked, tongue in cheek.

Libby rolled her eyes at him. "Something like that."

"Then why the English major?"

She shrugged, her expression slightly defensive. "I loved books. It was the one area of study where I could indulge my obsession with the printed word and no one would criticize the hours I spent in the library."

"Is that what your parents did?"

Her smile was bleak this time. "They told me no man would want to marry a woman who was boring. That I should learn to entertain and decorate a house and choose fine wines and converse about politics and current events."

"Sounds like a Stepford wife."

"I suppose. It became a moot point when my father decided to defraud the government. My standing in society evaporated, not that I minded. At least not on my own account. I did feel very sorry for what it did to my mother. She never signed on for coupon clipping and shopping at discount clothing stores. My father spoiled her and pampered her, right up until the day he was carted away in handcuffs."

"That's all behind you now. Nothing but good times ahead."

He heard his own words and winced inwardly. What did *he* know about the struggles Libby faced? Even several years ago when he decided to give up his career in Chicago, it wasn't a huge risk. The Kavanagh family had deep pockets. He had started Silver Reflections with his own money, but if he had run into financial difficulties, there would have been plenty of help available to him. Never in his life had he faced the challenges that had been thrust upon Libby.

She wiped her mouth with a napkin and reapplied her lipstick. Watching her smooth on the sultry red color was an exercise in sexual frustration.

When she looked up, she caught him staring. He must have put on a good show, because she didn't appear to notice how close to the edge he was. Instead, she grimaced. "Let's go see my building before I get cold feet."

The sentence would have made sense, even if the words had been literal. The temperature outside had to have dropped at least ten degrees since they had arrived in the city.

He hailed another cab and looked at Libby. "You'll have to give the address this time."

"Of course." She nodded, her expression hard to decipher. But as they whizzed through the streets of the city, he saw her anxiety level rise.

When he took one of her hands in his, it was ice-cold. "Where are your gloves?"

"I didn't have any that matched this coat, and I wanted to look nice for your business associates."

"Oh, for God's sake, Libby. Here. Take mine." The ones in the pocket of his overcoat were old and well-worn, but they were leather, lined with cashmere. At least they would keep her warm in transit.

She barely seemed to notice his offering, but she didn't protest when he slid the gloves onto her hands. Finally, the cab stopped. "We're here," she said. For a moment, she didn't move.

"Libby? Are we going to get out?"

She looked at him blankly.

"Libby?" He kissed her nose. "C'mon, darlin'. There's no bogeyman waiting for you. Nothing but bricks and mortar."

"I know that."

Even so, when they stood on the sidewalk, she huddled against him, pretending to shelter herself from the wind. But they were shielded by the building, and the biting breeze had all but disappeared.

He put his arm around her shoulder, at a loss for how to

help her. "Which floor was yours?" he asked...anything to get her to talk.

"The penthouse. Daddy liked looking down on Central Park."

Patrick stood quietly, holding her close. "I'm here, Libby. You're not alone."

At last, she moved. He thought she meant only to walk past the impressive building, but she stopped in front of the double glass doors and, after a moment's hesitation, stepped forward to open them.

Before she could do so, a barrel-chested, white-haired man in a gray uniform with burgundy piping flung them wide. "Ms. Libby. Good God Almighty. I've been worried sick about you. I'm so sorry about your mother, baby girl. Come let me hug you."

Libby launched herself into the man's embrace and wrapped her arms around his ample waist. "Oh, Clarence. I've missed you so much."

Patrick watched in bemusement as the two old friends reconnected. He entered the lobby in deference to the cold, but hung back, unwilling to interfere with Libby's moment of closure.

At last, the old man acknowledged his presence. "Come on, Libby. Tell me about this handsome young fellow."

Libby blushed, her face alight with happiness. "That's my boss, Patrick Kavanagh. Patrick, this is Clarence Turner. He's known me since I was in diapers."

Clarence beamed. "Sweetest little gal you ever saw. And she grew up as beautiful on the inside as she was on the outside. For my sixtieth birthday, she made me a banana cream cake from scratch. Nicest thing anyone had ever done for me since my wife died."

Patrick stuck out his hand. "An honor to meet you, sir."

Clarence looked at Libby, his face troubled. "I'd take you upstairs if I could, but I think it would upset you. The new owners redid the whole place. You wouldn't recognize it."

"It doesn't matter," Libby said. "Seeing you is enough. I always thought my parents and I would give you a big, awesome gift when you retired…maybe a trip to Hawaii… or a new car. Turns out you'll be lucky to get a card and a pack of gum from me now."

She smiled and laughed when she said it, but Patrick knew it troubled her not to be able to help her old friend in any substantial way. Patrick made a mental note to follow up on the situation and see what he could do in Libby's name.

Clarence shot Patrick an assessing glance. "I thought maybe the two of you were an item," he said, not so subtly. "A man could do a lot worse than to marry Libby Parkhurst."

Before Patrick could reply, Libby jumped in. "Patrick and I are just friends. Actually, I'm working for his company temporarily. Patrick's mother and mine were good friends. Maeve Kavanagh has been helping me get back on my feet." She hugged Clarence one more time. "We have to go. But I promise to write more often. You're still at the same address?"

"Yes, indeed. They'll have to take me out of there feet-first." He looked at Patrick one more time and then back at Libby. "You're going to be okay, Libby. I never saw a girl with more grit or more light in her soul."

"Thank you for that, old friend."

When Patrick saw Libby's soft green eyes fill with tears, he decided it was time to go. "Nice to meet you, sir. I hope our paths will cross again."

Though Libby glanced over her shoulder and waved one last time as they braved the cold again, she didn't protest. Patrick had a feeling that the emotional reunion had taken more out of her than she realized.

On the sidewalk, he tipped up her chin and kissed her forehead. "How 'bout we go on the hotel and check in? I think we both could use a nap. If we're going to have a night on the town, you need your beauty sleep. And now that I think about it, I probably should get some play tickets."

They climbed into a cab and Libby took his hand. "What if we skip a play and just go out to dinner? That way we'd be back to the hotel early."

He swallowed, aware that the cabbie was perhaps listening, despite the fact that he had his radio on. "I'd like that very much." He clenched his other fist. "I want to be alone with you," he muttered.

"We could skip the nap, also."

In her eyes he saw everything he wanted and more. "I booked two rooms," he said hoarsely. "I didn't want to take advantage of you."

"I'm not weak, Patrick. I can take care of myself. And I was mad when I asked for that second room. We don't need it. I don't expect anything from you except pleasure."

"Pleasure?" His mouth was dry, his sex hard as stone. His brain had for all intents and purposes turned to mush.

She leaned into him. "Pleasure," she whispered. "You're a smart man. You'll figure it out."

Fortunately for Patrick's sanity, it was a brief cab ride. He paid the fare, aware all the while that Libby watched him.

He couldn't bear to look at her. He was too close to the edge.

At the front desk, the polite employee didn't blink an eye when Patrick canceled one of the rooms. The clerk dealt with the credit card and handed over the keys. "We've been holding your luggage, Mr. Kavanagh. I'll have it sent up immediately, along with a bottle of champagne and some canapés. Is there anything else we can do for you?"

Patrick swallowed, his hand shaking as he signed the charge slip. "No. Thank you."

He turned to Libby. "You ready to go upstairs?"

Twelve

Libby linked her hand in his. "I'm ready." She was under no illusions. If she hadn't pushed the issue, Patrick might well have ignored the spark of attraction between them. He was wary of hurting Libby, and he had a healthy respect for his mother's good opinion.

Libby rested her head on his shoulder. They were alone in the elegant elevator. "No one will know about this but you and me, Patrick. You're not interested in a relationship, and I'm not, either. But that doesn't mean we can't enjoy each other's company."

His grip tightened on her hand when the elevator dinged. The bellman had come up on the service elevator, so there was a busy moment as Patrick opened the door and the luggage was situated. A second bellman came on the heels of the first, this one pushing a cart covered in white linen. The silver ice bucket chilled a bottle of bubbly. An offering of fancy cheese spreads and toast fingers resided on china dishes, along with strawberries and cream.

Once the efficient Carlyle employees disappeared, tips in hand, Patrick leaned against the door. "May I offer you a strawberry...or a glass of champagne?"

Libby nodded, her heart in her throat. "The latter please." She was accustomed to drinking fine champagne, but it had been a very long time. When Patrick handed her a crystal flute, she tipped it back and drank recklessly. The bubbly liquid was crisp and flavorful.

Patrick followed suit, although he sipped his drink slowly, eyeing her over the rim. "Have I told you how sexy you look in that dress?"

She was crestfallen. "I thought it was suitably professional."

"It *is* suitable," he said. "And professional. But the woman inside makes it something else entirely."

"Like what?" She held out her glass for a refill. Her knees were shaky. Was she going to chicken out now? She couldn't remember the last time she had experienced such genuine, shivery, sexual desire.

Patrick filled her flute a second time. But before he handed it to her, he took a sip...exactly where her lipstick had left a faint stain. "Tastes amazing," he said.

She kicked off her heels and curled her toes against the exquisite Oriental rug. Ordinarily, she hated panty hose with a passion, but the weather today had been a bit much for bare legs. There was no good way for a man to remove them...romantically speaking.

"Will you excuse me for a moment?" she asked, setting down her half-empty glass.

"Of course."

In the opulent bathroom, she covered her hot red cheeks with cold hands. She was going to have sex with Patrick Kavanagh. Casually. Temporarily.

Good girls didn't do such things. But then again, she'd

been a good girl for much of her life, and look where it had gotten her.

Rapidly, she stripped off her panty hose and stuffed them in a drawer of the vanity. She fluffed her hair and then held a damp cloth to her cheeks, trying to tame the wild color that was a dead giveaway as to her state of mind.

When she could linger no longer, she returned to the sitting room. It was lovely, with pale green and ecru walls. Antique French furnishings lent an air of romance. Patrick had even lit a candle, though it was the middle of the day.

He came to her and slid his hands beneath her hair, his smile holding the tiniest hint of male satisfaction. "Are you shy, Libby love?"

"Maybe. A little bit. I'm suddenly feeling rather unsophisticated."

"I don't want sophistication. I don't need it." His eyes had gone all dark and serious, the blue-gray irises like stormy lakes.

She curled her fingers around his wrists, not to push him away, but to hold on to something steady as her emotions cartwheeled. "What *do* you want and need, Patrick?"

He scooped her into his arms. "You, Libby. Only you."

On the way to the bedroom, he stopped to pick up the heavy pillar candle. But he couldn't manage it and Libby, too. Not without tumbling them all to the floor in a pile of hot wax. The image made her smile.

Patrick scowled. "Are you laughing at me?"

She looped an arm around his neck. "I wouldn't dare. I was merely contemplating all the ways I could use hot wax to drive you wild."

He stumbled and nearly lost his balance. His jaw dropped. Not much. But enough to let Libby know her little comment had left him gobsmacked. It felt good to have the upper hand, even if for only a moment.

The bedroom was something out of a fantasy…soft lavender sheets, fresh violets in a crystal vase…a Louis XIV chaise longue upholstered in sunshine-yellow and aubergine brocade. The ivory damask duvet had already been folded back. All Patrick had to do was gently drop Libby on the bed.

"Don't move," he said. "I'm going back for the ambience."

She barely had time to blink before he returned. He put the candle on the ornate dresser, a safe distance away. Then he closed the drapes, shutting out the gray afternoon light.

Libby propped her elbows behind her. "I thought you wanted a nap," she teased.

"Later," he said.

His jaw was tight, his cheekbones flushed. As he walked slowly toward the bed, he stripped off his tie and shirt and jacket with an economy of motion that was both intense and arousing…as if he couldn't bear to waste a single second. Libby's breath caught the first time she saw his bare chest.

"Nice show," she croaked. Her throat was dry, but the champagne was in the other room.

When he stood beside the bed, he unbuckled his belt and slid it free. Next went the shoes and socks. When he was down to his pants and nothing else, he crooked a finger. "Come here and turn around."

Trembling all over, she got up on her knees and presented her back to him. His fingertips found the top of her zipper and lowered it slowly. He cursed.

She looked over her shoulder, alarmed. "What's wrong?"

His expression was equal parts torment and lust. "You're too young. Too vulnerable. Too beautifully innocent."

"I'm not *entirely* innocent."

"I'm not talking about that kind of innocence," he said gruffly, stroking the length of her spine. He unfastened her bra, sliding his arms around her and palming her achy breasts. "It's *you*. All these things have tried to defeat you and yet you're still like a rosy-eyed child. As if nothing bad could ever happen."

She took one of his hands and raised it to her lips. "I'm only young in calendar years, Patrick. Life gave me an old soul, whether I wanted it or not. Now, quit agonizing over this and come to bed."

Patrick knew he was a lucky man. At this point in his life, he possessed most everything he'd ever wanted. But he had never wanted anything or anyone the way he wanted Libby Parkhurst. He wanted to be her knight, her protector, her one and only lover. The intensity of the desire overwhelmed him and left a hollow feeling in his chest. Because to have Libby in his life on a permanent basis would mean changes he wasn't prepared to make.

He wasn't in love with her. This was about sex. Nothing more.

He helped her out of the black dress. Underneath it, her bra and panties were pink lace. He'd never particularly been a fan of pink. But on her, it was perfect.

When she was completely naked, he sucked in a breath. "Get under the covers," he said gruffly. "Before you freeze."

He wondered if she saw through his equivocation. The room was plenty warm. But he needed a moment to collect himself. Turning away from the bed, he stripped off his pants and briefs. His erection could have hammered nails. He ached, almost bent over with the need to thrust inside her and find peace. When Libby flicked off the only remaining lamp, he turned around.

In the light from the single candle, her hair glowed like a nimbus around a naughty angel.

She curled on her side, the covers tucked to her chin. "I'm feeling nervous," she said quietly.

Did the woman have no filters? No emotional armor? "I'm feeling a bit shaky myself," he admitted.

Her eyes widened when she spotted the physical evidence of his excitement for the first time. "Really? 'Cause from over here it seems like you're good to go."

Her droll humor made him laugh. He flipped back the covers and joined her, his legs tangling with ones that were softer and more slender. "You have no concept of how much I want to make love to you."

"Why, Patrick? Why me?"

"Why not you?" He teased the nearest nipple, watching in fascination as it budded tightly.

"That's not an answer." She cried out when he bent to suckle her breast. But she must have meant for him to continue, because she clutched his head to her chest, her fingers twined in his hair.

She smelled like wildflowers and summer love affairs. In the midst of winter, she brought warmth and sunshine into this room, this bed.

He kissed her roughly. "Not everything in life can be explained, Libby."

Her arms wrapped around his neck, threatening to choke him. "Try."

"You give me something no one else ever has," he admitted quietly. "When I'm with you, everything seems right."

He saw in her eyes the recognition of his honesty. It wasn't something he planned. In fact, he felt damned naked in more ways than one. But if he couldn't give her forever, at least he could give her this.

"Make love to me, Patrick."

It was all he needed to hear and more. Later there would

be time for drawn-out foreplay and fancy moves. But at the moment, all he could think about was being inside her.

Reaching for the condoms he had dropped on the nightstand, he sheathed himself matter-of-factly, trying not to notice the way Libby's gaze followed his every motion. "Now, my Libby. Now."

He eased on top of her, careful to shield her from his entire weight. For a moment, he couldn't move. He was hard against her thigh, shuddering with the need to take and take and take.

Libby reached up and cradled his face in her hands. "I want you, too, Patrick."

"You wouldn't lie about not being a virgin…would you?"

Her eyes darkened with an emotion he didn't understand. "I don't lie about *anything*."

That was the problem. Few people in life were as transparent as Libby. If he hurt her, either physically or emotionally, he would know it. Immediately. Was he prepared for that responsibility? The first one, yes…no question. But the second?

Slowly, he eased inside her, pressing all the way until he could go no farther. Her sex was warm and tight. Yellow spots danced behind his eyelids. Every muscle in his body was tense.

Libby curled her legs around his waist, unwittingly driving him deeper still. "This is nice," she said, catching her breath.

"Nice?" He clenched his teeth. He was damned if he would come like a teenage boy—all flash and no substance.

Libby squeezed him inwardly, her mouth tipped up in a tiny smile that told him she enjoyed flexing her newfound power. "I give you high marks for the opening sequence. Very impressive delivery. Appealing package."

He choked out a laugh. "Haven't you ever heard of calling a spade a spade? You can refer to it as a co—"

She clapped a hand over his mouth with a move that was beginning to seem familiar. "No I can't."

"Where did you say you went to school?"

"Catholic everything. My parents were Protestant, but they liked the idea of surrounding their baby girl with nuns."

"Can we please not talk about nuns right now? It's throwing me off my game."

She nipped his chin with sharp teeth. "Proceed. You're doing very well so far."

When he flexed his hips, he managed to erase the smile from her face. "How about now?"

Libby tipped back her head and sighed, arching into his thrust. "Don't ever stop. What time is checkout tomorrow?"

The random conversation confounded him. As a rule, his bed partners were not so chatty. "Eleven. Twelve. Hell, I don't know. Why?"

Green eyes, hazy and unfocused, gazed up at him. "I want to calculate how many more times we can do this before we have to go home."

Libby was in deep trouble. She'd been lying to herself so well, she didn't even see the cliff ahead. And now she was about to tumble into disaster. Again.

At sixteen there had been some excuse. Not so much in her current situation.

Patrick was big and warm and solid, and that wasn't even taking into consideration the body part currently stroking her so intimately. He surrounded her, filled her, possessed her. The smell of his skin, the silky touch of his hair against her breasts. She could barely breathe from wanting him.

"Hush now, darlin'," he groaned, his Southern accent more pronounced as he ground his hips against hers. When he zeroed in on a certain spot, she cried out, her orgasm taking her by surprise.

The flash of climax was intense and prolonged, wave after wave of pleasure that left her lax and helpless in his embrace. But Patrick was lost, as well. His muffled shout against her neck was accompanied by fierce, frantic thrusts that culminated in his wild release.

When the storm passed, the room was silent but for their harsh breathing.

Coming back to New York had triggered an avalanche of feelings. And not only about her father's fall from grace. There was that other business, as well. The thing that still shamed her and made her question her judgment about men. She had never wanted to be so vulnerable again. But Patrick wouldn't hurt her, would he? At least not the way she'd been hurt before.

Thirteen

Libby was having the most wonderful dream. She was floating in the ocean, the sun beaming down in gentle benediction. The temperature was exactly right. A warm blanket cocooned her as the breeze ruffled her hair.

Some sound far in the distance brought her awake with a jerk. Every cell in her body froze in stunned disbelief. Patrick Kavanagh lay half on top of her, his regular breathing steady and deep.

Holy Hannah. What had she done? Other than make it perfectly clear to Patrick that she was ready for dalliance with no expectation of anything more lasting than a weekend fling…

She eased out from under her lover, wincing when he muttered and frowned in his sleep. Fortunately, he settled back into slumber. He wasn't kidding about the nap. On the other hand, he probably needed it. The preceding week hadn't been a walk in the park. Maybe Patrick had experienced the same disturbing nightmares she had.

Caves with endless tunnels. Suffocating darkness. Musty air. Crypts and death. That's what came from having a too-vivid imagination.

Tiptoeing around the bed, she made her way into the other room and found her carry-on with her toiletry bag. Since she was naked as a baby at the moment, it also seemed prudent to locate her gown and robe. Patrick didn't stir when she quietly opened the bathroom door.

Once she was safely on the other side, she exhaled shakily. Nothing in the course of her admittedly limited sexual experience—much of it negative—had prepared her for Patrick's lovemaking. He was thorough. And intense. And enthusiastic. And generous. Did she mention generous? She'd lost track of her own orgasms. The man was a freaking genius in the bedroom. Who knew?

She wrapped a towel around her hair to keep it dry, and took an abbreviated shower. The thought of getting caught in the act was too terrifying to contemplate. The man had seen her naked. But that didn't mean a woman didn't like her privacy.

When she was clean and dry, she put on her silky nightwear. The soft ivory gown and robe were old, but still stylish and comfy. The fact that they were very thin gave her pause, but it was better than being nude.

Her hair did well with nothing more than a good brushing. Now all she had to do was pretend to be blasé, make her way through a fancy dinner and convince Patrick to sleep on the sofa.

She needed to put some distance between them. A barricade against doing something stupid. He'd already told her that marriage wasn't in the cards for him. Which meant this relationship was going nowhere.

If she let herself share his bed again, all bets were off. She might end up begging, and that would be the final indignity. He'd already called her a misfit once. She was sure as heck not going to let him pity her for crushing on him like a teenage girl.

She sat on the edge of the bathtub for ten minutes, trying to decide how to stage her return to the bedroom. In the end, Patrick took the matter out of her hands. He jerked open the door without ceremony and sighed—apparently in relief—when he saw her.

"I didn't know where you were," he complained.

The man was stark naked, his body a work of art. His *penis*—she could whisper that word in the privacy of her own head—hovered at half-mast, but was rapidly rising to attention. And apparently, the man had no modesty at all, because he stood there in the doorway, hands on hips, and glared at her. Not seeming at all concerned with his nudity. His spectacular, mouthwatering nudity.

"Where would I go?" she asked, trying not to look below his waist.

He ignored the question and strode toward her, dwarfing the generous dimensions of the bathroom. "I fail to see why you're wearing clothes. Aren't you the one who was doing mathematical calculations about potential episodes of sexual activity per hour?"

"That wasn't me," she lied, leaning back as his *stuff* practically whacked her in the nose.

His good humor returned. Without warning, he scooped her into his arms. "For future reference, no pj's unless I say so. And now that I think about it, no pj's at all."

Her cheek rested over the reassuring *thump-thump* of his heart. "These aren't pajamas. It's a peignoir set."

"I don't care if it's Queen Elizabeth's royal dressing gown. Ditch it, my love. Now."

He set her on her feet and, without further ado, lifted the two filmy layers over her head, ignoring her sputtering protests. "Patrick!"

He tossed the offending garments aside and ran his

hands from her neck to her shoulders, to her breasts, and all the way down to her bottom. "God, you're beautiful," he muttered.

"Oh, Patrick."

"Oh, Patrick." He mocked her gently. "Is that 'Oh, Patrick, I want to have sex with you again' or 'Oh, Patrick, you're the best lover I've ever had'?"

She caught her bottom lip with her teeth, torn between honesty and the need to keep his ego in check. "Well, both. But to be fair, you're only number two, so there's still room for comparison down the road."

His gaze sharpened. "Only number two?"

"I'm barely twenty-three."

"Yes, but a lot of girls are sexually active at sixteen."

"Not in my family. You do remember the nuns, right?"

"There you go again. Mentioning nuns at inappropriate moments. For the record, I knew one or two good little Catholic girls who taught me a lot about life. And sex."

Her eyes rounded. "Well, not me."

He thumbed her nipples, sending heat streaking all the way down to the damp juncture between her thighs. "You were amazing, Libby. Who taught you that thing you did there at the end?"

She shrugged demurely. "I read books."

"I see."

"You don't believe me?"

"You're awfully talented for a relative beginner."

The compliment was unexpected. "That's sweet of you to say."

"You want to tell me about number one?" Patrick seemed troubled, though she couldn't understand why.

She didn't. Not at all. The memory made her wince. "Maybe another time."

"Fair enough." He tipped his head and nibbled the side of her neck. "This will be slower, I promise."

She shuddered, her hands fisting at her sides. "I had no complaints."

Again, he scooped her into his arms, though this time he sat on the edge of the bed and turned her across his knees. "Do you have any spanking fantasies?"

She looked at him over her shoulder. "I can't say that I do, but feel free to test the hypothesis."

The sharp smack on her butt shocked her, even as the heat from his hand radiated throughout her pelvis. "That hurt, Patrick."

He chuckled. "Isn't that the point?"

The truth was, there was more to the sharp-edged play than hurt, but she didn't want to give him any ideas. She wriggled off his lap and knelt on the floor, resting her elbows on his bare knees and linking her hands underneath her chin. "I'll bet you know all sorts of kinky stuff, don't you?"

He grabbed handfuls of her hair and tugged gently. "Like the scenario where the desert sheikh takes the powerless English woman captive."

"I'm not English," she pointed out.

Patrick smiled tightly, sending a frisson of feminine apprehension down her spine. "We'll improvise. For the moment, let's see how you do on the oral exam. If you don't object, how about getting a washcloth and cleaning me up?"

"You mean so I can...?" Her voice trailed off. His erection bobbed in front of her. "Um, sure." She scuttled to the bathroom, painfully aware of his gaze following her progress. When she returned, he had leaned back on both hands. He didn't say a word.

But his challenging gaze tested her mettle. The balance of power was already unequal. He saw her as naive. Susceptible to being charmed by a man of experience. Though any and all of that might be true, she was determined to knock him off his feet.

Feigning confidence she did not possess, she sat at his hip and ran the washcloth over his intimate flesh, squeezing lightly. She smiled inwardly when he gasped, even though he tried to pretend it was a cough. "Too hard?" she asked, her expression guileless.

"No." Sweat beaded his forehead.

She continued to do her job, around and around, up and down. When she was finished, his flesh had turned to stone, and his chest rose and fell with every rapid breath.

Dropping the wet cloth on the floor, she bent, placed a hand on each of his thighs and took him in her mouth.

Patrick was pretty sure he had died and gone to heaven. He'd had blow jobs before. But none like this. His skin tightened all over his body. Libby's mouth was in turns delicate and firm. He couldn't predict her next move, and the uncertainty ratcheted up his arousal exponentially. He had promised her slow this time around, but already, he was at the breaking point. "Enough," he said, the word hoarse.

She looked up at him, her wide-eyed innocence no doubt damning him eternally for the lustful thoughts that turned him inside out. Putting his hands under her arms, he dragged her up onto the bed and kissed her recklessly. "Tell me what you want, Libby."

"I've never been on top."

Sweet holy hell. He swallowed hard. "Is that a request?"

She shrugged. "If you don't mind."

He took care of protection and moved onto his back. "You're in charge," he said, wondering if it were really true. He would hold out as long as he could, but the odds were iffy.

Libby seemed pleased by his gruff words. "I don't feel

very graceful," she complained as she attempted to mount the apparatus.

"The view from this side isn't bad."

When she slid down onto him without warning, he said a word that made her frown. "That's what we're doing, but you don't have to call it that."

She leaned forward, curling her fingertips into the depressions above his collarbone. "Don't you like this position?"

No one could be that naive. He gripped her firm ass and pulled her against him more firmly. "I've got your number now, Libby. You think you can drive me insane. But that's a two-edged sword. Wait until later when I tie your wrists to the bedposts and tickle you with a feather. You won't be so smug then, now will you?"

Her mouth formed a small perfect O. Her eyes widened. "Isn't that kind of advanced? We haven't known each other all that long. I think we should take things slowly...you know, get comfortable with each other before we branch out."

"I'm pretty damn comfortable right now." He put his hands under her breasts and bounced them experimentally. "These are nice."

She flushed. "Why are men so obsessed with boobs?"

"Maybe because we don't have any. I don't know. But you have to admit, they're beautiful."

"Now you've made me all weepy." Suppressing a smile, she leaned down and rested her forehead against his. "I didn't know it would be like this with you."

"Like what?"

"So easy. But so scary."

"I scare you?" He lifted her and eased her back down, making both of them gasp.

Without warning, she went for the dismount, nearly unmanning him in the process. She bounced off the bed and stood there, arms flung wide, her expression agitated. "You're ruining me for other men. I won't be able to find a husband after this."

He frowned. "I thought you were concentrating on rebuilding your life. That you didn't want a husband."

"Not today. Or tomorrow. But someday." She shook her head. "Now every guy I go to bed with is going to have to measure up to *that*." She pointed at his erection, seeming aggrieved by its very existence.

"You're overreacting. My co—" He stopped short. "My male *appendage* is perfectly normal," he said. "And people have casual sex all the time. Once we leave this hotel, it won't seem like such a big deal."

She folded her arms around her waist, apparently forgetting that she was bare-ass naked. "You know this from experience?"

"I have more than you, apparently. So, yes. And PS—it's bad form to walk out in the middle of the performance."

"I'm sorry." But she stood there so long he began to be afraid that she was actually going to call a halt to their madness.

He sat up and held out a hand. "Come back to bed, Libby. Please."

Her small smile loosened the knot in his stomach. "Well, if you ask that nicely…"

When he could reach her hand, he tugged, toppling her off balance and happily onto his lap. Libby sputtered and squirmed and protested until he flipped her and reversed their positions. Staring down at her, he felt something break apart and reform…a distinct seismic shift in his consciousness. Fortunately, he was good at ignoring extraneous details in the middle of serious business.

"Tell me you want me," he demanded.

"I want you."

"That wasn't convincing."

She linked her hands at the small of his back. "Patrick Kavanagh…I'll go mad with lust if you don't take me… right now."

"That's better." He shifted his weight and slid inside her, relishing the tight fit, the warm, wet friction. This was rapidly becoming an addiction, but he couldn't find it in his heart to care. His brain wasn't in the driver's seat. "I want you, too," he said, though she hadn't asked.

Libby's expressive eyes were closed, leaving him awash in doubt. What was she thinking? In the end, it didn't matter. His gut instincts took over, hammering home the message that she was the woman he needed. At least for now.

He felt the inner flutters that signaled her release. At last, he gave himself permission to finish recklessly, selfishly. Again and again, he thrust. Scrambling for a pinnacle just out of reach. When the end came, it was bittersweet. Because he realized one mind-numbing fact.

Libby Parkhurst had burrowed her way beneath his guard. And maybe into his heart.

Fourteen

"Hurry up, woman. We have dinner reservations in forty-five minutes."

Libby laughed, feeling happier than she had in a very long time. "I'll be ready in five." She leaned toward the mirror and touched up her eyeliner, then added a dash of smoky shadow.

After asking her preferences earlier in the day, Patrick had made reservations at an exclusive French restaurant high atop a Manhattan skyscraper. The evening promised to be magical.

She resisted the urge to pirouette in front of the mirror. The dress Maeve had bought for her was sexy and sophisticated and exceedingly feminine. The fabric was black lace over a gold satin underlay. The skirt ended modestly just at the knee, but the back dipped to the base of her spine.

Patrick rested his hands on her shoulders and kissed the nape of her neck, his hot gaze meeting hers in the mirror. "We could skip dinner," he said.

He was dressed in an expensive, conservative dark suit. The look in his eyes, however, was anything but ordinary.

She put her hand over one of his. "We need to keep up our strength. And besides, it would be a shame to waste all this sartorial splendor on room service."

"I could live with the disappointment," he muttered. He lifted the hem of her dress and stroked her thigh. "You can't go bare legged. It's cold outside."

"I thought you would be a fan of easy access."

"Maybe in July. But not tonight. I care about you too much to see you turn into a Popsicle."

Despite her distaste for the hosiery, she knew he was right. With that one adjustment to her wardrobe, she was ready. At least her black coat was fairly dressy. At one time she had owned an entire collection of high-end faux furs. But those were long gone.

Their cab was waiting when they got down to the lobby. It was dark now, and the wind that funneled between the buildings took her breath away as they stepped outside. Patrick didn't have to say, "I told you so." At least her legs had a layer of protection from the elements.

On the way, he played with the inside of her knee. "We could stay another night," he said.

The words were casual, but they stopped her heart. Because she wanted so very badly to say yes, she did the opposite. Too risky. She was letting him too close. "I don't think so," she said. "Your sister-in-law Zoe offered to help me move to Dylan's apartment Sunday afternoon, maybe find a few pillows and pictures to spruce it up. You probably remember she did a stint as a vagabond for a couple of years, so she has a good eye for a bargain."

"I see. We'll go back, then."

Had she wanted him to talk her into staying? Was she hurt that he dropped the idea so easily?

She didn't want to answer those questions, not even to herself.

They made it to the restaurant with ten minutes to spare. An obsequious maître d' seated them near the floor-to-ceiling windows at a table overlooking the city. Patrick tipped the man unobtrusively and pulled out Libby's chair.

"Does this suit your fancy?"

"Perfect," she sighed. The restaurant was new. And crowded. Discreet music filtered from hidden speakers overhead. Their fellow diners—men and women alike— dazzled in stunning couture clothing. Expensive accessories. Flashy jewelry. At one time, this had been Libby's life.

Patrick touched her hand across the table. "You okay?"

She shook off the moment of melancholy. "Yes. More than okay."

Another puffed-up employee, this one their waiter, appeared at the table. "Would Monsieur like to order for the lady?"

Patrick shook his head, smiling. "I don't think so."

Libby picked up her menu, and in flawless French ordered her favorite dish of scallops and prawns in cream sauce. The man had the decency to look chagrined before he turned to Patrick. "And you, sir?"

"I won't embarrass myself in front of the lady. Please bring me a filet, medium, and the asparagus in lemon butter."

"My pleasure."

When they were alone again, Libby grinned. "You set him straight, but so very nicely."

"The owners probably taught him that spiel. It's not his fault."

Libby gazed out the window, soaking in the vista of the city she considered home. "I don't think I'll stay in Silver Glen after this summer," she said impulsively. It would be impossibly difficult to be around the man who didn't want marriage and forever.

Patrick, caught in the act of sipping his wine, went still, his glass hovering in midair. "Oh? Why not?"

The reality was too painful, so she fed him a lesser truth. "I need to be independent. If I lean on your mom or even the Kavanaghs in general, I won't know if I really have the guts to rebuild my life. Here in New York, at least everything is familiar. I know the turf…and I have contacts…maybe even friends if I can figure out which ones still care about me now that my bank account is empty."

"So you don't see yourself becoming part of a place like Silver Glen?" His expression was curiously blank.

"I think we've established that I'm not much of a country girl. The concrete jungle is more my speed. I know which deli has the best pastrami, and I can tell you the operating hours of the Met and Natural History. I memorized the subway system by the time I was fourteen. I've seen the Rockettes dance every December since I was three years old…well, except for this past one. New York is home to me."

"I see."

His gaze was odd, turbulent. Did he think she was somehow insulting his beloved hometown?

"Don't get me wrong," she said hurriedly. "North Carolina is incredibly beautiful. And I'm happy to be living there for the moment. But when I think about the future, I can't see myself in Silver Glen."

In the heavy silence that followed her pronouncement the waiter returned, bearing their meals. The food was amazing, the presentation exceptional. But the evening had fallen flat.

She was honestly mystified. Patrick should be glad she wasn't going to hang around. He was the one with the matchmaking mother. And he'd made no secret of the fact that he was not ever going to get married.

For Libby's part, it made sense to decide from the beginning that she and Patrick were nothing more than a blip on the radar. She had suffered enough trauma in her life during the past year, without adding a broken heart to the mix.

Falling in love with Patrick Kavanagh would be the easiest thing in the world. Maybe she was partway there already. But she wasn't a fool. People didn't change. Her father hadn't. Her mother hadn't. And in the end, their inability to be the people they could have been desperately hurt their only daughter more than they could have imagined.

Still, Libby was tormented by one simple question. She knew she wouldn't be satisfied until she knew the answer.

Over dessert, she took a chance. "Patrick…"

"Hmm?" Distracted, he was dealing with the credit card and the check for their meal.

"May I ask you a personal question?"

He lifted an eyebrow, his sexy smile lethal. "I think we've reached that point, don't you?"

Maybe they had, and maybe they hadn't. But she risked it even so. "I know what happened to you when you were in high school. And I get that it was deeply painful and upsetting. But why have you decided that marriage is not for you?"

For a moment, he froze. She was certain he was going to tell her to go to hell. But then his shoulders relaxed and he sat back in his chair. "It's pretty simple really."

"Okay. Tell me."

"I've already done it. And messed it up. I choose not to take it so lightly again."

"I'm confused."

He fidgeted with his bow tie, his tanned fingers dark against the pristine white of his shirt. "Five of my brothers have gotten married so far. They've each stood in front of

God and family and made a solemn vow to one particular woman. To love and to cherish…till death do us part… all that stuff…"

"And you don't want to do that?"

"I'm telling you," he said, his voice rising slightly. "I already did it. But I cheapened the meaning of marriage. I bound myself to a woman, a girl really, whom I didn't love. And I knew I didn't love her even while I was repeating the vows."

"But you weren't an adult…and you were doing what was expected of you."

"Doesn't matter. The point is, I had my chance, and I made light of a moment that's supposed to be sacred. So I'm not going to take another woman in front of the altar knowing that I've already betrayed her before we ever start."

It made a weird sort of sense.

Poor Patrick…chained by the strength of his own regrets to life as a bachelor. And poor Libby…on the brink of falling for a man who didn't want anything she had to offer in the relationship department. It might have been funny if it hadn't been so wistfully sad.

Over one last cup of coffee, they sat in silence. Her question and his answer had driven an invisible wedge between them. She played with the silver demitasse spoon, watching the blinking lights far below…the traffic that never ceased. The Empire State Building off to her left was lit up, but the colors puzzled her. "I wonder why they went for pink and white this weekend," she murmured.

Patrick leaned forward. "Seriously? Tomorrow is Valentine's Day, Libby."

"Oh. Well, this is awkward."

"Why? Because you don't know what day it is?"

She lifted her chin. "No. Because you and I are the last two people who should be having a romantic dinner."

"Humans are good at pretense." The tinge of bitterness was unlike him.

But since her Cinderella experience was winding down, she chose to ignore his mood. She reached for his hand. "I don't want to fight with you, Patrick." She rubbed her thumb across the back of his hand. "Let's go back to the hotel. Please."

Patrick was not accustomed to self-doubt. He made decisions and followed through. He was mentally, physically and emotionally strong. People respected him...admired his integrity.

Then why did he feel as if he were failing Libby on every level?

He was so rattled by his jumbled thoughts that he forgot to call a cab before they got down to the street. "Stay inside a minute," he said.

But Libby had already gone on ahead, calling out to him with excitement in her voice. "Come look, Patrick. It's snowing..."

He followed her and pulled up short when the scene slammed into him with all the force of a freight train. Libby stood in the glow of a streetlight, arms upraised, her face tipped toward the sky. She was laughing, her features radiant. The sheltered heiress who had lost everything and been forced by harsh circumstances to grow up in a hurry, still had more joie de vivre in her little finger than Patrick could muster at the moment.

She had made love to him...openly, generously. Never once holding back or trying to protect herself from his *rules* for relationships. Even knowing that he was an emotionally locked-up bastard, she gave him everything. Her sweetness...her enthusiasm...her amazing body.

He should be kneeling at her feet and begging her forgiveness. Instead, he was going to commit the unforgiv-able sin. He was going to let her go.

As the snowfall grew heavier and the wind stilled, the whole world became hushed. Although he was miles from home, this particular gift of winter was the same every-where. People stopped. Time stopped. Quiet descended. The swirl of white was an experience linked to childhood. Simple joy. Breathtaking wonder.

When he finally managed to hail a cab, he and Libby were coated in white. Strands of damp hair clung to her forehead, and her cheeks were pink. She laughed at him when he tried to brush the melting flakes from her shoulders. "Leave it," she said. "We'll be home soon."

He knew it was a slip of the tongue. A hotel, however lovely, was not home. But he was almost certain that Libby possessed a talent he lacked…the ability to make a real home with nothing more than her presence and her giving heart.

The trip from the cab to their suite seemed inordinately long. He shook, not from the cold, but from an amalgam of fear and desperation. This was it, most likely. His last chance to be with her intimately. His last opportunity to memorize the curve of her breasts, the softness of her bottom pressed to his pelvis as they curled together in sleep.

Libby's mood had segued from delight to quiet intro-spection. Perhaps she had picked up on the chaos inside him. But no matter the reason, she gave him space. Made no requests. He almost wanted her to demand something from him. To beg him to change. To plead with him to make an exception for her.

Libby, however, treated him like a grown man. She respected his choices, even as she made plans to go her own way. It was the most painful "letting go" he could have imagined.

As he fumbled with the key to their door, Libby slipped

her arm through his and leaned her head on his shoulder. "I think that last glass of wine was one too many," she murmured.

The door opened, and he scooted her through, backing her against it when it closed. His hands clenched her shoulders. His forehead rested against hers. "I need you." He meant to say more than that, but she understood.

She smiled at him as she unbuttoned her coat. "I know, Patrick. And it's okay, I promise. I won't ask for more than you're willing to give." She tossed the coat aside. "But we have tonight."

Fifteen

He undressed her reverently, as if she were a long-awaited Christmas gift. Either Libby was very tired, or she understood his need to be gentle in this moment, because there was no mad stripping of clothes, no sex-crazed fumbling to get naked. With her head bowed, she submitted to his hands, even when those hands trembled and even when he cursed a stuck zipper.

At last, she was nude. He lifted her in his arms and carried her a few steps to the settee. Depositing her carefully, he stepped back and removed his own clothing. She watched him drowsily, her green eyes glowing with pleasure.

Her gaze was almost tactile on his bare skin. At last, it was done. He held out a hand. "Come with me."

That she obeyed instantly messed with his head. Was she trying to win him over? Or was she humoring a slightly deranged man who temporarily held her captive?

Did it matter?

As soon as she stood up, he recognized the possibilities in the elegant piece of furniture. "How do you feel about playacting the emperor and the concubine?"

"On someone else's furniture?" She was scandalized. "Not without something to protect it."

"Don't move." He raced to the bedroom and grabbed the blanket off the foot of the bed, along with a strip of condoms. When he returned, Libby had taken him at his word.

She stood, arms at her sides, and stared from him to the settee and back again. "I never took gymnastics classes. So don't get any kinky ideas."

"Kinky ideas are the best," he said. Teasing her was almost as much fun as making love to her. She sputtered and blushed and scowled adorably. Giving her a moment to get used to the idea, he flipped the thick duvet out and over the settee and sat down, palms flat on his thighs. "I'm ready."

Libby tilted her head to one side and pursed her lips. "Clearly."

"Well, come on."

"And do what?"

"Sit on my lap."

He watched as she assessed every possible permutation of that suggestion.

"Umm…"

"Don't be a chicken. You're a fearless woman who survived a night in the mine. Surely you're not afraid of a little role-playing."

"I'm not afraid of anything," she said firmly.

"I know it. And now you know it, too."

The look on her face was priceless. Libby had changed. She had grown. She was no longer the same woman who had professed timidity during her job interview.

"I don't know what to say. Thank you, Patrick."

He tucked his hands behind his head. "Don't thank me. You're the woman who has been slaying dragons."

She inhaled, making her breasts rise and fall in a way that would turn any man's brain to mush. "Okay, then…"

"Wait. Stop." He'd forgotten the protection. But, within seconds, he was sheathed and ready to go. "Come and get me."

"Isn't that supposed to be my line?"

He tickled the insides of her thighs as she gingerly straddled his lap. "I think an emperor would expect more bodily contact." He grabbed her butt and kneaded her warm, resilient flesh. "We should have a mirror," he complained, wishing he had been more prepared.

Libby cupped his neck with her hands and leaned in to kiss him. "Focus, Kavanagh. You have a naked woman on your lap."

"That's my problem," he complained, thoroughly aggrieved. "I forget my name when I touch you. It makes decision-making dicey at best."

"I'll help," she promised. "Give me something to decide."

"Well," he drawled. "It would be nice if you could get a little closer."

Fortunately, Libby was a smart woman. "Like this, you mean?" She lifted up and lowered, joining their bodies perfectly.

He buried his face in her scented breasts. "Exactly like that."

This particular position might have been a miscalculation. The visual stimulation combined with a somewhat passive role on his part made his body burn. He had barely entered her, and already he wanted to come.

Damn it.

But as much as he wanted to move, the urge was strong to simply hold her there. And pretend she was his to keep.

She tapped him on the head. "Hello in there. The last emperor who wanted me was a bit more…um…*active.*"

"You want active, little concubine?" he muttered. "How about this?" He surged upward, burying himself so deeply inside her, he wasn't sure he could find his way out.

"Patrick!" Libby cried out, stopping his heart.

"Did I hurt you?" he asked, pulling back to examine her face.

"You didn't hurt me." She bit her lip. "But it was definitely…"

"What? Definitely what?"

One shoulder lifted and fell. "Wicked. Memorable. Deep."

He swallowed hard. "I see. Would you consider those positive adjectives?"

She wiggled her butt, making him squeeze his eyes shut as he counted to ten and tried to hold on.

"Oh, yes, my emperor," she whispered. "Very positive indeed."

Libby might have lied a little bit. That last move on Patrick's part left her hovering on a line between pleasure and pain. She had never felt more desired, nor more completely possessed.

He trembled against her…or maybe that was her own body shaking. Was good sex always this momentous? Her basis for comparison was woefully inadequate. She'd had one terrible experience and now this one.

She raked her teeth along the shell of his ear. "Make love to me, Patrick. I want it all. Don't hold back."

Her request tore through his last thread of restraint. He lunged into her once…twice…then a third time, before he tumbled them both onto the floor and lifted one of her legs over his shoulder.

Suddenly, she felt exposed…vulnerable. Their bodies were no longer joined. Patrick was talented, but even he couldn't manage that trick while airborne. He stroked a fingertip in her damp sex, making her squirm as he stared at her intimately.

"Do you trust me, Libby?"

"Of course, I do."

"Close your eyes."

"But I…"

"Close them."

She obeyed the command, quivering in his grasp. "What are you going to do?"

"Hush, Libby."

She sensed him moving, and then she arched her back in instinctive protest when she felt his hands spread her legs apart. Moments later, his warm breath gave her the first warning of what he was about to do seconds before she felt the rough pass of his tongue on her sex.

A groan ripped from her gut, shocked pleasure swamping her inhibitions. She tried to escape, even so. But he locked her legs to the rug and continued his lazy torture.

She came more than once…loudly. And in the end, she barely had the breath to whisper his name when he moved inside her and drove them both insane…

It was still dark when Libby awoke. She was sore and satiated but oddly uncertain. Some sound had dragged her from a deep sleep. Patrick breathed quietly at her back, his arms wrapped around her waist, his face buried in her hair.

"Patrick," she said, turning to face him. "I think your phone is vibrating." It had to be bad. No good news ever came at…what was it? Four in the morning?

Her companion grumbled, but reached for his phone on the bedside table. "What?"

Patrick sat straight up in bed. "How bad is it?"

The tone in his voice alarmed her. "What's wrong?"

He ignored her until he finished the call. "It's Mia…

Dylan's wife. She's in the hospital with a ruptured appendix. And there are complications."

"Oh, no..."

"There's nothing we can do to help."

"Are you trying to convince me or you? Come on, Patrick. You know we need to go back. At least we can be there to lend moral support. People die from a ruptured appendix sometimes. Dylan must be out of his mind."

"Thank you for understanding," he said quietly.

They barely spoke as they gathered up their things and dressed. Patrick hardly acknowledged Libby's presence. She forgave him his silence, though, because she knew what it was like to be sick with fear.

A car waited for them when they exited the hotel. Apparently nothing ruffled the overnight desk clerk, even guests rushing out with their hair askew and wearing rumpled clothing from the night before.

At the airport, the pilot was ready. The flight back to Silver Glen seemed endless. Patrick stared out the window. Libby dozed. By eight in the morning, they were touching down on the new airstrip.

James was waiting for them, the car warm and toasty, despite the frigid early-morning air. As James stowed their bags into the trunk, Patrick helped Libby into the backseat and then joined James up front.

"How is she?" Patrick asked. "And tell me what happened. I didn't wait for details earlier when Liam contacted us."

James grimaced. "Apparently, she started having severe pain sometime after midnight, but she didn't wake up Dylan, because she didn't want to have to get Cora out of bed. By three thirty, it was so bad she had no choice. Dylan didn't take her. She went by ambulance. She's in surgery right now."

"Damn it, women are stubborn."

"Yeah."

Libby stayed silent in the backseat, hearing the concern in the siblings' voices…and the faintest hint of panic. These were big strong men. But they loved their sisters-in-law and treated them as blood relations, integral parts of this large, tight-knit family.

At the hospital, Libby staked out a seat in the waiting room and tried to become invisible. Through the glass walls adjacent to the corridor she had seen Maeve, the brothers and most of their wives from time to time, pacing the halls. Still wearing her coat to cover her inappropriate clothing, Libby closed her eyes and leaned her head against the wall. This setting brought back too many painful memories of her mother's early suicide attempts.

When Patrick finally sought her out, almost two hours had elapsed. He plopped down in a chair across from her and rested his elbows on his knees, head in his hands. Wearing his tux pants and wrinkled white shirt, he looked exhausted.

"Patrick?" Alarm coursed through her veins. "Did something go wrong? Is Mia okay?"

He sat up slowly, his expression taut with stress. "She's going to be. At least I hope so. The surgery went well, but infection is a concern. She was in recovery for forty-five minutes. They've brought her up to a room now. We've been taking turns going in to see her."

"How is she?"

"Cranky at the moment. She hates being out of control."

"I'm sure it's scary for her."

"Yeah." He pushed his hair from his forehead, his eyes weary, but laden with something else, as well. "Dylan is an absolute wreck."

At that moment, Maeve walked into the waiting room. Normally, Patrick's mother was the epitome of vigor and elegance, never a hair out of place. This morning, how-ever, she looked every bit her age.

Patrick jumped up. "Here. Take my seat, Mom. I'm going to find some coffee."

Maeve managed a smile, but her hands trembled as she sat down and looked at Libby. "It's a hard thing to watch your children suffer. My poor Dylan is stoic, but I was afraid he was going to have a heart attack. He loves Mia deeply. And I do, too, of course. A man's love for his wife, though, is a sacred thing."

"I'm so glad it looks like Mia is going to be okay."

"Would you mind driving me home, dear? I told Patrick I was going to ask you. He's already had your things sent up to the lodge."

"Are you okay, Maeve?" The older woman was definitely pale.

Maeve nodded. "I'm fine. Just a little shaky, because I never ate breakfast. My car is in the parking lot."

They made their way downstairs, pausing to speak to various members of the family. But Patrick had not returned. As they exited the hospital, Libby's stomach growled. "Would you like to stop at the diner for a meal?"

"Actually, that sounds wonderful. Thank you, dear."

The little restaurant wasn't crowded. Maybe because it wasn't a weekday. Libby and Maeve grabbed a booth and ordered bacon and eggs with a side of heart-shaped pan-cakes in honor of the holiday. Coffee and orange juice came out ahead of the food. Libby drained her cup in short order, hoping the jolt of caffeine would kick in soon. Maeve did the same, but she eyed Libby over the rim.

"I'm glad you suggested breakfast, Libby. I wanted to ask how the New York weekend went. I see you're still wearing that lovely dress."

Libby drew the collar of her coat closer together, thank-ful that the temperatures justified her attire. "We left in such a hurry this morning, we both just grabbed our clothes from last night."

Maeve's smile was knowing. "I wasn't making a judgment call…merely commenting. So tell me…did things go well?"

"The orientation at Peabody Rushford was fascinating. Although it wasn't for *my* benefit, I learned a lot."

Maeve shook her head, her dark eyes sharp with interest. "I'm not really asking about Patrick's business dealings. My son is an astute entrepreneur. I would expect no less. Mine was a more personal question."

Most people wouldn't have the guts to pry. But Maeve was not most people. Libby could do nothing about the flood of heat that washed from her throat to her hairline. "I'm not sure what you mean."

The server delivered the food. Libby scooped a forkful of eggs, hoping the distraction would derail Maeve's interrogation.

But Patrick's mother was like a dog with a bone… a very tasty bone. "I don't expect a blow-by-blow description, but I would like to know if the two of you connected on an intimate level." She locked her steady gaze with Libby's flustered one.

Blow-by-blow? Good grief. Libby managed to swallow the eggs that had solidified into a lump in her throat. "Um…yes, ma'am. We did."

"But?"

"But what?"

"You hardly seem the picture of a young woman who has been swept off her feet by romance."

"I haven't had much sleep, Maeve. It's a long way from New York."

"Give Patrick a chance," Maeve begged. "I know he doesn't go in for big gestures and declarations of undying passion, but he's a deep man. You can unpeel the layers if only you'll be patient."

Libby reached across the table and took Maeve's hand, squeezing it for a moment. Then she sat back in the booth and sighed. The delicious breakfast had lost its appeal. "Patrick is an *amazing* man. But he's been very honest with me from the beginning, and I have to honor that. For you to interfere or for me to weave daydreams based on nothing at all, would be wrong."

Maeve's face fell. "But you care about him?"

"Of course I do. He's a lovely man. But that doesn't make us soul mates, Maeve."

"I don't want my son to spend his life alone."

Tears glistened in Maeve's eyes. Given Patrick's mother's talents for benign manipulation, Libby had to wonder if the tears were genuine. But then again, Maeve was capable of deep feeling. Everything she did came from a place of abundant love.

"Some people like being alone, Maeve. I know tons of single people who are very happy and content with their lives. Patrick has a rewarding career and a circle of intimate friends. You can't box him into a *relationship* corner he doesn't want or need."

"You sound awfully wise for a young woman of your age."

"Life is a tough teacher."

"So what you're telling me is that you won't even consider letting yourself fall in love with my son because he's told you he doesn't want to get married."

"That's about the sum of it. I may stay for the duration of Charlise's leave…as long as things don't get awkward. But I've already told Patrick that I'm thinking of going back to New York permanently. This weekend's trip told me I can handle it. I wasn't sure, to be honest. I didn't want to think about my mother's death and my father's crime every second of every day. But I think it's going to be okay."

"Well…" Maeve scowled at a strip of bacon. "It sounds like you know your own mind."

"Yes, ma'am. And don't worry about Patrick. He knows what he wants and what he doesn't want."

Maeve leaned forward. "So what *does* he want?"

"He wants to build his life here…among family. He wants to be close to you and his brothers, and their wives and children, both physically and emotionally. He wants to grow Silver Reflections and know that he's making a difference in people's lives. He wants to spend time in the mountains and to draw strength from this place you all call home."

"For a woman who hasn't found her soul mate, you surely sound as if you know a great deal about my son."

"Stop it, Maeve. I'm serious. This last year has taught me that I can't always bend the world to my will. I have to accept reality and deal with it as best I can. And even under those circumstances—sometimes difficult, sometimes tragic—I can be happy. Or at least content."

Maeve held up her hands. "You've convinced me. I'm officially done with playing Cupid…though it's awfully hard to say that on his special day."

Libby laughed, finishing her meal with a lighter heart. "Maybe *we* should be worrying about *you*, Maeve. You're still very youthful and attractive. I'm sure there are tons of eligible men out there who would like to find a woman like you."

Maeve blanched. "If that's blackmail, I stand forewarned. I like my life the way it is. I had one husband. That was enough."

"If you say so. Now please pass the syrup, let's finish breakfast so I can go back to the lodge and get out of these clothes."

Sixteen

Patrick kicked a log, not even flinching when pain shot from his toe up his leg. He liked the pain. It helped distract him from the turmoil in the rest of his body. It had been over twenty-four hours since he had seen Libby. Longer than that since they'd had sex. He was like a junkie jonesing for the next hit.

But therein lay his problem. He had to stay away from her.

The conviction had been born in an intimate New York hotel room and solidified in the antiseptic corridors of a hospital. He couldn't afford to fall in love with Libby Parkhurst. It was too dangerous.

Little memories of Friday slipped into his thoughts when his guard was down. The smell of her hair on his pillow. The humorous, self-deprecating way she spoke to his clients about sleeping in the great outdoors. Her delighted laughter as she tipped her face toward the sky while snowflakes fell on her soft cheeks.

Even the way she hugged an old man in a uniform and let him know that he was important in her life.

Libby made everything brighter, more special. If he'd been inclined to find a lover and hang on to her, that woman might be Libby. But he couldn't. He wouldn't.

Without realizing it, he'd been on his way to changing his life plan. Having Libby in his bed, turning him inside out, had begun to convince him that he might be smarter about marriage a second time. After all, he wasn't a kid anymore.

But then yesterday happened. Mia's emergency surgery. Patrick knew his brother Dylan as a laid-back, comfortable-with-the-world, confident man. But in Dylan's eyes yesterday, Patrick had seen raw terror. With the woman Dylan loved in danger, Patrick's older brother had been helpless… scared sick that he was going to lose his whole world.

Patrick didn't want that kind of responsibility or that kind of grief. He remembered well the bitter taste of failure and loss when his youthful marriage ended, and that was for a girl he hadn't even loved.

How much worse would it be if he let himself get addicted to Libby and then he lost her? Death. Divorce. Infidelity. There were any number of forces waiting to tear couples apart.

Why would he subject himself to such vulnerability?

The hours he'd spent with Libby in the Carlyle hotel had literally changed him. Her sweet, sultry beauty. Her gentleness. Her shy, eager passion. He could have wallowed in their lovemaking for days on end and never had enough.

But when he broached the subject of extending their stay, Libby hadn't jumped at the idea. Worse still, she'd spoken of returning to New York permanently. Of leaving Silver Glen. Of leaving him.

It wasn't too late to correct his mistakes. He hadn't

gone all the way into obsession. He could end this thing and walk away unscathed.

But to do so meant suffering through one very unpleasant conversation. Today was Sunday. Thank God, Valentine's Day had come and gone. There was no reason not to intercept Libby's plans before she returned to Silver Reflections Monday morning.

When he contemplated what he was about to do, the bottom fell out of his stomach. Much like the first time he'd stood atop the high dive as a ten-year-old and wondered if he had the guts to make the jump.

He took out his cell phone and started to punch in a number. Libby carried a cheap pay-as-you-go phone. But at the last minute he remembered that Zoe was helping Libby get set up in the apartment over Dylan's bar.

The two of them had vowed to hit up thrift stores and outfit Libby's new digs. Should he stop Libby before she spent any of her hard-earned cash on things she might not need?

Damn it. He'd never had to deal with any of this with Charlise at his side.

At last, he decided he had to make the call.

Libby answered on the first ring. "Hello?"

Her voice reached inside his chest and squeezed his heart. "Are you and Zoe still occupied with your move?"

"She had to cancel. But I may go over to the Silver Dollar later to get the lay of the land. What's up, Patrick?"

"We need to talk," he said gruffly. "What if I pick up some sandwiches, and you and I go for a drive?"

"It's not really picnic weather," she said, laughter in her voice.

The day was infinitely dreary, sheets of rain drenching the mountains, temperatures hovering at a raw 38 degrees.

"I know that," he said. "But I've eaten in my car before. It won't kill me."

"If you say so."

"Can you be ready in an hour?"

"Of course."

"See you shortly." Now that he had made up his mind, he wanted to get this thing done...

Libby had a good idea what was coming. Patrick was going to tell her that an intimate relationship was not a good idea since she was going to be working for him. The thing was, she sort of agreed.

At this point in her life, she needed a good job more than she needed a love interest. Maybe in time this physical attraction between the two of them might blossom into something stronger...something lasting. She was a patient person. And if that were never going to happen, then she would be a big girl and face the truth.

Despite her brave talk, the prospect of seeing Patrick again made her insides go wobbly. They had gone from sleeping in each other's arms, to panic, to rushed travel to the hospital, to nothing. Patrick had left to get coffee, and that was the last she had seen of him.

This afternoon, with one guarded phone call, he was evidently prepared to set her straight. A fling in New York was one thing. Now it would be back to business as usual.

Since they weren't going anywhere fancy, she dressed warmly in jeans, boots and a thick, forest green sweater. The pleasant weather when Patrick had taken her out in the woods was nothing but a memory. Winter had returned... with no sign of relenting.

She was waiting on the front steps of the hotel when Patrick pulled up in his sporty sedan. It didn't seem like a good idea to meet him inside where his mother might happen to see them and get the wrong idea.

Ever the gentleman, he got out and opened her door, despite the fact that a uniformed parking attendant stood nearby, ready to lend a hand. She wanted to smile at Patrick and say something light and innocuous, but the words dried up in her throat.

This man had seen her naked. He had done wonderfully wicked things to her and with her. They had slept like exhausted children, wrapped in each other's arms.

Looking at Patrick's stoic face right now, no one would ever guess any of that.

Once they were seated practically hip to hip in the interior of the car, things got worse. The windows fogged up and the tension increased exponentially. She literally said nothing.

Patrick followed her lead.

She wanted to ask where they were going. But Patrick's grim profile in the waning afternoon light didn't invite questions. Chastened, she huddled in her seat and watched as the world flew by her window.

He drove like a man possessed, spiraling down the mountain road at least ten miles above the speed limit, and then racing on past town and out into the countryside. If he had a destination, she couldn't guess what it was. Her gut said he was driving at random.

When thirty minutes had passed from the moment he fetched her at the lodge, he finally slowed the car and rolled to a stop. The scene spread out in front of them was the definition of *middle of nowhere*. If she hadn't known better, she might have been worried he was going to dump her out and drive away, leaving her to find her way back home.

Their meal was in the backseat, but she wasn't hungry. And since she'd never been one to put off unpleasant tasks, she decided to cut to the chase. "I've been expecting this conversation," she said quietly. "You're going to say that we can either be lovers or coworkers, but not both."

Patrick's hands were white-knuckled on the steering

wheel. "The rain has stopped. I need to get out of this car. Do you mind?"

His question was clearly rhetorical, because before she could respond, he had already climbed out. She joined him on the side of the road, her arms wrapped around her waist. Even with a coat over her sweater, she was cold. The graveled edges of the pavement were waterlogged and muddy. The tops of the surrounding mountains were invisible, shrouded in low clouds, though the sun was trying to peek through.

Patrick stood a few feet away, physically and emotionally aloof, with aviator sunglasses obscuring part of his face. His khakis were crisply creased. He wore a white shirt underneath a brown bomber jacket. The leather was soft and scarred, clearly the real deal. Who had given it to him? Maybe it had been a gift when he first earned his pilot's license.

A light breeze ruffled his hair. Though she couldn't see his eyes, she guessed they were more gray than blue in this light. "Are you asking *me* to decide? New York was incredible, Patrick. I want to pick sex with you and say to hell with everything else. But we don't know each other all that well, and I was serious about learning to stand on my own two feet."

"You've misunderstood me," he said, hands shoved in his pocket.

"Does that mean *you* get to choose? I have no say in the matter?"

His expression was grim, his jaw so tight he would surely have a headache soon if he didn't already. It wasn't the face of a man who was going to choose physical pleasure over their work relationship.

He held up a hand. "Stop, Libby." His voice was hoarse. "You're making this harder."

Disappointment set up residence in her stomach.

Clearly the sex that had seemed so incredibly intimate and warm and fun to her had meant nothing to him. Well, she wouldn't be an object of pity. If he thought she was going to pine away for him, he was wrong. As far as she was concerned, they could work together and pretend the past weekend never happened.

She mimed zipping her lip. "Say what you have to say."

He took off his sunglasses and tucked them in his pocket. In the battle between the clouds and the sun, the clouds had won. "I'm not asking you to choose, Libby. I think you were right. You should go back to New York."

Trembling began deep in her core and worked its way to her extremities. "I don't understand."

In his face, she saw no remnant of the tender, funny man who had made love to her so passionately and so well. He stared at her impassively. "You gave it your best shot, Libby. I admired your resolve in the woods and in the mine, but you're not who I need while Charlise is gone."

You're not who I need. The blunt statement took her breath away.

"And our physical relationship?" Now her entire body shook. She tightened her arms around herself, trying not to splinter into a million tiny pieces of disbelief and wounded embarrassment.

"One night does not make a relationship. We were great in bed, but I've already told you how I feel about marriage. If you stay in Silver Glen, and you and I *continue* to end up in bed, things will get messy.

"Messy..." She parroted the word, her thought processes in shambles.

"You have to go home, Libby. Your instincts were good about that. Silver Glen is not the place for you, and I'm not the man you want. It's better to put an end to this now with no harm done."

Somewhere, she found the strength to smile evenly,

even as jagged, breathless pain raced through her veins and threatened to cripple her. It was a hell of a time to realize she was in love with him. She inhaled and exhaled, calling upon all of her acting skills. "I can't say I'm surprised by your decision. I never really thought you were going to give me the job anyway."

He must have seen through her layer of calm. For the first time, something in him cracked…visibly. For a split second, she could swear she saw agony in his eyes. "Libby…" He took an impulsive step in her direction and reached for her arm.

She jerked away, backing up so quickly she nearly lost her footing in the loose gravel. "No. Just no. Please take me back to the hotel. I have plans to make."

The return drive seemed endless. In front of the Silver Beeches Lodge, Patrick rolled to a halt and locked all the car doors with one click. His chest heaved. "Libby…" he said her name again.

But his time she had no escape route. He leaned across the console and tangled his hands in her hair, pulling her to him for a hard, desperate kiss. It took guts and fortitude, but she didn't respond. At all.

When he finally released her and sat back, she slapped him hard across the face. In seconds, his cheek bore the dark red mark of her fingers. "You're a selfish, heartless jackass, Patrick Kavanagh…and an emotionally stunted shell of a man. I don't ever want to see you again…not even if your face is on a Wanted poster. Go to hell."

Seventeen

Patrick had known it was going to be bad…but not that it would hurt so damned much. He unlocked the doors and watched Libby exit his car and his life in one fell swoop. His throat tight, he lowered the window and called her name urgently. "Libby!"

She never hesitated…never turned around.

Patrick struggled through the next several days as if the hours were quicksand threatening to pull him under. Though he found a replacement for Charlise—a male grad student in desperate need of extra cash who was willing to work for five months and then go back to chipping away at the course work for his degree—Patrick felt no sense of relief.

He went through the motions of preparing for his first outdoor adventure group, but the tasks that normally energized and excited him felt burdensome.

Even worse, he was forced to hide out from his family.

He knew his mother well. She had surely put two and two together by now. As Libby's champion, she would have his hide for hurting her.

Even a scheduled trip to LA, a city he normally enjoyed, was torture. All he could see in his mind's eye was Libby sitting at the conference table in her stylish black dress, handing out advice to skittish executives.

Far worse were the two nights he spent in a California hotel, flipping channels when he couldn't sleep. Libby was everywhere. In the big king-size bed, the marble tiled shower, the love seat that was a close twin to a certain settee in New York.

As much as he wanted to avoid facing the music in Silver Glen, he quickly wrapped up his assignment and headed home. His mother's birthday was in two days. Zoe and Cassidy were coordinating a huge bash in the ballroom of Silver Beeches. Though Liam and Maeve had run the lodge together for years, Maeve had finally decided to step down and devote herself to her rapidly expanding crop of grandchildren.

There was no possible way for Patrick to miss such an event. Nor did he want to. But it went without saying that Libby would be in attendance, as well. Even thinking about the possibility of seeing her again made him hard. He hadn't slept worth a damn since she ran from his car.

He relived that moment time after time. In every way he spun the conversation, the truth was, Libby was probably right. But even if he had it all to do over again, he didn't think he could change. The prospect of loving her was too scary.

What if he let himself love her and something happened to her? He had watched Dylan come apart at the seams. Fortunately, Mia was on her way to a complete recovery, but even so, Dylan was probably hovering over her, making sure she obeyed doctor's orders.

Patrick was following the only possible path. He had to keep his distance. He wouldn't let love destroy him.

At last, he came up with what he decided was a rational, well-thought-out plan. He would go to the Silver Dollar—surely Libby had finished moving in by now. And she wouldn't have left town yet—not without taking a few weeks to make some plans about her future and to look for a place to live in New York. He would track Libby down in her upstairs apartment over the saloon and discuss how they would comport themselves during Maeve's celebration.

His heart beat faster at the thought of seeing her again. She wouldn't be able to call him out on the validity of his visit. Neither one of them wanted to hurt or embarrass Maeve.

To mitigate his nervousness and postpone the inevitable, he stopped downstairs in the bar first. It was midafternoon on a Friday. Only a handful of customers lingered after what would have been a predictable lunch-hour rush.

Dylan was behind the bar doing something with the cash drawer. He looked up when Patrick approached. "Howdy, stranger. I thought you'd left town. Nobody's seen or heard from you all week."

"Been busy." He sat down on a leather-topped stool.

Dylan poured him a beer. "You want to go in with Mia and me for Mom's birthday gift? We were thinking about getting her a three-day visit to that new spa over in Asheville…with the works. It's not something she would buy for herself."

"Sounds good. Just tell me how much I owe you." He drained half of his beer and felt his chest tighten. "Do you happen to know if Libby is upstairs at the moment?"

Dylan frowned. "What do you mean?"

"Well, she lives here now, doesn't she? I thought you might keep track of her comings and goings."

Dylan wiped his hands on a clean bar towel, his expression troubled. "She's not living upstairs, man."

"But she was planning to move her stuff here from the hotel. She told me."

"Libby stayed for one night. Then she went back to New York."

Patrick made some excuse to his brother and departed, scraped raw by the look of sympathy on Dylan's face. Patrick felt hollow inside. Life had kicked the heart out of him, and it was his own fault. He hadn't really thought Libby would leave. Granted, he'd told her to go back to New York, but he'd assumed Maeve had helped her get a more suitable job here in Silver Glen while Libby decided if a return to the big city was the right thing to do.

Why would she go back to New York and the friends who had shunned her after her father's arrest?

His stomach curled as he imagined innocent, openhearted Libby living in some roach-infested apartment in a bad part of town. Possibly in actual physical danger.

God, what had he done?

He raced home and packed a bag. Then he lay awake almost all night to make absolutely sure he knew what he had to do. This was his mess. He was going to make it right. Fortunately, the jet was not in use the next day.

In a moment of absolute clarity, he saw the arrogant blunder he'd made. He'd been so entrenched in the notion that he had no business marrying anyone, he hadn't seen how much he was hurting the one woman who meant the world to him. He loved her. Right or wrong. And he couldn't let her go.

He filed his flight plan and was airborne before 8:00 a.m.

LaGuardia was busy. He had to execute a holding pattern until he was given permission to land. By the time he made it into the city, it was almost noon. He took care of several errands, then checked into the Carlyle and left on foot to walk to Libby's old building.

His idea was far-fetched, but it was the only hope he had of finding her. Fortunately, the doorman was the same old guy Libby had hugged with such fierce affection.

The man recognized Patrick right away. Patrick's plan called for bold-faced confidence.

Patrick smiled. "Hello, there. I'm hoping you can help me. I've come to see Libby and surprise her at her new place, but somehow I lost the address she gave me. Do you perhaps remember what it is? I know the two of you are close."

The elderly gentleman stared at Patrick for the longest time, leaving no doubt that he saw through Patrick's lie. But at last, he relented. He reached in his pocket and took out a scrap of paper. "Don't make me regret this."

Patrick jotted down the information in the note app on his phone and sighed in relief. At least he knew where to start. "Thank you," he said. "I appreciate your help." He pulled a folder from his pocket and handed it to Clarence. "This is an open-ended reservation at my family's hotel. For a two-week stay. You've meant a lot to Libby, and she wanted you to have this."

Hopefully, the tiny white lie would buy him goodwill in both directions.

Clarence smiled broadly. "Tell Miss Libby thank you. And I'll talk to her soon. This is mighty nice. Mighty nice."

Unfortunately, the new apartment was not in walking distance. Patrick was forced to grab a cab and slowly make his way downtown in rush-hour traffic. Contrary to his worst fears, the address pointed him toward TriBeCa... and a trendy collection of redesigned lofts.

This was far beyond anything Libby could afford right now. Had she found a man...an old friend willing to take her in? His gut cramped at the possibility. He took the elevator and rang the bell for 2B. Moments later, he heard footsteps. But nothing happened. There was a security peephole in the door.

Taking a chance, he stared straight at it. "Open up, Libby. I know you're in there, and I'm prepared to stand out here all night."

Libby leaned her forehead against the door and fought back tears. To peek outside and see Patrick in the flesh decimated her hard-won composure. She'd thought she had herself under control.

Turned out, she was wrong.

She cracked the door open, but left the chain on. "Why are you here?" she asked, her tone carefully dispassionate. Obviously it wasn't to declare his undying love for her.

"Maeve's birthday party is tomorrow night. Are you planning to be there?"

The hand behind the door, the one he couldn't see, clenched in a fist. "No. It's too expensive to fly and I don't have a car."

"You're willing to disappoint your mother's good friend…the woman who has done so much for you?"

She was getting tired of trying to read his mood through the crack. But she knew him well enough not to let him in. "Maeve will understand. She knows my financial situation."

"I brought the jet to pick you up, so money is not really an issue."

"I said I'm not going. Goodbye, Patrick."

He stuck his large leather shoe in the opening, foiling her attempt to shut him out. "Now who's being selfish and emotionally stunted?"

Had her words actually wounded him? Why else would he remember them almost verbatim? What would it take to make him leave her alone? And more importantly, what would it take to convince herself she hadn't fallen in love with him?

"What do you want?" she asked. Her heart was in shreds, and she didn't have the will to fight. The past few days had almost done her in. She wanted the man on the other side of the door with every fiber of her being. But she wasn't going to beg. Her dignity was all she had left.

"Please let me in, Libby."

She glanced behind her at the clock on the wall. Spencer would be home soon. This awkward confrontation couldn't last too long. "Fine," she said. "But only for a moment. I have things to do."

After disengaging the chain, she stepped back and let him come in. The dimensions of the loft were generous, but Patrick's size and personality made an impact, even so.

"Have you eaten?" he asked.

"Yes, sorry." But she wasn't sorry at all. And she wasn't going to offer to cook for him.

"This is quite some place."

"Yes. It's very nice."

"I thought all your friends dropped you when your dad went to prison."

"Spencer was doing an eighteen-month stint with the Peace Corps in Bangladesh. Manhattan society news travels slowly over there."

"And now Spencer is back and took you in?"

"Yes."

"And your future employment?"

"Zoe loaned me some money. I interviewed today for a position as a personal shopper at Bergdorf Goodman. Turns out I have skills in that area. As soon as I'm able, I'll be paying her back…"

"And Spencer, too?"

"Of course."

Patrick's expression was moody, as if he resented the fact that she had landed on her feet. What was it to him? He hadn't been willing to give her a job or a place to live... or even a tiny piece of his heart.

"Shall I tell Maeve that I flew up here to get you, but you were too busy to come to her birthday party?" He leaned against the wall in the foyer, his hands shoved in his pockets.

"Why would you do that?"

"To get my way."

Wow. There it was. Not even dressed up.

At that moment, the door opened without ceremony and a large, handsome blond man entered. He stopped short when he saw Patrick. Then he lifted an eyebrow. "Libby?"

"Patrick was just leaving," she said hurriedly. She took the newcomer by the arm and dragged him toward the kitchen, but he refused to go very far. Instead, she had to whisper in his ear.

He straightened after a moment and eyed Patrick with distrust. "I see."

She squeezed his arm. "I'm going back to Silver Glen for a couple of nights. But don't worry about me. I'll be fine."

"You'd better be."

Ten feet away, Patrick practically vibrated with incensed testosterone overload. She had to get him out of the apartment. "You win, Patrick," she said. "But I need some time. I'll meet you at the airport in two hours. Take it or leave it."

He nodded once, scowled at her and walked out.

The blond man chuckled. "Poor bastard. He's madly in love with you and you let him think you're living with me."

"Well, I am living with you," Libby said, giving him a big hug.

"Yeah, but with me *and* Spencer, who happens to be my beautiful, sexy wife."

Libby winced. "I might possibly have led him to believe that Spencer is male…and that *you* are Spencer."

"That's stone-cold, love. But he probably deserved it."

Libby threw some things in a bag, her heart racing with adrenaline. She didn't have a gift for Maeve, but Maeve would understand. Coat, keys, phone, small suitcase. In forty-five minutes, she was running downstairs and out to the street.

Then she stopped dead, because leaning against a lamp-post was Patrick Kavanagh. "I said I would meet you at the airport," she protested.

He shrugged. "I didn't trust you not to run."

There was accusation in his voice…and something else. Fatigue? Sadness? What did he want from her?

"Well, I'm here."

They faced each other silently. Being this close to him ripped apart the web of lies she had told herself to keep going every day. The truth punched her with a ferocity that took her breath. She was madly, deeply, unfortunately in love with Patrick Kavanagh.

He raked a hand through his hair, for the first time revealing a trace of vulnerability. "The airport is shut down for fog. We can't leave until tomorrow morning."

She swallowed. "Okay. Call me and let me know what time." She turned to go back inside the building.

Patrick caught her in two steps, his hands warm on her shoulders. "We need to talk, Libby. Come back to the hotel with me. We'll have dinner there. Casual. Nothing fancy. I'll get you a room if you want it. Or—" He stopped short as if he hadn't meant to say that.

"Or what?"

"Nothing," he muttered. "Never mind. Come have dinner with me. Please."

He was the last person on earth she wanted to have dinner with. And the only person. He didn't deserve to be given the time of day. But she let herself be persuaded. And not because she was weak, and he smelled wonderful. She would hear him out, for Maeve.

After that, Patrick was a complete gentleman. He kept his distance in the cab. At the hotel, he handed her bag to a bellman and steered Libby toward the dining room. The restaurant was conservatively old-school, reminding her of birthday dinners with her parents.

She ordered the lobster bisque. Her appetite lately had been almost nonexistent, but the rich, warm soup was perfect. Patrick chose the duck. Because the captain and servers were attentive, it was easy to let conversation touch on innocuous topics.

But at last, over cappuccino and crème brûlée, Patrick made an overture she hadn't expected. "We need some privacy, Libby. Will you come upstairs with me?"

What did he mean, *privacy*?

Well, hell. She wasn't going to be a coward about this. "For talking? Or something else?"

His throat flushed dark red and his eyes flashed with some strong emotion. "I'll let you make that call."

When he stared at her with storms in his blue-gray irises, she was helpless to resist. Or maybe that was the lie she told herself, because she didn't *want* to resist.

She folded her napkin and set it on the table. "Fine. We'll go upstairs."

The tension in the elevator would have been unbearable except for the older couple who joined them during the brief ride to an upper floor.

At Patrick's door, Libby waited nervously for him to fish the key from his pocket. It was a different room, of course. But the furnishings were similar enough to remind her of every last thing she and Patrick had shared just days earlier in this same city…this same hotel.

Libby took a seat. Patrick stood and paced.

"If you're feeling guilty, I absolve you," she said, the words flat. "You were right. The job at Silver Reflections wasn't suited for me. But you needn't worry. I've landed on my feet, and things are going very well. I should thank you for firing me."

"I didn't exactly *fire* you," he protested, the muscles in his neck corded and tight.

"What would *you* call it?"

He exhaled. "A mistake. A bad mistake. I acted like a complete ass, and I hope you will find it in your heart to forgive me."

"I make no promises. What about the sex?" she asked recklessly, fighting for her happiness, unwilling to let a blindly stubborn man ruin what they had.

"I can't deny it was incredible. But my life was rocking along pretty damn well until you came along." His voice faltered.

"Well, mine wasn't. A thousand apologies, emperor." She made her tone as snide and nasty as she could manage. And she leaped to her feet, no longer content to sit and let him scowl at her.

He grabbed her wrist to reel her in, his chest heaving. "I will not fail at marriage again, Libby."

Eighteen

Her heart dropped to her feet until she looked deeply into his eyes and saw the secret he was trying so hard to keep. Her jaw dropped. "You love me…"

"No I don't." His denial was automatic but totally unconvincing.

She cupped his face in her hands. "I love you, too, Patrick. But we don't have to get married," she said softly, "if that's what scares you. We can live in sin. You'll be the black sheep of the family."

At last the line between his eyebrows disappeared. "It's the twenty-first century. You'll have to do more than that to get me ostracized."

"I'll try my best. But it will have to be something really awful, won't it? Like maybe you and I making a baby without a ring on my finger? Your mom would hate that."

She saw the muscles in his throat work. "I'd hate it, too," he muttered. "This isn't how things should be, Libby. I've already stood before a priest and repeated marriage vows.

You deserve a man who can come to you with a clean past, a blank slate."

Going against all her instincts, she released him and put the width of the room between them. Still, she couldn't sit down. Too much adrenaline pumped through her veins. She busied herself at the minibar. "Would you like something to drink?"

"No. Look at me, Libby. You know I'm right. You're young and sweet and you deserve all the traditional trappings of an extraordinary wedding. You deserve to be the perfect bride."

She set down the small unopened bottle of liquor. "Here's the truth, Patrick…the last year has taught me that life is seldom perfect. I won't have my father to walk me down the aisle, because he's in prison. My mother won't be at my side helping me pick out a dress, because she took a bottle of pills."

"I'm sorry about all those things."

There was one more secret she knew she should disclose. Something that might make him understand. "Patrick?" She forced herself to perch on the sofa. The gas logs in the fireplace burned cheerfully. "Please sit with me. I want to tell you a story."

His expression guarded, and with reluctance in every line of his body, he nodded. But instead of joining her, he took a chair opposite, putting a low antique table between them as a barrier. "I'm listening."

This was harder than she had thought it would be. But if she didn't tell Patrick, perhaps she would never be free. "You keep calling me innocent, but you had to realize that I wasn't a virgin when you and I made love."

"I knew that. But neither was I. I've never approved of the double standard for women. I don't care about the men in your past, Libby. It's not important."

She leaned forward, her hot face in her hands. Shame flooded her stomach. "Well, it sort of is," she muttered.

Patrick made some kind of motion. "I don't want to hear your confession."

She sat up and stared at him before looking away and shaking her head. "I'm not giving you a choice. I was a very rebellious teenager, Patrick. I'd been spoiled and pampered, and I thought the world was my oyster. I'd barely dated at all, because my parents were so strict."

Patrick inhaled sharply. "Libby…"

"Don't interrupt. Please. The thing is, my father's best friend was newly divorced that year. He began flirting with me every time he came over to the apartment. I didn't really think of it as flirting. But I was smug about the fact that an older, sophisticated man was interested in my thoughts and opinions. It made me feel very grown-up."

Beneath his breath, Patrick said a word that was succinct and vehement. She had to ignore him to get through this.

"I turned sixteen in February. That fall was the beginning of my senior year. Most of my classmates had boyfriends, but I didn't. So I started telling everyone about *Mitch*."

"Was that his real name?"

She shrugged. "His middle name. I wasn't entirely stupid. I didn't want to get him or me in trouble. But as time passed and no one ever saw my 'boyfriend' at parties or other social occasions, they began to accuse me of making him up. The more teasing I took at school, the closer I grew to my father's friend. The attention of this handsome, very masculine man soothed my adolescent feelings of inadequacy."

"A man old enough to be your father."

"It didn't seem that way. To me, he was close to perfect."

"So what happened?"

Apparently, in spite of himself, Patrick wanted to know.

"In October, my father had to go to a financial seminar in Chicago. He wanted my mother and me to accompany him. But the trip sounded beyond boring to a teenage girl, even though my mom promised me shopping. I insisted that I was almost an adult and that they could certainly trust me. I begged them to let me stay home for the two nights they would be away."

"Oh, Libby…"

"It wasn't really a big deal. I planned to watch *inappropriate* movies on cable and paint my toenails and text with my friends. Maybe even sneak into my parents' liquor cabinet and have a single glass of sherry. I felt very daring and independent."

"And then Mitch came over."

"How did you know that?"

"It's not that hard to figure out. He knew you were going to be alone."

Libby grimaced. "I was an easy mark. He pretended he dropped by to see Daddy, and then feigned surprise that my father wasn't home. Later on, of course, I understood that Mitch knew exactly where my parents were and that I hadn't gone with them to Chicago. But at the time, it seemed like a happy accident. I asked him to come in."

Patrick had gone white beneath his tan. "He raped you."

Even now, the memory of that night made her shudder. "I wish it were that simple. I didn't understand all that much about men. I certainly didn't know that when they started drinking they were more dangerous. But I was having so much fun and he was complimenting me on my looks and my intelligence…anyway, when he kissed me the first time, I thought it was okay. For a minute."

"And afterward?"

"Something inside me said I should go to my bedroom

and lock my door. But I didn't want him to think of me as a child. So I ignored that little voice. And I paid the price."

"God, Libby…"

Tears stung her eyes, though she didn't let them fall. "It was a long time ago. And I'm fine…really I am. I just wanted you to know that I wouldn't come to marriage unscathed, either. Not that you've asked me, but you know…"

Patrick staggered to his feet, his heart and his composure shattering into pieces like brittle glass. He went to the sofa and sat down, scooping her into his lap. For a long time, they just sat there…not speaking, her head tucked against his shoulder.

He stroked her fiery hair, wanting desperately to find the son of a bitch with the middle name Mitch and avenge Libby's honor.

At last, he drew a deep breath and let go of the past that had held him with invisible chains. "I adore you, Libby Parkhurst. How could I not? You're beautiful and brave and you have the most extraordinary outlook on life." He tipped her backward over his arm and kissed her, shuddering with relief as she kissed him in return.

When they separated and sat side by side, her green eyes were damp, but then his were, too, so they were even. "Don't move," he said.

Her face expressed first puzzlement and then astonishment when he slid off the sofa and onto one knee, pushing the table aside. Reaching into his pocket, he pulled out a turquoise leather box and flipped it open. "Marry me, Libby," he pleaded, the words hoarse, his throat raw.

She stared at the multicarat single stone as if it were a snake. "You have a ring?"

Her bewilderment made him feel lower than low. "Of course, I do," he said. "I'll change this for a diamond if you want, but I've always thought redheads should wear emeralds." Libby didn't protest when he slid the simple platinum band with the exotic jewel onto her finger.

She held her hand up, her eyes wide. "It's extraordinary."

"I have no doubts about us, Libby, not anymore. And it's not because of your confession. You've opened my eyes to how stupid I've been to deliberately throw away something so amazingly good. I'm sorry I insulted you and fired you and tried to break your heart. I was an idiot. I bought the ring this afternoon, but then I got cold feet." He rested his forehead against her knee. He'd said his piece. The outcome was up to her now.

Her silence lasted too damn long. When he felt her fingers in his hair, he braced for a refusal.

But Libby took him by surprise. She slid down beside him, her legs curled to one side. "This is a very beautiful rug," she said. "I suppose we shouldn't do anything to ruin it."

He scowled at her. "Damn it, Libby. Don't toy with me. I've had a hell of a day."

"And whose fault is that?"

"I know I said I didn't care about other men in your life, and I really don't, but tell me one thing. Is Spencer expecting to share your bed? He's a big guy, and I want to know if I'm going to have to fight for your hand."

Libby's eyes widened, and she laughed, staring down at her fingers as if mesmerized by the brilliant green stone Patrick had spent several hours choosing. "Spencer is my dear friend. She and I were best buddies in school. The man you met at the loft is her husband, Derek."

Patrick exhaled, torn between frustration at Libby's deliberate deception and relief that no one else had a claim on his fiancée. "You're going to lead me in a merry dance, aren't you? I'll never be able to turn my back. And when you gang up with my sisters-in-law, Lord help us all."

He stretched out his legs and banged his shin on the table leg. "Wait a minute," he said, aggrieved. "You haven't said you'll marry me."

"I didn't?" Guileless green eyes looked up at him.

He started to sweat. "Say it, Libby. Right now."

She sighed, leaning forward to unbutton his shirt. "Yes, Patrick Kavanagh. I will marry you. Now, are you satisfied?"

He kissed her hard, moving over her and pressing her into the sofa. But it was a damned uncomfortable position. "I'm not satisfied at all," he stuttered. "Bedroom. Now." He dragged her to her feet, trying to undress her and walk at the same time. They made it as far as the still-closed door, but his patience frayed.

He lifted her hands over her head, trapping her against the polished wood with the weight of his body. Her breasts, mostly exposed in a sexy bra, heaved.

Libby's gaze was dreamy. "Let's come here for our honeymoon," she said.

"But during the summer. When you don't have to wear so many clothes." He gave up on the wrist-holding thing and unzipped her pants. "Help me, woman."

Finally, aeons later, they were both nude. He held her tightly, his face buried in her hair. "This is forever. I hope you know that."

Libby sighed deeply. "I'm counting on it, my love."

Twenty-four hours later, Libby stood in one of the private salons at the Silver Beeches Lodge and hid a yawn behind her hand. The emerald ring hung on a chain tucked inside her dress. All around her, the Kavanagh family, along with an intimate circle of friends, laughed and danced and partied. Maeve, the guest of honor, beamed continuously, delighted to have all her loved ones under one roof.

By prior agreement, Patrick and Libby had arrived at the festivities separately. For the past two hours they had stayed on opposite sides of the room. Either Dylan or Zoe must have warned everyone not to make a big deal about Libby's presence after a weeklong absence, because no one said a word out of place. All the attention was centered on Maeve—as it should be.

Still, it was a good bet that all the Kavanaghs knew Libby was no longer working for Patrick, and that things had ended badly.

After a sumptuous dinner, Maeve opened gifts. Her family and friends showered her with offerings of love and affection. For a brief moment, Libby allowed herself to grieve the fact that her own children would have only one grandmother. But then the moment passed.

She was luckier than most.

At last, when the babies were asleep and even the grown-ups were starting to fade, it was clear the party was over. Patrick stepped to the center of the room and gave his mother a hug. "I have one last gift for you, Mom."

Maeve seemed confused. "But I thought the spa thing had your name on it, too."

Little by little, the room fell silent. All eyes were on Patrick. "This is something more personal," he said.

Unobtrusively, Libby removed the emerald from its resting place and slipped it onto her left finger. It had pained her not to wear it, even for this one brief evening.

Patrick stood—tall and strong—with an almost palpable air of contentment and joy surrounding him.

Maeve stared at her boy, her brow creased. "Well, don't keep me in suspense. Where is it?"

Patrick grinned broadly, crooking a finger. "It's not an *it*. It's a *who*."

Libby threaded her way through the crowd, smiling as

the swell of exclamations followed her progress. When she joined Patrick, he put an arm around her.

"Mom," he said. "I'd like to present my fiancée, Libby Parkhurst, soon to be the daughter of your heart."

Maeve burst into tears, and the entire room fairly exploded with excitement. Libby lost track of the hugs and kisses and well wishes.

When some of the furor finally died down, Maeve held her close and whispered in her ear. "Thank you, Libby. Look at him. He's beaming."

And indeed he was. Libby's heart turned over. If she had harbored any last doubts, seeing Patrick like this in the bosom of his family and so obviously exultant and happy made her own heart swell with emotion.

Patrick finally reclaimed his fiancée and dragged her out to the car. He leaned her against the hood and kissed her long and slow. "Come home with me, my love."

Libby wrapped her arms around his neck, feeling the beat of his heart against hers. "I thought you'd never ask…"

* * * * *

LET'S TALK
Romance

For exclusive extracts, competitions
and special offers, find us online:

- f facebook.com/millsandboon
- ⊙ @millsandboonuk
- 🐦 @millsandboon

Or get in touch on 0844 844 1351*

For all the latest titles coming soon, visit
millsandboon.co.uk/nextmonth

Want even more
ROMANCE?

Join our bookclub today!